"So how much, Cleo, to secure your services for the month? Four hundred thousand dollars? Would that be enough?"

The numbers went whirling around her brain. Four hundred thousand dollars for a month of pretending to be Andreas's companion? Was she nuts even to think about giving that up? She could go home, pay for the farm's leaking roof to be fixed, and she'd still have enough left over to buy a place of her own. But could she pretend to be this man's lover? She shook her head, trying to work it all out. "Andreas, I—"

"Five hundred thousand pounds! One million of your dollars. Will that be enough to sway your mind?"

One million dollars. She swallowed against a throat that felt tight and dry. "I don't know if I'm the right person for the job."

He smiled then, as he curved one hand around her neck. "You'll be perfect. Any other questions?"

She shook her head. His fingers were warm and gentle on her skin and setting her flesh alight.

"Then what say we seal this deal with a kiss?"

Dear Reader,

Welcome to the March 2010 collection of fabulous Presents stories for you to unwind with.

Don't miss the last installment from bestselling author Lynne Graham's PREGNANT BRIDES trilogy, *Greek Tycoon, Inexperienced Mistress.* When ordinary Lindy goes from mistress to pregnant, shipping tycoon Atreus Drakos will have no choice but to make her his bride!

We have another sizzling installment in the SELF-MADE MILLIONAIRES miniseries. Author Sarah Morgan brings us *Bought: Destitute yet Defiant,* where unashamedly sexy Sicilian Silvio Brianza has plans for the disobedient Jessie!

Why not relax with a powerful story of seduction, blackmail and glamour in Sara Craven's *The Innocent's Surrender,* and go from humble housekeeper to mistress for a month in Trish Morey's *His Mistress for a Million.*

Cassie's life changes altogether when her new boss turns out to be none other than the notorious Alessandro Marchese, the father to her twins in *Marchese's Forgotten Bride* by Michelle Reid. And when Eva finds herself married to the notorious Sheikh Karim, she discovers that her husband is having a startling effect on her in Kim Lawrence's *The Sheikh's Impatient Virgin.*

Don't forget to look out for more tantalizing installments of our new miniseries during the year, kicking off with DARK-HEARTED DESERT MEN in April! The glamour, the excitement, the intensity just keep on getting better.

Trish Morey

HIS MISTRESS
FOR A MILLION

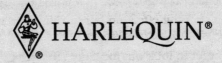

HARLEQUIN®

TORONTO • NEW YORK • LONDON
AMSTERDAM • PARIS • SYDNEY • HAMBURG
STOCKHOLM • ATHENS • TOKYO • MILAN • MADRID
PRAGUE • WARSAW • BUDAPEST • AUCKLAND

Recycling programs
for this product may
not exist in your area.

ISBN-13: 978-0-373-12904-1

HIS MISTRESS FOR A MILLION

First North American Publication 2010.

Copyright © 2009 by Trish Morey.

www.eHarlequin.com

Printed in U.S.A.

All about the author...
Trish Morey

TRISH MOREY wrote her first book at age eleven for a children's book-week competition. Entitled *Island Dreamer,* it told the story of an orphaned girl and her life on a small island. *Island Dreamer* also proved to be her first rejection. Shattered and broken, she turned to a life where she could combine her love of fiction with her need for creativity—Trish became a chartered accountant. Life wasn't all dull though, as she embarked on a skydiving course, completing three jumps before deciding that she'd given her fear of heights a run for its money.

Meanwhile she fell in love and married a handsome guy who cut computer code, and Trish penned her second book—the totally riveting *A Guide to Departmental Budgeting*—whilst working for the NZ Treasury.

Back home in Australia after the birth of their second daughter, Trish spied an article saying that Harlequin Books was actively seeking new authors. It was one of those "Eureka!" moments—Trish was going to be one of those authors!

Eleven years after reading that fateful article (actually June 18th 2003 at 6:32 p.m.) the magical phone call came and Trish finally realized her dream.

According to Trish, writing and selling a book is a major life achievement that ranks up there with jumping out of an airplane and motherhood. All three take commitment, determination and sheer guts, but the effort is so very, very worthwhile.

Trish now lives with her husband and four young daughters in a special part of South Australia, surrounded by orchards and bushland and visited by the occasional koala and kangaroo.

You can visit Trish at her Web site at www.trishmorey.com or drop her a line at trish@trishmorey.com.

To the Maytoners,
every one of you warm, generous and wise.
This one's for you, with thanks.
xxx

CHAPTER ONE

REVENGE was sweet.

Andreas Xenides eyed the shabby building that proclaimed itself a hotel, its faded sign swinging violently in the bitter wind that carved its way down the canyon of the narrow London street.

How long had it taken to track down the man he knew to be inside? How many years? He shook his head, oblivious to the cold that had passers-by clutching at their collars or burrowing hands deeper into pockets. It didn't matter how long. Not now that he had found him.

The cell phone in his pocket beeped and he growled in irritation. His lawyer had agreed to call him if there was a problem with his plan proceeding. But one look at the caller ID and Andreas had the phone slipped back in his pocket in a moment. Nothing on Santorini was more important than what was happening here in London today, didn't Petra know that?

The wind grew teeth before he was halfway across the street, another burst of sleet sending pedestrians scampering for cover to escape the gusty onslaught, the street a running watercolour of black and grey.

He mounted the hotel's worn steps and tested the handle. Locked as he'd expected, a buzzer and rudimentary camera mounted at the side to admit only those with keys or reservations, but he was in luck. A couple wearing matching tracksuits and money belts emerged, so disgusted with the weather that they barely looked his way. He was past them and following the handmade sign to the downstairs reception before they'd struggled into their waterproof jackets and slammed the door behind them.

Floorboards squeaked under the shoddy carpet and he had to duck his head as the stairs twisted back on themselves under the low ceiling. There was a radio crackling away somewhere in the distance and his nose twitched at a smell of decay no amount of bleach had been able to mask.

This place was barely habitable. Even if the capricious London weather was beyond his control, he had no doubt the clientele would be much happier in the alternative accommodation he'd arranged for them.

A glazed door stood ajar at the end of a short hallway, another crudely handwritten note taped to the window declaring it the office, and for a moment he was so focused on the door and the culmination of a long-held dream that he barely noticed the bedraggled shape stooping down to pick up a vacuum cleaner, an overflowing rubbish bag in the other hand. A cleaner, he realised as she straightened. For a moment he thought she was about to say something, before she pressed her lips together and flattened herself against a door to let him pass. There were dark shadows under her reddened eyes, her fringe was plastered to her face and her uniform was filthy. He flicked his eyes away again as he passed, his nose twitching at the combined scent of ammonia and stale beer. So that was the hired help. Hardly surprising in a dump like this.

Vaguely he registered the sound of her retreat behind him, her hurried steps, the thud of the machine banging against something and a muffled cry. But he didn't turn. He was on the cusp of fulfilling the promise he'd made to his father on his deathbed.

It wasn't a moment to rush.

It was a moment to savour.

And so he hesitated. Drank in the moment. Wishing his father could be here. Knowing he would be watching from wherever he was now.

Knowing it was time.

He jabbed at the door with two fingers and watched it swing open, letting the squeak of the hinges announce his arrival.

Then he stepped inside.

The man behind the dimly lit desk hadn't looked up. He was too busy scribbling notes on what looked like the turf guide with one hand, holding the phone to his ear with the other, and it was all Andreas could do to bite back on the urge to cross the room and yank the man bodily from his chair. But much as he desired to tear the man to pieces as he deserved, Andreas had a much more twenty-first-century way of getting justice.

'Take a seat,' the man growled, removing the phone from his ear long enough to gesture to a small sofa, still busy writing down his notes. 'I'll be just a moment.'

One more moment when it had taken so many years to track him down? Of course he could wait. But he'd bet money he didn't have to.

'*Kala ime orthios*,' Andreas replied through his teeth, *I'm fine standing*, 'if it's all the same to you.'

The man's head jerked up, the blood draining from his face leaving his red-lined eyes the only patch of colour. He uttered a single word, more like a croak, before the receiver clattered back down onto the cradle, and all the while his gaze didn't leave his visitor, even as he edged his chair back from the desk. But there was nowhere to go in the cramped office and his chair rolled into the wall with a jolt. He stiffened his back and jerked his chin up as if he hadn't just been trying to escape, but he didn't attempt to stand. Andreas wondered if it was because his knees were shaking too much.

'What are you doing here?'

Andreas sauntered across the room, until he was looming over both the desk and the man cowering behind it, lazily picking up a letter opener in his long-fingered hands and testing its length through his fingers while all the time Darius watched nervously. 'It's been a long time, Darius. Or would you rather I called you Demetrius, or maybe even Dominic? I really can't keep up. You seem to go through names like other people go through toilet paper.'

The older man licked his lips, his eyes darting from side to side, and this close Andreas was almost shocked to see how much his father's one-time friend and partner had aged. Little more than fifty years old, and yet Darius's hair had thinned and greyed and his once wiry physique seemed to have caved in on itself, the lines on his face sucked deeper with it. The tatty cardigan he wore draped low on his bony shoulders did nothing to wipe off the years.

So time hadn't treated him well? Tough. Sympathy soon departed as Darius turned his eyes back to him and Andreas saw that familiar feral gleam, the yellow glow that spoke of the festering soul within. And he might be afraid now, taken by surprise by the sudden appearance of his former partner's son, but Andreas knew that any minute he could come out snarling. Not that it would do him any good.

'How did you find me?'

'That's one thing I always liked about you, Darius. You never did waste your time on small talk. No "how are you?" No "have a nice day".'

'I get the impression you didn't come here for small talk.'

'Touché,' Andreas conceded as he circled the room, absently taking inventory, enjoying the exchange much more than he'd expected. 'I have to admit, you weren't easy to find.

You were good at covering your tracks in South America. Very good. The last we heard of you was in Mexico before the trail went cold.' Andreas looked up at the high basement window where the sleet was leaving trails of slush down the grimy glass before he turned back. 'And to think you could still be back there enjoying the sunshine. Nobody expected you'd be fool enough to show your face in Europe again.'

A glimmer of resentment flared in Darius' eyes, and his lip curled into a snarl. The hungry dog was out of its kennel. 'Maybe I got sick of beans.'

'The way I hear it, you ran out of money. Lost most of it on bad business deals and flashy women.' Andreas leaned over and picked up the form guide sitting on the desk. 'Gambled away the rest. All that money, Darius. All those millions. And this—' he waved his hand around him '—is what you're reduced to.'

Darius glowered, his eyes making no apology in their assessment of his visitor's cashmere coat and hand stitched shoes, a tinge of green now colouring his features. 'Looks like you've done all right for yourself though.'

No thanks to you!

Andreas' hands clenched and unclenched at his sides while he tried to remember his commitment not to tear the man apart. A deep breath later and he could once again manage a civil tone. 'You've got a problem with that?'

'Is that why you came here, then? To gloat?' He sneered, swinging a hand around the shabby office. 'To see me reduced to this? Okay, you've seen me. Happy now? Isn't that what they say—success is the best revenge?'

'Ah, now that's where they're wrong.' This time Andreas didn't restrain himself, but allowed the smile he'd been headed for ever since he'd set foot in this rat trap. 'Success is nowhere near the best revenge.'

The old man's eyes narrowed warily as he leaned

forward in his chair, the fear back once more. 'What's that supposed to mean?'

Andreas pulled the folded sheaf of papers from inside his coat pocket. 'This,' he said, unfolding them so that the other man could see what he was holding. '*This* is the best revenge.'

And Andreas watched the blood drain from the other man's face as he recognised the finance papers he'd signed barely a week ago.

'Did you even read the small print, Darius? Didn't you wonder why someone would offer you money on this dump you call a hotel on such easy terms?'

The older man swallowed, his eyes once more afraid.

'Did you not suspect there would be a catch?'

Darius looked sick, his skin grey.

Andreas smiled again. 'I'm the catch. That finance company is one of mine. I lent you that money, Darius, and I'm calling in the debt. Now.'

'You can't… You can't do that. I don't have that kind of money lying around.'

He flung the pages in Darius' direction. 'I can do it, all right. See for yourself. But if you can't pay me back today, you're in default on the loan. And you know what that means.'

'No! You know there's no way…' But still Darius scrabbled through the pages, his eyes scanning the document for an out, squinting hard when they came across the clause that proved Andreas right, widening as he looked up with the knowledge that he'd been beaten. 'You can't do this to me. It's no better than theft.'

'You'd know all about theft, Darius, but whatever you call it this hotel is now mine. And it's closing. Today.'

The shocked look on Darius' face was his reward. The man looked as if he'd been sucker punched.

Oh, yes, Andreas thought, revenge was sweet, especially when it had been such a long time coming.

CHAPTER TWO

ROCK bottom.

Cleo Taylor was so there.

Her head ached, her bruised shin stung where the vacuum cleaner had banged into it, and three weeks into this job she was exhausted, both mentally and physically. And at barely five o'clock in the afternoon, all she wanted to do was sleep.

She dropped the machine at the foot of her bed and sank down onto the narrow stretcher, the springs that woke her every time she rolled over at night noisily protesting her presence.

Karma. It had to be karma.

How many people had tried to warn her? How many had urged her to be careful and not to rush in? And how many of those people had she suspected of being jealous of her because she'd found love in the unlikeliest of places, in an Internet chat room with a man halfway around the world?

Too many.

Oh, yes, if there was a price to pay for naivety, for blindly charging headlong for a fall, she was well and truly paying it.

And no one would say she didn't deserve everything that was happening to her. She'd been so stupid believing Kurt, stupid to believe the stories he'd spun, stupid to believe that he loved her.

So pathetically naïve to trust him with both her heart and with her nanna's money.

And all she'd achieved was to spectacularly prove the award she'd been given in high school from the girls whose company she'd craved, but who never were and who would never be her friends.

Cleo Taylor, girl most likely to fail.

Wouldn't they just love to see her now?

A barrage of sleet splattered against the tiny louvred window high above the bed and she shivered. So much for spring.

Reluctantly she thought about dragging herself from the rudimentary bed but there was no way she wanted to meet that man in the hallway again. She shuddered, remembering the ice-cold way his eyes—dark pits of eyes set in a slate-hard face—had raked over her and then disregarded her in the same instant without even an acknowledgment, as if she was some kind of low-life, before imperiously passing by. She'd shrunk back instinctively, her own greeting dying on her lips.

It wasn't just that he looked so out of place, so wrong for the surroundings, but the look of such a tall, powerful man sweeping through the low-ceilinged space seemed wrong, as if there wasn't enough space and he needed more. He hadn't just occupied the space, he'd consumed it.

And then he'd swept past, all cashmere coat, the smell of rain and the hint of cologne the likes of which she'd never smelt in this place, and she'd never felt more like the low-life he'd taken her to be.

But she had to get up. She couldn't afford to fall asleep yet, even though she'd been up since five to do the breakfasts and it had taken until four to clean the last room. She reeked of stale beer and her uniform was filthy, courtesy of the group of partying students who'd been in residence in the room next door for the last three nights.

She hated cleaning that room! It was damp and dark, the tiny en suite prone to mould and the drains smelling like a swamp, and if she hadn't already known how low she'd sunk that room announced it in spades. The students had left it filthy, with beds looking as if they'd been torn apart, rubbish spilling from bins over the floor, and an entire stack of empty takeaway boxes and beer bottles artfully arranged in one corner all the way from the floor to the low ceiling. 'Leaning Tower of Pizza,' someone had scrawled on the side of one the boxes, and it had leant, so much so that it was a wonder it hadn't already collapsed with the vibrations from the nearby tube.

It had been waiting for her to do that. Bottles and pizza boxes raining down on her, showering her with their dregs.

No wonder he'd looked at her as if she were some kind of scum. After the day she'd had, she felt like it.

She dragged herself from the bed and plucked her towel off a hook and her bag of toiletries, ready to head to the first-floor bathroom. What did she care what some stranger she'd never see again thought? In ten minutes she'd be showered, tucked up in bed and fast asleep. That was all she cared about at the moment.

The bright side, she told herself, giving thanks to her nanna as she ascended the stairs and saw rain lashing against the glazing of the ground-floor door, was that she had a roof over her head and she didn't have to go out in today's weather.

"There's always a silver lining", her nanna used to tell her, rocking her on her lap when she was just a tiny child and had skinned her knees, or when she'd started school and the other girls had picked on her because her mother had made her school uniform by hand and it had shown. Even though her family was dirt poor and sometimes it had been hard to find, there'd always been something she'd been able to cling to, a bright side some-where, something she'd been able to give thanks for.

Almost always.

She sighed as the hot water in the shower finally kicked in and warmed her weary bones. A warm shower, a roof over her head and a bed with her name written on it. Things could always be worse.

And come summer and the longer days, she'd have time to see something of the sights of London she'd promised herself before she went home. Not that there was any hurry. At the rate she was paid, after her board was deducted, it would be ages before she could even think about booking a return airfare to Australia. God, she'd been so stupid to trust Kurt with her money!

A sudden pang of homesickness hit her halfway back down the stairs. Barely six weeks ago she'd left the tiny outback town of Kangaroo Crossing with such confidence, and now look at her. If only she could go home. If only she'd never left! She'd give anything to hug her mum and half-brothers again. She'd even find a smile for her stepfather if it came down to it. But when would that be? And how would she be able to face everyone when she did?

She would be going home humiliated. A failure.

The bright side, she urged herself, *look at the bright side*, as she pulled her eye mask down and snuggled under the covers, the cold rain lashing at her tiny window. She was warm and dry and she had at least ten hours' sleep before she had to get up and do it all over again.

'But you can't close the hotel,' Darius protested. 'There are bookings. Guests!'

'Who will be catered for, as will the staff we have on file from your finance application.' Andreas snapped open his phone, made a quick call and slipped the phone back into his pocket. 'I'm sure the guests won't mind being transferred to the four-star hotel we've chosen to accommodate them in and you can be assured the employees will be paid a generous redundancy.'

He cast a disdainful eye around the room. 'I don't foresee any complaints. And now I want you off the premises. I have staff coming in to take over and ensure the changeover is smooth. The hotel will be empty in two hours.'

'And what about me?' Darius demanded. 'What am I supposed to do? You're leaving me with nothing. Nothing!'

Andreas slowly turned back, unable to stop his lips from forming into a sneer. 'What about you? How many millions did you steal from my father? You happily walked away and left my family with nothing. What did you care about anyone else then? So why should I care about what happens to you? Just be grateful you're able to walk out of here with your limbs intact after the way you betrayed my father.'

A buzzer sounded, the security monitor showing a team of people waiting on the front step. 'Let them in, Darius.' The older man's hand hovered over the door-release button.

'I can help you!' he suddenly said instead, pulling his hand away to join the other in supplication. 'You don't need all these people. I know this hotel and I… I'm sorry for what happened all those years ago. It was a mistake… A misunderstanding. Your father and I were once good friends. Partners even. Isn't there any way you might honour that?'

Andreas dragged much-needed air into his lungs. 'I'll honour it in the same way you honoured my father. Get out. You've got ten minutes. And then I never want to see you again.'

Darius knew when he was beaten. Sullenly he gathered his personal possessions, the form guide included, in a cardboard box and slunk away even as the team filed into the office. Andreas took two minutes to go over the arrangements. Someone would email all forward bookings and advise of the change of hotels while the rest of the team would meet guests as they returned to expedite their packing and transfer to the new hotel. New guests would simply be ferried to the alternative premises nearby. There was no reason for the operation not to go like clockwork.

His cell phone beeped again as he dismissed the team to their duties and he reached for it absently, taking just a second to savour what he'd achieved. The look on Darius' face when he'd realised the truth, that he had lost everything and to the son of the man he'd cheated of millions so many years ago, was something he would cherish for ever. Doubly so because his father never could.

He frowned when he looked at the phone. Petra calling again? *Kolisi*, maybe there really was an emergency.

'*Ne?*'

Half a continent away, Petra's voice lit up. 'Andreas!' She sounded so bright he could almost hear the flashbulb.

'What's wrong?'

'Oh, I've been so worried about you. How is it in London? It is all going to plan?'

Andreas felt a stab of irritation. No emergency, then. Merely Petra thinking she had some stake in what was happening here. She was wrong. 'Why are you calling, Petra?'

There was a pause. Then, 'The Bonacelli deal! The papers are here ready to be signed.'

'I expected that. I told you I'll sign them when I get back.'

'And Stavros Markos called,' she continued at rapid pace, as if he hadn't spoken. 'He wants to know if they can book out the entire Caldera Palazzo for their daughter's wedding next June. It's going to be huge. They only want the best and I told them it should be fine, though I have to put off another couple of enquiries—'

'Petra,' he cut in, 'you know they can. You don't have to ring me to confirm. What's bothering you? Is there something else?'

There was silence at the end of the line, and then she laughed, an uncomfortable tinkle. Or at least, it made him feel uncomfortable. 'I'm sorry, Andreas,' she continued. 'It probably sounds silly, but I miss you. When do you think you'll be back?'

Something clenched in his gut, the pattern of her constant phone calls making the kind of sense he didn't want them to make. But there was no other option. She'd been checking up on him, making sure nobody else was occupying his bed or his attentions while he was in London and she was holding the fort back on Santorini.

He murmured something noncommittal before sliding his phone shut. What was wrong with her? He didn't do relationships. Petra, more than anyone, should have understood that. She'd witnessed the parade of women through his life. Hell, she'd been the one to organise the flowers for them when they were on the inner, the trinkets for them when they were on the outer. But he'd made one fatal mistake, broken his own rule never to get involved with the staff.

Drunk on success and the culmination of years of planning, he'd let his guard down when he'd heard the news that Darius had been found and the trap set. He'd been the one to insist Petra go out to dinner with him to celebrate. He'd been the one to order the champagne and he'd been the one to respond when she leaned too close, all but spilling her breasts into his hands. He'd wanted the release and she'd been there.

What a fool! He'd always assumed she was as machine-like and driven as he was. He'd always thought that she'd understood it was always just sex to him. And yet every time Petra called him now, he could almost feel her razor-sharp nails piercing his skin all over again. But why she'd want to be his mistress when she knew which way they invariably went…

Cold fingers crawled down his spine.

Or did she have something else in mind? Something more permanent she thought she was due after working alongside him for so many years?

Sto thiavolo!

What had his mother been telling him in her recent phone calls? That maybe it was time for him to settle down and find a wife?

And who did his mother like to talk to first, calling the office line instead of his cell phone, because 'her own son never bothered to tell her anything'?

Petra.

Had his mother also confided the news with her good friend's daughter that it was time for her only child to settle down? He'd just bet she had.

Damn. He didn't want to have to find a new marketing director. Petra was a good operator. The best at marketing the package of luxurious properties that Xenides Exclusive Property let to the well-heeled looking for a five-star experience in some of the most beautiful places in the world. She'd single-handedly designed the website that made his unique brand of five-star luxury accommodation accessible to every computer on the planet and made it so tempting that just as many booked through the website alone as booked by personal referral.

He didn't want to lose her; together they made a good team. But neither did he want her thinking she was destined to be anything more to him than a valued employee.

He sighed. What would she do when he found someone else, as he inevitably would? Would she leave of her own accord?

Andreas made up his mind on a sigh. It was a risk he would just have to take. Petra's departure from the business, while inconvenient, was preferable to her making wedding plans. All of which meant one thing.

He wouldn't be returning to Santorini without a woman on his arm and in his bed.

She would have to be somebody new, somebody different, someone who could step into the role of his mistress and then step out when he no longer needed her. No strings. No ties.

A contract position. A month should be more than enough.

Now he just had to find her before his flight back to Greece tomorrow.

He looked around the dingy room and sighed, the weight of years of the need for vengeance sloughing from his shoulders. His work here was done, an old score settled and Darius vanquished. There was no need for him to linger; his team knew what to do. He could hear them now knocking on doors and explaining the move, smoothing any objections with the promise of four-star luxury and their bill waived for the inconvenience. They would make the necessary transfers and see to the stripping bare of the furnishings in preparation for the builders and decorators that would turn this place into something worthy of being included in the Xenides luxury hotel portfolio.

Everything was under control.

And that's when he heard the scream.

CHAPTER THREE

THE earth-shattering sound rang through the basement, followed by a torrent of language Andreas had no hope of discerning. He was down the hallway and at the open door in just a few strides. 'What the hell is going on?'

One of his team was busy backing out of the small room, closely followed by a slipper that flew past his head and smacked into the wall behind. 'I had no idea there was anyone here,' he said defensively. 'It was marked on the plans as a closet. And it's barely six o'clock. What's anyone doing in bed at this time of night, least of all here?'

'Get out!' screeched the voice. 'Or I'll call the manager. I'll call the police!'

So much for everything being under control. Andreas ushered his red-faced assistant out of the way. 'I'll handle this.'

He stepped into the tiny room that smelt and looked more like a broom closet, ducking his head where the stairs cut through the headspace and avoiding the single globe dangling on a wire from the ceiling, under whose yellow light he found the source of the commotion. She was sitting up in bed, or on a camp stretcher more like it, with her back rammed tight against the wall, the bedding pulled up tight around her with one hand despite the fact her fleecy pyjamas covered every last square centimetre below her neck. In her other hand she wielded a second furry slipper.

Her eyes were wide and wild-looking under a pink satin eye mask reading 'Princess' that she'd obviously shoved up to her brow when she'd been disturbed. Some kind of joke, he decided. In her dishevelled state, with her mousy-coloured hair curling haphazardly around her face, she looked anything but princess material.

Then his eyes made sense of the smell. In the yellow light he saw the vacuum cleaner tucked at the end of the bed and the drab uniform draped unceremoniously over the radiator, and one question at least was answered. The cleaner, he surmised, the one he'd spotted earlier in the corridor who'd stunk of beer. No doubt she'd been trying to sleep it off when she'd been disturbed.

He tried to keep the sneer from his lips as he addressed her. 'I must apologise for my people startling you,' he began. 'I assure you, nobody means you any harm. We simply didn't realise you were here.'

'Well, I am *obviously* here and your *people* have a bloody nerve going about bursting into other people's rooms. What the hell are you playing at? Who are you? Where's Demetrius?'

He held up his hands to calm her. She was Australian, he guessed from her accent, or maybe a New Zealander, but her words were spilling out too fast to be sure.

'I think perhaps you should calm down and then we can discuss this rationally.'

Her hand lifted the slipper. 'Calm down? Discuss rationally? You and your henchman have no right barging into my room. Now get out before I scream again.'

Gamoto, the way she clung to those bedcovers as if her virtue were at stake! Did she really think he was going to attack her? It would take a braver man than him to tackle those industrial-strength pyjamas she was buried beneath.

'I'll leave,' he conceded, 'but only so you can get dressed. Come out when you're ready to talk. It is impossible to reason with a woman sitting in bed dressed up like a clown.'

Her jaw fell open, snapping shut again on a huff. 'How dare you? You have no right to be here. No right at all.'

'I have every right! I've wasted enough time here as it is. Now get dressed and meet me in the office. I'll speak to you then.'

He spun away, pulling the door closed behind him, but not before the other pink slipper went hurtling over his shoulder like a furry missile.

He'd barely started pacing the office floor, damning Darius for the spitting, snarling legacy he'd left behind, when he heard someone behind him. He turned to find a young woman in jeans and a top standing there, her expression sullen, her feet bare.

He sighed. *What the hell else*, he thought, *has Darius left me to clean up?* 'Can I help you?'

'You tell me. You're the one who demanded my presence.'

His eyes did a double take. This was the cleaner? The banshee ready to scream the house down in the broom closet? He didn't know what to be more impressed by, her speed in complying with his orders—the women he associated with couldn't effect a quick change if their life depended on it—or the radical change in her appearance.

He asked her to shut the door behind her and he leaned back and perched himself on the edge of the desk, watching her as she complied. She'd discarded the fleecy pyjamas and ridiculous eye mask and pulled on faded jeans and a long-sleeved T-shirt, and that brought the second surprise. She wasn't tall, but what she missed out on in height she made up for in curves. He'd never have guessed there was shape under that drab uniform or hidden away under a mound of bed clothes, but her fitted T-shirt and hipster jeans accentuated the swell of breasts and the feminine curve of waist to hip that had been completely disguised before.

Nor would he have guessed she would scrub up so well. Sure, there were still grey shadows under her eyes, but she looked years younger than the haggard wreck he'd seen struggling with the vacuum cleaner in the hallway, and much less frightening than the banshee he'd encountered so recently in the closet-cum-bedroom. With not a hint of make-up and with her damp hair tamed into some kind of loose arrangement behind her head, a few loose tendrils coiled around her face served to soften features that weren't classical in the least.

She would never pass for pretty, he determined, but if she bothered to make an effort she could probably do something with herself.

Although right now it looked as if she'd much prefer to do something with him, preferably involving knives.

He caught the glower as she folded her arms underneath her breasts and wondered if she had any idea that motion just accentuated their fullness. *Or that it drew attention to their peaking nipples.*

So she hadn't bothered to put on a bra? No wonder she'd been so quick to appear. He was surprised to feel his body stir, but then he'd never had a problem with such time-saving measures, or with breasts that looked like an invitation. Despite the inconvenience, he could only be intrigued by the closet-dweller. He was sure he'd seen no mention of her in the reports that had crossed his desk.

Cleo bristled under the relentless gaze. What was his problem? She'd done what he'd demanded—abandoned any hope of sleep to get herself up and dressed and met him in the office and for what? So his eyes could rake over her as if she were some choice cut of meat in a butcher-shop window?

So maybe the look was marginally better than the one he'd given her in the hallway earlier when he'd regarded her as some kind of scum before sweeping imperiously by, but it certainly didn't make her feel any more comfortable.

Quite the reverse. She rubbed her upper arms, not from the chill, but to ward off the prickling sensation his gaze generated under her skin. And if she was lucky the action might just break whatever magnet hold his eyes had on her breasts.

He only had to look at them for her nipples to harden to rocks.

Damn the man! Arrogance shone out of him like a beacon, but the only thing it was lighting up was her temper.

'Are you going to tell me what this is all about or would you prefer to keep ogling me?' She looked around the office. 'Where's Demetrius?'

'The man you know as Demetrius is gone.'

Of course he would speak in riddles. The man was insufferable. 'What are you talking about? Gone where? When will he be back?' She'd never much liked her boss, who'd seemed more concerned with his form guide than with how his hotel was falling down around his ears, but as far as she was concerned, the sooner he was back, the better.

'He won't be back. This hotel now belongs to me.'

His revelation slammed through her like a thunderbolt. Where did that leave her? Her rapidly chilling toes curled into the cracked linoleum while a shudder of apprehension wormed its way into her mind. Whatever had happened must have been sudden. She'd heard Demetrius on the phone to his turf accountant when she'd finished the last room, just before this man had appeared, larger than life. A bloodless coup. And the man in front of her, with his cold eyes and strong jaw, looked just the kind of ruthless man for the job. Ruthless— but also her new boss. She swallowed, horrified at the impression she'd made so far. Hadn't she flung a slipper past his ear? 'What is this, then, some kind of interview? Okay, my name is Cleo Taylor and I've been cleaning here for three weeks, and doing the breakfasts. Demetrius probably told you—'

'Demetrius told me nothing. There was no mention of you in the list of employees we had.'

'Oh? But then, Demetrius paid me in cash. He said it was better for the both of us.'

'He would no doubt think that.' Andreas understood why. So Darius could pay her peanuts and most likely deduct the majority of it in return for the cot she occupied.

She shrugged, looking confused. 'So… You'll still be needing a cleaner, right?'

'Not exactly.'

'Okay, I do more than clean. I get up at five for the breakfasts…'

'I'm not looking for a cleaner. Or a kitchen hand.'

'But the hotel—'

'Is closing.'

The fear that had begun as a shred of concern exploded inside her in a frenzy of panic. It might be the worst job with the worst pay in the world—but it was a job, and it came with a roof over her head. And now she'd have no job. *And, more importantly, nowhere to live.*

Her mouth was drier than a Kangaroo Crossing summer's day. 'You mean I lose my job.'

He gave the briefest of nods. It might as well have been the fall of the guillotine. Once more she'd failed. Once more she'd bombed. She almost wanted to laugh. Almost managed to, except the sound came out all wrong and this was no place or time for such reactions, not with him here, watching her every move like a hawk.

Oh, Nanna, she beseeched, closing her eyes with the enormity of it all, *where's the silver lining to losing the worst job in the world?* Unless that was it. She hated the job. Now she had no choice but to find something else. And hopefully, something better.

But it was so hard to think positive thoughts about losing her job when it also meant she'd be losing the roof over her head with it. She opened her eyes toward the window, the rain still pelting against the glass. A bright side. There had to be a bright side. But right now she was darned if she could see what it was.

'When?' Her voice was the barest of whispers. 'How much time do I have?' She would have to move fast to secure something. The little money she had wouldn't last long and if she had to use it for any kind of rental bond…

'Tonight. You need to pack your things and be gone in two hours. The guests are all being transferred to other premises. The builders and redecorators move in to gut the place tomorrow.'

'Tonight? You're closing the hotel so soon?' And panic turned to outrage. 'No. No way you can just walk in and do that!'

'No? And why is that? Surely not some misplaced loyalty to your former employer? I see he showed you none.'

'No, damn you. But it took me the best part of the day to clean this dump. Every single room from top to bottom and now you tell me you're closing it and I could have knocked off at ten this morning? Thank you very much. You could have saved me the trouble!' She flung out her arms to make the last point and then put a hand to her brow, pushing back the hair from her face. Although it was what the action did to her breasts that had his attention.

He didn't know what he'd been expecting, but it wasn't the impassioned response she'd given him. Or the swaying floor show. No sag. Her breasts were full and round and pointed high. Would they look as good uncovered? Would they fill his hands as generously as he imagined they would? Would he like to find out? He needed a woman…

He dragged in a breath, trying to cool his rapidly heating groin, and forced his eyes away. *Sto kalo*, she was a cleaner. A cleaner with a drinking problem if how she'd appeared earlier was any indication. Petra must really be getting to him if he was getting hot under the collar over a cleaner. 'You're mad at me,' he said, reluctantly dragging his attention back to her face, 'because you've spent all day cleaning? Isn't that your job?'

She choked back a sob. Yes, she probably sounded irrational, hysterical, but what did he expect—that she would turn around and calmly thank him for his bombshell? 'You try being a cleaner in a dump like this. I've just had the worst day of my life. How would you like it if you were a cleaner and someone booby-trapped their rubbish? How would you like it if you ended up smelling like a brewery and wearing someone else's dried pizza crusts and then somebody else told you that you hadn't had to clean it up at all, that you needn't have bothered?'

His ears pricked up. Maybe not a cleaner with a drinking problem after all. Maybe he wasn't quite so crazy... 'You don't drink beer? I thought you were an Australian.'

'So that makes me a drinker? No, for the record, I don't drink beer. I can't abide the taste of it. And,' she continued, without missing a beat, 'then I get hauled from my bed and told that my job is over and that I have to leave. And that you want to throw me out in that!' She pointed to the window, where the rain distorted the light from the streetlamps and turned it into crazy zigzags. 'What kind of man are you?'

He wanted to growl. This was supposed to be the most successful day of his life, a day he'd dreamed about for what seemed like for ever. And here he was, being challenged by the likes of this scrap of a woman, a mere cleaner. He ground out his answer between his teeth. 'A businessman.'

'Well, bully for you. What kind of business is it that throws innocent women out onto the street in the middle of the storm from hell?'

He'd heard enough. He turned and flicked an imaginary piece of lint from his sleeve. 'You must have somewhere else to go.'

'Yes. And it's twelve thousand miles away. Shall I start walking now, do you think?'

'Then why don't you just buy yourself a ticket home?'

'And you think that if I could afford my fare home, I'd be working in a dump like this?'

'Do you need to be so melodramatic?'

'No. I don't need to. I'm just doing it for laughs.' She dragged in a breath and threw her arms out by her sides. 'Look, why can't I stay here? Just for tonight. I'll go tomorrow morning, first thing. I promise. Maybe it will have stopped raining by then.'

'The hotel is closing,' he reiterated. 'It will be locked down tonight in preparation for the builders and redecorators coming in tomorrow. The deal was the hotel would be delivered empty.'

'Nobody made a deal with me!'

'I'm making it now.'

It didn't sound like much of a deal to her. 'So where are the guests going? Why can't I go there?' She held up her hand to stop his objection. 'Not as a guest. Surely they could do with a cleaner, with this sudden influx of additional guests.'

He uttered something in Greek, something that sounded to her dangerously like a curse. 'I'll call and ask. No guarantees. Meanwhile you get your things together. I assume that won't take long.'

She sniffed. 'And if they don't have a job?'

'Then you're on your own.'

'Just like that?'

'Just like that.'

She put her hands on top of her head and sighed, locking her fingers together, and turning her head up high, as if to think about it.

But Andreas couldn't think about it. He was too busy following the perfect shape of her breasts, her nipples pulled up high, their shape so lovingly recreated by the thin cotton layer that was all that separated him from them. Her waist looked even smaller now. Almost tiny in comparison as she pulled her arms high, the flare of her hips mirroring the curve above. His mouth went dry.

Damn it all! He yanked his eyes away, rubbing them with his fingers. Anyone would think he'd never had a woman. She was a cleaner. It wouldn't work. Clearly the day had taken more out of him than he'd realised.

'And what about my wages?' She was looking at him, her eyes wide, her arms unhooking. 'Demetrius owes me for more than a week! And surely I'm entitled to some kind of severance pay, even if he was paying me cash, seeing you're the one to terminate my job!'

Silently he cursed Darius again, along with his own team that had failed to pick up this stray employee. 'How much are you owed?'

Cleo did some rapid sums in her head. Math had never been her strong point, so the calculations were a bit rough, but an entire week and a half, less board, that was a considerable sum. 'Fifty quid,' she said, rounding it off, hoping he wouldn't balk.

He pulled a money clip from his pocket, withdrew a handful of notes and then added a fistful more before handing the bundle to her.

Her eyes opened wide as she took in the high-denomination notes and the number of them. Her math was still lousy, but it was more than clear he'd given her way too much. 'I can't take this! There's heaps more than that here.'

'Then consider it a bonus for doing what I ask and getting out of here. Call it your redundancy package, if you like, with enough for your accommodation tonight and probably for an entire week if you play your cards right. Now, it's time you started packing.'

She looked as if she'd rather stay and keep arguing, her mouth poised open and ready to deliver another salvo, but she must have thought better of it. She jammed her lips shut and wheeled around, marching purposefully towards the door, shoving the wad of notes into her jeans pocket as she went. Not that it was any distraction. He was already looking there, admiring the way her denim jeans lovingly caressed the cheeks of her behind as she went. But she stopped before the door and turned, and he was forced to raise his eyes to meet hers.

'I'll go and pack,' she said, colour in her cheeks and fire spitting from her eyes, 'and I'd like to say it's been a pleasure meeting you, but I'm afraid that isn't possible. I'll leave my key in the door. Not that you need it, apparently.'

And then she swept out with her head held high like the princess on her eye mask rather than a redundant cleaner.

There was no need for him to stay. But he sat there, leaning against the desk, thinking that he'd been wrong. She wasn't pretty by any measure, she wasn't tall and elegant like his usual choice of woman, but there was something about her, a fire in her eyes as she'd protested his closure of the hotel, something that had almost burned bright in the seedy air between them. Would she be as passionate in the bedroom, or would she go back to being the bedraggled mouse he'd seen lurking in the corridor?

Damn! Trust Darius to leave him to clean up his rubbish. But he should have expected it.

He rubbed the bridge of his nose, hating the way his thoughts were going. The woman had a point. He, more than anyone, knew what it was like to be left with nothing and without even a roof over his head. He wouldn't wish that on anyone.

He slid open his cell phone, found the direct number for the manager of the hotel the guests here were being transferred to and hit 'call'. It answered within a moment. 'It's Andreas. Have you a position for another cleaner or kitchen hand? There is one here who requires a position, preferably live-in.'

There was a moment's hesitation, but no argument, no

question as to qualifications or referees from the manager. That Andreas himself had enquired was all the assurance the manager required, the moment's hesitation all the time he needed to make the necessary rearrangements. Of course, they could use the help, came the answer. And there would be a bed the person could use in a shared room.

Andreas breathed deep with relief. When he'd thought of getting even with Darius, he'd thought they'd covered all the bases with everyone on the payroll. He'd not thought about any other fallout, the ones Darius had been paying on the sly. But now that fallout was well and truly taken care of. His father had been avenged and nobody had been inadvertently left homeless in the deal. It was the best of all worlds.

He tried to recapture the joy, the exhilaration of the day's events. After what he'd achieved after a lifetime of wanting, he should feel better than this, surely. But something still didn't sit right with him. Maybe it was just the adrenaline let-down now that he'd achieved his goal?

Or maybe it was because he wasn't sure that he wanted someone else taking care of fallout that came complete with sweet curves and lush breasts?

He sighed. He might as well go give her the good news. His car was waiting and he had work to do.

She was already struggling out of her room with an over-sized pack when he emerged and he wondered how she'd walk if ever she got it onto her back. It looked almost as big as her. He leaned down and took it from her, lifting its weight easily. Their fingers brushed and she pulled her hand away, tucking it under her other arm. 'So you pack as quickly as you get changed?'

She looked up at him, her cheeks flaring with colour again as he looked down at her, surprised by the extent of her reaction. Did she not want to touch him that desperately, or was it something else she was feeling? Resentment perhaps, or even hatred that he'd bowled her out into such a night. But she'd dragged on some kind of all-weather jacket and her breasts' reaction was hidden from him. 'Please, you don't have to take that. Not after—all those things I said about you. It was very ungracious after you were so generous. I'm sorry. It's been a long day.'

'I found you a job.'

Her eyes opened wide. 'You did?' They were blue, he realised for the first time, the kind of blue that came with the first rays of light on a misty Santorini morning showing all the promise of a new day. And then she smiled. 'But that's fantastic. Thank you so much. Is it a cleaner's job at the other hotel? Can I stay there?'

He'd never seen her smile. He got the impression she didn't use it a lot around this place, but it was like switching on a light bulb and for a moment it switched off his thought processes. He coughed, his mind busy rewinding, rethinking. 'The job comes with accommodation, yes.'

'Oh, I can't believe it. I'm so sorry for all those things I said back there. I really am.' She reached into her back pocket and hauled out the stash of notes he'd given her, pressing them into his free hand. 'Here. I can't take this now. I won't be needing your money.'

A woman who wouldn't take money when it had been given her? He didn't know many women who wouldn't be hanging around for more, not handing it back. So she worked as a cleaner—maybe she was better qualified than he'd assumed.

A month.

That was all he'd need. She wouldn't be the kind of woman to expect to hang around. She wouldn't want more than he was prepared to give.

A month would work out just fine.

CHAPTER FOUR

'KEEP it,' Andreas said, pushing her hand back, curling his fingers around it. 'You'll probably need some new clothes in your new job.'

Cleo solemnly regarded the notes still curled in her palm, her hand small and warm in his. 'Oh, you mean a new uniform.'

'Something like that,' he said, turning away quickly. 'Come on, my car's waiting outside, I'll give you a lift.'

He hauled her bag up the stairs as if it were a handbag and not stuffed full with all her worldly possessions and from there someone else took one look and relieved him of it, following in their wake, holding an umbrella over their heads as they emerged into the wet night. *Who is this man,* she wondered, *to have his own people to fetch and carry and clean out an entire hotel at his say-so?* A line of minibuses waited at the kerb outside, their exhaust turning to fog in the cold evening air. She recognised some of last night's guests being bundled with their luggage into one of the vans.

She started walking to the one behind. 'No,' he said. 'This one's ours.'

She looked where he indicated and did a double take. He had to be kidding. The black limousine stretched for what looked an entire frontage if not the whole block! She swallowed. She'd never travelled in such a vehicle in her life. She flashed a look down at her outfit. Worn farm boots, denim jeans and an old Driza-Bone coat. She looked longingly at the line of minibuses. She'd feel much more comfortable in something like that.

But the chauffeur had the door open, waiting. 'Are you sure we'll both fit?' she asked, but her companion didn't crack a smile, just gestured for her to precede him, and she had no choice but to enter the car.

It was like being in another world as the vehicle slipped smoothly into the traffic. It was bigger than her bedroom in the hotel and she wouldn't have been surprised to learn it boasted its own en suite. The plush leather seats were more like sofas with not a squeak of springs to be heard and they felt and smelled divine. A cocktail bar sprawled along one side, boasting spirits of every colour imaginable, a row of crystal-cut glasses held delicately in place, and then, just when she thought it couldn't get more amazing, there were stars, or at least tiny coloured lights twinkling all over the ceiling. And even as she watched they changed from blues and greens to oranges and reds and back to blues again.

And then there was him. He sprawled on the seat opposite, his back to the driver, one arm along the back of the seat, and with one leg bent, the other stretched long into the space between them. He'd undone his coat and the sides had fallen apart. Likewise the suit jacket underneath, exposing an expanse of snow-white cotton across his broad chest, all the whiter against the olive skin of his face and hands.

He was watching her, she realised. Watching her watching him. Her skin prickled. How could he do that with just his eyes? But it wasn't just his eyes, it was the slightly upturned mouth, the sculpted jaw and the attitude. Oh, yes, he had attitude to burn.

She pressed herself back into the seat, trying to look less

overwhelmed, more relaxed. 'I guess you've never met anyone who hasn't been in a stretch limousine before. My reaction must have been quite entertaining.'

'On the contrary,' he said, without moving his eyes from hers, 'I found it charming.'

Charming. Nobody had ever used that word around her before. She wouldn't have believed them if they had. He was no doubt being polite. More likely thinking *gauche*. She felt it. Maybe she should steer the conversation, such as it was, to safer territory.

'Is it far to the hotel?'

'Not far.'

'Do you know what kind of job it is?'

'I think you will perform a variety of tasks. I'm sure you will find them to your liking.'

'Oh.' She wished he could be more specific. 'But it's a live-in position?'

Across the vast interior he nodded, his dark eyes glinting in the light of a passing streetlamp, and for some reason she suddenly felt uncomfortable, as if she'd almost glimpsed something in their otherwise shadowed depths.

'There is just one catch.'

'Oh?' There had to be though, she thought. Why should her life suddenly turn around without there being a catch? 'What is it?'

'The position has a fixed contract. This job will last only one month.'

'I see.' She sank back in her seat. Well, a month was better than nothing. And at least she'd have time to sort something else in between now and then.

'But you will be well compensated.'

She blinked up at him. 'Thank you again for your generosity, Mr…' and she was left floundering, speechless. She was in a car heading who knew where with a man who'd promised her a job somewhere and she didn't even know his name. When would she learn? What the hell kind of mess was she heading for now? 'Oh, My God, I can't believe I'm doing this. I don't even know your name.'

He smiled and dipped his head. 'I assure you, you have nothing to fear. Andreas Xenides at your service.'

Her eyes narrowed. She was sure she'd heard the name, maybe even read something in one of the papers back home before she'd left. But that man had been a billionaire. She didn't tend to meet many of them in her line of business. Maybe this man was related. 'I think there's someone called Xenides with a huge hotel up on the Gold Coast in Queensland.'

He nodded. 'The Xenides Mansions Hotel. One of my best performers.'

She swallowed. 'That's your hotel? You own it?'

'Well, one of my companies. But ultimately, yes, I own it.'

She didn't so much sink back into her seat as collapse against it.

He frowned. 'Does that bother you?'

'Bother me? It terrifies me!' She put a hand to her wayward mouth. Oh, my, the man was a billionaire and she'd thrown a slipper at his head, right before she'd bawled him out in the basement and insisted he pay her wages and find her a replacement job. As a cleaner. And the amazing thing about it was that he had.

Mind you, the way people were running around after him at the hotel ready to do his bidding, he could probably have found her a job as an astronaut if he'd put his mind to it.

What must it be like to wield that much power? She glanced over at him, her eyes once more colliding with his dark driven gaze. So he was a billionaire. That answered a few questions. But it didn't answer all of them.

'There's something I don't understand.'

'Oh.' He tilted his head to one side, as if almost amused. 'What is it?'

'Why would you care about a tiny dump of a hotel three blocks from Victoria Station? Why buy it? There must be plenty of other hotels better suited to a posh outfit like yours.'

And his eyes glistened and seemed to focus somewhere behind her and Cleo got the impression he didn't even see her. 'I had my reasons.'

She shivered at his flat voice as if the temperature had just dropped twenty degrees. Whatever his reasons, Andreas Xenides struck her as a man you wouldn't want to cross.

Cleo looked away, wanting to shake off the chill, and was surprised to see how far they'd come. She'd expected a lift to another small hotel somewhere close by, as he'd intimated, but she could see now that the limousine was making its way towards Mayfair.

His cell phone beeped and she was grateful he had a distraction. She was happy just to watch the busy streetscape, the iconic red double-decker buses, the black taxi cabs all jockeying for the same piece of bitumen and somehow all still moving. 'Petra, I'm glad you called. Yes, I'm finished in London.'

She wasn't trying to listen to his call, but there was no way she couldn't hear every word, especially when he made no attempt to lower his voice, and it was a relief when he dipped into his native language and she could no longer understand his words and she could just let the deep tones of his voice wash over her. When he spoke English his accent gave his words a rich Mediterranean flavour, a hint of the exotic, but when he spoke in Greek his voice took on another quality, on the one hand somehow harsher, more earthy and passionate on the other.

Much like Andreas himself, she imagined, because for all his civilised trappings, the cashmere coat and the chauffeur-driven limousine, she'd seen for herself that he could be harsh and abrupt, that he was used to making the rules and expecting people to play by them. And definitely passionate. Hadn't he set her own body to prickly awareness with just one heated gaze?

It made sense that a man like him would have a Petra or someone else waiting for him. He was bound to have a wife or a girlfriend, maybe even both; didn't the rich and famous have their own rules? She looked around at the car's plush interior, drinking in the buttery leather upholstery with her fingers and wanting to apologise to the pristine carpet for her tired boots. She gazed out of the tinted windows and caught the occupants of passing cars trying to peer in, looks of envy on their faces, and sighed, committing it all to memory. What would it be like to be one of the Petras of this world? To move in such circles and consider this all as normal?

She smiled philosophically. This was not her world. Any minute now he'd drop her at the hotel to take up her new cleaning position and he'd be gone for ever, back to Petra or another, whoever and wherever she was.

'We're flying back tomorrow,' she heard Andreas say, abruptly switching back to English. 'Expect us around five.'

Cleo wondered at the sudden change of language but continued peering out at the scenery outside her limousine's windows, the magnificent park to their left, the lights from buildings and streetlamps making jagged patterns on the wet roads. Even on a dark, wet night the streets of London fascinated her. It was so different from the tiny town of Kangaroo Crossing, where the main street was dusty and almost deserted after six at night. Here it was so vibrant and filled with life at whatever time of the day or night and she would never get sick of craning her neck for a look at the everyday sights here like Buckingham Palace, sights she'd only ever dreamed about one day seeing.

'*Us*, Petra?' Andreas continued. 'Oh, I'm sorry, I should have mentioned. I'm bringing a friend.'

Something about the way he said those last words made Cleo turn her head, some loaded quality that spoke of a message she didn't quite understand. She didn't mean to look right at him, she intended to swing her head around as if merely choosing to look out of the nearside windows, but her eyes jagged on his and held solid. 'That's right,' he said, holding her gaze and her heartbeat, it seemed, in his. 'A friend. Please ensure Maria has my suite prepared.'

He clicked the phone closed and slipped it away, all the while still holding her gaze.

'Is it much further?' she asked with false brightness, wondering what it was she was missing and why she was so suddenly breathless and why he needed to look at her that way, as if she were about to be served up for his next meal.

'No. Not much.'

As if on cue the limousine pulled off Park Lane into a wide driveway and rolled to a gentle stop. She looked up at the hotel towering over the car. 'But this… This is Grosvenor House.'

'So it is.'

The door opened and cold air swept into the warm interior as the concierge pulled open the door. 'But why are we here? I thought… You said…'

'We're here,' he simply said, sliding one long leg out and extending his hand to her. 'If you care to join me.'

'But I can't go in there. Not like this. I look like I've just stepped off the farm.'

'They'll think you're an eccentric Australian.'

'They must have a staff entrance!' But still, she was already moving towards him, inexorably drawn by his assuredness.

'Come,' he said, taking her hand to help her out. 'These people are paid not to take any notice.'

It was no consolation. She felt like someone who should

be staying at some backpackers' hotel, not the poshest hotel in Mayfair. She caught sight of her reflection in the glass frontage and grimaced. She looked like a total hick. Why couldn't he have warned her? But Andreas didn't seem to care. The concierge staff swarmed like foot soldiers around him, taking orders, trying to please, while others ferried her backpack onto a trolley as lovingly as if it were the finest Louis Vuitton luggage.

She followed in his wake uncertain, sure someone was about to call Security and send her on her way, but worry soon gave way to wonder.

She stepped from the revolving door into a lobby of white marble and columns the colour of clotted cream and forgot to think. It was amazing. Luxurious. A fantasyland. It took every shred of self-control she possessed not to spin around in a circle to take it all in. Instead she slipped her Driza-Bone from her shoulders and tried to look as if she belonged. Fat chance.

Could it be possible that she'd soon be working here? At Grosvenor House? Andreas left her momentarily while he dealt with Reception, she guessed to inform the housekeeper she was here, and she drank in the luxury and the ambience. Now she would have a reason to call her mother and not feel as if she had nothing but bad news. After the disaster that Kurt had been and her mother worrying about her working long hours in a seedy hotel, she would be thrilled she'd scored a position in one of London's landmark hotels. She wouldn't tell her it was only for a month. If she played her cards right, she'd have a reference from one of London's top hotels and she would be set for another job.

And maybe some time soon she'd be able to save enough money to pay back the money her nanna had given her and she'd lost when she'd entrusted it to Kurt. At least now she had a chance.

Andreas returned and took her arm and steered her past a suite of red velvet chairs on a round signature rug that reeked money.

'Are you taking me to meet the housekeeper? I'm sure I can find her. I've kept you long enough.'

He didn't look at her, simply kept on walking her into a lift. 'I thought you might like to see your room first, see if it's suitable.' He pushed a button and she frowned. 'Did I tell you you'd have to share?'

His question distracted her. 'You think I mind? Just look at this place.' She paused as the elevator smoothly hummed into motion, suddenly making sense of what had niggled at her before. 'Hang on. We're going up. Surely they wouldn't give staff accommodation on a guest floor?'

He held off answering as the lift doors slid open, welcoming them into an elegant elevator lobby decorated in olive and magenta tones, before he directed her to a nearby door and keyed it open. 'It seems you're in luck.'

And the hairs on the back of her neck stood to attention. 'Tell me this is not my room.'

'Strictly speaking, it's not. Like I told you, you'd have to share.'

She swallowed. 'Then tell me whose room it is. Who would even have a room like this in the Grosvenor to start with—Prince Harry?' And even as she asked the question the chilling answer came to her, so unbelievable that she didn't want to give it credence, so insane that she thought she herself must be. 'It's your room, isn't it? There is no cleaning job. And you expect me to share with you?'

His dark eyes simmered with aggravation. 'Come inside and I'll explain.'

'I'm not going in there! I'm not going anywhere except down in that lift unless you tell me right now what's going on. And then I'm probably heading down in that lift anyway.'

'Cleo, I will not discuss this in public.'

She looked around. 'There's nobody else here!'

A bell pinged behind her, followed seconds later by lift doors sliding open. A group emerged, the women chatting and laughing, their arms laden with shopping bags, the men looking as if they could do with a stiff drink.

She looked longingly at the open lift door behind them. Took a step towards it and then realised. She snapped her head around. 'Where is my pack?'

'No doubt still on its way up. Now come in and listen to what I have to say and if you still want to go, you can go. But hear me out first. I do have a job for you.'

'Just not cleaning, right?' Cleo bit her bottom lip. What kind of jobs did Greek billionaires give girls who'd dropped out of high school and made a mess of everything they'd ever attempted? Definitely nothing you needed qualifications for...

But that made less sense than anything else. Her looks were plain, her figure had always erred on the side of full, and she'd never had men lining up for her favours. Cleaning was about all she was suitable for.

'Cleo.'

He made her name sound like a warning, the tone threatening, but maybe he was right. Maybe she should hear him out while she waited for her pack. Besides, if she was going to let fly with a few choice words of her own, maybe privacy was the preferred option.

And then she'd leave.

Spider legs skittered down her spine at the thought of going out into the cold wet night with no place to go. But she'd face that later. She wasn't going to let the weather dictate her morals. She strode past him into the room, cursing herself for choosing that particular moment to breathe in, wishing that, for someone so aggravating, he didn't smell so damn good.

Thankfully the room was large enough that she could put some distance between them. A lot of distance. She'd been expecting a bedroom, a typical hotel room. She found anything but.

The room looked more like a drawing room in a palace than any hotel room she'd ever seen, a dining table and chairs taking up one end of the room, a lounge suite facing a marble mantelpiece at the other with the dozen or so windows dressed in complementary tones of creams and crimsons.

But she wasn't here to appreciate the fine furnishings or the skilful use of colour. She didn't want to be distracted by the luxury she could apparently so easily take advantage of. Would it be easy? She wondered.

She dropped her jacket over a chair and turned, dragging in oxygen for some much-needed support. 'Okay, I'm here. What's going on?'

She almost had the impression he hadn't heard her as he headed for a sideboard, opening a crystal decanter and pouring himself a slug of the amber fluid it contained. 'You?' he offered.

She shook her head. 'Well? You told me I had a cleaning job at some hotel.'

Still he took his sweet time, taking a sip from the glass before turning and leaning against the dresser. 'While it's not exactly what I said, it is what I intimated. That much is true.'

'You lied to me!'

'I did not lie. I found you a job cleaning at another hotel. And then I decided better of it.'

'But why? What for?'

He drained the glass of its contents and placed it on the dresser in the same motion as he pushed himself towards her. 'What if I offered you a better job? More pay. Enough to buy your return ticket to Australia and a whole lot more. Enough to set you up for life.'

She licked her lips. If she could pay back her nanna what she'd borrowed… But what would she be expected to do to get it? 'What kind of job are you talking about?'

He laughed, coming closer. 'You see why I knew you would be perfect? Any other woman would ask how much money first.'

She sidestepped around the dining table, until it was between them. 'That was my next question.'

He stopped and started moving the other way, slowly circling, step by step. 'How much would be enough? One hundred thousand pounds? How much would that be in your currency?'

She swallowed, too distracted to concentrate on keeping her distance. Her maths might be lousy but even she had no trouble working that one out. Double at least. Her mouth almost watered at the prospect. But she'd heard plenty of stories about travellers being offered amazing amounts of money to courier a box or a package. And equally she'd heard of them getting caught by the authorities and much, much worse. She might have done some stupid things in her life, but she was so not going there. 'I don't want any part of drug money. I'm not touching it.'

He was closer than she realised, his dark eyes shining hard. 'Cleo, please, you do not realise how much you insult me. This would be nothing to do with drugs. I hate that filthy trade as much as you. I assure you, your work would be legal and perfectly above board.'

Legal. Above board. And it paid in the hundreds of thousands of dollars? Yeah, sure. There were jobs in the paper like that for high-school dropouts every other day. 'What is it, then?' she asked, circling the other way, pretending to be more interested in an arrangement of flowers set upon a side table. The red blooms were beautiful too, she thought, touching her fingers to the delicate petals, just like everything else in this room. Did he really expect her to share it with him? 'So what's the job?'

He didn't move this time, made no attempt to follow her, and because she was ready for it, expecting it, the fact he stayed put was more unnerving than anything. 'It's really quite simple. I just need you to pretend to be my mistress.'

CHAPTER FIVE

'PRETEND to be your *what*?' Cleo started to laugh. If ever there was a time for hysterical laughter, this moment was tailor-made, but shock won out in the reaction stakes, choking off the sound and rendering her aghast. 'You must be insane!'

'I assure you I'm perfectly serious.'

'But your mistress? Who even uses that word any more?'

'Would you prefer it if I used the word *lover*?'

'No!' *Definitely not lover*. And definitely not when it was said in that rich, curling accent. She didn't want to think about being Andreas' lover, pretend or otherwise. 'I don't know where you got the impression that I might say yes to such a crazy proposition, but I'm afraid you have the wrong impression of me, Mr Xenides. I'm sorry, but I'll have to turn down your generous proposal.'

'Call me Andreas, please.'

She looked over her shoulder anxiously, watching the door, before she looked back. 'And why would a man like you even need someone to act as his mistress anyway? It makes no sense.'

He shrugged. 'Maybe I just don't like to be seen as available.'

'Maybe you should just put out a press release.' She looked longingly at the door again. 'When is my bag supposed to arrive? I want to go.'

'At least think about it, Cleo. It's a lot of money to throw away. Can you afford that?'

'You're crazy. Just look at me.' She held her arms out at her sides, her heart jumping wildly in her chest, her words tumbling over her tongue. 'I'm a cleaner. I muck out bathrooms and rubbish bins and have the split nails and red hands to prove it. I'm short and dumpy and have never once in my life been called so much as pretty, and you're suggesting I could pretend to be your mistress? Who's going to believe that for a start? They'll think you've gone mad and they'd be right.'

He answered her with a raised eyebrow and a half-hearted shrug as he eased closer. 'I think you underestimate your charms.'

Charms? What planet was this man from? 'Why *me*? You could have any woman in the world. You probably already have.'

He turned her implied insult to his advantage. 'Exactly. Which is why I don't want just any woman in the world.' He was close now, so close she could see the individual lashes that framed his dark eyes, close enough to see his pupils flare as he held out his fingers to her cheek. She flinched but he kept coming, tracing the line of her cheek with the backs of his fingers. 'I want you.'

Her heart missed a beat or two. She tried to shake her head but still his fingers remained, his touch feather-light and yet bone-shudderingly deep in effect.

'I don't… I can't…'

And he pulled his hand away, concern muddying his eyes as if something had just occurred to him. 'You're not a virgin?'

The intimacy of the question threw her for a moment. She could feel her cheeks burning up as she fought to find an answer. 'I thought this was about pretending. Why should whether or not I've ever slept with anyone even be an issue?'

He shrugged. 'Because there will be nights we are forced to share a bed to keep up appearances. And it's not beyond the realms of possibility that as a man and a woman, together, we might wish to seek mutual pleasure in each other's bodies.'

Help! 'So you expect sex, then, as part of this deal?'

He frowned and drew away, as if the very idea of her asking offended him. 'Not necessarily. Just that it may well be a by-product of our arrangement.'

Sex as a by-product of our arrangement?

How formal that sounded. How impersonal. It sounded more like a business deal, which she supposed it was. Not that she'd been involved in too many business deals, especially where they included a sex clause.

'I don't want it,' she ventured, not entirely sure if she meant just the contract or the sex or both. Because there was something about Andreas' touch that sent her senses into overdrive, something about his touch that made a secret part of her ache in ways it shouldn't, especially not for a man she'd only just met, a man she knew nothing about.

'It's a good offer,' he continued, as gently and convincingly as a parent trying to get a child to drink its milk. 'It's a fixed-term contract and in one month you go home. All expenses paid. First-class travel naturally.'

He watched her face, searching for the crack in her resolve. 'And no sex, if that's what you want. Though if it did happen, I can guarantee it wouldn't mean anything.'

His words blurred. *"It wouldn't mean anything."* And all she kept hearing was the echo of the words Kurt had said to her when she'd told him she loved him. And he'd just laughed as he'd yanked up his jeans. *"What's your problem? It didn't mean anything. You really are stupid."*

And all she had felt was the bottom falling out of her world as her newly discovered heart had lain shredded. She'd made a pointless journey, thrown what she'd always believed to be special away on a deadbeat who'd taken everything he could get and left her high and dry.

'You have had sex? Can we be clear on that?' Andreas' uncertain voice came from a long way away and still it brought her hackles up. What did he think now, that she was a complete loser?

'Oh, sure, loads of times.' *Once.* But then why should it matter if he thought her a complete loser? It wasn't as if she hadn't thought the same thing herself.

'Then it's all settled.'

Her head snapped up. 'Hang on, what's settled?' She had a feeling she'd missed something somewhere. Had she said yes and somehow forgotten?

'Tomorrow you will fly with me to my home on Santorini.'

She knew the name. Kurt had wooed her with his promises of travel and sunsets, of short breaks they could take to the Mediterranean, to Corfu and Mykonos and Santorini, of crystal-clear waters and lazy summer days. It had sounded so romantic, but of course, it had all been lies designed to convince her that they had a future together in order to lure her to London. She'd all but given up any hope of seeing anything at all of Europe.

But now she had the chance to go there with Andreas. Was it enough of a reason to say yes?

A buzzer sounded and Andreas moved swiftly to the door, pulling it open to the porter at last with her luggage. 'We will leave at twelve. The morning will be busy with appointments so we will have to start early.

'In the bedroom, thank you,' Andreas directed the porter, pressing a note into his hand.

'No!' she called, surprising them both and causing the porter to wheel around. 'I'll take that.' She grabbed one of the shoulder straps.

'Leave it, Cleo.'

'But there's no point. I was just leaving anyway.'

The porter looked nervously from one to the other, Cleo tugging on the pack, knowing it was her hold on reality and on control, and Andreas glowering until finally the porter decided that discretion was the better part of valour and withdrew, uttering a rushed, 'Call me if you need anything more,' before making himself scarce.

Cleo heaved the backpack onto her shoulder.

'I thought we had a deal.'

'You thought wrong. I never agreed to anything. And I'm leaving.'

'But you have no job, nowhere to go.'

'I'll find something. I'll manage.' She retrieved her Driza-Bone from the back of a chair and bundled it in front of her before being game enough to steal one last glance at him.

Impossibly good-looking. That was how she'd remember him. Eyes of midnight-black and hair that waved thick and dark to collar length, an imperious nose and a passionate slash of mouth it was almost a crime for any man to possess. And a face like slate, just like she'd thought in the hotel, until it heated up and the angles took on curves she'd never seen coming.

But so what? She was leaving. It might be a huge amount of money to give up and already she could hear the girls from her high school singing out a familiar chorus of "loser, loser, Cleo's a loser". But she'd been hearing that chorus a long time and she was used to it. She'd been an object of pity ever since her father had walked out on her pregnant mother, never to be seen again.

And besides, she knew she was doing the right thing. For Andreas' proposal was flawed. She didn't want the chance of 'sex as a by-product' of anything. She'd had sex that didn't mean anything and she'd hated herself in the aftermath. It had made her feel cheap and disposable and had hurt her more than she wanted to admit. She didn't care for the chance of more, no matter how much he might be paying.

'I'll see myself out.'

'I need you,' he said as she turned for the door.

She halted, her fingers around the door handle. 'I get the impression, Mr Xenides, that you don't need anyone.' She twisted and pulled. She didn't belong here. Now she'd made up her mind, she couldn't wait to get away. Had to get away.

The door was open just a few inches when his palm slammed it shut. 'You're wrong!'

She turned to protest but the words sizzled and burned in the heat she saw coming from his eyes. 'How much will it take, then? How much do you want? I thought you didn't care about money, but you're just like the rest, one whiff and you want more. You're just a better actress. Which tells me you're exactly the woman I need.

'So how much, sweet, talented Cleo? How much to secure your services for a month? One hundred thousand clearly isn't enough, so let's say we double it. Two hundred thousand pounds. Four hundred thousand of your dollars. Would that be enough?'

The numbers went whirling around her brain, so big they didn't mean anything, so enormous she couldn't get a grip on them. Four hundred thousand dollars for a month of pretending to be Andreas' companion? Was she nuts to even think about giving that up? She could go home, pay back her nanna, pay for repairs to the farm's leaking roof that her mother always complained about but there was never enough money to repair, and she'd still have enough left over to buy a place of her own.

More than that, she'd be able to go home and hold her head up high. And for once, just once in her life, she didn't have to be a loser.

But could she do it? Could she pretend to be this man's lover and all that entailed and simply walk away in the end?

She shook her head trying to work it all out. She truly didn't know. If she just had some time to think it all out. 'Andreas, I—'

'Five hundred thousand pounds! One million of your dollars. Will that be enough to sway your mind?'

She gasped. 'You have to be kidding. That's an obscene amount of money.'

'Not if it gets me what I want. And I want you, Cleo. Say yes.'

She couldn't think, couldn't breathe, only one note of clarity spearing through the fog of her brain.

One million dollars.

How could she walk away from that? It was unthinkable, unimaginable, like winning the lottery or scooping the pools. And she'd even get to live on Santorini for a whole month, the island she'd longed to visit, the island Kurt had only talked about visiting for a day or two. Wasn't that some kind of justice? She licked her lips, once more feeling her hold on the world slipping, swaying. 'Just for a month, you say?'

The corners of his mouth turned up. 'Maybe even less if you play your cards right.'

'But definitely no sex. Just pretending. Is that right?'

A shadow passed across his eyes and was just as quickly gone. 'If that's the way you want it.'

'That's exactly the way I want it. No sex. And in one month I go home.'

'No questions asked. First class. All expenses paid.'

She swallowed against a throat that felt tight and dry and against a fear that he might soon discover he was making the mistake of his life and she'd be booted out with the week. 'I don't know if I'm the right person for the job.'

He slipped the pack from her shoulder and dropped it on the ground beside them before she'd noticed, relieving her of the weight on her back, but not even touching the fear in her gut. 'You'll be perfect. Any other questions?'

She shook her head. How could she expect him to make sense of anything going on in her mind when she couldn't unscramble it herself? 'No. Um, at least... No, I don't think so.'

He smiled then, as he curved one hand around her neck, his fingers warm and gentle on her skin and yet setting her flesh alight. 'Then what say we seal this deal with a kiss?'

She gasped and looked up at him in shock. That message cleared a way through the fog in her brain as if it had been shot from a cannon. 'We could always just shake hands.'

'We could,' he agreed, both hands weaving their magic behind her head, his thumbs tracing the line of her jaw while he studied her face. 'But given we will no doubt have to get used to at least this, we might as well start now.'

And he angled her upturned face and dipped his own until his lips met hers. Fear held her rigid, that and a heart that had taken on a life of its own and threatened to jump out of her chest. But as his lips moved over hers, gentler than she'd imagined possible, gentle but, oh, so sure, she sighed into the kiss, participating, matching him.

One hand scooped down her back, pressing her to him from chest to thigh, her nipples exquisitely sensitive to the chest that met hers, heat pooling low down between her thighs, making her more aware than she'd ever been of her own physical needs. They called to her now, announcing their presence with logic-numbing desperation until her knees, once stiff with shock, threatened to buckle under her. She trembled, reaching for him, needing something to steady herself as his mouth wove some kind of magic upon her own.

It was just a kiss. Tender almost, more gentle than she would ever expect this man to give, but, oh, so thorough in its impact. Her fingers tangled in his shirt, her fingertips drinking in the feel of the firm flesh beneath and she was sure she felt him shudder. Was this how a man felt, rock-hard and solid, as opposed to a boy? Kurt had claimed to be twenty-six and told her he worked out regularly, but his body had been white-bread soft and just as unsatisfying.

But Andreas felt as if he'd been sculpted from marble, firm flesh over muscle and skin that felt like satin and her fingers itched to feel more. Ached to feel more.

Then just as suddenly the kiss was over, his lips departing, and she was left bereft and breathless blinking up at him. He said nothing, just looked down at her, his dark eyes swirling with questions until a bubble of panic rose up inside her.

Had he spotted her lack of experience? Would he change his mind and toss her out, now that she'd finally agreed to his terms?

'I guess we have a deal,' he surprised her by saying, before letting her go. 'You might want to settle in. I have some work to do with the lawyers and I'll arrange for the necessary papers to be drawn up.'

'The papers?' She'd just been kissed senseless and he expected her to suddenly know what he was talking about. 'What papers?'

'The contract. This is a business arrangement. I think we both need the assurance it will stay that way.'

'Oh, of course.' She nodded as if she understood completely. When what she knew about business law would fit through the eye of a needle. Which was what had got her into her mess with Kurt. *A gentlemen's agreement*, he'd told her, and she'd been fool enough to believe he was gentleman enough to honour the terms. So much for trust.

Andreas clearly wasn't into trust or gentlemen's agreements, for which she should be thankful, even if it rubbed that he might not trust her. But if a contract meant she'd get her money and not get ripped off this time, she could live with it.

A wave of exhaustion suddenly washed over her, the adrenaline rush of the last half-hour, the events of the last twenty-four hours, especially the emotional upheaval of the last four when she'd been wrenched from her bed, catching up with her. She needed sleep and she needed it badly. 'Which way to my room?'

He'd already pulled his cell phone from his pocket and made the connection. He looked up and frowned before turning away, a torrent of Greek pouring into the phone.

Okay, so she'd find it by herself. She hauled her pack over her shoulder and aimed for one of the two doors she knew didn't lead to the hallway outside. One of them would be her room for sure.

She found a bedroom off the living room, a massive king-sized bed covered in almost a dozen pillows taking centre stage. She opened one cupboard and found a line of shirts and trousers hanging inside. Andreas' wardrobe, then. She took another door that led into a massive marble bathroom, complete with bath, shower and bidet, and then took another door out, only to find herself back in the living room where Andreas was still on the phone.

He raised one eyebrow when he saw her emerge and she raised her own. 'My room?' she mouthed quietly and he frowned and pointed to the door she'd first entered and her heart leapt into her mouth. Surely he wasn't expecting them to share? Even though he'd hinted that it might be necessary to maintain the illusion, there was no one else here to pretend for now. And hadn't she made it plain enough that she wouldn't sleep with him? She shook her head and her panicked thoughts must have been laid bare in her eyes. He covered the handset with one hand and pointed to a sofa. 'I'm sleeping there,' he growled. 'The bedroom is all yours.'

She retraced her steps to the bedroom and dug through her bag until she found her pyjamas and toilet bag and ducked into the bathroom, feeling embarrassed and stupid and relieved all at the same time. Of course he didn't want to sleep with her! What the hell had she been thinking? Their deal was for her to *pretend* to be his mistress, not be the real thing. One kiss had scrambled her brain completely. One kiss and she was practically expecting him to make love to her.

She adjusted the water temperature and stepped into the cloudburst of a shower. The pounding of the steamy water was like a salve to her weary muscles and tired body, but still she was out in record time, simultaneously pulling on her pyjamas and cleaning her teeth in case Andreas needed the bathroom. Her stomach rumbled and she realised she hadn't eaten since breakfast. But she was used to that. It was the one reason her jeans fitted her now, rather than stretching at the seams like when she'd first arrived in London. At least her mad job had achieved what ten years of New Year's resolutions had failed to deliver. Anyway, she was too tired to eat now. All she wanted to do was collapse into bed.

She pulled the hair tie from her hair, shaking the damp ends free as she surveyed the object in question. Compared to the camp bed she was used to, the bed seemed to stretch an acre in every direction. And it was all for her. But which side was his? Or did his lordship like to occupy the middle? He might be going to sleep on the sofa outside, but just the knowledge that he'd slept here last night and she could be sharing that same place seemed too intimate, too personal. She hovered at the side a while, before exhaustion got the better of her and she climbed into the closest side, finding herself enveloped in cloud-soft luxury, the scent of Andreas on her pillow, the comforter so soft and warm around her it was like a hug from her nanna.

The bright side, she thought dreamily, was that sooner than she'd expected she'd be home and hugging her nanna again. There was always a bright side.

She pulled her mask over her eyes to shut out the ribbon of light seeping under the door, feeling sleep tugging at her so hard that nothing could keep her awake tonight, not the occasional burst of Greek she could hear coming from the room outside, not regret at making the deal she'd done and not even the fear that, despite his assurances, at any moment Andreas Xenides could walk through that door and climb into this bed.

She yawned. She knew she should care. She wanted to. But not right now. In the morning she'd be able to think straight. In the morning they could set any necessary boundaries.

In the morning…

Andreas was still on the phone when Room Service arrived with the meal he'd ordered in between calls to his lawyers and to the concierge to arrange the round of appointments Cleo would need in the morning. He was hungry and he figured she must be too, and until she'd been thoroughly made over there was little point being photographed with her in any of the restaurants or bars. Before and after shots wouldn't help his cause. In any event, there was something to be said for taking a few hours in private to get to know one another. For, as much as he expected she'd be perfect for his purposes, the contracts needn't be signed until he'd made absolutely certain.

He pushed open the door to the bedroom to let her know their meal had arrived and found the room in darkness, lit only with the light spilling in from the room behind. And there she lay, looking tiny in the big wide bed, her flannelette pyjamas buttoned almost all the way up to her neck like a suit of armour with the quilt pulled up almost as high, and that damned Princess mask hiding her eyes.

The blood in his veins heated to boiling point. She was

sleeping? He'd just agreed to pay her a million dollars and she was sleeping as if it were no big deal and she could start earning her money tomorrow?

He was just about to rip the damn mask off when she stirred on a sigh and settled back into the mattress, her breathing so slow and regular that he paused, remembering.

She'd been asleep when his staff had woken her hours ago, he recalled, after being awake since the very early hours, the shadows under her eyes underlining her exhaustion. Maybe he should give those shadows a chance to clear and give the makeover experts a fighting chance to turn her into the woman he needed her to be?

Maybe he should just back out of here and let her sleep?

And maybe he should just climb right in there with her and make the most of his money? She'd said she didn't want sex but he'd never known a woman to turn him down. That she'd been so adamant grated.

There was a knock at the door outside. Housekeeping, no doubt, come to make up the sofa bed, and he turned and pulled the door closed behind him.

He had no need to take any woman. He had an entire month. She would come to him; he knew it.

CHAPTER SIX

IT WAS a strange dream, where people faded in and out of focus, the girls from school with their taunts of loser, her half-brothers hugging the father who looked on her as excess baggage, and Kurt laughing at her, his white chest quivering with the vibrations. From somewhere Cleo could hear the sound of her nanna telling her to look for the silver lining. She spun around trying to find the source of her voice, trying to pull her from the shadows and hang onto her message and drown out the chorus behind her, when a different shape emerged from the mist, tall and broad and arrogantly self-assured.

"I'm scared." It was her voice, even though she'd not said a word, and she wanted to run, tempted to turn back to the mocking chorus behind her, back to the world she knew and understood so well, back to the familiar, but her legs were like lead and she couldn't move and he kept right on coming until he stood head and shoulders above her. And he smiled, all dark eyes and gleaming white teeth. 'You should be,' and then he'd dipped his head to kiss her and she heard nothing but the buzzing in her ears and the pounding of her heart, and from somewhere in the shadows, the sound of her nanna's voice.

'Rise and shine.' The words made no sense until the blow

to her rump, cushioned with the thick quilt but enough to bring her to consciousness with a jump. 'You've got a busy morning.'

The alarm on the bedside table alongside snapped off and she drank in the scent of bed-warmed flesh. *His bed-warmed flesh.* So the alarm was the buzzing in her ears? But what was causing the fizzing in her blood?

She sat up and pushed her mask above her eyes, and then, remembering his comment about dressing like a clown, swiped it from her head. A moment later she wished she'd kept it on. He was naked. Unashamedly naked as he strode to the wardrobe and pulled out a robe. Too late she averted her eyes and, *oh, my*. She felt the blush rise like a tide as the truth sank in—he was huge! Only to have the blush deepen with the next wayward thought.

And if he looks that big now?

She swallowed, pulling her legs up like a shield, wondering why she should be suddenly tingling down *there*. How big he could be had nothing to do with her. It wasn't something she was planning on finding out.

'Hungry?' he asked casually, but her brain had ceased to function on that level. 'You missed dinner,' he explained, slipping into a robe and thankfully tying it at his waist. 'I thought you might be hungry. I've taken the liberty of ordering for both of us. You looked like you could have slept until noon.'

She unplastered her tongue from the roof of her mouth. 'I was tired.'

'Apparently. You slept like the dead. Breakfast will be here in a few minutes and then your first appointment is in under an hour.'

'What appointment?'

'Downstairs in the spa salon. You're booked in for the works by which time the stylist will be here with a selection of outfits. You won't have much time to decide. We're flying out at noon.'

Cleo glanced at the clock; it was only just after seven. 'That's hours away.'

'You'll need every bit of it, so eat up and don't wait for me.' His eyes raked over her and her skin prickled under his gaze. 'You're going to need your strength.'

She shivered as he disappeared into the bathroom. Why did she get the impression he wasn't only talking about her upcoming appointments?

He needn't have worried about her not eating. Room Service arrived with the heavily laden trolley a minute or two later, and the aroma threatened to drive her crazy. The porter had hardly finished serving the breakfast up on the dining table in the next room before she practically fell upon the feast. There was yoghurt and jam, pastries and rolls and toast, along with two massive platters of English breakfast. It was a feast. The coffee was smooth and rich with just the right amount of bitterness to wash it all down. She couldn't remember enjoying a meal more.

Andreas emerged from the bathroom while she was still eating, a towel lashed low around his hips and barefoot, moisture still clinging to his chest and beading in the hair that curled into his neck.

'That's what I like to see,' he said, sitting alongside her at the table. 'A woman with a healthy appetite.'

She managed to swallow her mouthful but it was hard to think about food after that. He was so close she could smell his freshly washed skin, the scent of fine soap and clean flesh challenging her appetite, steering it in another direction completely. He uncovered a platter of croissants, still steaming hot from the oven, and offered it to her.

Turning towards him was one mistake. Looking at him rather than the plate of croissants was a bigger one. His olive skin glistened with moisture under the lights and even as she watched a bead of moisture ran down over his sculpted chest, pausing at the bud of one tight nipple only to sit there, poised on the brink.

She could feel that droplet as if it were on her own skin, feel it rolling down her breast and teetering at her nipple, turning it tight and hard against the soft flannelette of her pyjamas.

She should reach out a fingertip and release it from the tension that kept it hovering. She could at least stretch out one hand and capture the doomed droplet in her palm.

She was too late for either. Gravity won and the droplet fell, swallowed up into his towel. 'Would you care for something?'

She blinked and raised her eyes to find his watching hers, amusement creasing their corners. 'A croissant, or perhaps there's something else you might enjoy more?' Now even his lips had turned up. He was laughing at her and she'd brought it on herself. Nothing unusual in that; she was used to making a fool of herself. It was just she wasn't used to making a fool of herself over a naked chest and a single droplet of water.

'N… No, thank you,' she managed, holding her pyjamas together at the neck as if that would defend her against… Against what? Throwing herself bodily at him? 'I should have my shower. Thank you for breakfast.'

'One thing,' he said, grabbing one hand as she made a desperate bid for freedom, his thumb making lazy circles on her palm as he held her. 'You don't have to thank me for anything. We have a deal. You will act like a mistress and take what is offered you, and I will take what is offered to me. Understood?'

Her hand was dwarfed by his, and so much paler now she'd lost her Aussie year-round tan, and the contrast seemed so much like the contrast between them. Andreas was strong and wealthy and darkly dangerous and she was broke and pale and reduced to making deals to survive. But did he really expect her to offer herself to him? He'd slept out here, the sofa bed still unkempt, sheets and blankets littering the floor, but from the moment he'd awakened her this morning, with his unashamed display of his naked body and his thinly veiled comments, she'd had the sense that sex wasn't far from his mind. *With her?* Surely not.

She swallowed. 'I'll do my job in accordance with the terms of our contract. I can't think what else I could possibly have to offer that would interest you.'

'Exactly what I meant,' he said, his words at odds with the look in his eyes as he let her go.

The rest of the morning passed in a whirlwind. She was ferried down to the salon and secreted away in a private room where it seemed a dozen staff were fully employed in transforming her into someone worthy of being seen on Andreas' arm. Nobody seemed to think it odd, or, at least, nobody made her feel that way and she wondered if Andreas had been right, that the staff were paid far too much to sit in judgement or to care about anything but the service they provided.

Before long, their skilful hands had her relaxing so much that she didn't care. How often did she have a treat like this? Never. She was determined to enjoy it.

In no time it seemed her hair was transformed into a thousand tiny tinfoil packages. A manicure and pedicure followed, along with waxing and a treatment over her new colour before she relaxed into a facial. She felt like a new woman even before the hairdresser studied her, reading her newly coloured hair as a sculptor read the stone, before a make-up artist took her attention, leaving the hairdresser to perform his art.

And finally they were finished. The team gathered around her smiling and waiting for her reaction, but she was too staggered to give one. In the mirror her once-mousy hair gleamed back at her in what looked like a dozen shades of copper to blonde to gold, the skilful cut using her natural wave for fullness while the artful layering somehow seemed to add inches to its length.

And that was just her hair. The make-up artist had turned her eyes into those of a seductress, their blue colouring intensified, the shadows beneath banished, and a woman who had never been pretty felt beautiful for the first time in her life. Tears pricked her eyes and she bit down hard on her lip, trying not to cry, not wanting to ruin all their good work. 'I can't believe what you've all done, thank you so much.' And to the make-up artist, she pointed to her eyes and asked, 'Can you show me how to do this?' and the girl nodded, her smile widening.

'I'd love to. You have such extraordinary eyes to work with. You just have to make more of them. They were just lost in your face before.'

Lost in her face? Or just lost? It could have been the story of her life. But a quick lesson later, Cleo was on her way back to the suite, armed with all the products and cosmetics she would need to reproduce the artists' work.

This time as she walked through the lobby towards the bank of lifts she didn't cringe, didn't expect Security to come running. She was still only clad in jeans and a casual top, but she held her head up high and moved with a confidence she'd never known. One or two heads turned as she passed, and it gave her an unfamiliar buzz. She couldn't keep the smile from her face. Likewise she couldn't wait to show Andreas the transformation.

Except he wasn't in the suite. She shoved aside a stab of disappointment. Of course, he was a busy man; he wasn't going to sit around waiting for her. Besides which, the suite had been turned in her absence into some kind of boutique, with racks of casual, resort and evening wear lining the walls and a stylist named Madame Bernadette who clearly took her job very seriously. No wonder he'd made himself scarce.

Mme Bernadette took one look at Cleo over the top of her glasses, and clucked her tongue. 'Hmm, let's get to work. This may take some time.' She snapped her fingers at an attendant, who meekly bowed and handed Cleo a robe. 'Put that on,' Mme Bernadette instructed. 'We have work to do.'

Two hours later, Cleo was exhausted. She'd lost count of how many times she'd changed, how many times the stylist had poked, prodded and pulled various bits of whatever she had on, analysing the fit, whether it was the sheerest lingerie or the most figure-hugging gown. But she obviously knew her craft, because by the end of it the racks had been depleted. Everything not still hanging was going with them. There wasn't a whole lot left hanging.

For someone who'd survived on the contents of one backpack for six weeks and lately just one pair of jeans and a couple of T-shirts, an entire couture wardrobe for one month seemed like overkill, but Andreas was clearly calling the shots as Mme Bernadette would not be swayed by any talk of moderation.

The dilemma of how it was supposed to fit in her luggage was soon taken care of, as another knock on the door heralded a trolley carrying a suite of designer luggage and two maids who curtsied as they entered—actually curtsied her—before getting on with the business of packing, letting her get on with her own preparations.

It was almost twelve. She had no doubt Andreas would expect her ready on the dot and had no doubt he would also expect to see the new collection put to good use. For that reason she'd chosen a creamy silk blend trouser suit with a silk camisole that skimmed her new shape, no doubt ably assisted with a new bra that was as sexy as it was an engineering masterpiece. It gave her both cleavage and support yet it looked sexy as sin and felt as if it were barely there. With the new slingbacks that added four inches to her height and showed off her newly pedicured toes to perfection, and a blue scarf Mme Bernadette had pressed upon her because it accented her eyes, she felt more feminine than she ever had, as if she'd grown up and made the transition from a child into a woman in the space of just a few hours. She couldn't wait to show Andreas the new her.

Twelve noon came and went. Then twelve-thirty and still there was no sign of Andreas, no calls. She sat in a wing-back chair surrounded by packed luggage, swinging one leg and clicking her newly manicured nails, increasingly nervous about what she was doing.

After a whirlwind morning where there'd been no time to wonder at the recklessness of what she was doing, of agreeing to fly off to somewhere in Greece with a total stranger, she wasn't sure she wanted a chance to think.

Nor did she need the time to wonder if Andreas had suddenly changed his mind, and, having totally sucked her into his plans, he'd left without her. She could imagine he'd worked out that nobody was worth one million dollars for one month of acting. She could equally imagine him laughing at her naivety as he soared thousands of feet above the earth back to his world.

Her stomach clenched. It wouldn't be the first time she'd been cast aside the moment she'd made a commitment. Kurt had chosen his moment with impeccable timing, offering to look after her money and taking everything she'd had to give, first her untested body and then her naïve heart, before cruelly rejecting both. She'd been no more than sport to him, a naïve girl lured overseas and out of reach of family and friends so she could be well and truly fleeced. Once he'd scored both her and her money, he'd discarded her to go in search of fresh prey.

Impatient with the direction of her thoughts, she pushed herself up out of the chair she'd specifically chosen because it was the first thing across the room Andreas would see upon entering, giving up any pretence of appearing cool and calm in favour of striding across the room to the windows, gazing down unseeingly across the busy street to the cool green serenity of Hyde Park beyond.

No, Andreas was no Kurt. He might be arrogant and autocratic, but he would never stoop to such a thing. He'd taken so long to convince her to come with him and he'd gone to such expense. Why do that if he wasn't going to go through with it?

Her hand went to the drapes and she rested her head against it. Although he'd shown no mercy yesterday. He'd invaded the hotel like an army general routing the enemy, the guests evacuated, the sleeping turfed from their beds, and Demetrius summarily vanquished. She shivered. How could a haircut and a suitcase full of new clothes make her blind to what had happened at his behest only yesterday? Was she so fickle?

No, Andreas might resemble a Greek god, but she'd be a fool to assume he would be a merciful one.

The buzzer sounded and she jumped, suddenly all pins and needles as she crossed the room and pulled open the door. The porter nodded. 'I'm here to collect the luggage for the airport. Your car is waiting downstairs, miss.'

She took a deep breath, trying to settle her quivering stomach. So she hadn't been abandoned? That was a good thing, surely? She grabbed her jacket and scarf, threw her bag over her shoulder and marched out, doing her best to play the cool, confident person she was supposed to be when inside even her blood was fizzing. My God, she was actually doing this! She was leaving England for a Greek island with a man she barely knew, a billionaire who needed a pretend mistress.

And yes, he might be arrogant and ruthless and used to getting his own way, and yes, she'd seen enough of him to know she didn't want to cross him, but it was just for one month. And at the end of that month, she'd walk away a millionaire herself.

How hard could it be?

She smiled as she made her way through the elegant lobby, the waves in her newly styled hair bouncing in time with the tapping of her heels on the marble floor. Finally her luck was changing. Finally Cleo Taylor was going to be a success.

A doorman in a top hat touched a hand to his brow as she emerged. 'Miss Taylor,' he said, as if she were some honoured guest he'd been waiting for and not the hick girl who'd walked in wearing cowboy boots less than a day before, and he pulled open the door to a waiting limousine.

She dipped her head and climbed inside, sliding onto the seat behind the driver, opposite where Andreas was sitting totally engrossed in some kind of report perched on his knees.

'I thought you could probably use the extra time,' he said by way of explanation, flipping over a page without looking up.

'You mean you're blaming me for you being late.'

He looked up at that, looked ready to take issue with her words, but whatever he'd been about to say died before it ever got to his lips. He didn't have to say a word, though, not with the way his eyes spoke volumes as they drank her in, slowly and thoroughly, from the tip of her coloured hair to the winking toenails peeking out at him from her sandals, a slow gaze that ignited a slow burn under her skin, the flames licking at her nipples, turning them hard, before changing direction and licking their way south.

'Cleo?'

'You were expecting someone else?'

The report on his lap slid sideways, forgotten. She smiled. 'Well? Do you think you got your money's worth?'

They'd done something with her eyes, he realised. They'd done something with her hair too, so it was no longer mousy and shone in what looked like a hundred different colours, and her clothes were a world apart from her jeans and cowboy boots, but it was her eyes that looked most different. Before they'd been the misty blue of a Santorini morning, but now suddenly it seemed the mists had cleared and they were the perfect blue of a still summer's day.

'Have I had my money's worth?' he mused, finally getting to her question. She was happy with the results, that much was clear, but not half as happy as he was. His hunch had been right. She would be perfect. 'Maybe not yet. But I fully intend to.' She gasped, colour flooding her cheeks almost instantly, and it was his turn to smile. Her reactions were so instantaneous, so honest. He hoped she'd never lose that. At least, not for the next few weeks.

He picked up the abandoned report and returned to his reading. He didn't want to have to work late.

Not tonight.

Tonight he hoped to have better things to do.

The Jet Centre at London City Airport ushered them through with a minimum of fuss, expediting immigration and customs requirements so that they were ready to board less than forty minutes after leaving the hotel.

She recognised the logo she saw on the side of the small jet they were approaching, the same stylised X she'd seen adorning Andreas' luggage. 'Isn't that your logo?'

Andreas nodded. 'You recognised it?'

She shook her head. He was missing the point. 'You own a plane? Your own jet?'

'Not entirely,' he responded, stepping back to let her precede him up the short flight of steps. 'The company leases it. Along with the helicopter we have for short-haul flights within Greece itself. It is a tax-effective arrangement.'

She shook her head. He imagined she was interested in his financing arrangements? For someone who'd only recently made her first ever flight in a commercial airline, and then cramped in cattle class with three hundred other tortured souls, the concept of having one's own plane at one's beck and call was mind-boggling. She'd thought the limousine was the height of luxury and here he was with his own private jet. *And* a helicopter.

'But there must be two dozen airlines flying between London and Greece every day.'

He shrugged. 'I expect so. But not when I want to.'

That was at the heart of it, she guessed, and what Andreas wanted, Andreas got. After all, wasn't that what she was doing here? And if he could afford to throw away a million dollars plus expenses on her, clearly a million dollars didn't mean very much to him. He had money to burn.

A smiling stewardess greeted her, directing her to a seat, showing her where to store her bag and taking her jacket before disappearing again. Cleo settled herself in, looking around the cabin in wonder and doing a rapid rethink.

The interior oozed comfort, a centre aisle flanked by no more than half a dozen ultra-wide armchairs in dove-grey leather that looked more suited to a fireside setting than to any plane travel she'd ever heard of. She thought about the cramped conditions on her flight to London, the lack of space to store her own things let alone the pillows, blankets and toiletry packs they weighed you down with so that you couldn't even sit down when you boarded, of the man in the seat in front who'd jerked his seat back the first chance he'd had and left it there the entire flight and the child two rows back with the spluttering cough. Who wouldn't choose flying like this over queues and delays and airline food if they could afford it? If you had money to burn, there were no doubt worse ways to spend it.

Andreas dropped his briefcase down on a timber table-cum-desk that extended from the other wall, slipping into the seat alongside her as the attendant reappeared, this time bearing a tray with two filled champagne flutes. 'Enjoy your flight,' she said. 'We'll be taking off shortly and I'll be serving lunch as soon as we're level.'

Andreas took both glasses, thanking her and passing one to Cleo as the plane started taxiing from the apron. 'This toast is to you,' he said, raising his glass, 'and to our month together. May it be mutually—satisfying.'

The glass paused on the way to her lips. How did he make just one innocent word sound so sinful? And what was it about him that provoked her thighs to suddenly squeeze down further into the seat? He watched her over the rim of his glass as he took a sip of the sparkling wine, his lips curled, his eyes charged with a heat that was soon washing through her, closely followed by a crashing wave of fear that sucked the air from her lungs.

He could be a panther sitting there, rather than a man, a big dark cat watching its next meal, waiting. She could even imagine the lazy flick of his tail as he pretended there was no rush…

Oh, God, what was she even doing here? She was an imposter, a charlatan. She'd had sex once in her life and it had been lousy. And here she was, contracted to play the role of this man's mistress for an entire month. Never had she been so unqualified for a position. Never so unprepared.

'You don't like the wine?'

Condensation misted the glass between her fingers. 'I'm not very thirsty. Maybe with lunch. How long is the flight?' She grasped onto anything that might steer the conversation, and her thoughts, into safer territory.

'Four hours, give or take. Unfortunately after our late departure we will have missed the sunset, said to be the most beautiful in all of Greece. You haven't been to Greece before?'

There was that sunset thing again. Maybe that was one

thing Kurt hadn't lied about, and now she'd have the chance to experience Santorini's sunset for herself. The bright side, she thought as she shook her head in answer to Andreas' question, definitely a bright side.

'Ah. Then you are in for a treat. I promise you will love Santorini.'

His enthusiasm was infectious and she found an answering smile with no hesitation. 'I look forward to it.'

The jet came to a brief halt at the end of the runway before the engines powered up and the plane moved off. Again Cleo was struck by how different this felt from the hulking jumbo jet that had seemed to take for ever to get going, panels vibrating and overhead lockers rattling as it lumbered along the runway before somehow managing to haul itself up into the air. This jet was small and powerful and accelerated as if it had been fired from a gun.

She held onto her stomach but there was none of the lurching motion that had made her feel queasy in the seven four seven. Instead the ground fell sharply away as the plane pierced the air like an arrow, and Cleo watched the rain-washed view in fascination until cloud cover swallowed both it and the plane. A few moments later they had punched their way through and bright sunshine poured through the large portholes, filling the cabin with light.

'I have some work I must attend to,' Andreas told her, retrieving his briefcase. 'But I have a copy of our contract for you to look over and sign. Will you be comfortable?'

Much more comfortable than if you didn't have work to do. The traitorous thought was as sudden as it was true. When he looked at her in that heated way that he did, it was impossible to think straight. And after the intensive morning she'd had, she could do with a few hours of quiet time curled up in a good book, or a good contract for that matter. 'I'll be fine,' she said a little uncertainly, taking the papers he offered.

He watched her a while, trying to search behind her eyes for what she was really thinking, but he found no hint of machination. Instead her clear blue eyes held without shifting or looking away. He nodded then, turning back to his report, before she might read too much into his gaze.

A woman who didn't need constant pandering, who didn't sulk and was content to let him work when he needed to? She was definitely a rarity. A pity about her 'no sex' demands. *If she were any good in bed, she'd be just about perfect.*

CHAPTER SEVEN

THE cloud cover cleared after lunch when they were somewhere over the south of France, revealing a coastline that was staggeringly beautiful even from this height, the world below like a rich tapestry of colour and texture of sea and land and mountains complete with their frosting of snow. Cleo watched the colours change below as they sped towards the night, the shadow moving over the earth as night claimed more and more for its own.

The contract had taken no time at all to deal with, the terms reasonably straightforward, even to her unbusinesslike brain. One month of partnering Andreas in exchange for one million Australian dollars and an all-expenses first-class fare home. Simple really, if she didn't let herself think about whom she was contracting with. No sex seemed such a crystal clear notion until she looked at him and felt that increasingly familiar tingle in her flesh, a tingle that felt too much like longing.

So she wouldn't look at him. Instead she pushed back in the wide armchair that felt more like a bed, shucking off her shoes and tucking her legs beneath her. Once in Greece she'd be four hours closer to home, a four-hour head start when she left in a month to return to Kangaroo Crossing. She smiled when she thought about seeing her mum and her nanna again, and her rough-and-tumble half-brothers who were happiest in their own company and probably hadn't even realised she'd gone yet. She'd send them a postcard the first chance she got, let them all know she was a few hours closer to coming home…

The next thing she knew, she was waking up with a start, struggling to sit up with her chair reclining to near horizontal, a weightless but snug mohair rug covering her.

'You're back with us, then,' Andreas said, putting away his laptop. 'We'll be landing soon.'

She put a hand to her hair, and then to her eyes, worried she'd just undone all the good work of the morning. 'I must have drifted off.' She looked outside her window but it was inky blackness outside, clusters of lights visible way down below, but, more importantly, no reflection to assure her she wasn't wearing panda eyes. Or, worse still, just the one.

'You look good.'

She blinked and turned slowly, not sure she'd heard right or that he was even talking to her.

He was stashing his briefcase away in the compartment alongside his knees, and for a moment she thought she must have misheard or been mistaken. Until… 'If that's what you were worried about.' Now he did turn, and once again she was staggered by the intensity of his gaze and the power he had to skewer her with just one glance. 'Stunning, in fact. I don't suppose I told you that before.'

Nobody had ever told her that before. Let alone a man whose five o'clock shadow only served to increase his eye appeal. Along with his white shirtsleeves rolled up and the dark V of skin at his unbuttoned neck, he looked more like a pirate now than a property magnate. She licked her lips. Boy, she could do with a drink. 'Um. Thank you.' She wanted to believe the butterflies in her stomach were all to do with the fact the pilot had chosen that second to commence his descent, but she'd be lying to herself. For the hungry look she'd seen in his eyes when she'd got his attention in the car was back again, and that had been enough to start the fluttering sensation, enough to switch on the slow burn inside her.

Nobody had ever called her anything approximating stunning before. Nobody. Even her own mother had never got beyond cute. Hearing Andreas say it made it all the more real.

And made him all the more dangerous.

She injected a lightness into her voice that was at odds with the pounding of her heart. Why let him know how much he affected her? That was never part of the deal. 'Well, it's good to know all this morning's work didn't go to waste.'

She unclipped her seat belt and stood, heading for the bathroom, and she was halfway to escape when the ground went from under Cleo's feet, her stomach suddenly in her mouth. With Cleo thrown offbalance, it took only a jerk of Andreas' hand to steer her towards him. She landed in his lap a moment later, appalled that he'd borne the brunt of her weight as she'd collided against him.

'This is no joking matter,' he warned, showing no discomfiture for her sudden landing, indeed, giving every impression that he welcomed it as he nestled her deeper into his lap. 'This is serious.'

She could see it was. She could feel it was. She looked up at his shadowed face, so supremely confident while she lay there breathless and terrified, her heart thudding like a drum as she battled to get her wayward stomach under control. She was no good in turbulence, she knew from experience, the unexpected motion flipping her stomach end to end.

And right now, sitting on Andreas' lap, was no ordinary turbulence. Flames under her skin licked and curled in all the places their bodies met—where his hands touched her and where her legs lay across his before they spilled over the arm rest, where her breast rested heavy and full against his chest and, most of all, where her bottom pressed tight into his lap. Where something growing and rock-hard pressed back.

She squirmed, embarrassed at the intimacy of the contact. He felt huge, so much bigger than he had looked this morning before his shower, so much bigger than Kurt, and she didn't want to know. Didn't need to know. 'Andreas,' she pleaded, not even sure what she was pleading for as she squirmed some more, the urge to escape such intimate contact warring with an inexplicable need to get even closer.

But his eyes were closed, a frown pinching the skin between his brows, the skin drawn tight across his cheekbones. 'You really should stop wriggling...' he said cryptically, and then he opened his eyes and she read desire in their swirling depths and it only served to confuse her more. 'Unless you're planning on rescinding that no sex condition.'

She launched herself from his lap, scrabbling to get herself upright and away from him. 'Don't flatter yourself! It was you who yanked me into your lap, remember?'

He smiled as she headed, chin up, for the bathroom. 'How could I forget? But it wasn't me who was wriggling.'

Clusters of lights clung to the hilltops off to one side, but it was the air Cleo noticed first as they stepped from the plane, so clear and fresh after London's heavy atmosphere, it seemed to have been washed with the very ocean itself. She inhaled deeply and tried to relax. It wasn't working. The plane might have landed but the flock of butterflies in her stomach hadn't come down with it.

'Welcome to Santorini,' Andreas said, drawing her into the circle of his arm and pressing his lips to her hair as they headed towards a waiting car, its headlights lighting their path. She shivered, as much from the cool night air as from his sudden and unexpected touch, and he squeezed her closer so she had to tuck her arm around him. Clearly the pretence had already begun.

It was no hardship to hold him, there was a firmness about his body that made him a pleasure to touch, and the closer she was to him, the more of his delicious masculine scent she could consume, but it was impossible to relax. Her legs felt stiff, her steps forced, her features tense. It was all for show, all to give the appearance they were lovers. And all of it was fake.

'Smile!' he ordered. 'Anyone would think you were about to meet a firing squad.'

Maybe not, but Andreas was paying her a million dollars to pretend to be his mistress and it was a role she had no concept of. A million-dollar mistress who couldn't sell what she knew about being someone's mistress for one dollar.

She should have told him, should have confessed that her experience with the opposite sex was limited to one lousy time instead of claiming to have had sex 'loads of times'. He'd expect her to know what was expected of her and how to act and he'd have every right to be furious when she didn't. She glanced up at him but his profile was set hard, his jaw line rigid as he scowled at the waiting car, and she thought better of it. Whatever he seemed so upset about, now was hardly the time to confess her inexperience.

Whatever was bothering him didn't stop him hauling her closer to him so that they were joined from shoulder to hip, their legs brushing every time they took a step, limb against limb, flesh against fabric until his heat radiated through her. She looked down at her feet and took a deep gulp of the clear night air. Did he feel it too, this delicious friction? Or was he so used to the feel of women that he didn't even notice? She was sure there was no way she would ever get used to the touch of him.

'Cleo?'

She turned her head up towards his. 'Yes?'

And suddenly he was kissing her. No tender kiss, this one; instead his mouth plundered hers with both savagery and skill that left her once-stiff knees jellied and her senses reeling.

She found her fingers in his thick hair, his breath in hers, and all she knew was that she wanted more. How could he do this to her with just one kiss? She could have been back on the plane, feeling the press of his erection hard against her thigh, the same desperate need building inside like a furnace suddenly given oxygen until she was thinking insane, irrational thoughts. Such as she needed to be closer. Horizontal. *Naked*.

He let her go just as abruptly and it was all she could do to stand. 'Wha…? What are you doing?' She clung to him, breathless, her lips swollen and aching as he scowled again even as he smoothed her hair where his fingers had tangled in it.

'Come on,' he said impatiently. 'There's someone I want you to meet.'

It was a contest which one was the most sleek. The Alpha Romeo had smooth fast lines and sexy red duco. The blonde leaning against the door with the amused look on her face was even sleeker. Skinny blue jeans, a white top and a gold belt all atop a pair of killer sandals had never looked less casual. Despite the new clothes, Cleo immediately felt lumpy and inferior and completely ill at ease.

'Cleo,' Andreas said, 'I'd like you to meet Petra Demitriou, my right-hand man, or, as it turns out, my right-hand woman.'

Petra laughed and shook her golden head, showing off her effortlessly sophisticated up-do and, courtesy of the same movement, the long smooth sweep of her neck. 'Oh, Andreas, and I thought you'd never noticed.' She elegantly unwrapped her long arms from over her ample chest and extended a hand to the visitor, while her razor-sharp eyes gave her the once-over. Cleo got the feeling she missed nothing. The way Petra blinked as her smile widened told Cleo she'd been found wanting.

It was hardly her fault. She was still battling to regain her land legs after that kiss. It hadn't been an air pocket she'd hit this time, it had been an Andreas pocket that had sucked the oxygen from the air and knocked her off her feet.

'Hello, Cleo, it's always nice to welcome another of Andreas' guests.'

The woman had an accent that sounded as smooth as honey and yet came with a chilli bite. So Petra wasn't impressed with Andreas' passing parade of women? But then, who could blame her? No doubt she'd be equally unimpressed if their roles were reversed. So instead of reading anything into the critical once-over and the clearly unwelcoming welcome, she thanked her and took the woman's hand.

Petra's fingers were long and slender and cool to touch and clearly weren't aiming to linger. In the next movement they'd been withdrawn and the other hand was holding out a car key to Andreas. 'I thought you might like to drive the new Alfa Romeo. It just came in today. Cleo and I can sit in the back.' Cleo caught something distinctly unfriendly in her expression the moment before her mouth turned into a smile. 'We could get to know one another while Andreas test-drives his new toy.'

Cleo did a rapid reassessment. Maybe she'd only imagined that sneer? She shrugged, confused by it all, confused by what was expected of her and not wanting to offend anyone. 'Lovely. Thanks.' Anything right now to escape the confusion the man alongside her could wreak with a single kiss.

'I wondered why you decided to meet us, rather than send Nick.' Andreas sounded annoyed, his words clipped.

Petra laughed his comment off as she offered the keys up at eye level like a temptation, her lips pouting seductively behind them. He remembered the pose. It was the same one she'd given when they'd been at that restaurant in Oia and she'd said she'd had too much to drink and asked if he could drive them both home, her hand on his thigh the entire way…

'I know how much you were looking forward to a ride. I thought you might appreciate the key.'

Breath hissed through his teeth. He hadn't had too much to drink tonight and the only ride Andreas was looking forward to right now was apparently off limits. But that Petra could be so obvious when it was clear he had found someone else to spend his nights with only served to confirm he had been right to bring someone home with him.

Thank God he hadn't turned up tonight alone. *Sto thiavolo*, he should have chosen someone who could be a bit more convincing! Cleo was as rigid and stiff in his arms as a store dummy. Even his kiss, designed to show Petra that they were completely and sexually into each other, had backfired. Your mistress wasn't supposed to ask what you were doing when you kissed her, as if you'd taken some liberty. No, it would take some doing to make Cleo more comfortable, and more convincing in her role, but if sex was off the agenda he didn't know what would do it.

He hadn't needed Petra turning up at the airport. Had she imagined that one look at her and his desire would be rekindled, the new lover forgotten? Or had she hoped he'd been bluffing, and that there was no woman? Why else would she dress so provocatively, in clothes that clung to her body like a second skin? He was suddenly beginning to get a new appreciation of his right-hand woman. She'd always been a good operator but he'd never realised just how cunning she was.

'Would you mind if I asked you to drive, Petra? Cleo and I have had such a long day. Haven't we, sweetheart?' The implication hung on his words that he'd had a long night and was expecting another to follow. The endearment was meant to convince Petra. Meanwhile a wide-eyed Cleo looked up at him like a rabbit caught in the headlights. He pulled open a rear door and ushered her in, wishing that just once she might act like the mistress he was paying her to pretend to be.

Petra, left with no other choice but to comply, smiled meekly and slid into the driver's seat.

'Have you eaten?' she asked a moment later as the car's powerful engine turned over. 'I've made you a booking at Poseidon.'

Andreas couldn't fault her logic. It was what he normally did if he arrived with a woman in the late afternoon or evening. Sometimes they'd be in time to catch the sunset, sometimes they'd miss it, but a platter of fresh seafood and a Greek salad filled with olives, feta and fresh tomatoes bursting with Greek sunshine ensured that they would be fuelled for the night ahead.

But not tonight. Not when his so-called mistress was as jumpy as a kitten. Maybe she might relax at the house.

'No, take us straight to the house. We had a late lunch. We will eat later.'

There was silence from the driver and yet Andreas could almost hear her mind ticking over, wondering just what was so important that they would rush back to the house and pouncing on the answer in the very next thought. He wondered how far Petra could be pushed. Would she leave if she could see her position was hopeless? He hadn't wanted to lose her expertise but maybe that would be for the best. No one was indispensable. And he couldn't have her thinking she had claims on him.

Likewise he couldn't have the woman alongside him thinking that she could just sit there, as far away from him as she could get and gaping out of her window like some tourist on a coach tour. Damn it, she was supposed to be interested in him!

He leaned across and wrapped an arm around her, cursing when her startled response earned raised eyebrows from their driver in the rear-vision mirror.

'It's not far to Fira,' he told Cleo as the car powered up the road from the airport.

It was as he said. Within a few minutes the car had climbed its way past small picturesque villages and scattered white-washed hotels to a road along the very edge of the island where it became more built up. On one side the land sloped down gently to where they'd just come, the lights of the airstrip bright in the dark night. On the other side, the land fell away steeply, to a dark flat sea. A scattering of lights shone across the waters while in front there seemed a sweeping curve of lights into the distance that curved in tiers down a hillside before being swallowed up by the darkness.

'It is hard to appreciate in the dark,' Andreas told her, the stroke of his thumb on her upper arm doing all kinds of crazy things to her breathing, 'but Santorini is actually a collection of small islands, the remnants of an ancient eruption. Fira, the capital, is built on the lip of the crater. The lights you see further on belong to the town of Oia. Like Fira, it is a very beautiful town, full of narrow cobbled streets and beautifully restored buildings, centuries of years old. Some say the sunset in Oia is the best in the world. I will take you there if you like.'

She suspected he was merely acting his part, she knew she should be, but still the very picture of sharing a sunset with this man worked its way into her soul so much that she almost wanted it to be real. Her voice, when she found it, was breath-less and short, and it was no trouble for her to inject into it the necessary enthusiasm. 'I would like that, very much.'

There was a strangled sound from the front seat, followed by a cough and a murmured apology. 'Andreas is right, Cleo,' Petra said, steering the car through a succession of narrower and narrower streets, past ornate iron gateways and walls of polished white set off with colourful bougainvilleas that caught Cleo's eye. 'It is only a small island, but there is much to see on Santorini. Will you be staying long?'

Cleo shot a look at Andreas, who was scowling again, and she wondered if it was because she'd made such a hash of things that he was already regretting their deal and the time he'd said they'd have together. 'Maybe a few weeks,' she offered nervously, 'maybe less…'

In the rear-view mirror she saw their driver's eyebrows shoot up as she pulled up before a private garage alongside a red-brick building that wouldn't have looked out of place in Venice and waited for the automatic door to roll up. 'That long? How lovely for you. It will be like a wonderful holiday.'

'Of course,' Andreas added with a growl as Petra steered the car into the garage and pulled to a stop. 'There's every chance she may stay longer.'

'Why did you say that?' Petra had bid them goodnight and left them in the lobby, retiring to her own suite, and meanwhile Cleo had been playing and replaying the words over in her head, so much so that she'd barely taken in the details of the house, other than just a handful of impressions. Grand proportions, furnishings that were both elegant and exquisite, it was more a palace than any humble home she'd ever seen.

'Say what?' Andreas sounded almost bored as he instructed the hired help to take care of the luggage and led the way to his suite of rooms, and yet there was too much coiled tension in his every step, his every movement, for her to believe that. Even his words were brimming with tension. The sound of her heels clicking on the terrazzo floor only served to ratchet it up.

'Why did you say I might stay longer?'

'Because you made it sound like you weren't planning on staying at all.'

'I wasn't sure you'd want me to.'

'And I thought we had a deal.'

Maybe so, but she knew he wasn't happy with her, knew she'd failed to impress him with her acting skills. But what did he expect when she'd never been a mistress, didn't know how a mistress was supposed to act? It wasn't as if she'd blown it in front of his business partners. It had only been his driver—his right-hand woman. *An exceptionally beautiful right-hand woman.*

Could the act all be for her benefit?

'Petra is very beautiful.'

He shrugged, but gave every impression of knowing who he was talking about. 'Is she? She's good at what she does.'

'And she lives here with you, in this—' she looked around her, at the exquisite wall hangings and period furniture '—this *house*?'

'The offices of Xenides Properties are here. I'm often away and Petra works long hours. It's an arrangement that works well for both of us.'

There was no hint of any attachment in his words or the tone of his voice. In fact he could have been talking about any employee. Maybe her hunch had been wrong. Maybe he was just aware of Petra's obvious resentment for his lifestyle and his constant change of companions? Or maybe he was just angry with her own hopeless acting skills. She could hardly blame him if he was.

'Here we are.' A pair of carved timber doors stood at the end of a passageway. He pushed them both open and her eyes opened wide. 'The sitting room,' he said, still moving.

She stayed where she was and let herself gape. By now she should have been used to the luxury—luxury suites in London hotels, a personal private jet with wrap-around leather and champagne on tap—but still the sheer opulence of his everyday lifestyle made her jaw drop. For this was no rented accommodation or flying office, this was his home. And this one room was large enough to house her entire family back home.

'How much money do you have?'

And he turned and looked at her, a cold expression charging his eyes. 'Does it matter?'

'Well, no. It's just…'

'Do not fear, I have more than enough to pay for you.'

His words shouldn't have stung but somehow they did. The notion he was paying to have her here, to stroke her hand with his thumb and kiss her when he needed to look as if he had someone to kiss.

It wasn't as if he were paying her for sex. She was merely acting. Pretending. And yet there was no pretence about the impact his touch and his kisses had on her. It made no sense. She'd been the one to insist on no sex, so why was it that his touch made her think of nothing else? Why did his kisses make her hunger for that which she had refused to entertain? Did he really not feel it too, this ribbon of desire that seemed to tug her ever closer to his side?

No! Andreas was right. This was a commercial arrangement, not some fairy-tale Cinderella story. In a month's time, or however long it took, she'd leave Santorini and go back to her home in Kangaroo Crossing, albeit a million dollars richer than when she'd arrived. For a girl with her background and her chances in life, surely that was fairy tale enough. And yes, clearly there was no question he couldn't afford it.

'Come on, then,' he said gruffly as he tugged off his tie, pointing towards a door on the far side of the room at the same time. 'Let's get this over with.'

CHAPTER EIGHT

'WHA…? What do you mean?'

Andreas sighed. What the hell had he been thinking to contract this woman to act as his mistress? As an actress Cleo was as stiff and unyielding as a block of cement. As a mistress, she'd been a total failure. And she would continue to be, until she got over this problem she had with being with him. He tossed the car keys Petra had given him onto a dresser where they slid straight off and fell with a clatter to the tiled floor. Behind him she did the startled thing again, jumping as if he'd just thrown the keys at her. And the quicker she got over it, the better. 'What do you think I mean?' He tugged off his already loosened tie and shrugged off his jacket.

Pointless!

She stood there in the doorway to the bedroom, knowing only that he was furious. Meanwhile Andreas had kicked off his shoes and peeled off his socks, tossing them into a corner. The shirt was next, exposing once again that muscled chest to her gaze. She wanted to look away, but she couldn't. She was transfixed.

'Couldn't you have even pretended to be my lover? Why do you have to jump like a startled rabbit every time I touch you?'

'Because you do startle me. I can't help it!'

He swore under his breath. 'We should have slept together last night. Instead we wasted a perfect opportunity to get comfortable with one another.'

His trousers hit the ground and he kicked them carelessly aside. She wanted to resent him for his arrogance, for his knowing that the hired help would pick them up, for his wealth that allowed him to be that way, and most of all for assuming that she would abandon the one condition she'd set on this arrangement. But he made it so hard, too hard, when, instead of mustering a defence, she was busy admiring his lean powerful legs and the way his muscles played under his olive skin with the action.

Her mouth was dry, her blood thick and thumping slow. 'I don't understand. I told you I wasn't prepared to sleep with you.'

He looked up at her then. 'No, you didn't. You said no sex. I told you there would be times where we would have to share a bed and you made no protest.' He looked up at her, her feet still stuck to the floor in the doorway. 'Go on, then, get undressed.'

Her mouth went dry. *Get undressed.* She could be in a doctor's surgery, awaiting an examination, but then the order would be a request and it would be gently and considerately done, with a curtain provided for her modesty and discretion. Here, she was somehow expected to take off her clothes and climb into bed with Andreas glowering at her, dissatisfied and unrepentant. 'Andreas, I…'

But he was already leaving the room, striding barefoot through a door to a room she could see brimming with marble and gilt. Seconds later he returned, stopping dead when he saw her still there, rooted to the spot. 'You're planning on going to bed fully clothed? At least I won't have to put up with that flannelette armour.' The black silk pouch that was his final barrier hit the floor next, leaving him gloriously naked before her. He was beautiful clothed, carrying himself with an authority and presence that turned heads, but naked he was magnificent, broad shoulders that tapered down to a tightly packed waist and lean hips. He was so beautiful, just the sight of him caused her blood to sizzle. She closed her eyes and swallowed hard against a throat filled with cotton wool as he flipped down the covers and slid into the bed.

'Last night,' she began. 'Last night I had my own bed. Why can't I now?'

'Last night we were in London. I told you we might have to sleep together, to keep up appearances. Given there is only one bedroom in this suite and the fact my offices are here, it wouldn't look good if word got out that my latest mistress was sleeping on the sofa, because I certainly don't intend to. Don't worry, I'm sure I can resist you.'

She didn't doubt it. But sharing the same bed as him, lying alongside his naked body when she already knew how his touch turned her flesh alight, she only wished she could be so sure she could resist him.

He pushed himself up on one hand. 'I'm losing patience, Cleo. Are you going to take your clothes off,' he growled, with more than a hint of menace in his voice, 'or am I going to have to come over there and do it for you?'

She shook her head, fear congealing like a ball in her gut. God no, the last thing she wanted was Andreas undressing her. She'd claimed she was experienced. She could do this. But she wasn't about to do it in front of him. She bolted for the bathroom, taking several minutes to calm herself, cooling her burning cheeks with water from the tap. Her luggage had not yet been delivered or if it had, Andreas wasn't telling, so she stripped herself down to the camisole, bra and knickers and wrapped herself in a voluminous robe she found hanging on the back of the door. It would have to do. This wasn't about sex, or so he'd claimed. So what she wore to bed shouldn't matter.

She emerged from the bathroom a good ten minutes or more after she'd entered to find the lights dimmed and Andreas facing away, his eyes closed as if asleep.

Please God he was!

She padded silently to the bed, stood there a second watching him breathe and decided this was it. She'd practically told him she was a woman of the world, claiming she'd had sex loads of times, so just sleeping with a man in the same bed should hardly throw her. She unlaced the tie at her waist and let the robe slip from her shoulders. Andreas didn't stir and she gained confidence. He wouldn't even know she was here. She turned off the light and slipped between the covers, hovering so close to the edge there could be no way he would feel her presence, and he gave no sign that he did, his breathing slow and regular, a pattern that calmed her own frantically beating heart.

On tenterhooks she lay there listening to his breathing, feeling foolish and naïve, even as the curtains of sleep descended one by one, closing around her and pulling her into their embrace, until she was surrounded by them, warm and comforting and reassuring.

And if those curtains felt as if they'd grown arms and legs and were fashioned of silken flesh rather than velvet, and breathed as if the mild night air moved through them, the brush of them on her shoulder like the warm brush of a lover's lips, she could feel no less comforted.

Cleo woke alone in the wide bed to the spill of sunshine through tall narrow windows and a feeling of disbelief suffusing her veins. She was here. She was really here, lying in bed in a centuries-old mansion on a Greek island and last night—last night she'd slept with a real Greek billionaire, a Greek billionaire who'd honoured her condition that sex was no part of this deal!

A shiver ran down her spine. Four weeks, the contract had stipulated. Four weeks she could be here, sharing Andreas' bed. After last night the prospect was suddenly more thrilling than threatening. Scattered remnants came to her then, of a warm hand and a silken touch, of the press of thigh and a puff of breath at her neck, and the press of lips…

She must have been dreaming again.

She pulled on the robe she'd left lying on the end of the bed just as the chimes of a clock on a mantelpiece rang out, drawing her eye. Ten in the morning! Even allowing for the two-hour time difference with London, she hadn't slept in so late for months. No wonder Andreas wasn't here. He'd probably gone to work hours ago. And no wonder she was so hungry, it was hours since they'd eaten on the plane. She was halfway to the bathroom when it caught her eye, a patch of blue through the whisper-thin gauzy curtains billowing in the soft breeze, so blue that she was compelled to draw the curtain and investigate.

What she saw took her breath away. There was a terrace outside the window, whitewashed and dazzling in the morning sun, and then the earth must have fallen away beneath them, for a long way below shimmered a sea of the brightest blue she'd ever seen, a sea that stretched before another island that rose, tall and long and dusted with white buildings. And to the left sat another islet, low and wide and dark.

So this was Santorini? No wonder Kurt had raved about it to her. Even if he had never visited, even if he'd never intended bringing her here, maybe for once he hadn't been lying. It was breathtakingly beautiful.

And now she had four weeks to enjoy it, to share it with Andreas…

'You're up, then.'

She turned with a start to see him standing in the doorway.

He looked as fresh as the morning, his hair damp at the ends where it curled over his collar, a white shirt and fitted trousers making the most of his lean shape.

And suddenly she wasn't sure what to be the more embarrassed about, finding herself staring hungrily at the delicious V of olive skin where his shirt was unbuttoned, or the knowledge that without intimacy they'd slept together and would do again, tonight. Damn it if her nipples hadn't already tightened under the robe in anticipation, her pulse sending blood to all the places that shouldn't even know he existed, but seemed to anyway. It was only sleep with him they had to look forward to, but that seemed to make no difference; she tingled all over.

'I thought you'd gone to work.'

'There were some things I had to attend to.' He stopped in front of her and curled a hand under her hair, skimming her neck with his fingertips and drawing her closer, his eyes on her mouth. She sensed he was going to kiss her and she made no move to shift away, her eyelids fluttering closed on a sigh. Why should she when his touch felt so good, and when he'd agreed to her terms? Sex might be out but a kiss was definitely within the bounds of conditions she'd set. She could deal with that. Surely this was the best of all worlds?

'Good. You didn't jump,' he said, abruptly letting her go before their lips had even connected.

She blinked, swaying momentarily until she regained her bearings. 'I what?'

'We seem to be curing you of your habit of jumping every time I touch you. This is a good start. Perhaps now you will be more convincing.'

'Oh, of course.' She studied her toes, while she pushed her hair back behind her ears, feeling a total fool for thinking he wanted to kiss her, a total fool for being so eager. 'That is good.'

He was already turning to go when he turned back. 'Breakfast is being served on the terrace if you're hungry.'

She nodded, looking to his eyes for a hint, hoping to find a trace of the warmth and comfort she'd felt last night in her sleep, but there was nothing there and she knew what she'd felt had been a dream.

'I'll be along as soon as I'm dressed.'

There was nothing to feel disappointed about, she told herself as she took a shower in the luxurious marble bathroom, the spray from the shower more like a downpour, raining down sense on an otherwise wayward brain. What was her problem? She had a job to do for four weeks and then she would return home, a millionaire. Tenderness didn't come into it.

She stepped out onto the sun-washed terrace and any remaining sense of disappointment evaporated in the wonder of the place he'd brought her to. What she'd glimpsed through the bedroom window had been magical. But outside on the terrace the view was simply breathtaking.

She could see from one end of this island to the other, the sweeping curve of dark cliffs topped with whitewashed villages that clung to the very edge of the cliff like icing spilling over the sides of a cake.

Andreas sat at the table already but, despite her growling stomach, she was too excited right now to sit and eat. How could she even think about eating when there was so much to devour with her eyes?

A breeze toyed with the ends of her hair as she stood at the balustrade, the air pure and clean as she gazed out across the sapphire-blue waters. The light was wonderful, more like the bright sunlight of home rather than the grey misty blanket that so often shrouded London, defining everything with sharp detail, so that even islands far beyond this ring of cliffs could be clearly seen.

Either side of her, the town of Fira spread across the

clifftop, a jumble of closely packed buildings, some adorned with splashes of colourful bougainvillea and punctuated by stairways and narrow paths that somehow combined harmoniously to create a picture of charm, while far below two sleek cruise ships sat anchored. For a second memories of Kurt once more invaded her thoughts, but only for a moment. She was no day visitor here; she was living here for a month.

'What do you think?'

Andreas appeared at her side, his arm looping casually around her shoulders. *Appearances*, she told herself, willing away the jag in her heart rate, *he's merely keeping up appearances for the maid busy filling up coffee cups.* But it didn't matter so much any more, not when she was being treated to a place of such amazing beauty that the man-made seemed not to detract from but to complement the natural.

'It's the most beautiful place I've ever seen. I don't know how you can bear to leave it.'

He smiled as if pleased with her reaction. 'It is always good to come home. Come.' He drew her further around the terrace, pointing out the various islands. 'This is the main island, known as Thera. The island across the water is called Therassia, and the tiny one between is known as Aspronisi.'

'What about that one?' She pointed to the low dark isle she'd noticed earlier.

'That is Nea Kameni, the volcano.'

Her head swung around. 'Volcano!'

He laughed, a rich deep sound that in normal circumstances would allay her fears. But these were hardly normal circumstances. He expected her to live on the edge of a volcano? 'Like I was telling you last night, this ring of islands and these cliffs are the remains of the caldera after an eruption thousands of years ago. The empty chamber filled with sea water causing a massive explosion into which the volcano collapsed. This ring of islands is all that's left.'

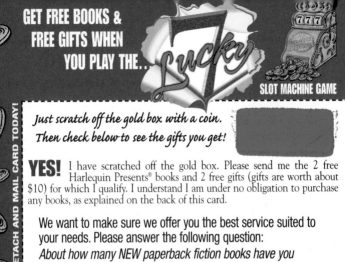

GET FREE BOOKS & FREE GIFTS WHEN YOU PLAY THE... *Lucky 7*

SLOT MACHINE GAME

Just scratch off the gold box with a coin.
Then check below to see the gifts you get!

YES! I have scratched off the gold box. Please send me the 2 free Harlequin Presents® books and 2 free gifts (gifts are worth about $10) for which I qualify. I understand I am under no obligation to purchase any books, as explained on the back of this card.

We want to make sure we offer you the best service suited to your needs. Please answer the following question:

About how many NEW paperback fiction books have you purchased in the past 3 months?

❑ 0-2
E4AD

❑ 3-6
E4AP

❑ 7 or more
E4AZ

❑ I prefer the regular-print edition
106/306 HDL

❑ I prefer the larger-print edition
176/376 HDL

FIRST NAME	LAST NAME

ADDRESS

APT.	CITY

STATE / PROV.	ZIP/POSTAL CODE

Visit us online at
www.ReaderService.com

7 7 7	**Worth TWO FREE BOOKS plus 2 BONUS Mystery Gifts!**
🍒🍒🍒	**Worth TWO FREE BOOKS!**
🔔🔔🍒	**TRY AGAIN!**

DETACH AND MAIL CARD TODAY!

The Reader Service — Here's how it works:

Accepting your 2 free books and 2 free gifts (gifts valued at approximately $10.00) places you under no obligation to buy anything. You may keep the books and gifts and return the shipping statement marked "cancel". If you do not cancel, about a month later we'll send you 6 additional books and bill you just $4.05 each for the regular-print edition or $4.55 each for the larger-print edition in the U.S. or $4.74 each for the regular-print edition or $5.24 each for the larger-print edition in Canada. That is a savings of at least 13% off the cover price. It's quite a bargain! Shipping and handling is just 50¢ per book in the U.S. and 75¢ per book in Canada.* You may cancel at any time, but if you choose to continue, every month we'll send you 6 more books, which you may either purchase at the discount price or return to us and cancel your subscription.

*Terms and prices subject to change without notice. Prices do not include applicable taxes. Sales tax applicable in N.Y. Canadian residents will be charged applicable provincial taxes and GST. Offer not valid in Quebec. Credit or debit balances in a customer's account(s) may be offset by any other outstanding balance owed by or to the customer. Please allow 4 to 6 weeks for delivery. Offer available while quantities last. All orders subject to approval.

Despite the warming rays of the sun, Cleo shivered. The island cliffs formed a crater that was enormous. That something so beautiful could be created from something so devastating beggared belief. 'But it's safe now, isn't it?'

'Oh, yes, the volcano hasn't erupted for some decades.'

Cleo wrapped her arms around her midriff. 'You mean it's still active?'

Andreas shrugged, a wry smile on his face. 'The volcano is rebuilding itself. Sometimes the island rumbles with the reconstruction, and sometimes she makes herself known in more obvious ways and lets off a little steam, but for the most part the earth is quiet. You are no doubt much safer here than on the streets of London.'

She breathed out. 'Maybe you're right, but Kangaroo Crossing is looking better by the minute. We lack the views of course, there's nothing but red dust and Spinifex bushes as far as the eye can see, but at least it comes with no nasty surprises.'

'You mean you don't have poisonous spiders or snakes? What part of Australia is this?' And she had the grace to blush.

'Come,' Andreas said, 'let's eat, and then I must return to work. There is a pool on the lower terrace where you can swim or you can explore the town on foot. Do you think you will be able to amuse yourself during the day?'

'I'm sure I will,' said Cleo, surprised by his apparent interest in her, but her attention snagged as she sat before the breakfast table laden with what looked more like a feast. There were bowls of creamy yoghurt drizzled with honey and platters of pastries and rolls along with a selection of cheeses and fruit from which to choose.

'Good,' he said, 'and then tonight I will show you the sunset and you will see it's not so bad to live on a cliff top overlooking a volcano.'

'I'll take your word for that,' she said, ridiculously pleased with herself when she caught his answering smile.

Refreshing was the word, he decided as he headed towards the suite of offices housed within the mansion. There was an innocence about her, a lack of sophistication that was charming.

Did she really fear for her safety here on Santorini when she came from a country with a reputation for its dangerous wildlife? It was laughable.

'Andreas, you're back at last.' Petra perched herself on the edge of his desk, crossed her legs and smiled, flashing two rows of perfect white teeth between blood-red lips. 'Your mother called.'

He didn't miss the show of leg revealed by the split in the skirt, a skirt he'd never seen before. Was it his imagination or was Petra putting up a fight for his attention, first with her skin-tight clothes display last night, and now a skirt that was split to her thigh? 'Did she leave a message?'

'She said she'd like you to visit, said she hasn't seen you for ages. I said you'd call her back later.'

Andreas wondered what else she might have said. 'Was there anything else?'

Petra looked miffed, the coffee she'd brought them both forgotten. Coffee together in his office around this time of day had been almost a daily ritual, where they would discuss whatever business had arisen or opportunities that might be in the offing. To him, there'd been nothing more in it than one colleague talking to another. Clearly Petra had read things differently. 'No, nothing.' She eased herself off his desk, straightening her skirt with her hands, the motion accentuating her cleavage. So different from Cleo's ingenuous innocence that he almost felt sorry for her. Cleo didn't have to play games to draw attention to herself. He'd noticed her attributes even before the makeover experts had woven their magic. Hers was a natural beauty, fragile, buried under a lifetime of feeling not good enough.

Cleo was more than good enough. Having her in his bed last night and trying not to touch her had been sheer torture. Only when he had been sure she'd drifted off, he'd allowed himself to gather her against him and breathe in the subtle scent of her skin and hair. Without even realising, she'd spooned her body next to his and it had taken every shred of self-control he owned to leave her sleeping when every part of him had been screamingly awake.

'Although,' Petra continued so abruptly that he looked up, surprised to see her still there, 'I guess I should remind you about the Kalistos ball tonight. You'll be taking Cleo, I imagine. Otherwise you and I could travel together…'

'Of course, I'm taking Cleo,' he barked as he sent her on her way. He suppressed a groan as he leaned back in his chair. What was wrong with him? It was clearly marked on his diary, but at breakfast he'd forgotten all about the ball and was thinking in terms of sunsets with Cleo instead. He knew what he'd rather do. But with Kalistos still to give his decision on Andreas' latest proposal to tie their businesses together, a proposal that could benefit both companies to the tune of millions of Euros, there was no way he couldn't show up. As for taking Cleo, she was starting to relax with him, but ideally he'd like another day or two before he could be sure she'd be completely convincing on his arm.

Another day or two he didn't have.

Cleo had never been more nervous in her life. She'd wondered why Mme Bernadette had insisted on her taking the numerous gowns and had half suspected she'd been merely feathering her own nest—a Greek island sojourn surely wouldn't require ball gowns?—and yet here she was, dressed in the pale gold halter-neck gown, her hair piled high on her head with coils trailing around her face courtesy of the hairdresser Andreas had sent to their suite, curtailing her sightseeing plans for today.

Andreas hadn't helped relax her when he'd taken one look at her and whistled low through his teeth, sending her pulse and her senses skittering. And he certainly wasn't helping relax her now as they drove down the windy switchback road to the port.

'Constantine Kalistos is not only one of the major business and political leaders on the island, but also owns the largest charter boat operation in Greece,' he told her, in a tone that suggested she should be taking notes. 'He's considering a business proposal I put to him and he's the main reason we're here tonight. He's the perfect host but, at the same time, he's a man you don't want to offend.'

Cleo battled to absorb the information, growing more nervous by the second as the car pulled closer to a wharf lit with coloured lanterns, music spilling from the massive yacht moored alongside, couples dripping with jewellery and designer fashions emerging from the limousines and sports cars lined up before them.

Help. She'd never been on a boat bigger than a canoe and she'd never been to any function more glamorous than the Kangaroo Crossing Bachelor and Spinster Ball, where Akubras were just as likely sighted as bow ties. She swallowed. There were no Akubras here.

Andreas followed her from the car, his hand collecting hers, and she'd never been more grateful to have him alongside. She was so nervous she was sure she was going to wobble straight off her gold kidskin spike-heeled sandals, especially as she stumbled with the gentle movement of the gangplank under her feet.

'Relax,' Andreas whispered, setting her coiling hair

dancing around her ear. 'And smile. You'll be fine.' And then he was tugging her forward, onto the brightly lit boat with the even more brightly lit people, and they were greeting Andreas and giving her openly curious glances and she wondered how a girl from Kangaroo Crossing got to be here, in a softly swaying yacht filled with Santorini's who's who with clearly the most handsome man on the island. One look around at the glittering attendees was enough to confirm that.

'Are you okay?' Andreas asked softly, breaking off a greeting to someone, and she looked up into his dark eyes, confused. 'I thought you wanted something,' he added. 'You squeezed my arm.' And she smiled and nodded, not even having realised she'd done it. 'I'm fine,' she told him, wishing for nothing more than for the butterflies in her stomach to settle down.

Something passed between them then, some spark of approval or warmth, she didn't know what to call it, but she felt it in his glance all the way down to her lacquered toenails, and she knew from his answering smile that he'd felt it too. So what if the only thing that bound them was a business contract? Would it be so wrong to like the man into the deal?

Someone slipped a glass of champagne into her hand as the boat slipped from port and Cleo felt the first uneasy twinge as the vessel rocked sideways before pulling away. Slowly it built up speed in preparation for its circuit of the islands and Cleo prayed that they'd soon find calm water as the butterflies turned to moths. Somersaulting moths. She forced a smile to her lips as Andreas introduced her to more and more people, all of whom seemed oblivious to the motion, and all the while shuffling on her stiletto heels in search of the ever-elusive balance as the boat sliced through the gentle swell.

She abandoned the barely touched glass of champagne, exchanging it for water, which still failed to settle her stomach.

The fresh air on deck didn't help, not when all she could notice was the line of lights atop the cliffs moving up and down and the passenger catamaran skipping away from them on the seas. When perspiration started beading at her forehead, she knew she was in trouble.

'Andreas,' she said, one hand on her stomach as they moved between groups on the deck. 'I don't feel—'

'Andreas! There you are.'

Cleo stepped back, wondering if she could just slip away as Andreas was swept into a man's embrace, his back slapped by one beefy hand. It was no mean feat given the man barely came up to Andreas' shoulders, his black jacket widest around his ample stomach, and his features creased and heavy with age and excess.

'Constantine,' Andreas said, 'it is always a great pleasure. Allow me to introduce Cleo Taylor, all the way from Australia.'

'Ah,' said the beaming Greek, his eyes sizing her up and taking her hand gallantly. 'Then it is in fact my pleasure.' He held out a hand and gestured around him. 'Tell me, what do you think of my little runaround?'

It was hitting the ferry's wake that did it. Her stomach felt as if it had speared into the sky only to be slammed down again and she knew it was too late. If she opened her mouth, she was lost. She pushed her glass into Andreas' free hand, shoved a path between the two men and bolted for the bathroom.

CHAPTER NINE

WHAT had he been thinking? Cleo was hopeless. A blow-up doll would have made a more convincing mistress. And the look Constantine had given him when they'd been offloaded back on shore had spoken volumes. Andreas wasn't holding out for good news in that department any time soon. The 'I told you so' look Petra had thrown his way as they'd disembarked hadn't helped.

The car slowly wound its way up the cliff-face road, the lights of Con's yacht heading once more for the sea, the music and laughter drifting upwards on the breeze, rubbing salt into his wounds, while alongside him Cleo sat hunched and looking despondently out of her window.

Damn it, was it too much to ask to get *something* for his million dollars?

Carrying her shoes in one hand, Cleo made straight for the bathroom where she spent at least five times the recommended daily time with her toothbrush and at least that again holding a cold towel to her red and swollen eyes. Andreas had thankfully kept silent all the way home, although she'd known that simmering silence would erupt at some stage, especially after the pleasure boat had had to make a special trip back to the wharf to drop them off.

So be it. She knew she was already a disappointment to

him. And now she'd probably blown a million-Euro business deal. But she'd warned him she wasn't the right woman for the job. Maybe now he might listen. Maybe now he would let her go. If he didn't throw her out first.

She sniffed, close to tears again. Did it matter? Either way, she was going.

He was sitting on the bed, flinging off first one shoe and then the other when she emerged. Following them with his silk socks. Without following her progress across the room, he spoke. 'Why didn't you tell me you get seasick?'

She stopped, just short of pulling open the wardrobe door. So the volcano was about to erupt? She was surprised he'd kept quiet this long. 'Maybe I didn't know.'

This time he did look up, disbelief plain on his features. 'How could anyone not know?'

'I've never been on a boat before. There's not a big call for boats where I come from.'

He answered with nothing more than a grunt. 'It could have been worse,' she offered, trying to sound light but having to bite down on her lip to counter the prick of tears.

'Do you think? Do you really think it could have been worse?'

'Sure. I could have thrown up all over the both of you.'

'You might just as well have, for all the good taking you tonight is going to do me.'

She closed her eyes and swayed against the door, liquid spilling from her eyes, and the sound of his clothes hitting the floor piece by piece like a series of exclamation marks. 'I know. I'm sorry.' She took a deep breath and reached in, hauling out her pack from the depths of the wardrobe. 'It won't happen again. There's no way it will happen again.'

Andreas seemed to come from nowhere, his arms forcing her around even as she clung onto the pack. 'What the hell are you doing?'

She couldn't bring herself to look at his face. But it was no compensation that her eyes were met by the wall of his naked chest, a naked chest she'd never see the likes of again after tonight. 'I can't do this, Andreas,' she said as her mind set about imprinting every square centimetre of his perfect skinscape on her memory while he slipped the pack from her hands. 'I'm going home.'

'You can't go. We have a contract!'

'I can't do this. I'm sorry, I'm hopeless in this role, and you know it.'

'No! That's not true.' He didn't know where the words came from. Hadn't he thought the very same thing himself tonight? But he had no answer for that mystery. All he knew was that he couldn't let her go, couldn't let her walk out of his life. Not like this. Not when he knew the sunshine of her smile. Not when he knew he was the one who had taken it away from her.

She tried to shrug away, even as his thumbs stroked her collarbone. 'You don't have to try to be nice to me. I know you're angry and you have a right to be. I told you I wasn't the right person for this job. I'm a cleaner. A cleaner who jumps every time you touch her. A cleaner who's just discovered she gets seasick. Not exactly an asset to you.'

'Not every time.'

She blinked up at him, frowning. 'What?'

'You don't jump every time. You're not jumping now. And I'm touching you. And I'd like to go on touching you.'

Her blue eyes widened. 'Andreas?'

And he answered her question the only way he knew how. With a kiss that he hoped would tell her he wanted her to stay. That he didn't want her to leave. He drew her closer against him, until the silk of her golden gown pressed warm and slippery and seductive against his skin. He managed to prise his lips away from hers long enough to say the words. 'I want to make love to you, Cleo.'

She was gasping for breath, and no doubt searching for reason. 'The contract…' she uttered.

'This is nothing to do with the contract. This is between you and me. Make love with me, Cleo.'

Did he mean that? Her thought processes were blurred, her senses packed to overload. What he could do to her skin with the touch of one thumbnail. What he could do to her breasts with just the brush of one fingertip. What he could do with one whispered request…

'Make love with me.'

He wasn't playing fair. Sex as a by-product of their arrangement—it should be clinical and dispassionate, surely. And then she could be rational and sensible in her rebuttal. But this assault was like a drug, winding logic into sensual knots, feeding into those parts of her that longed for more of what Andreas could provide.

His hands slid down her arms, captured her breasts and forced the air from her lungs. *'Make love with me.'* And the only answer she could find was to lift her hands behind her neck and unclip her halter top, so that the fabric slid down over the hands that now supported her breasts.

He growled then, and swept her into his arms, carrying her like a prize and laying her down on the bed, peeling down the silk until her breasts lay exposed to his gaze. She watched him watching her, her hands around his neck, his dark eyes heavy with longing, and never had she wanted anything more.

And then she felt nothing beyond the ecstasy of his hot mouth on her breast, his tongue hungrily circling her nipple.

'Andreas,' she implored, not knowing why or what she wanted. He growled a laughing response and she almost cried out in despair when he withdrew and cold air replaced where he'd been, only for his mouth to claim the other. His hands scooped her sides, moulding to her flesh, drinking it in as his lips drew her breast deeper into the furnace of his mouth.

Somewhere in some vague recess of her mind, she was aware of his hand at her back, and the downward buzz of a zipper, but it was the sensation of the silken gown sliding down her body that took precedence and the feel of his hot mouth at her belly.

Some time, she couldn't remember when, she'd wrapped her arms around his neck and tangled her fingers in his hair. It was thick and silky, the waves curling around her fingers possessively.

And then there was nothing between them but underwear, nothing that could disguise his need or hide her want.

Oh, God!

The panic welled up even as his hand scooped down her body, from shoulder, over breast, to stomach, to *there*, where she forgot about panic and ached instead with something that felt like desperation. His fingers slipped under the lace, scooping low, driving her crazy with his feather-light touch.

And then so gently, so tenderly he parted her and her back arched from the bed. She could feel what he could, her slickness, the moistness that let his fingertips glide against her tender flesh like satin over silk, while his thumb circled a tight bud of nerves that combined agony with ecstasy, the pressure building and building until they screamed for release.

His lips found her nipple and it was Cleo who screamed, Cleo whose world fractured and split apart in a blinding explosion of colour and sensation that left her shattered and gasping in his hands.

She was more responsive than he'd imagined and now he wanted her more than ever! He dispensed with his underwear and reached for protection in almost the same movement. The scrap of lace hit the floor in the next as he kissed his way up her still-shuddering body, positioning himself over her. He'd known he would enjoy her body. She was lush and curvy and her breasts filled his hands better than he could have hoped.

His erection bucked, eager now, and more than ready. Still, he took a moment to lap at one rose-coloured nipple, to nuzzle at her neck before brushing the hair from her turned-away face and pressing his lips to her cheek, only to taste salt.

He took her chin in his hand and pulled it around to face him. Tracks stained her cheeks, moisture clung to the lashes of her closed eyelids and her lips were firmly pressed together. 'You're crying? Did I hurt you?'

Reluctantly her blue eyes opened to him. Awash with tears, they looked the colour of the sea as she slowly shook her head, swiping at her eyes with one hand. 'I'm sorry,' she sniffed, 'but that's never happened to me before. I didn't know…'

Never happened? Confusion clouded his mind for a moment, clearing just as quickly as a wave of fury rolled over him. He sat up. 'You are a virgin!' *Vlaka!* He was such a fool. He left the bed and strode across to a wardrobe, plucking out a robe that he lashed around himself, giving the tie a savage tug. No wonder she had been so coy, so sensitive to his touch. No wonder she had been so bad an actress! She had been touched by nobody!

He rounded on the bed, to where the girl now sat huddled over her knees, scrabbling for her golden gown in an effort to cover her nakedness. A virgin! That was the last thing he needed. 'You told me you had slept with men before! You told me you were not a virgin. What the hell are you doing here?'

She dropped her head onto her knees as a fresh flood of tears spilled from his eyes, only magnifying his fury.

'What kind of woman are you? Were you so hungry for money that you would risk that which is most precious to you?'

'No,' she cried, raising her tear-stained face up at him, 'because I'd already thrown that away for nothing!'

She sniffed again and swiped the back of one hand across

her cheeks, swinging her legs over the side of the bed and standing, the gown bunched ineffectually around her. 'I'm not a virgin, if that makes you feel any better. So you don't have to worry about deflowering me. Somebody else got there first.'

He supposed he should have been relieved. He watched her flight for the bathroom while he stood there wondering why all of a sudden that thought was somehow so very unappealing.

'You made out like you'd had sex plenty of times.'

She didn't even turn around. 'So sue me.'

'But you've never even had an orgasm.'

This time she did, glaring over her shoulder at him. 'I don't recall seeing that condition in the fine print.'

He consumed the distance between them in a handful of purposeful strides, catching her by the arm just short of the bathroom door and swinging her around to face him.

'So why not? How many times have you had sex? How many men?'

She looked down at his hand on her arm, before turning her face slowly up to his. The tracks of her tears had messed up whatever had been left of her make-up. There were dark smudges under her blue eyes and her hair was still tangled and messy from thrashing her head around when she'd climaxed. *When she'd climaxed for the very first time.*

He'd given her that. Despite the tears and smudges and tangled hair he saw only that. He felt the thrum of blood return, the heaviness building once again in his groin.

'How many?'

'One.'

And he felt himself frown. 'One man?'

Her eyes looked sad and pained at the same time, before she blinked and turned her head away and he knew.

'Why didn't you tell me?'

She flinched and tried to pull away and he couldn't blame

her. He'd growled out the words so harshly that even to his own ears his question had sounded more like an accusation. But damn it, she was supposed to be pretending to be his mistress. 'You should have told me, instead of making out you'd had sex plenty of times.'

Her head snapped around, her blue eyes blazing. 'You think it's easy to admit to someone you barely know that you've had sex only once and it was so lousy anyway you really wish you hadn't bothered? Especially when sex isn't part of the deal.' She gave an exaggerated shrug to accompany a wide-eyed look of innocence. 'And you so understanding. Heck, why didn't I tell you?'

He wanted to shake her. He wanted to tell her she'd been wrong ever thinking she could pull this off, that she should have admitted the truth when he'd first put his proposition to her, and maybe he would do both of those things, but first of all there was a raw pain in her liquid eyes that made him want to tear somebody else limb from limb first.

'Who was he?'

'It doesn't matter. He was just some guy. It was just for a laugh.'

But her eyes told him differently.

He cupped her neck in one hand and drew her head to his shoulder. For a moment she stayed stiff but the strumming of his fingers on her skin soon soothed away her resistance. 'But it was no good. At least, not for you.'

She gave what he suspected was meant to be a laugh, but came out more like a hiccup. 'It was awful. It hurt and it was over in no time but I thought…'

He drew her closer into a hug. What kind of man was so uncaring of an innocent? 'You thought what?'

She shrugged and tried to lift her head. 'It doesn't matter.' Her voice was flat and lifeless but her body was warm and pliant against his, as if she'd forgotten to be afraid. His fingers stroked her neck, tracing the bones of her spine up into her hair and then down again.

Her scent surrounded him, the smell of her hair, the remnants of her fragrance and the warm scent of her earlier arousal. She had come apart in his arms. His and nobody else's and the knowledge made him hard. She was almost a virgin and she needed to know it could be better. He kissed her hair and breathed deep.

'He was a fool. He did not deserve the gift he'd been given.'

She raised her face and blinked up at him. 'I thought you would be mad with me. *Were* mad with me. And you'd have every right. I'm sorry. I know I should never have agreed to do this.'

He listened to her words and nodded on a sigh. 'You're right. You clearly do not have the experience necessary for the job.' And he felt her stiffen in his arms and try to pull away.

'But perhaps that is something we could remedy together.'

It felt as if her heart had skipped a beat. Or maybe it had just stopped altogether. But no, she was still standing and there was her heartbeat, pounding louder than ever in her ears.

She looked up at him, afraid she'd misconstrued what he meant, afraid in case she hadn't.

Afraid.

And he took her face in his hands and pressed his lips to hers.

'I promise you your second time will be better.'

She was in his arms in the next moment, bundled still with the golden dress tangled around her and feeling strangely disjointed and other-worldly.

'Andreas,' she whispered as he placed her like a treasured prize in the centre of the bed. 'What if I can't? I mean—' She felt the heat flood to her face. 'You're so…big.'

And he smiled as he unwrapped her from the coverlet, uncovering her bit by bit until she lay naked on the bed before him. 'I will not hurt you,' he said, and his dark eyes held a promise as intense as their desire so that even when he untied his own robe and revealed the full extent of his arousal she believed him.

Time became irrelevant in the minutes following. Colours blurred and merged with her feelings into a sensual overload. And nothing mattered but the sensations Andreas conjured up inside her as he worked his brand of slow magic upon her body.

No part of her escaped his attention. Nowhere was ignored by his clever fingers or his heated mouth or the hot flick of his tongue.

Until she was burning with a need that she'd never known. Burning for completion.

'Did he do this to you?' Andreas asked as he parted her thighs and dipped his head lower. And she tossed her head from side to side, the sensations inside her robbing her of the power of speech.

'Did he make you feel this way?' He wanted to know as he pressed his hot mouth to her very core, almost tipping her over the edge.

'Did he make you call his name?' he demanded.

Her cry was torn from her, his name on her tongue as he sent her once again over the edge. 'Did he?' he demanded, raining hot kisses on her eyes and on her mouth. Hot kisses that tasted of him and of her.

'No' she breathed when finally she could talk once more, her head still spinning, her body humming. 'No.'

'Then he was not a man. He gave you nothing and so what he took from you was nothing.'

She shuddered under him, though whether from the intensity of his message or from the obsidian gaze meeting hers, she couldn't tell. Nor could she think as she felt the nudge of him against her.

She gasped and felt a moment of panic but his eyes stayed her.

'You are ready,' he told her. 'Trust me.'

Strangely she did. And this time there was no stab of pain, no discomfort. This time she felt her muscles slowly stretching as he eased his way inside, until he filled her completely, all the time his dark eyes not leaving hers.

He kissed her then, a slow, deep kiss that spoke of possession as he started to move inside her. She gasped into his mouth as he slowly withdrew. She gasped again when he returned, awakening nerve endings she'd never known she possessed, inviting their participation in this sensual dance.

Every part of her felt alive. Every part of her awake to his slow seduction, welcoming him as he increased the pace and the rhythm. And still his eyes didn't leave her face.

She clung to him, inside and out, feeling it building again, that relentless ever-increasing tension as he took her higher and still higher with each deep thrust until there was nowhere left to climb, nowhere left to go.

And then her world exploded, shattering into tiny fragments as he pushed her over the edge. And this time she wasn't alone. This time he came with her.

Clearly the man had been a fool. Andreas lay there listening to the sound of her deep even breathing as the moonlight spilled through the long window and over her creamy skin, giving it a pearl-like sheen. He'd always made a point of not bedding virgins. He didn't want to build false hopes. He didn't want attachments based on first times. He didn't want attachments full stop.

So whoever had clumsily relieved Cleo of her virginity had handed him a gift. She was unbelievably responsive, her delight in an unfamiliar act refreshing and light years away from that of the women he normally associated with, who tended to go mechanically through the motions with a brisk, businesslike efficiency. Not that there was anything wrong with that; it was no different from the way he himself operated. But now that he had been handed this prize, it would be refreshing to spend a few weeks having sex with someone who wasn't quite so practised, someone for whom the art of love-making would be more of a novelty.

Far from being the disaster he'd been contemplating earlier tonight, his four-week plan had been inspired, now that she'd clearly dispensed with that no-sex clause. A few weeks with Cleo in his bed would suit him perfectly and then she'd depart back to wherever she'd come from and meanwhile Petra would have well and truly got the message.

He sighed, congratulating himself as he relaxed back into the bed, the scent of a woman's hair on his pillow, the scent of their love-making in his bed.

A few easy-to-take weeks with Cleo, and life would be back to normal.

CHAPTER TEN

ANDREAS started work early the next day, hoping to work out a way of getting Constantine back on side, but he wasn't returning calls and with growing frustration Andreas picked up a file from his desk, flipped it open and found documents he'd been waiting on since before his trip to London. Good. He glanced over them once and frowned when he couldn't remember a thing he'd just read. Took a second look and still nothing stuck. He closed the file, pushing it away as he leaned back in his chair, spinning it around to face the view of the caldera from his office.

What was Cleo doing today? He'd left her snug in bed, the scent of their recent love-making perfuming the air. Had she decided on a late breakfast and a swim? Or had she decided to explore the streets of Fira on her own after he'd curtailed her exploration yesterday? She didn't speak Greek. Santorini's tourist venues catered for tourists of course, but still…

'Where are you going?'

'I'll be back,' he told Petra as he strode past. 'Later.'

An hour later he *was* back, his mood foul because he'd missed her, still no call back from Con and still the damned papers made no sense. He opened another file. Signed some papers awaiting his signature, relegated some more marked

for his attention to the out-tray, read and reread another batch
of files before he decided his heart wasn't in it and he pushed
his chair back with a rush.

Where was she? He'd told the staff to let him know the
moment she returned, and he'd heard nothing. Surely they
couldn't have forgotten his instructions.

Maybe they had. By four o'clock he'd had enough of
waiting and guessing. How much time did one woman need
for shopping? Fira wasn't *that* big a town.

He found her in the suite preparing to take a shower,
already in her robe, and he knew he'd been right to suspect
she was up to something because not one shopping bag
littered the room. 'Where the hell have you been?'

She turned, startled, her cheeks reddening. 'You told me
I could go out.'

And he had. He exhaled, trying to rid himself of hours of
frustration in one single breath. 'You were gone a long time.
You clearly weren't shopping. What were you doing?'

Her face brightened again, warily at first, gaining enthusiasm as she spoke. 'Fira is amazing! The paths and the
houses and even the gates. Did you realise how wonderful the
doorways are here? They beckon you with a glimpse of
paradise, a snatch of view, like some wicked temptation, and
opening to stairs you don't even know are there and that lead
to terraces hidden below. It's incredible. I've never seen
anything like it.'

She was like a powerhouse, so lit up with the joy of her
discoveries that her joy fed into him. He should be used to
the everyday sights that surrounded him but she made them
all fresh and new and now he wished he'd been there to see
it through her eyes and feel the joy of her discovery with her.

'And there are donkeys with ribbons and beaded head-
bands that carry people all the way up and down to the port…'
For a moment her blue eyes misted and lost a little of their

joy. She shook her head. 'I walked. I felt a bit sorry for them. But then,' she said breathlessly, her eyes lighting up again as if she'd discovered the meaning of life itself, 'then I found the Archaeological Museum.'

'You what?' He smothered a snort of disbelief, but it was only just. Nobody he'd ever brought to Santorini had bothered to look it up. Not one of his former women had ever been interested, preferring to shop for the gold jewellery the island was renowned for or designer trinkets to take home. 'Why did you go there?'

'I was curious about Santorini, and it was amazing! I couldn't believe the history of this place. There was an entire city buried under ash. A whole city buried, just like Pompeii, but thousands of years earlier and they'd found pots and urns and the most incredible artworks.' She held out her hands and sighed, her blue eyes bright with discovery, her cheeks alive with colour and all he knew was that he wanted that enthusiasm and joy wrapped around him. He wanted her. *Now.*

He saw the change in her eyes as she realised, saw the movement in her chest as she hauled down air and felt the air crackle between them as if it were alive. 'Andreas?' And then she was in his arms as they tumbled together onto the bed.

Last night's tenderness was history. They came together in a heated rush, Cleo grappling with his shirt buttons and his belt while he plundered her mouth with his kisses and drove her to the edge with the hot sweep of his hands before plunging into her depths. It was brutal and savage and fast but they both wanted it that way, needed it to be that way, the all-consuming fire of their need driving them on. Her cries melded with his as he drove into her one final time, sending them both spinning and weightless and once more into the crater.

Panting and slick with sweat, he cursed himself for his lack of control. That was no way to take a woman with so little experience. 'Are you all right?'

She blinked her blue eyes up at him, eyes that were still dizzy and lacking focus. 'Wow.'

'Was I too fast? Did I hurt you?'

'Oh, no. Just, wow.'

Strangely, in a place he didn't even know he had, he felt a surge of pride. Still inside her, not caring that he was still half dressed because he didn't want to be apart, he cradled her face in his hands and kissed her softly. 'What was that for?' she breathed.

'Just because.' He traced a hand down her throat and up the incline to one perfect breast. 'Did you see the women, how they were portrayed in the wall paintings?' She gasped as his fingers circled her nipples, her flesh firming, responding to his touch. He growled in appreciation. So responsive and yet she'd just come. And in turn, so was he. He felt the change in direction in his blood. Felt the heat return. 'Did you see how they were dressed?'

She blushed the delightful way she did. 'Did the women really go bare-breasted? I wasn't sure.'

He arched over her and flicked her nipple with his tongue. 'They did. The Minoans celebrated life and nature and all things beautiful. And these…' he dipped his head to her other breast '…are beautiful. You would have been a goddess in those times,' he said, feeling himself swell once again, feeling the need to take her once more. 'A fair-headed goddess from across the seas.'

This time the rhythm was slower, more languid and controlled and he watched the storm once more build inside her, her arms woven around his neck, her legs anchored at his back. He watched her face as she neared the summit, he watched her azure eyes widen as the waves of pleasure lifted her higher and ever higher and then he watched her features freeze into that mask of ecstasy as her muscles clamped down around him and took him with her.

It seemed like for ever until he could breathe normally again. Slowly, gently, he withdrew and found reason to curse himself all over again.

Vlaka! Like some hot-under-the-collar schoolboy he'd forgotten to use protection. What the hell had he been thinking? But he hadn't been thinking, not beyond being inside her and sharing that glorious enthusiasm that had streamed out of her like sunshine.

'Cleo, are you safe?'

The words made no sense in the context of their love-making. She was safe. She felt safe being with Andreas. Until a cold wave of realisation washed over her. They hadn't used protection!

'Oh. I...' When was her last period? Was it three weeks, or only two? 'I don't know. I can work it out, though.'

'So work it out,' he said gruffly as he tore off what was left of his clothes and headed for the shower.

She curled up behind him on the bed. 'You make out like it's my fault.'

He took a deep breath. In a way it was. He'd never lost control like that before. Never been so obsessed with being inside a woman that he'd forgotten something as basic—as necessary—as protection. Who else's fault was it?

His.

He looked over his shoulder to where she now sat, huddled on the bed, her robe drawn back tightly around her like a shield. 'You're right.' He forced the words through his teeth. 'I'm sorry. But sorry isn't much good if you become pregnant.'

Pregnant? Oh, God. She'd been so blown away by Andreas' love-making that she hadn't stopped to think of the consequences. Pregnant. No wonder he was so angry. It couldn't happen, could it? Surely life wouldn't be that unfair when she was going home in just a few weeks.

Although knowing her luck...

She swallowed. She'd be going home pregnant and unmarried. A loser. Again.

Or would she?

The bright side, she thought, knowing she was probably being irresponsible to even think this way. The bright side was she'd be going home with Andreas' baby. Would it matter that she was pregnant if she had something of Andreas to keep for ever? Was it wrong to think that way? At least the money she was going home with would ensure that their baby would want for nothing.

And the chances were, nothing would happen, and she would go home alone.

She jacked up her chin. 'We'll deal with that *if* it happens. But I don't have stars in my eyes, Andreas. I know I have a use-by date. I'm not looking for more.'

He nodded and told her she was welcome to join him before stepping into the bathroom. He didn't expect she would now, he thought as he turned on the powerful jet of spray and adjusted the temperature, the familiar smell of salt from the mineral-rich water thick in the steamy atmosphere. Which was a shame. He would enjoy her body slick with soap and water.

Another time.

He could see he'd hurt her and that bothered him. Not that he'd hurt her, but that he even cared. Especially when her words should have given him comfort. She didn't want any more from him. That was good, wasn't it?

He lifted his face up into the stream of water and soaped his body. He'd make it up to her. Petra could hold the fort for a few days. He'd show Cleo his Santorini, the world that he loved, seeing as she was interested in more than just the usual souvenir shops.

After all, if they only had a month, they might as well enjoy it.

* * *

The next few days passed in a blur for Cleo. Andreas surprised her by wanting to tour the island with her and he was a consummate tour guide. He took her to the town of Oia at the very tip of the island and let her explore the narrow laneways and discover the blue-domed churches and the elegant remnants of Venetian occupation and the windmills that clung to the sides of the cliff.

And then he delighted her by taking her to the mountain of Mesa Vouno where hand in hand they climbed the path to the ruins of Ancient Thera, the remnants of an ancient Greek and later Roman city. With the wind whipping in her hair she discovered more of that fascination for the ancient that she'd found while touring the museum. People had lived here, thousands of years ago. They had left their mark on the earth in the walls and the columns still standing and in the engravings on the rocks, of eagles and dolphins and strong-featured men.

Andreas could be one of them, she thought, chiselled and strong-jawed and handsome beyond belief. He caught her watching him, the wind in his hair so that it looked alive. 'What are you thinking?'

And she smiled and celebrated a brand-new discovery: that a girl with no education and no career wasn't necessarily doomed to clean rooms all her life, that she'd found something she could be passionate about. 'I'm going to go home,' she announced, on the top of a mountain overlooking the entire island, 'and study. I'm going to find a course where I can learn about the people who lived here and left these marks on the rocks. I want to know more.' And she spun around laughing.

And he laughed too, because her mood was infectious, even though he suspected she'd go home and the memories would fade and she'd forget all about a bunch of old rocks on the top of a mountain somewhere halfway across the world.

They stopped for lunch at a *kafenio* in a nearby village on the way back and enjoyed simple fare of the freshest vegetables and seafood cooked superbly and that tasted better than anything she'd ever eaten before, and they walked it off again along a black sandy beach.

And wherever they went, it was to a backdrop of azure seas and sky, black volcanic rock and whitewashed buildings that all melded with incredible beauty.

'You are so lucky,' she sighed later that night as together they watched another fiery sun sink into the ocean, the sky a painter's dream of scorching red and gold. They hadn't missed a sunset since that aborted ball and she knew that she would never get sick of the sight.

She turned to see if he'd heard and caught him watching her, the intensity of his eyes sending vibrations down her spine that converged on her heart and made it lurch. 'The sunset. You're not watching.'

And he smiled. 'I'm watching it reflected in your expression. I never knew how beautiful our sunset was until this moment.' He curved a hand around her neck, drawing her closer into a kiss. 'How long do we have left?' he murmured, his lips in her hair, his breath tickling her ear.

She trembled against him. She knew exactly what he was asking. She'd been counting off the days and nights since she'd arrived, at first with enthusiasm, and lately with a sense of dread. 'Um, two weeks and four days.'

And he pulled her closer until their bodies were aligned, length to length. 'Then let's not waste a minute of it.'

Half an hour in the mornings was all he needed these days to clear his desk of anything needing his attention. He was sick of looking at files that meant nothing, sick of worrying about unreturned calls and he'd discovered the joy of delegation and the freedom it brought. Half an hour was enough to clear his desk and his day for Cleo. So it was lucky she chose then to call.

'Sofia.' He grimaced, remembering he was supposed to call his mother back days ago. 'I was just about to call you.'

'We need to talk,' she said. 'It's been too long.'

It had been. And he had things he needed to tell her, things he'd meant to tell her when he'd returned from London. 'Aren't we talking now?'

'Come to Athens,' she said. 'I need to see my son. I have news I can't tell you over the phone.'

Ice slid down his spine. 'What's wrong?'

There was a moment's hesitation and he sensed her wavering, almost able to see his mother holding onto the edge of the table for support. 'Come to Athens.'

There would no doubt be a breeze later, she'd learned enough about the weather since she'd been here to know that it would whip up over the clifftops around midday, but for now the waters of the caldera showed barely a ripple under the perfect spring sun, and the waters of the infinity pool stretching out before Cleo showed even less. In the distance she could hear the odd group of tourists passing by, exclaiming over the perfect photo opportunity—there seemed to be one around every corner on Santorini—but the pool deck was private and tucked away from the main tourist trails and their voices and snatched words drifted away and all was quiet again. She was breathless from the slow laps she'd done but that was good. She had a pile of books on Santorini, its history and archaeological treasures to read, and that was good too. She needed to keep busy, given Andreas wouldn't be back until at least tomorrow.

She clamped down on the stab of disappointment that accompanied that thought. Soon enough she wouldn't see him at all. Surely she could live with his absence for a couple of days?

But after the bliss of their last few days and nights together, the news that Andreas had taken the helicopter to Athens and would be away overnight had been a major disappointment. She liked being with him. She liked his company and his conversation and she'd surprised herself by loving being in his bed. Then she'd received the message he would be another night at least.

Two days to fill. Two nights alone in his bed, with the smell of him on his pillow and the empty space alongside her where he should be.

How quickly she'd become accustomed to his touch. And how quickly she'd abandoned the concept of pretending to be his mistress.

Every night they made love. As far as she was concerned, she didn't have to pretend. To all intents and purposes, she was his mistress, in every sense of the word.

She put down the book she couldn't concentrate on and dived back into the pool. She needed to do more laps. The more tired she was, the less she would notice the empty space beside her in bed and the better she would sleep. And the better she slept, the less she would miss his magic touch.

Strange, how she could think his touch so magic after just a few nights. But for the first time in her life, she had felt like a woman. Andreas had done that, unleashing sensations within her that she'd never imagined were there, sensations that yearned to be released again.

Lap after lap she drove herself until, weak limbed and gasping, she staggered from the pool and collapsed into a lounger. She closed her eyes and tried to blank her mind, but it was still pictures of Andreas she saw, pictures of what they might do together on his return. She'd already decided it was time to be more proactive, to take matters into her own hands.

She could hardly wait to surprise him.

'*Kalimera*. I hope I'm not disturbing you.'

Cleo came to with a start. With Andreas away she'd assumed Petra would be busy in charge of the office. She hadn't expected her to turn up poolside wearing the black-scrap-of-nothing bikini with tie-around skirt that, given its brevity, did nothing to protect her modesty and everything to accentuate her endless legs.

'*Kalimera*,' Cleo replied with almost the extent of her Greek, instantly on edge. Her own bikini was a Moontide original that Mme Bernadette had insisted she take, swirls of blue and green that accentuated her eyes and complemented her skin now that it was starting to take on the tan she'd lost while in England. She knew she looked good in it, but compared to the tall, slender Petra she felt awkward and lumpy. And definitely too exposed. 'I didn't expect to see you,' she said, reaching for a towel to cover her on the pretext of drying her knotted hair. Anything to protect her from the other woman's laser-sharp scrutiny. 'I thought you'd be flat out in the office with Andreas away.'

Petra unhitched the tiny skirt and let it flutter to the lounger alongside, an action clearly designed to draw attention to her legs. It worked. Cleo instantly felt short and squat. 'It is very busy, of course, but I was feeling a little queasy this morning and thought a swim would refresh me before the afternoon's appointments.' She put an impeccably manicured hand to her waist.

Cleo followed the movement and wished she hadn't. Did the woman not have a bulge anywhere? 'You're not well?'

The woman gave a shrug and checked her hair. 'We had a reception with lunch yesterday. Most likely just something that disagreed with me.' She walked lithely to the water's edge, descending the stairs into the pool's liquid depths as regally as a Miss Universe contestant, where she breast-stroked two lengths of the pool without a splash, emerging from the water with her hair as sleek and perfect as when she'd gone in.

'Ah, that's wonderfully refreshing,' she said as she lowered herself to the lounger. 'And finding you here is even better. We haven't had much of a chance to get to know one another, have we? Andreas selfishly keeps you all to himself.'

'I guess not.'

'I love your swimsuit,' Petra said, patting herself dry with a towel. 'Those colours are wonderful on you.'

Cleo blinked. The words sounded sincere enough, and she wondered if she'd misjudged the woman. All she'd had to go by was one car trip from the airport and she'd been tired. Maybe she'd imagined the snippiness. 'Thank you. Yours looks gorgeous too.'

Petra smiled and nodded her thanks. 'You're Australian, aren't you?'

Cleo relaxed a little. At least here was a safe topic. 'That's right. From a little outback town called Kangaroo Crossing. It's dry and dusty and nothing at all like here.'

'I've always wanted to go to Australia. Tell me about it.'

Cleo obliged. It was good to talk of home, of a place that was so much a different world from this one that it could have been on another planet, of a place of endless drought and struggling families and mobs of kangaroos jumping across paddocks of red dust. And the more she spoke of home, and the more the other woman smiled and laughed, the more she relaxed. It was good to talk to another woman. She'd missed that in London.

'Now I simply must go and visit your homeland. But Andreas said you met in London. What were you doing so far from home?'

Cleo shook her head. 'You really don't want to know. You'd think me a total fool if I told you.'

'Oh, no, never.' She reached one long-nailed hand over to Cleo's and patted it. 'It's all right. You can tell me. I'll understand, I promise.'

And then, because it had been so long since Cleo had been able to pour her heart out to anyone, it all came out in a rush, how she'd found Kurt through an Internet chat room and how he'd seduced her with his promises of romance and travel and how she'd fallen for it, hook, line and sinker. She didn't tell her about his making love to her, of relieving her of her virginity and then casting her aside. She'd had no choice but to tell Andreas, but that part was nobody else's business.

'So you were stuck in London? You poor thing. But surely you had a return ticket?'

She shook her head. 'I'd only enough money for one way. I never thought I'd need to head home so soon. Except my nanna had lent me the return fare just before I boarded the bus to the city, just in case the worst happened. Only I didn't have a bank account so Kurt said he'd look after it for me…'

'And he took your money? What kind of man was he?' She patted her arm again. 'You are much better off without him and here in Santorini.'

'I know.' She took a deep breath. It felt surprisingly good to get that all off her chest. All the emotions and guilt and self-flagellation that had plagued her every day since he'd dumped her felt as if they were sloughing away, as if she'd confessed her sins and all would be right with the world.

'And how fortunate for you to meet Andreas after all that had happened to you. You must feel very lucky.'

'I do,' Cleo agreed, sure Petra hadn't meant that to sound as it had.

'So how are you enjoying Santorini, then?' she asked, changing tack. 'This is your first time here?'

Cleo relaxed again, certain she'd been reading too much

into the other woman's tone. Santorini was another topic she could easily and honestly enthuse about. 'It's so beautiful! You're so lucky living here, being surrounded by all this—' her arm swept around in an arc '—every day. The sights and atmosphere, even the history is amazing.'

'I'm so glad you're enjoying it. We're very proud of our island home. We want visitors to be happy here.'

'I'm very happy. The sunsets are amazing.'

'Honeymooners come here just to experience Santorini's sunset. It's supposed to be very romantic. What do you think?'

Cleo suddenly felt too tied in knots to answer. It was romantic, or it would be, if you were here with the right person. But Andreas wasn't the right person, was he? They'd just been forced together by circumstances and soon she would leave. Although the way he'd looked at her the other night on the terrace… 'I guess it could be, if you were here with the right person.'

'Oh, I'm so sorry. I'm making you uncomfortable.'

'It's okay. It's not like I'm here for the romance exactly.'

The other woman's eyebrows arched approvingly. 'No? Well, I guess in your place that's the best way to think about it. Andreas has quite a reputation for moving on. And now I must get back to work. Thank you so much for talking with me. I feel like we're going to be good friends while you're here.'

'Are you feeling any better?' she asked as Petra retied the tiny skirt around her hips.

'Oh, I'm feeling *much* better, thank you.'

Cleo watched her slip on her gold sandals and wander away, wondering why it should be that she was suddenly feeling so much worse.

'It's just a lump, Andreas. There's no need to go on about it.' Sofia Xenides stiffened her spine and sat her slim body higher on the chaise longue, her ankles crossed demurely beneath her, her coffee balanced on her knees. Andreas knew the posture, recognised it as his mother closing the subject down again.

To hell with that.

'You should have told me.'

'You were busy. In London apparently. And then with who knows what?'

He bristled. 'You could have called me on my cell phone.'

'And told you what? That I had a lump? And what could you have done besides worry?'

'I would have made you see a doctor.'

'Which is exactly what I did do. And tomorrow I will get the results of the biopsy and we will know. There was no point worrying you unnecessarily before, but I am glad you will be with me tomorrow. And now we have more important things to discuss. When were you planning on telling me what exactly you were doing in London?'

Andreas sighed. 'You know, then?'

'Petra tells me you found Darius. Is that true?'

'I found him. He'd gambled the last of the money away, all he had left was a seedy hotel filled with mould and rising damp. He was ripe for a low-interest loan in order to fund his gambling habit.'

'So you found him, and you exacted the revenge you have been looking for all these years. I imagine you ruined him in the process.'

'It is no more than he did to us!'

'Andreas,' she sighed, 'it is so long ago. Perhaps now you can put the past behind you?'

'How can you say that? I will never put the past behind me. Don't you remember what he did to us, what it was like back then? He destroyed Father and he walked away and left us with nothing. *Nothing!*'

She shut her eyes, as if the mention of her late husband was still painful, but a breath later she was still firm. 'And it has driven you all these years, my son. Now that you have achieved the goal you have aimed for all your life, what are you going to do with the rest of your life?'

Andreas stared blankly out of the window and shrugged, the question unnerving him. Hadn't he been feeling an unfamiliar lack of motivation lately, avoiding the office because suddenly it was all too uninspiring? Below the terrace lay the rolling expanse of Athens city, apartment blocks jostling with antiquities in the sprawling city. No, he was just temporarily distracted with Cleo, that was all. Soon she would be gone and he would refocus on his work again. 'I will go on with my business,' he said, resolutely. 'Already the Xenides name is synonymous with the most prestigious accommodation on offer across all of Europe. I will make it even bigger, even better.'

She gave another sigh, except this one sounded less indulgent, more impatient. 'Maybe there is another goal you might pursue now.'

'What do you mean?'

'Perhaps it is time you thought about family.'

'I have never neglected you!' Even though he felt a stab of guilt that he'd never returned her call as he'd intended.

'Did I say you had? But the time for looking backwards is past. It is time to look to the future, and to a family of your own.'

He sighed. If this was about getting married again... And then something he'd never seen coming hit him like a brick. 'You want grandchildren.'

'I am a Greek mother.' She shrugged. 'Of course, I want grandchildren. Maybe now you have satisfied this lifelong quest for vengeance, you might find the time to provide me with some, while I can still appreciate them.'

'Mother—'

She held up one hand to silence him. 'I am not being melodramatic. It is not just that I have had this scare and I must face the prospect of the results not going the way I would prefer, but you are not getting any younger, Andreas, and neither am I. I do not want to be too old or too sick to appreciate my grandchildren when they eventually come.'

'Stop talking this way! I'm not about to let you die.'

'I have no intention of dying! At least not before you bestow upon me the grandchildren I crave. I am not blind. You have quite a reputation with the women, I believe. After all this experience, do you not know what kind of woman would suit you for a wife?'

It was ridiculous to feel like blushing at something his mother said, and he wouldn't, but still her veiled reference to his many lovers made him so uncomfortable he couldn't bring himself to answer. Besides, could he in all honesty answer? The women he had through his bed had one resounding attribute, but it hardly made them wife material.

'Petra said you have a woman staying with you.'

He almost growled. Petra had always been like family, they'd practically grown up together, but there were times he resented the closeness and the fact Petra knew his mother so well. This was one of those times.

'It's none of Petra's business. Or yours, for that matter.'

'Tsh, tsh. Who else can ask if I can't? Petra said she's an Australian woman. Quite pretty, in her own way.'

She was more than pretty, he wanted to argue, until another thought blew all thoughts of argument out of the water.

And she could be pregnant.

They'd had unprotected sex. Twice. Right now she could be carrying his seed.

A baby. His mother could have the grandchild she yearned for. And as for him? *He would have Cleo.*

Strange, how that thought didn't send his blood into a tailspin.

But marriage? Was that what he wanted? He took a deep breath. But his mother would expect it, and, besides, there was no way he could not marry the mother of his child. Especially not now.

Granted, they'd shared but a few short days, less than two weeks, but those days had been good. The nights even better. Surely there could be worse outcomes?

'Petra said—'

He snapped away from possibilities and turned back to the present. 'Petra talks too much!'

'Andreas, she only wants the best for you, just as I do. In fact, I once wondered if—'

It was like a bad soap opera. Or a train wreck where you couldn't look away. He had to keep going till the bitter end. 'Go on.'

'Well, you and Petra have lived together for a long time now.'

'We share a building, not a bed!' And the mood his mother was in, he wasn't about to confess that they had. *Once.*

'And,' she continued, without missing a beat, 'you have so much in common.'

'She works for me. Of course, we have a lot in common.'

'Anyway,' Sofia said with a resigned shrug of her shoulders before she turned her attention to pick at an invisible speck of nothingness alongside her on the sofa, 'sometimes we don't realise what's right there in front of us, right under our noses. Not until it's gone.'

His teeth ground together. 'I'm not marrying Petra.'

She smiled up at him, blinking innocently as if his outburst had come from nowhere. 'Whoever said you would? I just wondered, that's all. And there's nothing wrong with a mother wondering, is there, Andreas? Much better to consider the options than to let the grass grow beneath your feet.'

The grass was feeling comfortable enough where he was

standing right now. Or it had been, until his mother had laced its green depths with barbs that tore at the soles of his feet and pricked at his conscience.

'About this appointment tomorrow to see your doctor…'

'I get the point, Andreas. But enough about doctors too. Would you like some more coffee?'

CHAPTER ELEVEN

CLEO was in the pool resting her elbows on the edge, one of her glossy history books perched in front of her. Hungrily Andreas' eyes devoured her, from the streaked hair bundled up in a clip behind her head, her bare shoulders and back, and her legs making lazy movements in the water. She looked browner than he remembered, her skin more golden. Clearly the weather here suited her better than that dingy hotel in London where her skin was never so much as kissed by the sun.

And an idea, vague and fuzzy inside him, found dimension and merit. She could be pregnant with his child, even now. And even though the news for his mother had been good, the tests had come back negative, that still didn't change the fact that his mother yearned for grandchildren.

Sofia was right. She wasn't getting any younger, although he'd never thought of his mother as a number with a finite span. And he'd never thought of his own age and the possibilities of family. Because he'd thought of nothing beyond the one thing that had driven his life for more than a decade.

Retribution.

And now he'd achieved it all, he'd built himself up from nothing until he could exact the revenge he'd been planning for twelve long years, and yet somehow he didn't get the same buzz from the achievement any more. He didn't even care any more if Constantine turned his proposal down flat, and that had never happened before. But the prospect that the grandchild his mother hungered for could already be in the making caused a new and unfamiliar buzz.

Fate? He shook his head. You made your own opportunities in this life, he knew. He'd lived by that mantra for years. He believed in it. It had been what had kept him focused, until he'd found Darius and pulled what was left of him down.

He'd made this opportunity. And like any other, he'd make the most of it.

He padded noiselessly to the side of the pool. He doubted she would hear him anyway, even if he had made a noise. The books she'd bought on Santorini and its ancient civilisations seemed to have her completely in their thrall. Maybe it wasn't just talk, maybe she really was interested in more than a superficial picture of the island. Or maybe she was just killing time until his return.

Option B, he much preferred.

She turned a page, the angle of her head shifting, still totally oblivious to his presence.

She wouldn't be for long.

He dived into the water and crossed the pool, taking her by the waist as he erupted like a sea god from the water.

'Hey!' She turned, her fright turning to delight when she saw who her assailant was. 'Oh, you're back.'

Her legs were cool where they tangled with his, her shoulders deliciously warm from the sun and her lips so slick with gloss he wanted to find out if they were as slippery as they looked. 'Did you miss me?' he asked, his hands caressing curves they had sorely missed.

'Not really,' she lied, unable to keep the smile from her face or the tingling from her skin. 'I was kind of busy here, catching up on my reading. You know how it is.'

'Liar!' he said. 'Believe me, I know how it is—' before pulling her into a deep kiss that had them both spinning together into the depths. They came up gasping but Andreas wasn't finished with her yet. Already he'd untied her bikini top, one hand at her breasts while the other pushed at her bikini bottoms.

'Andreas…'

'Do you realise how long I've dreamed about having you in water?'

'Andreas…' She clung to him. She had no option but to cling as he brought her flesh alive and made her blood sing. His hands pushed inside her bikini, rounded her buttocks and delved deeper.

'I've missed you,' he growled, burying his face at her throat, his words so heavy with want it made her head spin. 'And I want you, so badly.'

'I… I got my period.'

He lifted his head slowly and gazed at her, his vision blurred by a rush of blood. Bad blood. 'I see.'

'But that's good news, isn't it? I thought you'd be pleased. Now there are no complications. That's what you wanted.'

He let her go and turned towards the edge of the pool, powering himself up with his hands to step from the pool like an athlete. He pulled a towel from a nearby stack and buried his face in it. 'Yes, it's good news. Of course.' Only it didn't feel like good news. It felt as though all the shifts he'd made, all the changes he'd made in his thinking were for nothing, and he was left stranded. He didn't like the feeling.

He could have done with the odd complication. It would have suited his purposes well.

So much for making opportunity happen.

Petra brought them both coffee as he checked his files the next day. Or she brought him one. Her nose twitched as she deposited the cup on his desk. 'You're not having one?' he queried, surprised she wasn't joining in with this long-time ritual.

Her nose twitched again. 'I seem to be off coffee. Don't know what it is. Probably just that time of the month.'

Andreas blanked out. He was over that time of the month, big time, and he certainly didn't want to hear about Petra's. He was irritable, he was short-tempered, and the sooner he got Cleo back where he wanted her, the better for all concerned. And maybe he'd even forget to use protection all over again. Only she'd probably be gone before she was fertile...

Damn.

Mind you, he could always change the contract terms... His mood brightened considerably. That was definitely one option worth pursuing.

'Poor Cleo,' Petra said, sifting through mail as she perched herself on the edge of his desk in her usual way, 'what a dreadful thing to happen, being cheated of her money like that.' She slapped a couple of papers down in front of him. 'Though I guess she brought it on herself to a large extent.'

His ears twitched at the mention of Cleo's name. He'd almost forgotten Petra was there again, already working out how best to tackle the subject of an extension to their terms. 'Brought what on herself?'

She shrugged. 'She must have told you. She went to London to meet this guy she'd hooked up with on the Internet and he ripped off the money for her return fare and left her with nothing. Awful. Mind you, you'd have to be pretty stupid to fall for something like that.'

Andreas sat back in his chair, letting the silence fall between them like an anvil. He knew for a moment that his scowl would say everything he needed to while he untangled the threads of his anger in his mind.

'Are you saying Cleo's stupid?'

'No! I mean… Well—' she shrugged and screwed up her nose, like she was making some kind of concession '—maybe just a bit naïve.'

'Or are you saying that my father was stupid?'

'Andreas! It's hardly the same thing.'

'Isn't it? My father trusted someone and lost everything to him. Cleo trusted someone and suffered the same fate. Tell me how it's different.'

He stood up and peeled his jacket from the back of his chair, shoving first one arm and then the other into it. 'You deal with the mail, Petra. I've got more important things to do.'

'Andreas, I didn't mean anything, honest.'

No? He was sick of the niggling, sick of Petra's snippy put-downs of Cleo with just a look or a snide remark. He'd been wrong to think she would take a not-so-subtle hint. Maybe it was time for a more direct approach. 'It's not going to happen, Petra, so don't think it is.'

She looked innocent enough, but he knew there was a computer inside that was as sophisticated as it was devious. 'You and me. That night was a mistake. It won't happen again.'

He found Cleo sitting out on the terrace overlooking the caldera and reading another of her books. In spite of the still-smouldering anger that simmered inside him, he smiled. In a lemon-coloured sundress that made the most of her newly acquired tan, she looked both innocent and intent at the same time.

She looked around, almost as if she'd been able to feel his eyes on her, and she smiled that heart-warming smile as her azure eyes lit up with enthusiasm. 'Back already? You'll never guess what I just read.'

Her enthusiasm was infectious. So infectious he didn't want

her to leave in however many days they had left. It was to his advantage she was in a good mood. It would be easier to convince her to stay. 'Tell me,' he said, pulling up a chair alongside.

'Well, when the volcano erupted going back three thousand years or so ago, it wiped out not just the cities on the island itself, but some think it brought down the entire prehistoric Minoan civilisation with it.'

'It's possible,' he acknowledged with a nod. 'Nobody knows for certain, but it could explain why the Minoans were such prosperous sea traders one minute and wiped from the face of the earth the next.'

Her azure eyes sparkled like the waters of the caldera itself. 'But this is the really exciting bit. Some say that the eruption and the fallout are the origins of the legend of Atlantis. A world that sank beneath the sea—and this is where it all happened! Do you believe it? Do you think Santorini is actually what's left of Atlantis?'

His cell phone interrupted them and he pulled it out, took one look at the caller ID and switched it off. Petra could wait.

'I think it's highly possible,' he conceded, repocketing his phone.

She sighed, hugging the book to her chest, and looked over to where the volcano, now silent, spread dark and low in the midst of the waters. 'I believe it. I did a Google search and found a Classics course in Sydney.'

'Cleo…'

'I'm going to enrol in it as soon as I get home. I'll be able to afford to live there now, thanks to you.'

'About going home.'

She turned her head, the spark gone from her eyes. 'Do you want me to leave earlier? I… I don't mind, if that's what you want.'

And he almost laughed at the idea. He shook his head. 'No. I don't want you to go earlier.'

'Then, what is it?'

He took a second to frame his thoughts. 'What's waiting for you at home? I mean, you've never talked about your family. Are they close?'

She gave a curious smile, her eyes perplexed. 'Well, not really. My mum's great, but the twins, my two half-brothers, keep her pretty busy and she's got a baby coming apparently.' She screwed up her nose. 'And then there's my step-dad, of course.'

'What's he like?'

She shrugged. 'He's okay, a bit rough around the edges maybe, but a lot of blokes are like that out there, but Mum loves him and he's good to her.'

'And to you?'

Excess baggage. The words were indelibly inscribed on her psyche. She sucked in a breath. 'We moved out there when Mum got the job as his housekeeper. I think he always saw me as a bit of an add-on, always hoping I'd make something of myself and move out. He'll be relieved I'll finally be off his hands.'

'Is that why you took off for the UK?'

She put the book she'd been holding up on the table and rubbed her arms. 'What's going on?'

'What do you mean?'

'Why all the questions? You've never bothered about all this personal stuff before.'

'Maybe we had something else to keep us busy then.' And even under her tan she managed to blush the way she did that made him warm all over. 'And maybe I'm just interested.'

She looked up at him warily through lowered lashes, as if she still didn't quite believe him. 'Okay. I guess wanting to prove myself was part of the reason I left. The job opportunities at home were non-existent and I kind of fell into cleaning, like Mum had.' Her hands knotted in her lap, her grip so tight it sent the ends of her fingers alternately red then white. 'I thought meeting Kurt was the opportunity of a lifetime and the chance to escape. I was so desperate to make a success of myself, I made every mistake in the book. I was such a fool.' She fell silent on a sigh, moisture sheening her eyes.

He reached over and untangled the damp knot of her hands, taking one of them between his own, lifting it, and pressing his lips to its back. 'It's no crime to trust someone.'

She blinked up at him, trying to clear her vision. Why did he have to be so kind? It had been easier when she'd thought him completely ruthless, easier when she remembered the way he'd taken over the hotel, issuing orders like a general in battle.

But lately he'd been beyond kind. The way he'd abandoned his work to escort her around the island, the way he'd watched sunset after sunset with her because she didn't want to miss a single one because she wanted to store them all up and remember when she went home, and the way he'd woken her softly just this morning with a kiss and brought her to climax with his clever fingers and his hot mouth.

And now he was listening to her as if what she said mattered. As if he cared for her as much as she was beginning to care for him.

She gulped down a breath.

Oh, no, don't go there! Don't imagine it for a minute. Because once before she'd thought someone cared for her. Once before she'd fallen for him because of it. Look where that had got her.

No, she'd made a deal. Under the terms of their contract, she would leave here in little more than two weeks and they'd never see each other again.

She turned her eyes away from the thumb now stroking her hand, his long, tapered fingers and neat nails, up, and up to his face, knowing he was waiting for some kind of response, something to show that she'd put what had happened in the past behind her. But it wasn't what had happened in the past that was bothering her. It was what lay ahead that scared her most of all.

Two weeks of sharing Andreas' bed and pretending to be his mistress, *being his mistress.*

Two weeks of guarding her fragile heart.

And two weeks to work on not falling in love with Andreas Xenides.

She dragged in oxygen to steel her resolve. She'd learned from her mistake with Kurt. It wouldn't happen to her again. She wouldn't let it. She couldn't afford to let it.

'Thank you,' she managed at last, trying to keep things as impersonal as possible. 'I appreciate it.'

'How much?'

It had taken her ages to form a response. She wasn't ready for his. 'Pardon?'

'How much do you appreciate it?'

She shook her head, still uncertain. 'What do you mean?'

'Would you consider an extension to our contract?'

'No.' This time it was her rapid-fire response that took him by surprise. He jerked back, as if she'd fired a shot from a gun. 'I mean, I'm not sure that's possible, with this course, and everything I've got planned.' She plucked at a crease in her dress, her mind in turmoil. Leaving after another two weeks would likely be hell. How would she calmly walk away if she stayed longer?

'I'll double what I'm paying you. Two million Australian dollars.'

'It's not about the money!' And it wasn't. Just lately the thought of being paid for what she was experiencing here on

Santorini sat uneasily on her. If he'd been a bully and as ruthless as he'd first seemed, she might have felt as if she deserved it for putting up with him, but he wasn't like that. He was kind and generous and he seemed as if he cared.

'But you like it here. You like being with me.'

She pushed herself out of her chair, striding to the balustrade, her hands grasping at its reassuring solidity. The season was warming up. Three cruise ships lay at anchor today, lighters zipping through the spring mist between them and the port with their cargo of today's photo-hungry tourists.

'It's no crime to trust someone.'

His words came back to her. Andreas was right. It was no crime to trust someone. Once. But it was a fool who let themselves be burned a second time.

How could she tell him she was scared? He was a businessman. He dealt in contracts and clauses and certainties. Those he understood. Those he lived by. And that would have to be her angle.

She sensed when he joined her at the terrace edge, on the very lip of the ancient crater where the fresh salty wind met the sky. Her skin prickled, her blood fizzed and her flesh became alive with want.

'You *do* enjoy my company, don't you?'

There was no point answering his question. The truth would get her nowhere. 'We have two weeks left, Andreas. Maybe we should just make the most of them.'

A noise alerted him, something other than the cry of seabirds or the distant buzz of conversation and exclamation as tourists wended their way through the narrow paths and came upon another magnificent photo opportunity. He swung his head around and saw her standing there, in the doorway leading to the terrace. *Gamoto*. How much had she heard?

'Petra, what can I do for you?'

'*Kalimera*, Cleo,' she started. 'I'm sorry to interrupt,

but, Andreas, your phone was switched off and I had to talk to you.'

'Can't it wait?' He didn't care if he sounded rude. The last thing he needed was Petra spying on them. Already she'd somehow wormed more information out of Cleo than he had wanted her to, and if she'd been here while he'd been talking about the contract…

'I am sorry. But you must excuse me. I'm not feeling very well, Andreas. I wanted to let you know I really think I'm not much good in the office today. I'm hoping it's all right with you to go to my apartment and lie down.'

Damned time of the month again, he supposed, though why all of a sudden she had to fall victim to the curse, he didn't know.

'Are you still feeling unwell?' Cleo asked, moving away from him to take Petra by the arm. 'Can I get you anything?'

'I really don't want to interrupt you,' Petra protested, and then with a smile, 'but that would be so sweet. I am feeling a little dizzy.'

And Andreas watched in bemusement and not a little frustration as the woman he had brought here to deflect the attentions of another was now giving that woman all of hers.

'Come straight back,' he called out to her. 'I want to take you shopping.' And she waved her hand to him, acknowledging she'd heard, even as she shepherded Petra into the building. It wasn't really a lie, he thought as he paced the length of the terrace waiting for her, watching the last of the morning mist burn off the deep blue waters of the flooded crater. She wasn't big on shopping, preferring to explore the churches and villages than the flash boutiques and jewellery stores, but there was something he wanted to buy her, something special he knew would remind her of the intense blue of the sun and sea of Santorini and would at the same time be the perfect complement to her eyes.

And something that might even help persuade her to stay.

Why she was so vehement about leaving, he didn't understand. She loved it here, she loved all of it, even coming to terms with the fact the islands were part of a volcanic system that had been changing over thousands of years and would keep on changing.

But he was determined to make her change her mind and he was confident he could do it. Everyone had their price. A million dollars had got her here.

He didn't care how much it took to keep her.

An hour later, Andreas excused himself to make a phone call and Cleo happily agreed to wait, a rack of blue-beaded key rings catching her attention. It was probably time she thought about buying a few souvenirs to take home. The last two weeks had gone in a flash. The next couple of weeks would probably fly past even quicker.

She dodged out of the way of a group of tourists taking up the width of the street. The streets of Fira were busy today, the day tourists growing in number by the minute, making the narrow lanes and streets even more crowded. If she'd known, she might have stayed at home.

Home.

Now there was a notion. Since when had the mansion she was temporarily occupying ever been her home?

A silver donkey key ring caught her eye, strung on blue cotton with blue beads that looked like eyes. She selected two. Her half-brothers would both love one. She found another, with spinning letter beads that spelt out SANTORINI with more of the eye beads and a beautiful blue stone at the base. Her mother, she decided instantly, slipping it from the rack.

Now she just needed something for her step father. She looked over the racks and decided that with the blue beads there was nothing 'blokey' enough, so her gaze widened, her eyes scanning the contents of the store for that perfect easy-to-pack memento.

And that was when she saw him.

CHAPTER TWELVE

HE WAS checking out the postcards, his face and chest puffier than Cleo remembered, or maybe that was just because they were both pink from the sun, and his arm looped around the shoulders of a girl who looked as stringy as her hair.

He was here.

The key rings slipped from her fingers, clattering to the floor.

'I'm sorry to leave you so long.' She registered Andreas' voice, clung onto the sound like a lifeline even as he bent down to pick up the items she'd dropped. 'Cleo, what's wrong? You look ill.'

'That's him,' she croaked through a throat clamped as tight as every muscle and organ in her body. 'That's Kurt.'

Kurt chose that moment to widen his own search, scanning the shop for opportunities. He looked around, the skin between his eyes creasing into a frown when he saw Andreas scowling at him, a frown that became confused when he looked at the woman alongside the stranger, until the moment he recognised her and his expression became one of abject terror. He tugged, already half outside the shop himself, at the girl next to him who was busy trying on sunglasses. Kurt didn't care, the need to escape clearly paramount, as he dragged his protesting girlfriend out with him, the unpurchased sunglasses still covering her eyes.

'Stay here,' Andreas said, barking out orders to the proprietor in Greek in the same breath before he took off after Kurt. A moment later a woman brought Cleo a chair, insisting she sit down, clucking over her like a mother hen as she pressed a bottle of spring water into her hands. Cleo didn't argue. She was still punch-drunk from seeing Kurt.

So he'd come to Santorini. All that talk of the Greek Islands hadn't been for nothing. But who was the girl? Someone he'd picked up on the Internet who did make the grade? She didn't want to feel hard done by, she had had a complete wardrobe and cosmetic makeover, but surely even before all that she'd been a cut above her?

God, was she that much of a loser that she couldn't even hang onto a man like Kurt?

The woman returned to her side, pressing a small plastic Santorini shopping bag into her hands. The key rings of course, she thought as she felt the beads inside. Andreas must have passed them on to her. She reached for her purse but the woman waved her away. 'No charge,' she said, smiling, bowling Cleo over with more of the warmth and hospitality she'd found everywhere on the island, so that her eyes threatened to spill over with it.

It seemed to take for ever but it was probably only fifteen minutes and Andreas was back. She stood to greet him. 'How are you feeling now?' he asked, collecting her inside his arm.

'Better, thanks. What happened to Kurt?'

'I'll tell you once we're alone.' And she understood why. There was a crowd gathered around the store now, sensing the excitement, wanting to find out what was happening and be part of the action, a crowd that seemed suddenly fascinated in blue-beaded key rings and postcards and bookmarks featuring church domes and cats.

She turned to the beaming proprietor, who was busy exchanging Euros for trinkets, but not too busy to be able to do two things at once. *'Efharisto poli,'* she said, in her slowly improving Greek, repeating it in English in case she'd made a complete hash of the words. 'Thank you, so much,' and the woman beamed and nodded and replied with a torrent of words Cleo was at a loss to understand. 'What did she say?' she asked as soon as they'd re-entered the busy street and he'd steered her towards the mansion.

Andreas didn't look at her, his gaze fixed somewhere ahead, his jaw tight. 'She said we would have beautiful children.'

'Oh. How…quaint.'

Andreas didn't answer. He was too busy wanting to believe it.

'I believe this is yours.' Staff had brought coffee and pastries to a table on the mansion terrace overlooking the caldera that Cleo knew should be listed as one of the wonders of the world, when Andreas handed her the envelope.

She eyed it suspiciously. 'What is it?'

He pressed the envelope into her hands. 'Take a look.'

She opened the flap and peered inside. A stack of notes sat plump and fat inside. She frowned. 'What is this?'

'I had a chat to your former friend.'

'You mean Kurt? You're kidding! You got Nanna's money back. I don't believe it!'

'It seemed he was only too happy to refund you the money he'd borrowed from you in order to escape a charge of shop lifting, plus a bonus for the inconvenience he caused you along the way.'

'Shoplifting?'

'The sunglasses. His girlfriend didn't have time to put them back on the rack. It ended up being a handy levering device. It seems he didn't want to hang around on Santorini and explain it to the police when his cruise ship was sailing tonight.'

It really didn't matter how or why, it didn't matter that soon Cleo would have more than enough money to repay her many times over, the simple fact was it was her grandmother's money she was getting back, the money she had entrusted to Kurt and haplessly thrown away in the same instant. And getting it back was as if she hadn't lost it at all. 'Thank you,' she said, throwing her arms around his neck. 'I love you so much.'

It wasn't so much hearing her own words. It was feeling his hands still at her sides that alerted her. She slid down his body, appalled at the gaffe she'd just made. 'That's just a figure of speech in Australia. A kind of thank you. Because I really appreciate what you've done.'

'I understand,' he said, but still putting her away from him as he was suddenly craving distance. 'I need to drop by the office, check everything is all right, given Petra is sick. Will you be okay?'

She nodded stoically, thinking that if Andreas had wanted her to stay longer before, he'd no doubt now want her gone tomorrow. 'Of course. I'll see you later.'

And then Andreas was gone and Cleo was left alone, in the sun and breeze and clear blue sky. There were clouds gathering in the distance, she noted absently, thinking that maybe they were in for a storm, while at the same time wishing that one day she would learn not to be so impetuous and admit things she didn't really feel.

Because she hadn't really loved Kurt. She could see that now. She was in love with the idea of being in love and being loved and she'd wanted it to work. So desperately that she'd thought that once they'd had sex, she should tell him that she loved him.

And she didn't really love Andreas either. Not really. He was just kind and she was just grateful and it was crazy to think, that just because he had behaved better to her than Kurt, this gratefulness she felt for him was somehow love.

Liar.

An inner voice brought her to task. She didn't want to stay because she knew what would happen. Not that she was at risk of falling in love with him, but because she would be at risk of loving him more.

Because she already loved him.

The wind whipped stronger around her, the cruise ships below straining at their chains. Kurt was down there, she realised, on board one of those ships and soon to sail once more out of her life.

But Kurt was nothing to her now. As Andreas had said, that first night they'd made love—*had sex*—Kurt had given her nothing.

It was Andreas who had given her everything. It was Andreas who had opened her heart.

It was Andreas she loved.

Andreas reread the fax with increasing frustration. There was a problem with the paperwork on the takeover of Darius' hotel. The bank needed more signatures. His. Or the papers could not be processed and the transaction could not proceed and Darius would retain ownership by default.

He would have to go to London.

It would take no time. A day. Two at the most. Cleo could come with him.

'I love you so much.'

Her words came back to him in stark relief. Sure, she'd tried to explain it away, to get him to accept it was some kind of Australian equivalent for thank you. But he wasn't buying that.

There was no way he could take her. As much as he wanted her and hungered for her, as much as he'd wished she'd been already incubating his child—maybe it was better that she didn't come with him.

Maybe, he thought with a tinge of reluctance, maybe it was even better that he sent her home early. He'd never wanted to get involved with virgins and with good reason.

Cleo had been the closest he'd got to having a virgin and maybe this experience had proven him right. Virgins and almost virgins. They were looking for someone to love, looking for someone special to make this huge physical leap they were taking into something emotional. Even if there was nothing there.

Except that his mother wanted a grandchild.

Cleo would be beautiful pregnant, her body rounded and blooming, her belly swelling with his seed, but she didn't want to stay and now he wasn't sure she should.

Maybe his trip away would do them both good, and put things into perspective, a perspective he was admittedly having trouble with himself. And then it would all make sense when he came back.

The idea appealed. Logic appealed.

Although, strangely, leaving her again didn't.

She'd blown it. Whatever sense of camaraderie had been building between them, she'd blown it with a few thoughtless and ill-timed words. He'd told her he was leaving in one breath and he was gone in the next, with barely a backward glance and even less warmth. She hadn't even rated a peck on the cheek.

It hurt, his physical withdrawal from her. It hurt more than the fact he would be gone for a day or two, because eventually he would return to Santorini, but things would be different between them.

At least it would be easier for her now to leave. Now there was no way he would want her to stay.

Restless and unable to settle into her books, she wandered into the town, to a small travel agent she'd seen tucked away alongside a heaving souvlaki shop. There was no reason why she shouldn't make enquiries about flights to Australia, the two weeks she had left would soon pass, but still she felt guilty, as if she were going behind Andreas' back. Which was ridiculous, she told herself as she forced herself to enter the narrow shopfront. It was not as if he didn't know she was going to leave. Not as if he didn't know when. What harm would it do to ask?

Then she saw it on the cover of one of the faded and tatty brochures that lined the walls, a picture of Ayers Rock amid a sea of red dust, and a wave of homesickness crashed over her. That was her world, a dusty, hot land where it never seemed to rain. That was where she belonged, not this island paradise, with its to-die-for-views and romantic sunsets and a man who would never really be hers.

A little over two weeks and she could be home.

Maybe it would be wise to make a booking now.

She found Petra in their suite, rifling through the drawers on Andreas' side of the bed. 'What are you doing here?'

'Ha!' the woman said, clearly not feeling guilty in the least as she turned, holding up a fistful of papers. 'There was nothing in the office but I knew I'd find it here.'

'What is it?' she asked, while fear uncurled in her stomach like a viper, hungry and hissing. 'What have you got?' But Cleo knew what it was. Andreas' copy of the contract. Their contract. And she remembered being out on the terrace and discussing an extension and them turning to see Petra watching them. Listening. She swallowed as the woman's greedy eyes drank in the details. 'That's none of your business.' She marched across the room and tried to snatch it from Petra's hands, but Petra whipped it away, staring at Cleo with such a look of triumph that Cleo was momentarily afraid.

'One million dollars! He's paying you one million dollars to sleep with him?'

'No, he's not! Give that back!'

'What does that make you? Some kind of high-priced whore?' Her eyes raked her as effectively as a blast of burning-hot Kangaroo Crossing dust. 'More like an over-priced one.'

'It's not like that. I didn't have to sleep with him.'

'No? But you are, aren't you? I've seen the way you look at him. I know what you're doing. How is that not selling yourself? How is that not whoring?'

'Get out! It's nothing to do with you.'

'Isn't it? I wondered where Andreas had dredged you up from, acting more like some frightened schoolgirl than one of his women. I knew something was up the minute you stepped from the plane. It was all a charade, all for my benefit.'

'What are you talking about? Why should it be for your benefit?'

'Because Andreas was my lover, until you showed up!'

Cleo reeled, feeling blind-sided. 'What?'

'And he didn't know how to tell me it was over. So he employed you—' she gave a theatrical toss of her head '—to be his whore.'

'Andreas wouldn't do that.' But even as she put voice to the words, the doubts she'd had from the start doubled and redoubled in her mind. Why had he needed someone to act as his mistress? To deflect gold-diggers generally, or one woman in particular? She couldn't believe it. Didn't want to believe it.

'But why couldn't he just tell you? Why go to so much trouble?'

'To totally humiliate me, why else?'

The other woman glared at her, as if she belonged here in

this place and Cleo didn't, and a wave of revulsion rolled over her. Had Petra occupied this bed in this room before her arrival? Had Petra spent the nights lacing her long legs around Andreas' back as he drove himself deep into her? She closed her eyes, trying to block the pictures out.

No wonder the woman didn't like her. She'd been right from the start: Petra's edgy friendship had been laced with hidden meaning and snide digs.

But whatever his tactics and however repugnant they might be, Andreas had clearly made up his mind. It gave Cleo a much-needed foothold in the argument. 'So Andreas didn't want you, then.' It was her turn to smile. 'And you just can't take no for an answer.'

'You bitch! Do you really think he wants you, a woman who is so stupid she falls for someone over the Internet and loses everything? Do you really think he would prefer your type than someone who can talk business with him and understands his needs?'

Even while Cleo berated herself for revealing so much to this woman—too much—she was so grateful she hadn't revealed absolutely everything. And at least she had the advantage of knowing Andreas wanted her, at least for now. 'Clearly,' she countered, 'you ceased being one of his needs some time ago! Did you overhear while you were eavesdropping on the terrace that he'd asked me to stay longer? Tell me then, who is it he needs—you, who are so loyal to your boss that you skulk around in his bedroom looking for dirt, or me, who he would happily part with another million dollars to have stay?'

And Petra pulled out her trump card. She collapsed on the bed and burst into tears, the contract slipping from her fingers onto the coverlet. Cleo reached down and snatched it up, although the damage had already been done, the cat well and truly let out of the bag. But as for what to do next? Comfort the hysterical woman after the things she'd said and the names she'd called her? Not likely.

'Do you want me to call a doctor?'

Petra sniffed and shook her head, for once her perfect hair unravelling at her nape like the woman herself. 'There's no point. I know what's wrong with me.' She snatched a tissue from the holder on the bedside table and blew her nose.

Maybe she really was heartbroken, thought Cleo. Maybe she'd really loved Andreas and thought he'd loved her back and she couldn't bear the thought of someone else having him.

'I guess it wasn't easy seeing me here.' She wasn't hoping for conciliation. She still hadn't sorted out how she felt about being used by Andreas to ward off his previous lover.

Petra responded with a snort. 'You could say that.'

'It's always hard when the person we want doesn't want us.' Hell, she'd been there herself. 'But sometimes it's for the best. Sometimes they're not the right choice for us after all.'

The woman looked sideways at her, her eyes red-rimmed and swollen. 'So now you're giving me advice. How sweet. Perhaps you might give me advice on another matter?'

Okay, so she probably wasn't the best person to be comforting this particular woman. But at least she was trying. 'I'll do my best.'

'Do you think I should have an abortion?'

CHAPTER THIRTEEN

LIGHTS swam behind her eyes, blood crashed in her ears and Cleo felt the urge to run. Run as fast and as far as she could. Run till her lungs burst and her legs collapsed under her. Run till she hurt so much she couldn't feel any more pain.

'You're pregnant, then.' It all made sense, Petra's morning queasiness by the pool, her dizziness this morning and her mood swings and tears.

'How clever you are. And have you similarly worked out whose child it would be?'

And Cleo's fantasy world crashed down around her. Andreas' child. His baby.

It's not a crime to trust someone.

Maybe not. But it should have been a crime to make the same mistake, over and over and over, like a broken record. *The bright side, Nanna, where's the bright side?*

You have a booking to go home in two weeks, a voice in her head told her. *Change it.*

And Cleo knew that was what she had to do. She had to leave, and now, while Andreas was away. Staying was pointless. She didn't want anything to do with him any more, a man who could treat women as he had, pitting one against the other like queens battling it out on some chessboard.

Besides, there was Petra to consider, and a baby. Andreas' baby.

She put a hand to her own stomach. For a few days there, the possibility had existed that it could have been hers. That she too could have been pregnant.

Thank God it had never happened! What a mess that would have been.

'He doesn't know, then?'

'Not yet. I only just found out myself.'

'I think you should tell him as soon as he comes back. I'm sure… I'm sure he'll do the right thing.'

Petra nodded, still looking at the floor. 'I know he will. His mother desperately wants grandchildren. At least she will be delighted.'

Oh, God. More words she didn't need to hear. More words that rocked the foundations of her soul. Andreas had forgotten to use protection with her that time. Surely not intentionally? And yet he'd seemed almost annoyed when he'd learned she wasn't pregnant. He'd offered her more money to stay— to give him more time to get her pregnant? It didn't bear thinking about. She didn't want to know the answer.

'I'm leaving,' Cleo told the woman still hunched and bowed on the bed. 'I'll pack my things and be gone this afternoon.' It was still early in the day. She was sure she could get some kind of link to Athens, be it by plane or ferry. She'd get out now, before Andreas returned and threw her out because there was no point continuing with their charade. She'd get out now while she still held some shred of pride intact.

Petra sighed and sent her a watery smile. 'That's probably for the best.'

Halfway to London, Andreas was growing restless, still searching for the answer to a question that had been plaguing him for hours. Why had she told him she'd loved him? Why would she do that?

She'd turned down a million-dollar offer to stay. Turned him down flat, talking about returning home as if she couldn't wait to be out of there.

And then he'd given her an envelope full of Kurt's money and she'd told him that she loved him. It made no sense, no sense at all.

He toyed with the plate of dips and antipasto, took a sip of his cold *Mythos* beer and watched the landscape beneath his window slowly roll by. What did she want by saying such a thing?

He sighed and pushed back into his seat, smiling about how excited she'd been when she'd told him what she'd learned about the legend of Atlantis. Why did she want to go home so badly to study when all she wanted was all around her here? She couldn't study in a more perfect place. No, she had to stay, there was no question.

But she wouldn't take his money. What else could he offer?

Family.

The idea was so simple! If she were part of his family she would stay. And she could bear him the children his mother so desperately wanted. He wasn't interested in looking for a wife. He couldn't even think about it with Cleo occupying his bed and his thoughts. And she had said that she loved him. It was perfect.

He took a celebratory swig of his beer and sighed. He'd marry her. Hadn't he come to terms with that very idea when he'd thought she could be pregnant? So what was to stop him marrying her when she was not? She would be pregnant soon enough then.

It was all settled.

He picked up the phone that connected him with the pilot. 'Change of plans. We're going back to Santorini.'

There was no argument, no question from the flight deck. They were turning around. So he wouldn't make it to London to sign those papers, but did he really care about Darius anyway? He'd put the fear of God into him. Wasn't that enough? He could do what he damned well liked with the hotel; one more wasn't going to make any difference to the Xenides portfolio. And the kicker would be that Darius would still have to pay him back the loan.

He put his hands behind his head and leaned back into the soft upholstery. It was perfect.

'Three weeks, Mother, that's right. Are you busy that weekend?'

'Too busy for my son's wedding? Tsh. Of course not.' Even here, standing at the window to his office overlooking the caldera, he could hear the tremor of excitement running through her voice, could imagine that five minutes after this conversation the entire who's who of Athens would know about the upcoming nuptials. 'Although I have to admit to being a little surprised.'

'Really?' Not half as surprised, he'd bet, as he had been when he'd returned home to find Cleo gone and a teary Petra apologising, not making any sense. Petra and tears. He'd never expected to see the day.

He'd been about to head straight back to the plane and follow Cleo when Petra had dropped the bombshell that she was pregnant. He wouldn't wish the news she'd given him on his worst enemy. It wasn't the world he'd imagined so perfect, with Cleo sitting on the terrace, her belly swelling, ripe with their child. But it was a child. *His child.* And there was no way he could walk away. 'Why's that?'

'Well, you seemed so sure when you were last here that you weren't planning on marrying Petra.'

'It was something you said,' he said, clutching at the

excuse. 'Something about not realising what was right there under your nose.'

'Oh.' There was a short silence and for a moment he thought the line had dropped out. 'I guess I did say that.'

Strange, Andreas thought, as one of his staff slipped a note to him. He'd imagined his mother would be delighted with that little snippet. He could see her even now telling all her friends at bridge that she'd played matchmaker.

'Anyway, I'll send over the helicopter for you a few days in advance.'

'That would be lovely. I'll enjoy coming over to help with everything. And, Andreas?'

'Yes?'

'It all seems such a rush. I know I put some pressure on you and, while that's a mother's prerogative, I'd hate to think you were rushing into something you might regret later. Are you sure you're making the right decision?'

His head collapsed back, his hand going to his brow. It was the right decision, wasn't it? Morally. Ethically. For the sake of his child. He was doing the right thing. The note in his hand fluttered against his brow. He looked at it, trying to focus, trying to make sense of the words it contained in the context of the query he'd sent to the clinic.

We are unable to provide information on our patients but can advise that we have no patient by the name of Petra Demitriou.

And it was signed by the very doctor Petra had claimed had confirmed her pregnancy.

No wonder she hadn't wanted him to accompany her!

'Andreas? Are you still there? I asked if there was any chance you were making a mistake.'

He was, but his teeth were grinding together and it took a

force of will to prise them apart. *Thank God he hadn't told his mother why it was all such a rush!* 'Very possibly, Mother. I'll have to call you back.'

'Possibly? What do you mean?'

'I'll call you back.'

Right now he had something more important on his mind.

He found her in his suite, supervising the removal and packing of Cleo's clothes. 'What the hell are you doing?'

'Andreas! I didn't hear you coming.'

'Who asked you to take Cleo's clothes away?' He gestured to the staff, clearing the room with a click of his fingers.

'Andreas, Cleo's gone. I thought I should make room for my things, seeing as I'll be moving in soon.'

He swallowed back on a surge of revulsion. He hadn't been able to stomach the thought of Petra back in his bed when he could still smell Cleo's scent on his sheets, the smell of her hair on his pillow. Although Petra had made it clear she'd like to resume sexual relations ten minutes after she'd dropped the double-barrelled blast that Cleo had gone and that she was carrying his child.

And now she was planning on moving in. It was all he could do to keep a tenuous hold on the contents of his stomach.

'When's your next appointment with the clinic?' he asked disingenuously. 'I'd like to come too.'

She smiled and closed the wardrobe doors, he guessed so he couldn't see how empty they now were. Empty of Cleo. As empty as he now felt. 'There's no need for that. It's just routine. Tests. You know.'

'No, I don't know. And neither, it seems, does Dr Varvounis.'

'Wha…? What do you mean?'

'You're not registered at the clinic. He's never heard of you. You haven't been, have you?'

'You probably have the wrong clinic—'

'I think I have the wrong fiancée.'

'What's that supposed to mean? I'm the one who's having our baby!'

'Are you? Or is it as fabricated as your affection for me? You made it up, didn't you? Made the whole story up in one final desperate attempt to get rid of Cleo and get your talons into me. And it nearly worked. Well, no more. The wedding is off. And you are no longer in my employ. I want you out of here.' He turned on his heel and strode out of the room and suddenly she was there, tugging at his arm.

'But I love you, Andreas! We can make a baby just like your mother yearns for, I know we can.'

Fury flared inside him. 'What did you say? Did she tell you that? Is that how you came up with this plan to trap me? I'm sorry, Petra. Maybe I wasn't clear enough before. I don't want you. I never really did. I want Cleo.'

'She wasn't good enough for you. She was young and naïve and stupid.'

'I love her!'

And her eyes went wide. 'You couldn't. You can't. Andreas, please, listen to me—'

'Get out, Petra. I never want to see you again.'

And then she was gone and he was alone. Alone to the realisation that had shocked him as much as it had Petra.

He loved Cleo.

And he was going to get her back.

CHAPTER FOURTEEN

SO MUCH for autumn. Cleo wiped the sweat from her brow as she lugged the vacuum cleaner along the balcony of the Kangaroo Crossing Hotel, the last pub, the sign boasted, this side of the Black Stump.

It might be April but a last hoorah from summer had the sun shining down like a blowtorch, turning the already parched earth to yet more red dust. As if they needed more. A convoy of four-wheel drives roared down the main street, turning the air red and rich with diesel fumes.

Welcome to the outback, she thought as she tackled the sticky doors of yet another balcony room.

Inside was thankfully cooler, the thick stone walls protecting the rooms from the worst of the heat, but still she managed to work up a sweat as she cleaned the last of the rooms.

She'd been lucky to score this job. Her mum had had to give up work as her pregnancy was now quite advanced and she was happily awaiting the arrival of her baby. Cleo couldn't help but be excited for her, not only because she'd been able to take over the cleaning job from her. She could even supplement her income by pulling beers in the bar at night.

And the best thing was the job came with its own accommodation. True, it was in the basement, but it was nothing like

he poky closet she'd endured in London. This was a real room
vith a real bed, and so much the cooler for being underground.

She'd save up now she was home and when she had
:nough she'd enrol in that Classics course in Sydney. She'd
liscovered she could do it by correspondence and hopefully
he'd be able to start next semester. She could hardly wait.
The books from Santorini she'd brought home were so well
ead they were dog eared and slipping from their covers.

She looked around and gave a small sigh of satisfaction
us she straightened the last kink out of the queen bed's
:overlet and stopped to smell the roses she'd salvaged from
he twisted climbers covering the beer garden. A VIP had
)ooked for tonight, the manager had proudly advised, the
'oom had to be perfect. And it was. Dubbed the honeymoon
;uite because it boasted its own bath and loo, it was the
grandest room the hotel had to offer. She smiled. Some honeymoon suite. Nothing at all like the suites she'd shared with
Andreas in London and Santorini. But then, this was
Kangaroo Crossing, and if she was ever going to have a honeymoon herself this was the best she could hope for.

Not that that was likely. Since coming home, she'd sworn
)ff men for good. Clearly she had no idea how to fall in love
with the right one. She hauled the vacuum cleaner and her
gear back out into the hot still air, allowing herself just a
second to remember what it had been like in those first few
giddy days and nights she'd shared with Andreas on Santorini,
when there'd been times she'd actually believed he'd cared
about her, those perfect days before she'd discovered she was
being used as some sort of shield between him and Petra, the
woman who was carrying his child, the woman he was
probably already married to.

The vacuum cleaner thumping almost reassuringly against
her shin brought her back to reality. Her time with Andreas
had been nothing more than a fantasy. This was her life now.

This was her world, a world that had shrunk in the last two weeks to one big wide dusty stretch of highway lined with low timber-board buildings.

Another car was making its way through the town, a trail of red dust behind it, a car impossibly shiny and as low slung and inappropriate for the outback roads as you could imagine. She stopped to watch for a moment, expecting it to keep right on going, only to see it slow to a halt, pulling up alongside the hotel in the shade of an ancient gum tree. Could this be their VIP, then? Kangaroo Creek didn't get many of those. She put down the machine and rested her arms on the timber balustrade to watch. And then the driver stepped out and the air was punched from her lungs.

Andreas.

Dressed in light-coloured chinos, a white shirt unbuttoned halfway down his chest and a gold watch glinting against his olive-skinned wrist, he looked cool and urbane. And then she thought of what he'd done to her, of his hot mouth and his clever tongue, and the very concept of cool and urbane tripped into overload.

Dry-mouthed, she clung to the railing now, knowing that if she didn't her legs would never hold her up. Why was he here? What could he possibly want?

Unless it was to show off his new wife…

The honeymoon suite. A VIP. It all made sense. But why bring her here? Surely Andreas wouldn't stoop that low?

But he was alone, and as she watched he tugged a single leather holdall from the boot. She should go before he saw her. She should disappear back to the basement and hide.

And then he looked up, and their eyes jagged, and her heart flipped over. *Please*, she thought, *please, I want to hate you for what you did. I want to be angry about how you used me. I want to forget. Please don't make me remember…*

But just one look at him was enough to know that she still

hungered for him, and then he pulled the sunglasses from his face and she knew that he wanted her too.

Oh, God, why was he here? What could it mean? And why did she have to look such a bloody mess? She pushed back from the railing, preparing to flee, when he raised a hand and spoke.

'*Kalimera, Cleo,*' he said, in that gorgeous accent that always made her insides quiver. It was probably the first time the greeting had ever been uttered in Kangaroo Crossing. And probably the last, if she had anything to do with it.

'What the hell are you doing here?'

'I love Australian women,' he shouted from below. 'They always speak what's on their mind.'

There was a murmur of agreement from below, no doubt from the blokes lining the verandah watching the occasional car go by, but she was already intent on her reply. 'Have you known that many to know?' And instantly she wished she'd fled when she'd had the chance because it seemed as if half the pub's contents had suddenly spilled out onto the verandah below to watch the proceedings.

'Only one,' he admitted. 'But that was more than enough.'

A ripple of laughter drifted up from the crowd. They'd all seen the car, they'd all seen the man that had stepped from it like some Greek god dripping with money and influence. She didn't have to see their glances to know what they were all thinking. That anyone would be mad to turn this man away. But they didn't know what he'd done. They didn't know he had a woman back home pregnant with his child.

'Go to hell, Andreas!' Damn him. She battled the vacuum cleaner down the outside stairs, thankfully in the opposite direction from where he was standing, and headed inside for the basement stairs, her mind too confused to deal with whatever was going on, her heart too filled with hurt to assist.

She was too slow. He met her in the lobby, where the

entrance hall met the stairs going down to the basement. 'Cleo.'

'How ironic,' she said, her feet riveted to the ground, 'that we should meet like this again. Have you plans for taking over the Kangaroo Crossing Hotel, then? Should I start looking for another job?'

'I didn't come for the hotel.'

'No?' She clutched the rounded stairway newel like a safe haven. If she hung onto that, surely her legs would keep working. Although maybe she should be more worried about her heart. Right now it felt so big it was a wonder it didn't spill right out of her mouth. 'Then what are you doing here?'

'I came here to see you.'

There was no way her legs were going to get her down those stairs, not with the way he was looking at her now.

'And what if I don't want to see you?'

The noise from the bar next door was almost overwhelming as the customers spilt back into the cool interior, one topic of conversation and conjecture clearly discernible amongst the shouts and laughter.

'We need to talk. Not here. Somewhere private. Have dinner with me tonight and I'll explain.'

'Mr Xenides, I presume?'

Daphne Cooper, the manager's wife, primped her hair and giggled like a schoolgirl as she spun the register around to face him. 'If you'd just sign here, please. And if you need somewhere private,' she continued with a wink in Cleo's direction, 'I can serve dinner for two in the honeymoon suite?'

'I would appreciate that very much,' she heard him say before Daphne's answering giggle, and Cleo took advantage of the interruption to flee.

She slammed her door, grabbed her bathroom gear and escaped to there before he would have a chance to follow her. Why was Andreas here? Why now, when he hadn't bothered to contact her in all the days since she'd fled Santorini and she'd made a start at a new life and forgetting…?

Who was she trying to kid? she asked herself, when she stepped under the shower. She would never forget those perfect few days and nights in paradise.

There was a card under her door when she returned.

Join me for dinner, it simply said, with a time and a room number. The honeymoon suite. What a joke. For a moment she was tempted to send a note back, telling him what he could well and truly do with his kind invitation, before sense got the better of her.

Why shouldn't she listen to what he had to say, the excuses he had to offer? Why shouldn't she hear him out? And then she could tell him exactly what she thought of him and tell him to get the hell out of her life once and for all.

She refused to hang around the hotel wondering what he was doing all afternoon, so instead she hitched a ride out to the homestead to see her mum, thinking that helping her with the washing or just sorting out the twins would distract her for a few hours. Nanna was there too, full of baby stories that made her laugh and made her almost forget the queasy feeling inside. She didn't tell them about Andreas. She didn't want to hear Nanna's take on the bright side. Because there wasn't one. Not this time. There couldn't be, except that soon he would be gone.

Her stepfather, Jack, wandered in for afternoon tea around four, his khaki work clothes dusty, his hair plastered to his scalp where his hat had been stuck all day. 'G'day all,' he said as he plonked his big frame down on a chair, and as Cleo's mum fussed with getting more tea and cutting slabs of cake. 'Bit of a commotion down at the pub. This mate of yours, Cleo, what's he doin' here?'

Her mother and nanna swivelled their heads simultaneously, their voices in chorus. 'What mate?'

'This rich bloke, from Greece, they reckon. Come to see our Cleo.'

Her head swung around to look at Jack. *'Our Cleo'?* Where had that come from?

But everyone else was apparently more interested in the rich bloke. Questions fired at her from all sides. They'd known it had all gone wrong with Kurt, but this job she'd had in Santorini she'd said precious little about. What was her former boss suddenly doing here? And why?

She fended them off the best she could. After all, she didn't know the answers herself. But she promised she'd let them know. First thing tomorrow when she came out on her day off. By then he'd be no doubt long gone and might cease to be a topic of conversation.

Her stepfather offered to run her back into town, another surprise. But the biggest surprise was when he pulled up outside the hotel. She was halfway out the door when a big beefy hand landed on her arm. She jumped and swung her head around. Her stepfather's face looked pained, preferring to study the steering wheel than look at her. 'Cleo, one thing. Close the door, love.' He suddenly nodded towards the line of men sitting outside on the verandah, sipping their beers. 'There's a pack of vultures out there waiting for any hint of gossip to brighten up their sad lives.'

She pulled her leg back in and closed the door and he resumed his scrutiny of the steering wheel, crossing both his wrists at the top.

'I know we've never been close. I know I've never made you feel welcome. And I should have. Because you're family. I was glad when you came back. Your mum was beside herself with worry and…' He sighed. 'Well, it was just good to know you were home, safe and sound. And I just want you to know that if this bloke tries to take advantage of you, or tries to hurt you, I'll wipe the bloody floor with him myself.' He swung his head around. 'Understood?'

She'd never known Jack to make such a long speech. She'd never known him to more than grunt in acknowledgement, and here he was, letting her know he'd defend her. As part of his family.

She flung her arms around his beefy neck and hugged him. 'Thank you.' And then, because she was as embarrassed as he was, and close to tears, she flung open the door and was gone before either of them could say goodbye.

She dressed carefully, or as carefully as she could given her now limited wardrobe. A wraparound skirt and vest top with mid-height sandals were the best she could do, although she could still use the make-up she'd been given in London to make the most of her eyes. She wasn't interested in seducing him, she told herself as she applied mascara. She just wanted him to see that she was surviving, and surviving well.

And then she was ready. She took one last look at herself, took a gulp of air and headed upstairs.

He was waiting for her knock, opening the door and standing there, all Greek god and potent male, so potent that the words almost dried in her throat and would have, but that there were questions she needed answers to. 'What are you doing here, Andreas? What is it that you want?'

He looked at her hungrily, as if she were the meal. 'Dinner is served,' he said, fuelling the feeling, and despite the desperate logical waves from her brain that told her to cling to her anger, to hold onto her hatred of what he'd done, her body hummed with his proximity as she let him usher her inside.

The door closed with a snick behind her, the table laden with dishes awaiting. The steaming dishes could have smelt good, the cooking here was renowned as the best country cooking could offer, but right now her senses were full of the scent of him, and nothing incited her appetite more. Oh, no. She had to get out of here. She couldn't do this!

She turned suddenly, 'Andreas, I—', and was surprised to find him so close behind her that they almost collided. He reached out and steadied her with his hands at her shoulders, warm and strong, and the feeling was so intoxicating, so real after the memories she'd been hanging onto, that she forgot what it was she wanted to say. She felt the tremor move within him then as he exhaled, as if she wasn't the only one fighting their demons. But that was crazy. What demons could possibly plague Andreas?

Unless he felt guilty about seeing a woman while his child grew within another.

'Come,' he said at last. 'Sit.' And so she did, watching him pour them both wine, knowing she dared not touch it for fear of losing her resolve. 'How are you?'

'Andreas. Can we please cut to the chase? What are you doing here?'

He took a deep breath, and placed an envelope before her plate. 'You left without this.'

With trembling hands she picked up the envelope and pulled the paper from inside. A cheque. For five hundred thousand pounds. 'You left without your money.'

She stared at the cheque feeling sick. So that was what this was about. Mr Businessman handling the money aspect, ensuring all the i's were dotted, all the t's crossed. Of course. Strange, though, when he could have just posted it. Although then she would never have had the opportunity to do this…

She slipped it back in the envelope and pressed the flap down with her thumb, her eyes not leaving his. His mouth was halfway to a smile, as if he was expecting her to pocket it, which in turn made her smile. And then, over a snowy china plate, she ripped the envelope in half, and tore those two pieces into half again, over and over, until the tiny fragments fluttered to her plate. And then she stood. 'I don't want your money. So if that's all?'

He was on his feet, blocking her exit, 'What the hell is wrong with you? We had a deal. The money's yours. You earned it.'

'No. I didn't. I left before the contract term expired. Besides which, even if I had stayed, I wouldn't want your money anyway. I don't want anything of yours, don't you understand that?'

His features looked strained, the flesh across his cheek-bones drawn tight. Clearly a man unused to not getting his own way. 'I pay my debts, Cleo. We had a contract and I—'

She wanted to scream, suddenly grateful for the foresight Daphne had had to organise dinner for them here in a private room as opposed the dining room, where this discussion would have provided gossip for the next decade at least. 'I will not take your money! You will not reduce those days I spent with you, making me feel like some overpriced whore!'

It was Andreas' turn to stand. 'I never thought of you like that!'

'No? But Petra did. She found the contract in your suite and made it clear that's what I was. Remember Petra,' she charged, 'the mother of your child?'

'You don't have to remind me about Petra,' he said, his teeth clenched. 'Petra was the woman who took you away from me.'

How could he be so blind? How could he avoid the truth that had sent her away? The truth that meant he shouldn't be here with her now or ever, whatever the reason. 'She never took me away from you. You did that all by yourself, when you got her pregnant and used me as some kind of human shield. How do you think that made me feel? Knowing that all the time I was in your bed, your previous lover was already carrying your child!'

'She was never my lover and she was never carrying my child!'

Cleo felt the wind knocked out of her sails. 'She what? But she was pregnant. She told me… And she said you were paying me to humiliate her…'

His hand raked through his hair; the other rubbed his neck. 'We had sex. Once. It was a mistake and I told her. But she knew my mother wanted grandchildren, and that she'd had a cancer scare and was worried I'd never get around to it. She admitted as much to Petra, who decided she'd have to bring out the big guns if she was going to get rid of you and clear the way for her. She faked the pregnancy to trap me.'

'But she was sick, dizzy…'

'All of it put on. All of it designed to make everyone believe it was true.'

It was too much to take in. Too much to accept. And there was still so much that didn't make sense.

And yet hadn't Petra said the very same thing—that Andreas' mother wanted grandchildren? And hadn't Cleo remembered his unexpected response when she'd informed him her period had arrived?

She swallowed. 'Is that why you're back here? Because you need a child and you think I'll provide it for you?'

'What? Cleo, what are you saying?'

'You wanted me to be pregnant, didn't you? You seemed strangely disappointed that I wasn't. That was right after visiting your mother, wasn't it? She told you then that she wanted grandchildren.'

He took a step closer, knowing the bridge between them was much longer and way more fragile than he'd realised. 'Cleo—'

'And then you asked me to stay longer, offered to pay me more. Why do that if you weren't going to try and get me pregnant?'

'It wasn't like that.' Except he knew that it was. Hadn't that been his exact plan? Keep her longer, get her with child. *Make his mother happy.*

'And then you discover Petra was faking it and you turn up on my doorstep.'

'No! I'll admit—' He spun away, troubling his hair again with his fingers, raking his scalp with his nails until he flung himself back, his arms slashing through the air. 'Yes, I'll admit I was hoping, that it seemed like an easy option. I'll admit that I wanted you to stay because I thought you might fall pregnant. But that's not why I'm here now. I didn't come for a child, Cleo, I came for you.'

Her chin kicked up, her blue eyes liquid and shimmering in the rays from the sun setting outside the window. 'And you expect me to believe that?'

'Cleo, I know I don't deserve your trust. I know I'm the last person to deserve that. But on that flight to London when I'd left you behind, I learned something. That I wanted you. That I wanted to marry you. And so I turned the plane around and came home.'

Her face was paler now, her fingers clawed around the back of her chair. 'Isn't it the same thing? Why decide to marry me, unless it was to keep me around longer and increase your chances of having a child?'

His features were tight, his jaw line growing even tighter before he conceded in a nod. 'Okay, that's what crossed my mind—initially—and no, I'm not proud of it. And then I got home and learned you'd already left and was about to follow you and bring you back, except there was Petra saying she was pregnant and I knew I had no choice but to let you go.'

He held out his long-fingered hands in supplication. 'Do you have any idea how that feels? To bow to responsibility when it feels wrong and when your heart wants something different, even if it doesn't understand why?'

She swallowed again and he followed the movement in her

throat and down to where she crossed her arms under the breasts he'd missed so much, but not just because of their perfection, he'd learned, but because of the woman he missed more.

'So tell me, Mr Businessman, what is it that your heart wants?'

He took a deep breath. 'You once said you loved me.'

'A figure of speech—'

'So you said. I promise you, at the risk of thoroughly humiliating myself here, my declaration won't be.' He watched her perfect blue eyes, saw the questions, the suspicion and maybe, maybe, just a flicker of hope to mirror his own. 'I love you,' he told her. 'I don't know when it happened, or how, or why it took me so long to realise that that was the reason I couldn't let you go, that you had to stay. And you will probably never forgive me for the way I treated you and for being so blind for so long, but I pray you will, because I love you, Cleo, and I had to come and ask you, beg you if necessary, if you would do me the honour of becoming my wife.'

Time stood still. There was the odd shout from the verandah downstairs, the odd drift of laughter through the French doors and outwardly her world hadn't changed. But inside it was as if someone had taken the pieces of her world and rearranged them and everything was suddenly new and unfamiliar.

'Cleo, for God's sake, say something.'

And she blinked to find Andreas still there, not a dream, not some wild imaginings of a woman who'd been too long in the sun.

'Me? You love me?' Cleo, the high-school dropout. Cleo, the cleaner, who would never amount to anything. A bubble of hope burst from her heart. 'You want to marry me?'

And she must have looked so shaky that he snatched her in his arms and held her so close that she could feel his heart thudding powerfully in his chest, but still she couldn't quite trust him. 'And babies, then. I guess you want babies.'

And he stilled for a moment and held her away from him with his big broad hands until he could see her face. 'Right now, all I want is you. I love you, Cleo. And if a child never happens, so be it, my mother will have to deal with it. Because it's you that I want, nothing more. '

Her eyes swam with tears, happy tears, as she looked up into his perfect face. 'I guess you've got me, then, Andreas.'

His dark eyes still looked uncertain. 'Is that a yes?'

And she flung her arms around his neck and held him tight. 'Yes!' she cried. 'Because I love you, Andreas, I love you so much!'

And he kissed her and swung her into his arms and carried her, the meal laid out for them forgotten, to the soft embrace of the queen-sized bed.

Later, much later, when the passion of their reunion had temporarily abated, they stirred. 'There's something else I brought you,' he whispered, nuzzling her cheek, before disappearing for a moment to withdraw a small package from his jacket. He didn't hand the box to her; instead he snapped on her bedside light before holding the pendant up before her. She loved it immediately, the geometric Greek pattern in gold surrounding a circle of amazing blue gemstone that looked as if it were on fire.

'I bought this in Fira,' he said as he clipped the chain around her neck, 'but I never had a chance to give it to you. But I think it signifies everything about us. For this,' he said, tracing one finger around the gold border where it lay on her chest, 'is the Greek, while the core, the inner beauty is an Australian opal, that shows, like your eyes, every colour of the sea and sky.'

'It's so beautiful,' she said, lifting and cradling the pendant in her hands so she could study its colour and depth.

'It's you and me,' he said. 'The Greek and the Australian, together.'

And they kissed and held each other tight.

'There's one thing I still don't understand,' she murmured a little while later as she nestled against him.

'What is it?'

'You said you turned the plane around. Didn't you go to London? I thought you had to go or you could lose the hotel deal.'

His fingers stilled momentarily in her hair, and she nestled closer, allowing her own hand to explore the perfection of his chest, the feel of his satin skin, the wiry dusting of dark hair that coiled around her fingers, the nub of a masculine nipple. 'It was important, as you say. But suddenly the hotel didn't seem to matter any more. And neither did getting even with Darius—or Demetrius, as you knew him.'

'What happened to the deal, then?'

He shrugged. 'Last I heard, he was back in charge. Probably still losing money hand over fist to his turf accountant.'

It was her fingers' turn to still. 'You let the deal fall through? I thought you hated him so much.'

He sighed. 'I did. Once.'

Troubled now, she let her fingers resume their exploration, down his chest and circling his navel with her fingertips. 'But why? What did he do to deserve that?'

'Does it matter?'

'I need to know the kind of man I'm marrying. I need to understand. You seemed so ruthless then, so driven.' She shivered and he tucked her in closer, his thumb stroking the nipple of one goose-bumped breast and flicking her thermostat to simmer.

'A long time ago he was my father's partner. They'd built a strong business together and everything seemed to be going well. But he'd asked my mother to marry him once, a long time before my father had married her. It seems he'd never forgiven him for that. Or her. So he bided his time watching the business grow and waiting for the perfect opportunity, when the business was cashed up and ready to make a major investment. He took the lot and left us with nothing. My father died barely a year later, a broken man, and I swore on his grave that I would one day get even.'

'Oh.' He'd tensed with his words, and her fingers worked to massage the pain away, stroking his flat belly and following the trail of hairs that arrowed downwards where she encountered him, thick and pulsing once more into life. 'I understand now,' she said, and she did. 'I can see why you needed to get even.'

He flipped over her then, so suddenly that she didn't see it coming. 'It's history,' he said as he buried his face in her neck and settled between her legs. 'And it doesn't matter any more. My mother tried to make me see that, but it was you who made me understand.'

She shook her head as his hot tongue circled her nipples, first one and then the other, his breath like a heated caress where his tongue didn't touch. 'How?'

But she did see the foil packet he had ready in his hand. She shook her head. 'I want you, this time,' she whispered. 'It's you I want to feel inside me, your flesh against mine.' And he cast it aside and kissed her, hot and desperate and soul deep.

She gasped into his mouth as he entered her in one tight, fluid stroke, gasped again when he started to move inside her, the delicious friction of his increasing rhythm sending tremors through every part of her. 'For too long,' he muttered through teeth clenched tight, 'I was looking to the past. But in you…' He stilled for a moment, poised at the brink as he looked down at her, caressing her face with the pads of his thumbs. 'In you, I found something different. In you I found my future. I love you, Cleo.'

And he lunged into her again, his cry rent from him like a cry of freedom, as together they spilled into their future.

EPILOGUE

HER mother was hanging out sheets on the line, her nanna sitting in the shade of the ancient peppercorn tree, when Andreas' car pulled up alongside the homestead late the next morning. Cleo had warned them they were coming but still her mother turned and stared, while the twins bowled around a corner of the house, shooting each other up with guns they'd improvised from sticks and rubber bands and skidding to a halt when they saw the red sports car Andreas was unfolding himself from. 'Wow,' they said in unison. 'Is that your car?'

Andreas turned on his million-wattage smile as he pulled off his sunglasses and shook his head. 'Sadly no, it is a hire car,' and the boys' faces dropped. 'But I have one much better than this back on Santorini,' and they wowed again and positively drooled as they circled the car like a couple of sharks.

'I'll give you a ride a little later,' he said. 'That is, if you like.' Their eyes lit up on their combined, 'Awesome!' Cleo laughed and wondered how he could read children so well when he'd had so little to do with them. Maybe he'd make a pretty good father, she figured, if his reaction to her half-brothers was any indication. Maybe having his babies wouldn't be such a hardship.

Making them, she already knew, would be nothing but sheer pleasure.

Her cheeks colouring into a blush she suspected she shouldn't be brandishing when she was about to introduce the man she loved to her family, she slipped her hand in his and led him to where her mother stood, her eyes as wide as her expanding stomach, while Nanna's watched on keen and interested. 'Mum, Nanna, I'd like you to meet Andreas Xenides, the man I love, and the man I intend to marry.'

'That is,' Andreas added, turning on his dazzling smile again and bowing as he took first her mother's and then her nanna's hand in greeting, 'if you permit me your daughter's hand in marriage.'

'Oh, my,' her mother said, the concerned look she'd had on her face when they'd driven up transforming into her own wide smile. 'Jack!' she called as the screen door slammed and her husband emerged from the house. 'Jack, come and meet Andreas. Cleo's getting married!'

Jack didn't rush. He took his own sweet time, Cleo thought, as he let his laid-back stride carry him closer, his beefy arms swinging loosely by his sides and his eyes narrowed by the sun and still drinking in the scene, missing nothing. He pulled up a metre shy and the two men faced each other off, the Greek billionaire in the white shirt, with money clearly at his fingertips, and Jack in his moleskins, his sandy hair for once not flattened by his hat, and who clearly felt that out here, even being the dirt-poor farmer he was, he was king.

He nodded, extending a wary hand. 'Mr Xenides, Jack Carter.'

'Call me Andreas, Mr Carter.'

He nodded. 'Andreas, it is. And just plain Jack is fine with me. I hear you made quite a ruckus in town with your fancy car. And now, I hear, you want to marry Cleo.'

Beside her Andreas smiled. 'That's about the size of it, if you'll allow me to, that is.'

And Jack turned to Cleo. 'And is this what you want, lovey?'

Cleo beamed at the endearment. 'It's everything I want, but only on one condition.'

Her stepfather's face turned dark and he looked ready to take Andreas on, in case he took issue. 'And what's that?'

'That you walk me down the aisle and give me away.'

And she could have sworn her sun-hardened stepfather melted right there before her eyes.

'Well,' said her mum with a tear in her eyes, wiping her hands on her apron and looking for something to fill in the stunned-mullet silence from her husband, 'you will both be staying for lunch? I've got a lamb roast on.'

And they did stay, and afterwards Andreas rang his mother while his new family were busy with dessert, knowing it was morning now in Athens. 'I have a surprise for you,' he told her.

'You're marrying the Australian woman after all?'

And he did a double take. 'You knew?'

She laughed. 'Didn't I tell you? Sometimes you don't know what's right there under your nose until it's gone.'

Andreas laughed then too. 'You did,' he told her, wondering if somehow she hadn't known all along but still not understanding how.

Then after dessert he took the twins for a spin in the car, after which they put their own two and two together.

'You're leaving again?' they asked Cleo, almost simultaneously, sounding disappointed that with Andreas gone they might be deprived of an occasional ride in a sports car.

And their nanna nodded wisely, as always. 'But look at the bright side, boys, you'll be able to visit Cleo and Andreas on Santorini and have a ride in his sports car there. Isn't that right, Andreas?' And Andreas nodded and Cleo laughed and knew right then and there she could stop looking for her own bright side, because she'd found it.

Love.

There was no brighter side.

* * * * *

Harlequin offers a romance for every mood!
See below for a sneak peek from our
paranormal romance line, Silhouette® Nocturne™.
Enjoy a preview of REUNION
by USA TODAY bestselling author Lindsay McKenna.

Aella closed her eyes and sensed a distinct shift, like movement from the world around her to the unseen world.

She opened her eyes. And had a slight shock at the man standing ten feet away. He wasn't just any man. Her heart leaped and pounded. He reminded her of a fierce warrior from an ancient civilization. Incan? She wasn't sure but she felt his deep power and masculinity.

I'm Aella. Are you the guardian of this sacred site? she asked, hoping her telepathy was strong.

Fox's entire body soared with joy. Fox struggled to put his personal pleasure aside.

Greetings, Aella. I'm the assistant guardian to this sacred area. You may call me Fox. How can I be of service to you, Aella? he asked.

I'm searching for a green sphere. A legend says that the Emperor Pachacuti had seven emerald spheres created for the Emerald Key necklace. He had seven of his priestesses and priests travel the world to hide these spheres from evil forces. It is said that when all seven spheres are found, restrung and worn, that Light will return to the Earth. The fourth sphere is here, at your sacred site. Are you aware of it? Aella held her breath. She loved looking at him, especially his sensual mouth. The desire to kiss him came out of nowhere.

Fox was stunned by the request. *I know of the Emerald Key necklace because I served the emperor at the time it was created. However, I did not realize that one of the spheres is here.*

Aella felt sad. Why? Every time she looked at Fox, her

heart felt as if it would tear out of her chest. *May I stay in touch with you as I work with this site?* she asked.

Of course. Fox wanted nothing more than to be here with her. To absorb her ephemeral beauty and hear her speak once more.

Aella's spirit lifted. What *was* this strange connection between them? Her curiosity was strong, but she had more pressing matters. In the next few days, Aella knew her life would change forever. How, she had no idea....

Look for REUNION by USA TODAY *bestselling author Lindsay McKenna,
available April 2010, only from Silhouette® Nocturne™.*

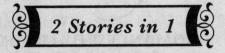

2 Stories in 1

HER MEDITERRANEAN PLAYBOY

Sexy and dangerous—he wants you in his bed!

The sky is blue, the azure sea is crashing
against the golden sand and the sun is hot.

The conditions are perfect for
a scorching Mediterranean seduction
from two irresistible untamed playboys!

Indulge your senses with these two delicious stories

A MISTRESS AT THE ITALIAN'S COMMAND
by *Melanie Milburne*

ITALIAN BOSS, HOUSEKEEPER MISTRESS
by *Kate Hewitt*

Available April 2010 from Harlequin Presents!

HARLEQUIN® *Romance*®

ROMANCE, RIVALRY AND A FAMILY REUNITED

THE BRIDES *of* BELLA ROSA

William Valentine and his beloved wife, Lucia, live
a beautiful life together, but when his former love Rosa
and the secret family they had together resurface,
an instant rivalry is formed. Can these families
get through the past and come together as one?

Step into the world of Bella Rosa
beginning this April with

Beauty and the Reclusive Prince
by
RAYE MORGAN

Eight volumes to collect and treasure!

OLIVIA GATES

BILLIONAIRE, M.D.

Dr. Rodrigo Valderrama has it all...
everything but the woman he's secretly
desired and despised. A woman forbidden
to him—his brother's widow.
And she's pregnant.

Cybele was injured in a plane crash
and lost her memory. All she knows is
she's falling for the doctor who has swept her
away to his estate to heal. If only the secrets
in his eyes didn't promise to tear
them forever apart.

Available March wherever you buy books.

Always Powerful, Passionate and Provocative.

LARGER-PRINT BOOKS!

HARLEQUIN *Presents*~

PASSION GUARANTEED SEDUCTION

GET 2 FREE LARGER-PRINT NOVELS PLUS 2 FREE GIFTS!

YES! Please send me 2 FREE LARGER-PRINT Harlequin Presents® novels and my 2 FREE gifts (gifts are worth about $10). After receiving them, if I don't wish to receive any more books, I can return the shipping statement marked "cancel". If I don't cancel, I will receive 6 brand-new novels every month and be billed just $4.55 per book in the U.S. or $5.24 per book in Canada. That's a saving of 13% off the cover price! It's quite a bargain! Shipping and handling is just 50¢ per book in the U.S. and 75¢ per book in Canada.* I understand that accepting the 2 free books and gifts places me under no obligation to buy anything. I can always return a shipment and cancel at any time. Even if I never buy another book, the two free books and gifts are mine to keep forever.

176 HDN E4GC   376 HDN E4GN

Name	(PLEASE PRINT)	
Address		Apt. #
City	State/Prov.	Zip/Postal Code

Signature (if under 18, a parent or guardian must sign)

Mail to the **Harlequin Reader Service:**
IN U.S.A.: P.O. Box 1867, Buffalo, NY 14240-1867
IN CANADA: P.O. Box 609, Fort Erie, Ontario L2A 5X3

Not valid for current subscribers to Harlequin Presents Larger-Print books.

Are you a subscriber to Harlequin Presents books and want to receive the larger-print edition?
Call 1-800-873-8635 today!

* Terms and prices subject to change without notice. Prices do not include applicable taxes. Sales tax applicable in N.Y. Canadian residents will be charged applicable provincial taxes and GST. Offer not valid in Quebec. This offer is limited to one order per household. All orders subject to approval. Credit or debit balances in a customer's account(s) may be offset by any other outstanding balance owed by or to the customer. Please allow 4 to 6 weeks for delivery. Offer available while quantities last.

Your Privacy: Harlequin Books is committed to protecting your privacy. Our Privacy Policy is available online at www.eHarlequin.com or upon request from the Reader Service. From time to time we make our lists of customers available to reputable third parties who may have a product or service of interest to you. If you would prefer we not share your name and address, please check here. ☐

Help us get it right—We strive for accurate, respectful and relevant communications. To clarify or modify your communication preferences, visit us at www.ReaderService.com/consumerchoice.

HPLP10

HARLEQUIN®

INTRIGUE®

WILL THIS REUNITED FAMILY
BE STRONG ENOUGH TO EXPOSE
A LURKING KILLER?

FIND OUT IN THIS ALL-NEW
THRILLING TRILOGY FROM TOP
HARLEQUIN INTRIGUE AUTHOR

B.J. DANIELS

WHITEHORSE
MONTANA

Winchester Ranch

GUN-SHY BRIDE—*April 2010*

HITCHED—*May 2010*

TWELVE-GAUGE GUARDIAN—
June 2010

HARLEQUIN *Presents*

Coming Next Month
Available March 30, 2010

Ashlyn Kane

FAKE DATING
THE PRINCE

PUBLISHED BY

Published by
DREAMSPINNER PRESS

5032 Capital Circle SW, Suite 2, PMB# 279,
Tallahassee, FL 32305-7886 USA
www.dreamspinnerpress.com

Fake Dating the Prince
© 2019 Ashlyn Kane
Editorial Development by Sue Brown-Moore.

Cover Art
© 2019 Alexandria Corza
http://www.seeingstatic.com/
Cover content is for illustrative purposes only and any person depicted
on the cover is a model.

Paperback ISBN: 978-1-64108-187-0
Digital ISBN: 978-1-64405-442-0
Library of Congress Control Number: 2019930016
Paperback published June 2019
v. 1.0

Printed in the United States of America
∞
This paper meets the requirements of
ANSI/NISO Z39.48-1992 (Permanence of Paper).

ASHLYN KANE is a Canadian former expat and current hockey fan. She is a writer, editor, handyperson, dog mom, and friend—sometimes all at once.

On any given day she can usually be found walking her ninety-pound baby chocolate lapdog, Indy, or holed up in her office avoiding housework. She has a deep and abiding love of romance novel tropes, a habit of dropping too many f-bombs, and—fortunately—a very forgiving family.

Twitter: @ashlynkane
Facebook: www.facebook.com/ashlyn.kane.94
Website: www.ashlynkane.ca

By Ashlyn Kane

DREAMSPUN BEYOND
#26 – Hex and Candy

DREAMSPUN DESIRES
#59 – His Leading Man
#84 – Fake Dating the Prince

Published by **DREAMSPINNER PRESS**
www.dreamspinnerpress.com

For Amy, Kate, and Amanda,
this book's biggest cheerleaders.

Acknowledgments

WITH special thanks to Sue Brown-Moore and Liz Fitzgerald for their excellent editorial polish.

Chapter One

FLIP had toggled his phone screen on and off so many times that the battery had run down even though it was still plugged into the charger in his armrest. That didn't stop him from pressing the button again, scanning his thumbprint, and reopening the same message he'd been stewing over for the first two hours of his seven-hour flight from Toronto to Paris.

You are cordially invited....

He reminded himself he was too well-bred to sigh.

Just in time too—the flight attendant trundled by with his cart of champagne and spirits, and Flip would've hated to be maudlin. God forbid he evoke *pity*. His great-grandmother would turn in her grave.

"Your usual, sir?" Brayden asked with characteristic cheer.

Flip wouldn't have admitted it to a tabloid, but his mood lifted too. "Yes, that would be lovely." A thought occurred to him. "Perhaps a double? I'm feeling self-indulgent." An extra helping of Macallan would do him far more good than a gusty exhale.

Brayden grinned, showing off a deep dimple that measurably improved Flip's mood. "My kinda guy." He poured the drink and set it on Flip's tray table with a serviette. "Would you care for a snack as well?"

His laughing blue eyes twinkled as he said it, perhaps because Flip had guiltily asked for the same snack on every flight they'd shared—twice a month for the past six months while Flip was setting up the office in Toronto. Around him, other passengers picked at the cheese-and-fruit plate the airline deemed as appropriate snack fare in first class, but….

"Yeah, silly question, I know," Brayden said before Flip could ask, and he stealthily delivered three packets of economy-class peanuts to Flip's tray. "The heart wants what it wants."

Flip's lips twisted into an involuntary smile. "You take good care of me."

"You're easy to please. I like that in a man." If only that were true. Brayden provided a hot towel for Flip to wash his hands. The little things made flying first class a worthwhile expense. "Do you need anything else at the moment?"

Flip shook his head. "Thank you, Brayden." High-class booze and a couple hundred bags of peanuts. He was set for an hour at least.

"Send up the Bat-Signal if you change your mind."

Flip absolutely did not watch as Brayden rolled his cart down to the next row, but he imagined it in great detail—another harmless indulgence, like his second helping of Macallan. Anyway, it kept him from brooding on weightier topics.

Almost automatically, he flicked his phone screen on.

You are cordially invited to the Night of a Thousand Lights hosted by His Highness Prince Antoine-Philippe of Lyngria.

Flip had originally intended to bring a date, of course. He could host a charity ball without one—if his parents hadn't met at the same charity ball thirty-odd years ago when his mother was hosting, or if he didn't mind that every introduction made over the night would sound like a singles ad. But Adrian had broken up with him when Flip refused to give up travel and work... or maybe Adrian had broken up with him when Flip hadn't put a ring on it quickly enough or taken him on enough vacations in the Maldives.

Anyway, Adrian had broken up with him months ago, the ball was in less than a week, he couldn't back out because it was the biggest royal charity in Lyngria, and the press would have him married off to six different people or suffering a psychotic break by Sunday.

Maybe both.

He could've had his mother arrange someone, but that seemed pathetic. He could've asked his Lyngria-based bodyguard, Celine, whom he'd known since they were in diapers, but that seemed worse. And he could have asked any number of friends and acquaintances, except most of them weren't single—and they'd do it anyway and have their names dragged through the mud for their trouble.

If only he weren't completely pants at meeting people.

Days like these, he envied his cousin Clara, who didn't have to worry about any of this nonsense despite her place in the line of succession. Of course, she was nine.

Maybe she could host next year.

Flip put his phone away again. He had a briefing and a subsequent press conference to prepare for, and the remainder of this flight plus his puddle jumper to Virejas to do it in. But if he started reviewing international policy now, he'd need an Ativan and a lot more of that Macallan to keep him sane for the next ten hours.

He cracked open the first of the illicit peanut packages and unfolded the entertainment screen to peruse the in-flight menu.

By the time Brayden came around to collect trash, Flip had found exactly nothing that he could convince his brain sounded appealing.

"Five hundred channels and nothing's on?" Brayden asked sympathetically as he retrieved the peanut bags with gloved hands.

"I think I have decision fatigue." Flip rubbed his forehead. He'd spent most of the past week doing the last round of employee evaluations, trying to decide who was the most trustworthy to handle the company. He wanted to sleep, but he knew he didn't have the self-discipline to clear his thoughts; his mind was always too busy on these returns to Lyngria. "Choosing what to drink was the last straw."

"Gotcha." Brayden perched on the armrest of the empty seat opposite him. "Mindless but cute, or zany but riveting?"

Flip handed him the tiny remote, bemused. Well, it wouldn't be the first time he'd let someone schedule his life. It wasn't like he had anything better to do right then, and if something could hold his attention, the flight would pass more quickly. "Rivet me."

Flip was three episodes into *Dirk Gently's Holistic Detective Agency*, deeply invested in anyone on the show realizing the girl was in the dog, by the time Brayden came around with dinner. He didn't ask which meal Flip preferred—though he probably didn't need to, since the in-flight meal options didn't vary much—but he did ask, "Good choice?"

"That depends." Pulling the headphones down around his neck, Flip met Brayden's eyes. "How many seasons are there?"

BRAYDEN bid goodbye to his favorite guest at the jet bridge at Charles de Gaulle. He was polite—some would even say reserved—but he treated everyone well, and Brayden had a bad habit of tossing decorum to the wind in order to win a smile now and then. He couldn't help it.

"Safe connecting flight," Brayden said cheerfully, and Antoine Philippe, seat 3A, lifted his fingers in a wave and smiled as he left.

Joanna, the head flight attendant, elbowed him in the side when first class had emptied. "So he's cute," she whispered.

Brayden grinned as the business-class passengers began to depart, and varied his farewells between English and French. "I've no idea what you're talking about," he told Joanna out of the side of his mouth. "My interest in 3A is completely professional." It wasn't even a lie—the man was good-looking, with his smooth amber skin and movie-star-quality smile, but Brayden had a policy of leaving work at work.

"Checking out his butt as he went by is a funny definition of 'professional.'"

Brayden covered his laugh with a cough. She'd caught him there. "What can I say? Some days I love my job."

Joanna shook her head minutely as business class finished disembarking and the main cabin passengers started their exit. "Where are you off to this time?"

"Lyngria." A tiny country tucked between Germany and Poland on the Baltic Sea. In his three years as a flight attendant, Brayden had never been to a Baltic country, at least not beyond the airport. "I've got three weeks, but I don't know. It's not a big country. I might make my way over to Berlin or Prague."

"You said that when you went to Madrid," Joanna pointed out. "And Sarajevo. And Budapest. And Zagreb. Every time. 'Oh, if it sucks, I'll just go back to the last place I loved.' And every time you love the new place even more."

Brayden shrugged. "What's not to love?" Every country, every city had a different vibe, a different culture, a different take on what made life worth living. He didn't have this job to ogle hot rich guys. He was in it for the travel. "Bon voyage," he added to a departing five-year-old who was hiding her face in her father's shoulder. She waved shyly, and a pang hit him. He missed working with kids—not a lot of those in first class.

Deboarding finished, and Brayden and the rest of the crew completed their checks.

"One man left behind," Luis said mournfully, holding up a stuffed animal that had been loved into ambiguity. "42B."

Brayden took it while Joanna looked at the passenger manifest. "What do you think? Is it a sheep?"

Squinting, Luis proclaimed, "A capybara."

Before their argument could devolve into further silliness, Joanna made a sharp noise. "They're off to Lyngria as well," she told Brayden. "Might be on your flight, if you make it off Standby. You want to play hero?"

Brayden clutched the maybe-opossum to his chest. "I accept the assignment."

By the time he'd retrieved his wheeled bag, he didn't quite have to run to make it to the next flight, but only because he had the luxury of flagging down a cart—he was still in uniform and with the possibly-panda, he was technically on official airline business—to drive him across the sprawling nightmare spiderweb of Charles de Gaulle.

He made it to the departure gate just as general boarding began and made his way to the counter. "Room for two more?" He waggled the dubious bear's paw.

In the boarding line, the little girl who'd waved at him raised her head from her father's shoulder. "Alain!" Well, damn—that didn't do much to help figure out what kind of creature it was. She let go of her father and stretched out her arms toward Brayden.

"He thought you might get lonely without him, so he asked me to track you down," Brayden told her in French.

The girl's father looked over, startled at first and then visibly relieved. "Thank you, monsieur. You've saved us some very difficult nights."

Brayden waved off his thanks as the gate attendant checked the flight ability. "You're in luck—one seat left, in business class."

Perfect.

Brayden waited for the paying passengers to finish boarding, and then he wheeled his suitcase down the jet bridge. Just two short hours and he'd be on the ground in Virejas, ready for his next adventure.

This flight was too small for a proper first class. Brayden had seat 3B—a slight disappointment, since he wouldn't be able to check out his temporary home from the sky, but he'd live. He rolled his bag to his seat and lifted it into the overhead bin—

Only to realize the man in 3A looked very familiar.

"Fancy meeting you here." Brayden smiled and folded himself into the chair. So much better than the jump seats. "Hope you don't mind slumming it with me for a few hours. I promise I can occupy myself." He held up his phone as if for proof.

"Well, that's fortunate—these puddle jumpers haven't been fitted with the full arsenal of in-flight entertainment options yet." Antoine gave him a rueful smile. "No *Dirk Gently.*"

Brayden couldn't help but smile back. Joanna had a point—this guy was *handsome.* "Oh God, a travesty. I'll take it up with management. But not for another three weeks."

"Vacation?" Antoine inquired. "In Lyngria? In the dead of winter?"

Brayden shrugged. "Most of my family is going on a Christmas cruise, but I get seasick, even on the biggest ones. Besides, I've always wanted to check out the winter markets and the light festival. And I know it's a long shot, but maybe I'll even get lucky and catch a glimpse of the aurora. That's bucket-list stuff, you know?"

"Fair enough. But I hope you packed your woollies."

Brayden had a spare uniform, two civilian changes of clothes, a winter jacket, and some heavy boots. "I'm Canadian."

Antoine smiled, a sly, knowing thing that reminded Brayden that as of twenty minutes ago, he was officially on vacation. "So you know about thermal underwear."

Laughing, Brayden admitted, "Yes, but I'm too vain to hang up my Andrew Christians over a little cold weather."

It was a perfect setup—Brayden could list five or six witticisms off the top of his head—but instead of choosing any one of them, Antoine briefly opened his mouth and then offered that reserved smile he used when Brayden asked if he wanted anything else, and said, "I see."

Which was… weird. Then again, they'd just had a long flight, so maybe he didn't want to talk. Brayden could respect that. He buckled his seat belt, ignored the little frisson he felt when Antoine handed over the buckle, which had been tucked under his leg, and thumbed open his phone to his travel guide.

By beverage service Brayden had forgotten all about his seatmate's hot-and-cold act. He looked up as the hostess parked her cart next to their row, but she looked right over his head at Antoine. "Welcome home, sir. I hope your flights have been agreeable?"

That measured, practiced smile again. "I've no complaints, Bridget, I assure you."

Bridget poured coffee and handed it over with one cream and one sugar. "We're all looking forward to the Night of a Thousand Lights. My nephew is one of the charity scholarships this year—fine arts. He's studying in New York."

Antoine set the coffee on his tray. "That's wonderful. He must be very talented."

Obviously Antoine wasn't just some ordinary rich guy. Not like Brayden's uncle, who'd won the lottery this past April, but like, really rich—the kind of rich where you couldn't ever spend all the money you had.

And important too, if he was somehow associated with the Night of a Thousand Lights, whatever that was.

"We're all so proud of him," she gushed, but she caught herself—Brayden could see it in her face as professionalism took over and her tone changed. "Can I get you anything else, sir?"

Antoine shook his head. "No, just the coffee, thank you, Bridget. Oh, but I don't know about Brayden?"

"Also coffee," Brayden said too quickly, a bit embarrassed at being caught eavesdropping. "Thank you."

"Cream and sugar?"

"Both."

Bridget left them after that, and Brayden turned his cup this way and that, watching the liquid slosh up to the rim, lost in thought, until Antoine cleared his throat. "Well. Now you know my secret."

Brayden looked up. "Secret? What, that you're the sort of posh person who attends fancy charity balls and who people recognize on international flights? I figured out most of that on my own, actually."

"Touché." Antoine shook his head and peeled back the corner of the creamer. "I meant that I'm…."

After a few seconds, when he still hadn't finished the sentence, Brayden took a sip of his own coffee. "That you're…?" he prompted.

Antoine sighed and shook his head, perhaps deciding he didn't want to talk after all. But then a curious expression came across his face and he looked at Brayden, eyes narrowed in assessment. "Three weeks in Lyngria, you said? Any plans in particular?"

FLIP couldn't quite believe his own nerve. Then again, he'd been raised to weigh boldness and caution, and perhaps he'd been afforded a rare opportunity. He'd be a fool not to take advantage.

"You see," he went on, when Brayden confirmed that he had no particular agenda, "you might have heard I'm hosting an event later this week. The Night of a Thousand Lights?"

Brayden's generous mouth twitched in an aborted smile. "I think I heard something about that. Going to be on national TV and everything."

Well, the crown owned the national TV station, so yes. Flip cleared his throat. "I find myself in the unenviable position of playing host without an escort of my own to pull me away when conversations become tedious."

Brayden had been sipping his coffee, and he spluttered a bit and reached for his napkin. "Uh, when you say *escort*—"

Damn North American euphemisms anyway. "I meant a date," Flip clarified quickly. "Not the other sort."

"A date, huh? To a fancy dance?" He licked his lips, chasing away a stray drop of coffee. "To be clear, are you asking me?"

Flip nodded once and resisted the urge to wipe his palms on his suit pants. Why was it suddenly so warm in business class? "Yes, I—if you're still available." As though Brayden could have made plans in the three minutes since the conversation had begun, but Flip felt as though he owed the man a graceful exit. "I know you're only in town for a few weeks, but I would enjoy your company, and your presence would shield me from a number of well-intentioned matchmakers. I would, of course, take care of all the details."

"Details?" Brayden echoed. "I, um. I'm flattered, and actually, rescuing you from people who want to bore you to tears sounds like it might be fun, but I definitely didn't bring a suit, and I imagine this kind of event has a strict dress code."

"Black tie," Flip admitted as Brayden winced. "Don't make that face. It was white tie last year. This was a major concession on the part of the royal tailor."

"That is not a real thing."

It was, but Brayden likely wouldn't believe it until he met the woman. "If you're amenable to an evening of dancing and canapés, I will of course provide a suitable ensemble, including access to the royal tailor." Bernadette would love to get her pins on Brayden's figure. "No strings attached," he added in an uncharacteristically desperate bid to secure Brayden's agreement.

"Dancing and canapés and a free tux," Brayden mused. "That does sound pretty awesome."

Flip's spirits lifted. "So you'll come?"

He realized the innuendo too late, but Brayden took pity on him and didn't comment. "Yes," he said and held out his hand. Flip shook it eagerly. Brayden's grip was strong and sure. "It's a date."

Oh *bollocks*. It really was.

Chapter Two

BRAYDEN had scrupulously researched his vacation, eager to squeeze as many new experiences out of it as he could. But like every time he went somewhere, he found himself captivated by the novelty of his surroundings.

His hotel, located in a former palace, boasted thick stone floors and high ceilings and plumbing that creaked and groaned charmingly, as though it were a friendly ghost. A few minutes' walk and he could be in the main square, with its multicolored facades and the Gothic spire of the cathedral stretching into the sky. Though the sun rose late and set early, Brayden found the glow of the shops and streetlights warm and welcoming—fortunate, since the temperature was hovering around freezing. But for a boy who'd grown up in Scarborough, it wasn't too bad—until the wind kicked up off the Baltic, at least.

Also, market stalls lined all the pedestrian streets, offering roasted nuts, pickled fish sandwiches, and mulled wine, as well as handmade gifts—hats and scarves, slippers and sweaters, pottery and tree ornaments and fruitcake. Brayden spent the whole first day walking from stall to stall, sampling everything, until the time change and the cold and dark caught up with him and he dragged himself back to his hotel to upload the highlights to Instagram.

The next day he awoke to his hotel phone ringing, and he blinked disoriented into the darkness and managed to clear his mind enough to answer. "Hello?"

"Good morning. I hope I didn't wake you. Is this Brayden?"

Brayden decided not to cop to still being asleep at—he glanced at the bedside clock—past nine. The day was getting away from him already. "Yes, hi." He stifled a yawn. Drat. "I don't suppose you'd believe me if I said I'd been awake for an hour already."

On the other end of the line, Antoine backtracked gracelessly. "I apologize. If this is a bad time—"

"It's fine," Brayden assured him as he swung his legs over the side of the bed and looked around for the hotel-provided slippers. These stone floors were a bugger on warm feet. "I prefer to get up earlier than this, actually, but the late sunrise is throwing me off. What can I do for you, Antoine?"

"Please, my friends call me Flip."

"Flip." Brayden smiled despite himself. Antoine was so poised and proper that the incongruous nickname felt perfect. "What can I do for you at quarter past nine in the morning?"

"I was hoping you remembered our agreement for Friday night, and I was able to clear my schedule until lunch. I don't suppose you could make yourself available for some shopping?"

"At the royal tailor's?" Brayden teased.

"Bernadette informs me that we've already cut things very close by giving her only four days to prepare," Flip said, his voice grave. "I would hate for you to miss out on your bespoke-dinner-jacket experience."

"And I would hate to embarrass my horrifically posh date by wearing something off the rack." Brayden slid into the slippers. "Give me ten minutes to shower and then—should I meet you somewhere?"

"No need," Flip assured him. "I have a car. I'll see you soon, Brayden."

With no time to waste, Brayden got acquainted with the shower, which did gurgle and hum a bit but had excellent water pressure. He wished he had time to test out the different settings on the expensive-looking showerhead, but that would have to wait until after his appointment.

He didn't realize until he was dressed and standing outside the lobby that his hotel was on a pedestrian-only street. Wondering if he'd been had, he glanced from the cheerfully decorated potted cedars that bookended the hotel doors to the Christmas lights that adorned the lampposts. A bakery down the street exuded the smell of cinnamon and sugar, reminding Brayden he hadn't eaten since last night. A handful of people strolled down the cobbled street, oblivious to Brayden's indecision. Should he go back inside? Maybe Flip had the wrong hotel?

But then, from two blocks down, came a low rumbling of tires on stone, and a long car with blacked-out windows rolled serenely down the street as curious passersby turned to look.

Brayden didn't blame them. If James Bond had a sugar daddy, he would drive a car like this—shiny and black, sleek, badgeless, with an immaculate chrome grill and a back seat that seemed to go on forever. Not that Brayden was getting any ideas.

At least not until the rear passenger-side door opened and Flip stepped out, hotter than any James Bond in a pale gray peacoat that probably cost more than Brayden's first year of university tuition.

"Dear God," Brayden muttered, glad the cold provided an excuse for his flush.

Then Flip *smiled* at him, and Brayden nearly melted into a puddle. "Brayden. There you are. I didn't keep you waiting too long, I hope."

"No, I really just got out here," he promised. "Though I did worry that maybe you had the wrong hotel, since you said you were driving. I hope I'm not going to cost you a ticket."

Flip laughed as though Brayden had said something charming… or maybe as though traffic tickets happened to other people. "If you do, the favor you're doing me will be well worth it. Shall we?"

Once upon a time, Brayden's mother had warned him about getting into cars with strange men. He didn't know if ultra-rich regular passengers counted as strange, but what his mother didn't know wouldn't hurt her.

Inside, the car was luxuriously appointed in leather and polished wood and utterly silent, even as they pulled away from the curb. A tinted-glass divider separated the passenger compartment from the driver.

The center bore a very subtle insignia—a crown in a circle made of two twisted loops, and below it the monogram AP.

Oh. *Shit.*

"Sooo." Brayden cleared his throat and wiped his palms on his best jeans, which seemed incredibly shabby just then. "When you said we were off to the royal tailor…."

Flip's answering smile held both sympathy and rue. "Les Fils Royaux has been the tailor for His Highness Prince Antoine-Philippe since he was in diapers." The smile turned wry. "Though I don't believe the diapers were tailored. That seems excessive even for us."

Oh *shit.* "So you're…."

"The crown prince of Lyngria, heir presumptive, et cetera. Sorry. You really didn't know?"

"Honestly gobsmacked, promise." Wow. *Wow,* Brayden was dumb. His sister was going to laugh her ass off when he told this story. Airline captains were supposed to brief them on passenger VIPs, but maybe they had no idea either. And now Brayden was doing a *favor* for a prince. "Are you sure I get to call you Flip? That's not, like, an offense worthy of, I don't know, deportation or ritual fruit-throwing?"

"Well, we do have an annual food fight, but I reserve the rottenest tomatoes for people who insist on calling me Antoine."

Brayden snorted and then had to cover his face in embarrassment that he'd made such an undignified noise. But that didn't last long, because this situation was honestly too cool to dwell on his many faux pas. "Right. I apologize for that. I'll bring that up at the next managers' meeting too. 'Maybe we can add a preferred-name section on those manifest lists. Also Prince Flip says we need to get on adding more *Dirk Gently*.'"

"I'd appreciate it."

They grinned at each other in silence for a few seconds before Flip shook his head minutely and continued. "In any case, I thought, well, now that you know the full extent of what you signed up for, I ought to give you a graceful way out."

"Are you kidding? How many guys can say they've gone to a fancy charity ball with a real-life prince? That's almost as good as the tux."

Flip laughed. "Not nearly. You haven't seen Bernadette's work. But you do understand the scrutiny you'll be under? Everyone will want to know who you are, how we met. They'll think you're after my title or wealth…."

"Not your hot bod?" Brayden teased, but the once-over was 100 percent genuine. He shrugged. "I don't even live on this continent. My family doesn't follow the tabloids, and I doubt charity-ball news from a tiny backwater European country is going to make even the International section in the *Toronto Star*. Uh, no offense."

Flip looked vaguely amused but waved it off. "None taken."

"So the only way they're going to find out about it is when I go home in a couple weeks and tell them about the one extremely cool date I went on with the prince of Lyngria. And I'll have my swanky tux to prove it. As long as you don't mind that I'm probably going to eat with the wrong fork or whatever, I'm game."

The car pulled to a very quiet stop. "I think the monarchy can weather a cutlery scandal," Flip said. "Shall we?"

BRAYDEN'S eyes went as wide as saucers when Flip opened the door to Bernadette's shop. "Oh wow. It literally smells like money in here."

Flip carefully controlled his smile. Brayden didn't have a filter on his mouth, and while that might be a problem come Friday night, right now Flip was having a hard time minding. "Paper, coin, or plastic?"

"*Silk*, darling," said Bernadette as she walked from the back of the shop.

Les Fils Royaux had all the trappings of an exclusive club. But Flip looked right past the dark-stained wood furnishings, bright, flattering lighting, limited inventory, and, of course, the shop's logo, specially granted by Flip's ancestor to Bernadette's—a crown threaded with a sewing needle, encircled by a loop of thread.

Bernadette fit in exactly, from her flawless dark skin and perfectly applied makeup to a three-piece suit that fit impeccably despite the fact that she was about seven months pregnant.

"Antoine-Philippe," she said to Flip—one of a few people from whom he didn't mind the use of his full name—and he bent to perform the customary triple cheek kiss. "Qui m'as-tu amené?"

"Bernadette Villiers, please meet Brayden Wood," Flip answered in English. "Brayden agreed last-minute to attend the Night of a Thousand Lights with me, and he tragically doesn't have any formal wear in the country."

"Hi," Brayden said, pink-cheeked, as he extended his hand to Bernadette. She shook her head at him and kissed his cheeks: left, right, left. "I'm sorry I'm so hopeless. Flip says you might be able to help me?"

Bernadette took a step back and looked him over head to toe, holding his shoulders. Then she looked at Flip. "Are you allowed to bring a twink as your date?" she asked in French.

"I should probably mention he speaks perfect French," Flip continued as though he hadn't heard.

"And I'm too muscular to be a twink," Brayden sighed, put-upon. "I used to rock the look, but then my metabolism slowed down and it was either stop eating everything or start going to the gym." He looked at Flip and fluttered his eyelashes. "Are you allowed to bring a twunk?"

"I'm the crown prince. I can do whatever I like," Flip said with forced loftiness. Brayden grinned at him, but Bernadette rolled her eyes. He should have known the two of them would get along.

Clucking, Bernadette plucked at Brayden's coat. "Well, take this off and let's get your measurements."

Normally Bernadette took measurements in a private back room. But when she suggested that to Brayden, his face fell and he gestured toward the windows. "Look, I saw you lock the door when we came in. This place is definitely by appointment only, right? We could just close the blinds. This is the coolest store I've ever been in. I don't want to miss a second."

Flip suspected he simply wanted to parade around an opulent location in his underwear, but he could hardly say so in front of Bernadette, who didn't offer any objections.

"The lighting is better out here anyway," she said with a smile. "And if you stand on the podium there, it'll save my back and my knees. I don't like to complain, but getting up and down gets harder every day."

Suddenly Flip worried he'd asked too much of her. "I'm sorry. I should have thought. You shouldn't be working so hard in your con—"

The look Bernadette shot him shut his mouth. "Your Highness," she said icily, "as you are well aware, I am pregnant, not ill, and perfectly capable of deciding whether I am fit to work."

Well, at least there weren't any cameras to document Flip's mortification. "Of course. I didn't mean—" Bollocks, how was he supposed to extricate his foot from his mouth when he'd shoved it in past his tonsils? He sighed. "I apologize."

"Apology accepted," Bernadette said primly as she relieved Brayden of his chunky green sweater. "In any case, as if I'd have let anyone else dress your date. There's such a thing as professional pride." She gazed up at Brayden, now clad only in his boxer briefs. That was unfortunate for Flip's sanity, because *twunk* about summed it up. Brayden had a youthful face and a sweet smile and thick, flirty eyelashes but the broad shoulders and defined muscular bulk of someone who wouldn't be easy to throw around in bed unless he wanted to be.

And Flip needed to focus.

"Actually, while you're here…."

He'd wondered how long it would be before she directed him to take *his* clothes off. "The usual dressing room?"

"Please and thank you."

He wasn't sure whether he ought to thank her for the distraction or take 10 percent off her bill.

As he expected, the latter idea disappeared from his mind when he saw the jacket hanging on the rack.

Despite his high profile and busy schedule in Lyngria, until recently Flip had lived a fairly regimented life—set hours at the Toronto office, set meals delivered by his meal service, set reps in his home gym, set meditation hours. And Bernadette was easily the best tailor in the country, if not Europe. So he wasn't surprised when the shirt and trousers fit perfectly or when he found the perfect set of cuff links—shaped like bellflowers—already waiting in the sleeves.

The waistcoat was deep blue silk, with lotus flowers embroidered one shade lighter—a subtle, intricate design Flip's father would love. The cravat was made of the same material. He tied it automatically as he tried to tear his mind away from the barely clothed civilian in the next room.

Easier said than done.

Flip usually favored a traditional-style dinner jacket, but this time Bernadette had done something a little different—a matte jacket in the darkest blue, without lapels, almost Nehru style, with a polished-looking trim. Wearing it, he looked much like his father. The blue complemented his dark skin in a way he had often avoided in the past, tired of reading about his divided loyalties in the press, as though he was less Lyngria's prince because his father was Indian, as though he couldn't love two countries and cultures at one time.

The Flip in the mirror now seemed to prove he could.

He shot the cuffs enough to show off the national flower and stepped out of the dressing room just in time to hear Bernadette ask, "Left or right?"

Still on the podium in his underwear, Brayden seemed perplexed. "Um? I think that one might be lost in translation."

Flip fought down a blush. Maybe he could escape back to the dressing room unnoticed?

But no, because Bernadette looked up just then from measuring Brayden's inseam, looked right at Flip, and switched to English. "Left or right?" she repeated, winking at Flip. "You know, when you dress. Which way do you... tuck?"

Brayden's mouth dropped open. "I... that *matters*?"

Flip wanted to groan. Tailors asked that question so they could measure an inseam without accidentally copping a feel. But Brayden was out there in his underwear—Bernadette knew exactly where his dick was. She just had a sharp sense of humor when it came to her craft.

Bernadette nodded seriously. "Yes, of course. One leg will be sewn slightly wider to accommodate... you."

Now Brayden threw his arms wide in exasperation, showing off excellent muscle definition across his back, shoulders, and chest. Flip swallowed. "What kind of guys have you been dressing, if you have to put extra dick room in their pants?" He gestured down at his boxer briefs, which hid nothing—not that Brayden had anything to be ashamed of. "I mean, you can basically see it. It doesn't need its own trouser leg."

Flip raised a hand to his mouth to smother a laugh. He didn't want Brayden to think he was laughing at him—or at his dick, which Flip was trying very hard not to look at.

Bernadette similarly restrained herself, though she did betray the sliver of a smile. "They're very closely tailored trousers, Mr. Wood." She indicated his underwear with a tilt of her head. "These will be quite unsuitable. I'm sure Antoine-Philippe can vouch for that."

Damn her. Now Brayden turned to find Flip watching him, only Brayden didn't seem at all concerned about it. In fact, though his eyes widened and his cheeks went even rosier, the slack set of his mouth and the way he licked his lips suggested an entirely different emotion from embarrassment.

"Oh my God. I cannot believe I didn't know you were a fucking prince. It's basically tattooed on your forehead. I am an idiot."

Flip had to clear his throat. An answering heat rose in his own cheeks. "I take it you like the suit."

"Let's just say I am regretting my choice to stand here in my underwear." Brayden put his palm over his face, but a second later he put it down again and grinned. "Bernadette, can you make me look that good?"

"I'm a tailor, not a miracle worker." She rose from her crouch with more grace than Flip expected and smiled at Brayden. "But I think I can work with these materials." She gestured to indicate—well, Flip assumed she meant Brayden's hair, his smile, his physique, his general unassuming charm.

Brayden fist-pumped. "I am gonna look bangin'." Then he glanced sideways at Flip. "I mean, I will look *totally appropriate* for a prince's *escort*."

Flip would probably be lucky if he didn't show up in a leopard print, from Bernadette's gleeful expression. She loved crafting suits for him, but as a member of the royal family, Flip couldn't wear anything too flashy. She'd have more fun with Brayden. He looked forward to the results.

Having finished with her measurements, Bernadette let Brayden down and sent him to the fitting room with a few more-or-less stock garments to double-check the accuracy. Bernadette opened the blinds, and Flip unlocked the door, only to find his driver and bodyguard, Celine, wearing an apologetic expression.

Resigned to his fate, Flip opened the door. "Your demeanor suggests my free morning has been rescheduled."

"Apologies, Your Highness." She sounded as contrite as she looked. "Only your aunt called.

Apparently Princess Clara is having a difficult time, and she wondered if you might stop by, seeing as you have a special bond."

A special bond. Flip supposed that was what developed between members of the aristocracy who were deemed unsuitable for rule by right-leaning media. Flip failed to impress them, being gay and having the wrong color skin for European royalty. Clara, on the other hand, had been born with a congenital limb defect, and was— or would be, one day—a woman, to boot. Hardly an improvement over the current monarch and her prince consort, from a Neanderthal's point of view.

Flip would have liked to spend the morning with Brayden as he'd planned, maybe even have lunch with him somewhere and go over what he could expect on Friday night. But Clara was, and might remain, his heir, and he knew a little about being a royal brat. She had to come first.

"I'll go, of course," he said, holding in a sigh. "Let me finish here and I'll be ready."

Bernadette gave him a knowing look as he walked away from the door, and quickly picked her pincushion off the desk as he made his way to the platform. "Bad news?" she asked as she briskly checked the fit across his shoulders and chest.

"Clara wants my help bullying her mother over something. Or vice versa."

Bernadette nodded and gestured for him to remove the jacket. She took it and set it aside to check the waistcoat. "Duty calls."

"Yes."

She was perfecting the hem of his trousers when Brayden sashayed out of the dressing room, halfway between rakish and resplendent in a very traditional

American-style tuxedo that Flip never expected to see
again, at least not on Brayden.

"Haven't worn one of these since my high school
prom." He tugged at his cuffs and grimaced a bit, whether
in discomfort at the formalwear or some distant memory.

He would have made an awkward teenager, Flip
thought, before he grew into his body.

"You're probably going to have to tie the tie for
me. I've only ever done a clip-on."

Bernadette shuddered. "Not on my watch." She
finished fussing with Flip's trousers and stood to take
in Brayden.

Flip stepped off the platform so Brayden could take
his place. "As much as I was looking forward to our lunch,
Brayden, I'm afraid I'm needed elsewhere. I apologize."

Brayden shrugged eloquently. "Hey, you're an
important guy. I get it. Bernadette can help me pick out the
right color and pattern for this thing without you, I bet."

"Count on it, Mr. Wood," Bernadette answered in
a voice that certainly meant *she* would be doing the
choosing.

"I'll send Celine back to get you once she's dropped
me off, and she can take you to lunch wherever you want
to go. Are you available Thursday? I'd like to make it
up to you." Even a single, simple date with no romantic
intentions was impossible to accomplish uninterrupted.
Perhaps Adrian had been right to break up with him.

"I think I can work you into my busy sightseeing
schedule," Brayden said with a shake of his head. "Go
on, get on your white horse and get out of here."

"Put your regular clothes back on first," Bernadette
said. "If you get horsehair on those trousers, I'll make sure
Clara's your only option for the line of succession."

Chapter Three

BRAYDEN filled his Wednesday with cultural experiences—a morning at the national museum, a boat ride through the city's canals, and then a guided walking food tour. The food tour was his favorite. The guide pointed out well-kept local secrets and places that didn't make TripAdvisor lists, and recommended specialty dishes in each restaurant or café. And at the end, he mentioned he was celebrating his first anniversary of starting the company, and he bought everyone a round of drinks.

Brayden clinked glasses of lingonberry beer—apparently a Christmas specialty—with his fellow travelers and didn't think at all about the country's crown prince or what he might be up to.

Well. Not *much*, anyway. Not until he got back to his hotel and found a neatly wrapped parcel waiting for him at the foot of his bed. Curious, he removed the lid of the box and brushed aside a sheet of tissue paper to reveal—

Underwear—basic black underwear in a boxer-brief cut. One pair, with a smooth, satiny sheen along the waistband.

Brayden didn't know what these very normal-looking underwear had done to warrant the fancy presentation until he lifted them from the tissue and realized they were made of some kind of space cotton or something, because no material made on earth had ever felt so soft and smooth. The legs had no visible hem, but the fabric seemed unfrayable.

James Bond underwear.

He couldn't decide whether to be amused, flattered, or offended. Maybe he should try them on and decide afterward.

But no—integrity first. He took out his phone and composed a text, taking a moment to appreciate how completely absurd it was that he had a mobile number for the crown prince of a European nation. *I know I have to let you buy me a tux*, he wrote, *but the underwear are more an escort thing than a date one. FYI.*

He didn't expect a reply—for all he knew this wasn't even Flip's direct line, and oh God, maybe he'd just aired the crown prince's dirty laundry to some poor PA or something and Flip would be mortally embarrassed… if embarrassment happened to royalty. But his phone chimed a moment later and answered almost all of his questions. *Bernadette sends a pair with every suit purchase to ensure we don't ruin the lines of her art. I'm sorry. I should have warned you.*

Well, that made Brayden feel better, but also worse because he'd bugged Flip about something when the guy was obviously busy. *I feel so important—the royal tailor micromanaging my underpants.* He paused and debated whether to continue. What the hell. Flip wasn't obligated to respond. *Hope whatever damsel you rescued yesterday appreciated your intervention.*

He set the phone on the nightstand and went to clean up before bed, because he still had jet lag and that lingonberry beer had him feeling warm and drowsy. When he returned, his phone flashed with a few new messages.

The first was a picture of Flip sitting in an armchair with a lapful of child, probably a girl from the length of the blonde hair. Based on her pose and the hour, Brayden guessed she was fast asleep.

The royal etiquette handbook frowns on selfies, but I had Johan take this one, so it doesn't count. Princess Clara thanks you for yielding your claim on my time.

Brayden went warm at being trusted with the photograph. Maybe this date was just a favor and a once-in-a-lifetime experience, but still. He'd earned the trust and friendship of a prince. That was pretty special in itself… and a prince who was sweet with kids too. Brayden was soft for that. *Etiquette handbook, eh? You can give me the cliff's notes tomorrow. Bedtime for me. Good night to you and Princess Clara.*

Good night, Brayden.

HE woke up to an email from his sister. Part of him wanted to avoid opening it, but if he did, she'd just message him on WhatsApp or stalk his Instagram.

Apparently she'd already been stalking his Instagram, because she opened with *Hey little brother, that's a nice tux you're wearing… what's up with that?*

Sometimes Brayden needed to use his brain before his phone.

Lina went on with:

Everyone's getting really excited for the cruise. Mom and Aunt Pat have been on the phone for an hour every day planning all the stuff they want to do. Me, I'm going to take my Kindle full of pulpy historical romances, park my butt on the sun deck, and do as little as possible for ten glorious days. In the Caribbean.

I get why you're not coming. I do. But I'm going to miss you. Uncle Walt sprung for king rooms for all of us (though everybody else is doubled up—guess we're the only two bachelor(ette)s left), so if you change your mind, you can bunk with me. I barely even kick in my sleep anymore. Seriously, anytime. I'm attaching the cruise schedule. I know you can get a flight. Meet us in Nassau. I don't care.

If not, I hope you're having fun in Lyngria... and that you didn't just spend your travel budget on formal wear (seriously wtf).

Your big sister,
L

Brayden had plenty of time before he had to meet Flip for lunch, so he rolled over in bed and debated his reply.

Hey sis.

I can't come.

For a moment he just left it at that and squirmed. He'd lied when he told Flip he got seasick, but the truth was too complicated to explain to a near stranger. Even his family only mostly got it.

Next year we'll do Christmas in November like we usually do, and I'll be there. I promise.

That would satisfy her... he hoped.

As for the tuxedo, well, you know how I am about experiencing new things. Turns out someone I know from my flights needed a date to a fancy event here in town and was so desperate he promised to spring for a tux!

Wow, that sounded way different written out than it did in Brayden's head.

WE ARE NOT HAVING SEX (I totally would, but he's not interested, and he's so far out of my league no one would even believe I was his sugar baby). It's just a favor that sounds fun. Get to see how the other 1 percent lives, you know? Besides, it's good to have a local guide to recommend things.

Tell everybody I say hi, and don't you dare forget to bring them my presents.

Brayden

He hit Send, and then he lay in bed for a little longer, staring at the ceiling and feeling sorry for himself. He missed his family, but he couldn't spend Christmas with them... not yet.

Maybe next year.

Eventually he noticed the time and had to hustle into the shower, where he let the water wash away most of his thoughts. Then he shoved his feet into his boots, wrapped up in his jacket, and grabbed his phone from the nightstand so he could flip open the directions Flip had sent yesterday.

Outside, the sun was out and the sky was a rich, deep blue, as though it knew it had only a few hours to lift people's spirits and was making the most of them. Brayden checked his map and the time and then stopped for a mug of mulled wine from a vendor, which he sipped as he walked along the cobbled streets.

He turned left to go toward the main square and then took the middle street of three that branched off it in the direction of the water. A few feet later, he was there—a two-story café in a bright pink building. The brass plaque outside read TEMMEL EIS.

Flip's instructions said to come up to the second floor, so Brayden ducked inside. He noted the cheerful glass display cases and the black-and-white checkered floor as he walked through the café and took the worn stone stairs at the back. Celine, Flip's driver from yesterday, waited at the door in a smart suit.

"I'm not late, I hope," Brayden joked as he got to the top of the stairs. Unless his phone was lying to him, he wasn't.

"His Highness insisted we arrive early," Celine replied, expressionless. She pulled open the door for him and let him through. "Have a pleasant lunch, sir." Then she let it fall closed again.

Flip sat at a table by the window, evidently engrossed in something on his tablet. He didn't seem to register Brayden's presence until Brayden took the seat opposite him.

Flip looked up with a start, and the tablet clattered to the table. "Brayden. I'm sorry. I was off in my own world. Obviously." He looked a little upset with himself, and his fingers convulsed into fists and loosened a few times.

"Do you want me to stand up and come back in so you can pull my chair out?" Brayden guessed, and Flip flushed guiltily. "No, that can't be it. A crown prince can't be pulling chairs out for plebs like me. And a handshake is too formal, so we'll have to deal."

Flip visibly, consciously relaxed. "I suppose you're right. Did you have a good day sightseeing yesterday, Bernadette's surprise notwithstanding?"

Brayden gave him a quick rundown of the day, with special emphasis on the lingonberries, and finished with, "How was your commitment on Tuesday? I hope everything turned out okay."

"Ah, well." Flip offered a tight smile. "I actually went to visit my cousin. She's nine. Minor crisis about her wardrobe for tomorrow night, and she needed my backup against her mom and royal tradition."

Brayden thought about Princess Clara asleep in Flip's lap, and warmth suffused him. Flip would be a great king one day. "A true hero."

Flip's cheeks went a bit pink. That was cute too, that Brayden could make a crown prince blush, when he must be used to flattery. "Even if I did leave the horse in his stall this time?"

"If Clara can forgive it, I can as well."

"Excellent. With the forgiveness out of the way…." Flip brandished the tablet. "Shall we order lunch?"

Brayden took it and glanced down at the screen to find it was a menu—a strange one, with pictures that looked like familiar dishes, but off somehow. After a moment he realized. "Are these all ice cream?"

"I hope you're not lactose intolerant," Flip said as though it had just occurred to him. "I know it's silly, but I try to come here every time I'm home, even in the winter. This is my first chance now that I've moved home permanently. Usually I just come by myself, eat, and leave, but…."

Brayden tapped to flip the menu to the next page. Was that poutine? Stark yellow ice cream shaped into french fries, smothered in caramel sauce and flakes of white chocolate. The next page had "pizza"—a crepe covered in a red jelly, with ice cream mozzarella and circlets of chocolate that looked like olives. He was six pages deep before he realized Flip had trailed off and was waiting for a response, and it took another twenty seconds to realize Flip must have just shared something with Brayden that he rarely did with anyone else.

Pushing the tablet away, Brayden looked into Flip's eyes. "This is the best lunch ever. What's good?"

The tablet apparently could send their order through for them, and a few moments later Celine entered with—

"That ice cream is bigger than my head," Brayden said faintly. "I think I'm in love."

"Taste it first, before you propose," Celine admonished, but she set their plates down, returned to her post, and closed the door behind her.

Flip met Brayden's eyes across the table and quirked his lips in a smirk. "Not bad advice."

Brayden lost half a second wondering if that was an innuendo before he shrugged it off and reached for his spoon—and his phone. This masterpiece needed to be documented. *Lunch fit for a king!* he wrote, amused at his own joke, even though no one would get it. He caught Flip looking at him as he put the phone away, and shrugged sheepishly. "I don't Instagram all my food or anything. But I travel a lot, and my family likes to know what I'm up to. It's an easy way for them to follow along without me spending hours on the phone every night."

Nodding, Flip picked up his spoon to dig into a bowl of "spaghetti." "Do you have a big family?"

"Kind of." He shoveled in a scoop of ice cream, delighted to find the "fries" were a rich vanilla, the caramel sauce a lovely complement. He made an involuntary noise of delight, closing his eyes as he savored it. When he opened his eyes again, Flip was busily arranging his chocolate "meatballs" on one side of the plate, his cheeks flushed. Maybe Brayden shouldn't make sex noises while at lunch with a prince. "In my immediate family, it's just my grandmother, my parents, and my sister. But my dad's brother, Walt, has a blended family, and there's seven kids, and they're all partnered off, and a lot of *them* have kids."

"I'd call that a big family." Flip's voice took on a wistful tone as he spooned up a chocolate chunk. "I'm something of an anomaly—a royal only child. Tradition dictates you need an heir and a spare"—he rolled his eyes as he quoted that—"but it wasn't in the cards for my parents. I've always wondered what it would be like."

"I mean, speaking mostly from secondhand experience? Chaos." He scooped up another half french fry and toppings and gestured automatically with his spoon. "Uncle Walt's family is so big we usually do Christmas in November. This year they're doing that cruise because he won a couple million on a scratch-off ticket and wanted to treat everyone."

Flip nodded thoughtfully, his brow furrowing, and then said, "Didn't you go on a boat tour yesterday? I thought you were here because you get seasick, so no cruise?"

Shit. Brayden fumbled his spoon and almost dropped it into his plate. "That, yeah, I…." He took a deep breath and let it out slowly, trying to calm his racing heart. He hated that Flip caught him lying, and he hated even more what he'd lied about. Most of all he hated that he was about to explain something he never talked about to anyone outside of family. "The seasickness thing, I just said that because the real story is sordid and I didn't want to get into it with someone I didn't know very well."

For all that Flip probably had professional schooling in how to maintain a neutral expression, he looked as though Brayden had slapped him. "Oh. I apologize. I didn't mean to pry."

Interesting—whenever Brayden said something to put Flip on his guard, he reverted to formality. But to hell with it. He wasn't going to let his weird friendship with Flip—who was not only a goddamn crown prince, but a nice person Brayden connected with despite their vastly different experiences—get screwed up over something that happened almost ten years ago.

"No, it's fine, it's a fair question. I...." Brayden frowned at what he was about to say, realizing it was true. "I think it'll be good to get it off my chest, actually. Though like I said, it's not a nice story." He shoveled in another bite of ice cream to fortify himself, but it tasted like ash, so he put down the spoon. "When I was sixteen, my best friend and I were inseparable. We arranged our school schedules so we'd be in the same classes, we joined the soccer team together. We even had a band, though Thomas couldn't carry a tune in a basket and I was dubious at best on guitar. But we had killer dance moves.

"Obviously I was in love with him." Proud when his voice didn't crack, Brayden took another cleansing breath and kept going. "I finally figured out he might feel the same, so on Christmas Day, between breakfast and dinner, I invited him over. I was gonna come clean."

Flip had stopped eating too, though he was still holding his spoon loosely in his right hand. He didn't say anything, just waited with bated breath for Brayden to finish.

"He never made it." There it was—the crack he'd been expecting. "Four-car pileup on the 407. He died instantly."

If he expected Flip to offer platitudes, to tell him it wasn't his fault, he was disappointed. "That must have been awful."

Brayden jerked his head in agreement. "I don't much feel like celebrating on that anniversary, so." He usually spent the day consumed by guilt that Thomas's family would never be whole. But that was definitely too much to saddle Flip with when they'd only really known each other a few days. And a prince would probably think Brayden's problems were pretty dumb compared to the scale of issues he had to deal with.

"No, I imagine not." He pushed his plate away. Evidently he'd lost his appetite too. "Do you travel every year on Christmas?"

"Nah. Couldn't afford it until I became a flight attendant. But my family understood—they all knew how I felt, even if I never said anything, and they leave me alone for the most part. Usually early in the evening my sister shoves a plate of leftovers in my hand and puts on the stupidest comedy she can find."

"Not a bad tradition, if a little unorthodox. Does she have a favorite?"

Brayden snorted and then admitted, "Actually, these past two years it's been *Thor: Ragnarok.*"

Flip coughed to conceal a laugh. "Well, I can't fault her taste."

"Right?" Brayden found himself grinning too. He still felt a little raw, but he felt lighter too. "What about you? Any weird holiday traditions?"

"Define 'weird.'" He twisted his mouth in a wry expression. "Every country in Europe has their own holiday traditions. And in our family, there's an added spin since my dad is Hindu and we celebrate those holidays too. Sometimes we have to compromise."

Brayden set his plate aside and found himself leaning in over the table automatically. "Like how?"

"Well, the traditional Christmas meat pie is never made with beef, for one thing." Flip shrugged. "And this year Gita Jayanti falls on Christmas—that's the Hindu celebration of the Bhagavad Gita. So Mom will do her usual Christmas address for the public, and Dad will be there, but he'll spend most of the day fasting and reciting verses."

"What about you?" Brayden propped his chin on his hand. "What do you do? Or, what *will* you do, I guess?"

As soon as he said it, he wondered if it weren't too personal a question. But Flip didn't bat an eyelash. "The same as my father, probably—meditate in the morning, then presents with Clara and my aunt and mother. And then Dad and I will listen to a webcast from India, probably."

That sounded nice. Different than what Brayden was used to, but nice. And…. "You're really close to your dad, aren't you?"

Flip flushed. "When you're the only two brown people in the entire European royalty collective, you share a lot of experiences that others don't understand."

"I get it. I mean, I don't get it, obviously, white commoner over here. But that makes sense. It seems like it's more than that, though. You look up to him."

This time Flip did seem taken aback. He paused completely and tilted his head as though reassessing Brayden's motives. "He's happy. Considerate. Kind. He and my mom, they're… I guess you haven't heard the story."

"The way you say that, I'm the only person in the country who hasn't." Brayden batted his eyelashes. "You want to fill me in, or should I google it?"

"God, no. Promise me you won't google. I'll never live it down if I get the details wrong." Flip shook his head. "My parents met at the Night of a Thousand Lights some—I guess it has to be thirty-five, thirty-six

years ago now. Have I explained what it's about? It's…
actually kind of terrible."

Brayden had his elbows on the table; he couldn't
help it. "I feel like I need popcorn. Tell me."

"My mother's… *ancestors* is too far back, but
some of her relatives were British nobility who went
on, let's generously call it a colonization tour. And
they were so consumed with white guilt they began a
scholarship program."

"I feel like this is definitely more colorful than
the Google version." He really wanted that popcorn,
though. "What kind of scholarships?"

"Arts—music, theater, drama, dance, and later
cinema." *Cinema.* God, he was so unbearably posh.
"All ages—children, teens, young adults—in the UK
but also here in Lyngria. But of course all the recipients
of these scholarships in non-European countries went
abroad to train."

Brayden didn't bother fighting the eye roll. "Oh, of
course." Because how could a worthy school exist in a
place like India.

"Obviously my parents and I have made some
fundamental changes to the scholarships. But that's how
it used to work, in a nutshell. And every year there'd
be a Night of a Thousand Lights, and top students and
alumni from all over the world were invited to attend and
perform and rub elbows with various important people."

By that Brayden inferred directors, conductors,
choreographers, producers, and the rest of the -ers and
-ors. "I'm with you so far."

"Well, imagine this—it's the 1980s. My mother
has just assumed the throne at the young age of twenty-
seven, after her parents stepped down due to my
grandmother's ailing health. It's her first time hosting

this huge event all by herself. She's nervous, but she's faking it really well.

"Before the event opens, it's traditional for the host to meet all the scholarship recipients in attendance for the event. So Mom put on her tiara and her gown a little early and went down to the ballroom to meet everyone, only she was so nervous she was actually *really* early— like an hour early. And she decided a queen couldn't be so indecisive as to go back upstairs thirty seconds after she'd just come down, so she was stuck there when my father came in, lost and looking for a restroom."

"And he couldn't leave once he'd seen her either," Brayden guessed.

"It would have been a bit rude to try to escape the hostess of the party that raises money for the scholarship that gave you your livelihood," Flip agreed. "Though he readily confesses he didn't want to escape. Well." He smiled so broadly the corners of his eyes crinkled, and Brayden was glad he was sitting down so he didn't swoon. "He did *really* have to pee by the time the party started."

Brayden snorted in surprised laughter—not just a little one either but a great piglike honk. He should probably have been mortified, but he caught Flip's eyes at exactly the wrong moment and saw the humor register there before Flip's good manners could cover it up. That only made him laugh harder. He snorted again and dissolved into giggles. Across the table, Flip had his hand over his eyes and his shoulders were shaking in silent mirth.

The first time Brayden caught his breath—"Okay, come on, it wasn't *that* funny"—Flip *hiccupped*, and that set them both off again. They had a few more false starts before they managed to get themselves under control, and Flip wiped tears from the corners of his eyes as Brayden clutched his stomach. "I think I have a cramp," he admitted.

Flip cleared his throat once and then grabbed a napkin from the dispenser on the table and blotted his face. "I haven't laughed like that in years."

Something warm and sweet and possessive swept through Brayden—a sense of accomplishment that he could bring that kind of joy to someone who had everything. It left him feeling tender under the ribs. "Me neither."

"No?" Flip cocked his head. "I would've thought…. You seem like the kind of person who lives every moment to the fullest."

"I am." Brayden shrugged, suddenly self-conscious, the back of his neck prickling. He smoothed a hand over it. "I do. But I guess…." He frowned, suddenly realizing the truth. "I'm alone for a lot of that. Hard to make yourself belly laugh."

"I suppose so."

"Anyway." Brayden pushed that tender, raw feeling to the side and centered himself. They'd been talking about how Flip's parents met. "The royal meet-cute. Your mom's the queen, and your dad—a scholarship kid, you said."

"He was thirty when they met, and well established in his career. But yes." When Flip talked about his parents, his eyes took on a kind of dreaminess. Obviously they were all very close. "Mom had never seen any of his films, of course."

Brayden sat up straighter. "Films?" he echoed. Something in his brain clicked into place. "Your dad's a *movie star*?"

"He was, in India in the seventies and eighties. Now he's prince consort of Lyngria." Flip gave him a strange look. "You didn't know any of this? Really?"

Okay, so most people would have googled, but…. "I didn't want to read up on you and come off like a creeper or embarrass myself reading some fake website."

Brayden's ears went hot. "Besides, I figured it was just as easy to get the information right from the source."

"Well, you'll be pleased to know that my father's entire body of work is available on Netflix in this country."

That sounded dangerous. Brayden had sights to see, and he didn't mean a television screen. "Maybe if we get a rainy day." Besides, a movie star with a son who looked like Flip? 1970s Flip's Dad was probably super hot, and lusting after him would be super weird, especially since he was likely to meet the man tomorrow. No, thank you.

"Fair enough. The day must be seized." Flip straightened his posture and folded his hands neatly on the table. "Anything else you need to know for tomorrow?"

Brayden thought for a moment. "Yeah, just one thing. What exactly are you doing, flying back and forth between here and Toronto every month?"

"My second job." Flip looked around as though to verify they were alone, which seemed ridiculous, but maybe he was about to divulge a state secret. "The crown owns a diamond operation here in Lyngria. I've been setting up a satellite office in Toronto because we're looking to break into the Canadian market. The plan is to turn the company public so that it will directly fund a universal childcare initiative, but letting go of control means I have to trust the people in charge, and I'm… having trouble with that part."

"Understandable." Brayden wondered if that meant that Flip would stop being on his flight a couple times a month. "Sounds like my job will get a lot less interesting soon."

He must have sounded more bitter than he meant to, or else something showed on his face, because Flip cocked his head. "You don't like your job?"

Brayden shrugged. "It's complicated." It provided a great excuse when his mother asked when he was going to settle down—*Mom, I'm never home. Who'd want to date me?*—and that's exactly why he chose it.

Perhaps Flip understood, if the wry smile he gave was an indication. "Isn't it always."

Brayden supposed being a prince would have a lot of its own pitfalls. "I guess so." God, when had the conversation gotten so heavy? They needed to get back on some lighter topics. He pulled the tablet toward himself and forced some brightness into his voice. "So... dessert?"

They chatted a little more about tomorrow and about Brayden's plans for that evening. Tonight was the light festival, when the people of Lyngria gathered in the streets with candles and sang to welcome the dark in hopes that it would take their troubles with it when it receded. Brayden didn't put much stock in that, but it was as unique a festival as he'd ever heard of. Just the description gave him goose bumps.

"You'll enjoy it," Flip promised. "Just make sure you get an electric candle, or else one of the no-drip ones so you don't end up with a burn. Ask me how I know."

Brayden smiled. "Thanks for the tip."

Before he could say anything else, there was a knock at the door and Celine poked her head in. "Your Highness, I hate to interrupt...."

Flip didn't sigh, though his expression suggested he might want to. "No, you're right. Thank you, Celine. Brayden, I hate to leave in the middle of our conversation again...."

Brayden waved him off. A real-life crown prince had taken time out of his day to eat lunch with him. He could hardly complain. "Go on, I know you have important things to do. I'll see you tomorrow."

Flip smiled. "Yes, you will."

Chapter Four

FLIP didn't realize how late it had gotten until the light came on in the hallway, startling him into nearly falling out of his desk chair.

He must have startled his mother too, because she pressed a hand to her breastbone and shook her head. "Flip. I didn't expect to see you in this part of the palace so late. Don't tell me you're working."

"All right, I won't tell you." It was an old joke between them, one they'd each been on both sides of. He glanced at the clock and wished he were surprised by the late hour, but he was exhausted. He'd intended to go to bed hours ago to be well rested for tomorrow, but he had a few things he wanted to accomplish first. And then he kept getting distracted wondering how Brayden was faring at the light festival, whether he'd gotten swept up in the moment or if he felt like an outsider. Probably the former. Brayden seemed to fit in pretty seamlessly anywhere. He took things in stride in a way totally unfamiliar to Flip.

He was probably having a lot more fun than Flip was with the personnel files of everyone who worked in management at the Crown Mining Co.

His mother sighed and came into the library. She leaned down to press a kiss to the top of his head. "I wish you hadn't inherited my work ethic."

Inherited? His years of tutors and lectures on the responsibility of privilege had drilled it into him. But maybe that was the same thing. He'd inherited the title, at least. "I want to get this proposal ready." He slid his laptop away and closed it, resisting the temptation to knuckle at his eyes. "I think I'm almost done."

His mother took a seat on the piano bench a few meters away and watched him. "It can wait until after the weekend. Parliament's not in session again until January anyway."

"I know." He took a few deep breaths and ran through one of the breathing exercises his father had taught him in order to release the tension from his body. "I'm just nervous."

"You still believe everything can be perfect." She smiled—not her public expression but one she only allowed in the privacy of their residence at the palace or at their summer home on the island. "That's why you don't know when to stop."

"I know when to stop," Flip murmured, but maybe he didn't. For months he'd been working on this proposal, a plan to turn the royal family's biggest asset, the diamond factory a few kilometers south of the city, over to the government to be run as a public holding. Before that could happen, he wanted to assure himself that the people in charge were competent, capable, incorruptible agents who would serve the public's best interest.

Signing off on people's integrity was hard.

She chuckled. "I see that. I hear Celine has a new background check to run." She crossed her legs in a way that indicated to Flip she didn't intend to stand for some time.

He turned away from the desk and faced her. As usual, her expression betrayed nothing—not to a casual observer. But she was Flip's mother, and he knew her better than almost anyone. The slightest curve of her mouth, that was hope. The single line on her forehead, easily mistaken for a wrinkle if you didn't know better, that was tension. She worried too much.

"She's already run it, as I'm sure you know." And Brayden was as squeaky clean as anyone could wish for. "You'll meet him tomorrow, if that's what you're worried about."

"I'm *worried* that my only son has a new man in his life and didn't tell his mother."

"What am I, chopped liver?" Flip's dad entered the library from the back door, clad in a kurta pajama and his usual house slippers. "When do I get to give the shovel speech? I've been practicing." He put on an exaggerated Southern US drawl. "You treat my son with respect and have him home by ten—"

"Irfan," his mother admonished, but her voice was warm. It seemed to serve more as an invitation. Flip's dad crossed the library to press a kiss to her cheek, sit beside her, and take her hand.

"You're right, we wouldn't want to cramp his style. 'Make sure you feed him breakfast before you send him on his walk of shame'—is that better?"

Flip groaned and ran his hands through his hair. "Thanks, Dad."

"Hey, I have your back."

"I know that. But seriously, there's a reason I haven't introduced him."

"Why, is he hideous?" Irfan addressed this question to his wife. "I know we're an intimidatingly good-looking family—" He cut off and made gestures to indicate her face, her figure, et cetera. Flip loved his dad.

"Irfan." She was laughing outright. "Stop. I want to hear his explanation." She lowered her voice. "Besides, I saw his new man's photograph."

Oh boy. "It's just a date," Flip said helplessly. He meant to tell more of the truth, that it was just a favor, that Brayden was in Lyngria on vacation for a few weeks and that nothing would come of it, but it got stuck on his tongue. "He didn't even know who I was when I asked him to come."

"Oh, so you're ashamed of us," his dad began, mock indignant.

But Flip couldn't take any more. He didn't know why it should bother him that his parents were excited to meet his date—why he didn't want to tell them it was nothing more than a convenient arrangement—but he didn't want to lie more than he had to. "Dad," Flip pleaded.

Irfan sobered. "All right. But you don't have to hide him from us, you know. No one is upset you're not marrying Prince Harry or whomever."

"Remember when you used to date that Belgian duke's son—what was his name?"

"Armand," Irfan supplied with a shudder. "I don't think I ever saw him crack a smile."

"He smiled," Flip said defensively, though it truthfully hadn't been very often. Armand had been a poor match in that regard, not that many people could keep pace with his father's sense of humor.

"Or that executive from Toronto you brought home a few years ago. He was nice enough, but—what's the phrase—he was dull as a post?"

"It's dumb as a post, dear."

"No, I mean he was boring. I thought I was going to have to learn to sleep with my eyes open."

Irfan had never missed a single beat during a state dinner, which Flip knew because they'd discussed at length how important it was to be engaged and informed, especially because certain factions would be hypercritical of them regardless. Trevor really was fairly boring, though.

"Can we be done dissecting my love life?" Flip pleaded. "You can meet Brayden tomorrow. But no shovel talk. We're taking it slow."

"I'd expect nothing less," his mother said, and though her tone was warm, Flip could have sworn it held a hint of disappointment. She stood, patting her husband's leg as she did, and crossed to the desk to kiss the top of Flip's head again. "Get some sleep, sweetheart. I won't have you begging off dances because you're tired. You don't want to fall asleep on your date."

In fairness, Brayden had probably already seen him asleep with his mouth open on one of their transatlantic flights together. But still. "That would be rude of me."

Irfan stood too and squeezed Flip's shoulder. He waited until Mom was gone and then for Flip to meet his eyes. "Whatever happens with this boy, your mother and I just want you to be happy."

Flip's throat tightened. "Thanks, Dad."

Then he was left alone.

He had a feeling sleep could prove elusive tonight.

BRAYDEN was half terrified when his phone rang at eleven o'clock in the morning. He was just puttering out of the shower, debating how fancied up to get when he knew Celine would be picking him up in an hour to be professionally fussed over.

He was so flustered that he answered without checking the caller ID—rookie mistake.

"So this party you're going to with this guy who's not your sugar daddy," Lina said, without waiting for him to say hello.

Brayden blinked and then checked the time. "Isn't it, like, four in the morning where you are?"

"I wanted to make sure you didn't have an excuse to blow me off." She yawned into the phone. "Anyway. Talk."

Brayden sighed, plucked his fancy new underwear from the box, and put them on. Then he immediately took them off and put on regular, plebeian underwear, because they felt entirely too good to wear while he was on the phone with his sister. "About what?"

"*About what*, he says. I don't know, about whatever event you're going to that's so fancy you're not only going to wear a tuxedo, but having someone tailor one for you?"

Brayden decided he'd better not tell her that actually, he was pretty sure Bernadette was going to make the whole thing from scratch. "It's a charity ball. A fundraiser for a scholarship program that sends underprivileged kids all over the world to art school, or something." He could have described it better, but that ran the risk of Lina googling the thing and realizing who Brayden must be attending with. No, thank you. He could do without his sister marrying him off to a prince, even in her head.

"Mm-hmm. So we're talking multiple thousands of dollars a head. Not including your tuxedo."

"Look, I met him at work, okay? He flies my usual Toronto to Paris and back. First class every time. Yeah, he's rich. So what? A couple grand means nothing to him."

Lina huffed. "Must be nice."

"Right?"

"But okay. He's rich. And you said he's super hot."

"Like the face of the sun," Brayden confirmed.

"And this is just a favor. You're not his real date, and he doesn't expect you to put out at the end of the night, even though you totally would."

"Succinctly put, thanks."

He could practically hear her rolling her eyes. "Shut up. I'm trying to understand. He's rich, he's hot, he dates… but not *you*. He's been recommending local places for you to go, so he's obviously not a total asshole."

"So…?"

"So what's wrong with him, Bray? Is he a serial killer? Does he have BO so bad you need a hazmat suit to get within ten feet? If he's so great, *why doesn't he have a real date*?"

Brayden opened his mouth to reply, then realized: "I have no idea." Put like that, it *was* a bit strange that Flip didn't have a cadre of suitable men on tap. Certainly he had to know someone more appropriate than Brayden, who was going to spend the whole night using the wrong fork, making crass jokes, and probably being a royal embarrassment. Why *didn't* Flip have a date?

But why did it matter? It wasn't like *Brayden* was looking to date him, no matter how hot and charming he was. That was punching above his weight.

"I'm just saying," Lina said. "Why you? Is it just coincidence? Or is there a story there? You know I love you, bro, and I'd never ask you to change. But, like, consider that maybe this guy does actually like you and maybe try not to break his heart."

Brayden had not yet recovered from that bombshell when the hotel phone rang, probably to announce his ride had arrived. *Shit.* "Okay. I promise I'm not running away from this conversation, but I have to go. My car is here."

"Your car that your mystery man sent for you," Lina deadpanned.

Because he's a prince! Brayden wanted to say. *He doesn't have time for stuff like that! He's used to having people do things for him!* But he couldn't tell her. She'd never believe him anyway. "Love you," he said desperately. "Bye!"

"Remember what I said," she admonished and then hung up.

Brayden answered the hotel phone and promised he'd be right down, only to realize he was still mostly naked and wearing the wrong underpants. He'd better move fast.

BY the time Brayden had dressed for his final fitting at Les Fils Royaux, he'd talked himself down from his panic. Lina didn't know anything. There were plenty of good reasons for an eligible person not to date. Such as not being interested in dating, like Brayden. Such as being asexual or aromantic. Such as significant past trauma. Such as having the paparazzi all up in one's business.

Brayden really didn't blame Flip for doing his solo thing, though obviously, if this tux didn't make him want to bone Brayden, he was hopeless.

"Well," Bernadette said as she stood back after adjusting the hem of his pants over his shiny new shoes, "what do you think?"

Brayden looked at his reflection in the mirror, at his broad shoulders framed in a perfectly tailored jacket, then turned ninety degrees so he could see the curve of his ass. Unsurprisingly, Bernadette had been right about the underwear. He looked at the slim-fit trouser leg. He looked at Bernadette. "I look hot."

She snorted, one hand on the curve of her stomach. "You're all right. Nothing pulling funny? It's not good for business if your pant seam busts on national TV."

"I promise you left enough third-leg room," Brayden said, rolling his eyes. Bernadette rolled hers right back, and Brayden returned his gaze to the mirror.

The crisp black lines of the tuxedo lent him a gravitas of posture he didn't normally carry, but the semigloss damask on the lining kept it from feeling stifling. And Bernadette had let Brayden inject some personality in the form of a raw silk vest, tie, and pocket square in bright amethyst.

"Then my work here is done." She dusted off her hands theatrically. "Now go take all that off so I can package it up. I don't trust you not to wrinkle."

And then Celine brought the car around to ferry him to the palace, to Flip's private apartments, where presumably valets and butlers and professional hair and makeup people would primp Brayden until he was fit for public consumption by the caliber of public who consumed Flip.

Okay, that sounded like he was going to an orgy and not a fancy charity ball. But still.

Brayden hadn't made it to the palace yet. Only parts of it were open to the public, but the tours had good reviews on TripAdvisor, and apparently the holiday decorations were something special to see. Driving up to the place, Brayden could believe it.

The palace sat a kilometer or two outside the city proper, surrounded by a topiary garden that was a little brown with the season. A crushed-gravel driveway a good five or six cars wide went on forever, lit on either side by old-fashioned streetlamps, each adorned with a wreath and bow. And there, at the end of it, with a dormant fountain in front, sprawled the palace itself—a mostly rectangular building three stories tall, sheathed in gray stone, with a copper roof. Cheerful yellow light poured out the windows into the already-darkening afternoon.

It would look like the perfect postcard if they got a little snow.

By now Brayden was used to waiting until Celine came around to let him out, but that didn't happen. Instead, the partition behind her rolled down and she turned to face him. "I'll have your things sent up," she promised, and then the door opened to reveal a man in what could only be described as a butler's uniform.

"Mr. Wood, I presume," the man said. He stepped back at attention as Brayden eased himself out of the car. "You are expected, sir. If you'll follow me?"

Brayden couldn't have said exactly what he expected. At some point he'd thought Flip would show up and they'd get ready together, or maybe he'd get to meet the royal family (and wasn't that insane, that that was a legitimate thought). Instead the butler—he introduced himself as Johan—led him through the wide marble halls of the palace, swiping a key card now and again to access areas that obviously weren't open to the public. Their footsteps echoed up to cavernous ceilings adorned in more crown molding than Brayden had ever seen in his life.

Someone had decorated the common areas with a heavy hand toward Western Christian iconography, even if some of it was the modern, secular variety with fat Father Christmases and reindeer and much of the rest was just trees and wreaths, but behind private doors, things were more subdued, as though real people might live there rather than demented holiday elves.

A handful of cards, including one obviously handmade by a child, adorned a mantel that wouldn't have fit in Brayden's apartment back home. No professionally decorated fifteen-foot tree in here either, just an eight-footer with a hodgepodge of ornaments. And though Brayden wasn't an expert on Indian culture, he thought he detected some elements of the décor with that influence. They passed by an alcove with soft lighting, the focus of which seemed to be an intricately carved table that might have been an altar. On a side table farther down the hallway sat a bluish statue with four arms.

After another moment or twelve of gawking, Brayden was led into a bland blue-gray room with good natural lighting and no carpet on the stone floor. A round-faced woman a few years older than he was smiled at him and extended her hand. "Mr. Wood? I'm Irina."

Her French had a noticeable accent—Polish, maybe, the country's fourth official language, even though from what Brayden had read, very few people living here spoke it as their native tongue. He shook her hand. "Nice to meet you. Please, call me Brayden."

"Brayden." She nodded and smiled and took a step back. "I will do your hair and makeup."

That sounded more like an order than a question, but honestly, Brayden was probably due for a haircut. He sat when she indicated the sole chair in the room.

He still hadn't seen Flip by the time he'd been snipped and coiffed and shaved—just his face, fortunately—and powdered, which made him sneeze.

Then Johan returned to escort him to a dressing room, and Brayden thanked Irina and went to dress.

"His Highness sends his regrets that he was unable to greet you personally," Johan intoned. "I was given to understand he had duties elsewhere."

"Princess Clara didn't like her dress again?" he guessed.

Johan's face betrayed nothing, but Brayden thought he detected an aura of affirmation. Brayden tried again as he stepped behind a screen for modesty to start the process of getting into a tuxedo. One had to be on one's best behavior in a palace, surely. "So when will I see Flip?" He flung his sweater over the top of the screen, mostly because he'd seen it in a cartoon, and then wondered what he was going to do with it. Then he realized that was stupid—Flip would probably have it laundered and delivered back to Brayden's hotel room. But he was starting to worry he'd have to enter the party solo, and while he didn't generally have a problem making small talk, he also didn't generally hang out with the uber-rich and famous.

"His Highness has arranged for your driver to bring you to a private anteroom at the opera house prior to the ball."

Well. That was better than nothing. Brayden knotted his tie—badly—buttoned his waistcoat, donned his jacket, and then stepped out for inspection. "How do I look?"

Johan ran him up and down with an appraising eye. "If I may?"

Brayden inclined his head, and Johan retied his tie and dismissed invisible lint from Brayden's shoulder with an actual brush. "Very good, sir."

Very good, Brayden echoed in his head. So why were his palms sweating? God, had he put on enough deodorant? This was absurd. Tonight had zero stakes for him, and Flip was a crown prince. Whatever Brayden did, Flip would be fine. He couldn't possibly commit enough faux pas to permanently damage Flip's reputation in one night.

That was just it, though—Brayden didn't want Flip to just be *fine*. He didn't want to make his life difficult. He wanted his friend to enjoy his evening, but he also didn't want to do anything that would embarrass Flip.

"This would have been easier if we never became friends," he muttered under his breath as Celine slowed the car around the back of the opera house. Belatedly he remembered to turn off the ringer on his phone. God forbid Lina tried to call him in the middle of this or Brayden got drunk enough to let her in on what was really happening. Nope. He needed his head in the game.

"Good luck," Celine told him, and with that Brayden went inside.

FLIP didn't mean to spend half the afternoon with Clara, reassuring her she looked beautiful in her dress. He certainly didn't mean to have to mediate a diplomatic incident with Poland after having his hair cut and before going over his introductory speech for the evening.

Worst of all, he didn't intend for Brayden to spend the afternoon in the palace by himself, neglected, potentially unprepared for the media frenzy that was Flip's life.

He had a thoughtful, erudite, heartfelt apology composed and ready to deliver, and then Brayden walked into the anteroom, laughing over his shoulder at something the opera house guide had said, and Flip forgot every last word of his five languages.

It only lasted a second—long enough for Flip to be able to enjoy the way Brayden's trousers clung to his hips and backside, the way the slim, tapered leg made him look taller than his six feet, and the way the well-cut material emphasized his broad shoulders and narrow waist. Even the loud amethyst waistcoat, tie, and pocket square suited him perfectly; Brayden should never attempt to be demure. For the moment, his flyaway hair had been tamed in a style reminiscent of classic Hollywood, in that modern retro way that seemed to be in fashion once again. With his eyes crinkled at the corners in laughter, he looked particularly dashing.

Fortunately, before Flip could embarrass himself with more staring, Brayden's laugh turned into a smile and broke the spell, leaving behind a moderately good-looking man with more than his share of charisma. "Hey," Brayden said, brimming with his usual cheer. He held his arms out at his side and spun around once. "How do I look?"

Flip didn't have it in him to obfuscate. "Like one of the scholarship alumni. I expect everyone will spend the night wondering which film they've seen you in."

Brayden grinned. "Let's hope they don't find the video from my cam-boy days."

Flip must have blanched, because Brayden hastened to add, "Oh my God, no. I'm kidding. I promise I'm not in any internet porn. Or other porn."

Laughing off the worst of the adrenaline, Flip shook his head. "This should be an interesting evening."

Brayden sobered. "I promise I'll be on my best behavior—or a whole other person's best behavior, even. I'm not going to do anything that will reflect badly on you. I'll just… keep to myself." He looked so earnest and determined.

Flip thought about the possibilities, about the different ways the night could go, and found that

Brayden's promise presented something of a worst-case scenario. "Don't," he said, surprised when it came out forceful. "I mean, maybe don't make any pornography jokes to anyone but me"—Brayden grimaced sheepishly—"but don't be someone else."

I like you.

Except Flip couldn't say that. Could he?

"Brayden lite, then," Brayden said as he nudged his shoulder against Flip's. "Slightly more personality than work Brayden, 90 percent fewer dick jokes than off-the-clock Brayden."

"Maybe eighty-five," Flip returned, biting back a smile.

"Good deal." Brayden made as though to put his hands in his pockets, but immediately stopped himself. Bernadette had probably read him the riot act. "So. Do we have a game plan? How exactly does this work? I assume you have schmoozing to do and I'll just slink off to the bar for a thirty-dollar martini?"

Flip's stomach twisted. He didn't especially want to explain. "Actually, ah, I need to talk to you about that."

"Sounds ominous." But he didn't seem worried. "What's up?"

There was nothing for it. Flip steeled himself and blurted out the truth. "My parents saw Celine had orchestrated a background check on you and assumed that we're dating. I mean, beyond this single engagement."

Brayden froze, expression unreadable. "Oh?" he said neutrally. "A bit upset, are they?"

Shit. Oh no, he was angry. Flip knew he'd bollocks it up. "Actually they're very excited to meet you. It turns out they've hated every boyfriend I've ever introduced them to, and even on paper, you're more interesting than any of them."

Brayden let out a breath that turned into a quiet laugh. "For a second I thought you were going to tell me I'd been disinvited."

That wasn't the reaction he anticipated. "So you're… fine with my parents thinking you're my boyfriend."

Brayden shrugged. "I mean, lying to your parents isn't ideal, but from my perspective, what's the big deal? We have fun tonight, tomorrow you can tell them I did something unforgivable in a boyfriend but not bad enough for a guest pass to the palace dungeon, and that's it." His face lost some of its openness, but not before Flip noted the thin set of his mouth and a tightening around his eyes. "Too bad, though. I've enjoyed having a local guide."

Flip forced himself to relax. "I… me too. Not that I've had a local guide. I mean." He sighed and then immediately regretted his lack of self-control. "You know what I mean."

Brayden rubbed his shoe against a scuff mark on the floor. "So… you want me to put on a show for your parents?"

"No," Flip said quickly. He didn't want to think about why that idea horrified him. "Just… be you, like we talked about."

The shuttered look eased somewhat, and Brayden's shoulders crept down from where they'd risen around his ears—probably the best Flip could hope for. "All right. So I'll meet your parents. When?"

"Soon." Flip fought the urge to check his watch. "They're supposed to meet us here before we go in. Which will be… well."

Brayden raised an eyebrow. "Which will be what?"

Closing his eyes, Flip took a moment to center himself. "You're not, I don't know, shy of attention, are you?"

Brayden raised the other eyebrow, and Flip realized his mistake and laughed. "No, you're right. Stupid question. Because my parents think we're…. Anyway, you're going to be formally introduced by the royal herald to everyone at the party as my date. Surprise!"

Brayden laughed. "God, you are so lucky you picked me up on that flight. No, you don't have to worry about me being the center of attention. Shockingly, I enjoy that. The only part I'm worried about is making sure I don't make you look like an ass by mixing up the titles for dukes and barons and—I don't know, eating with the wrong fork."

"'Sir' and 'ma'am' will work fine in a pinch. Most people don't know that stuff these days. And you don't need to worry about the forks—"

"It took me a year to figure it out," said Flip's father from the door to the main hall, where he and Flip's mother had just entered. "And I had tutors. What do they say in North America? Fake it till you make it."

A little on the nose, Dad. Flip cleared his throat and stood up straighter. He didn't think about how easy it was to let instinct take over, to put his hand on Brayden's back as they stepped forward to meet his parents halfway. "Because tonight is canapés only. Mom, Dad. This is Brayden. My boyfriend."

Chapter Five

DESPITE his assurances to Flip, Brayden blanked out most of meeting his parents and the introduction to a ballroom full of important people he didn't know. The curved baroque ceiling went up three or four stories, with arched balconies on all sides. Brayden had never seen so much finery in one place.

But by the time he and Flip had descended the marble staircase arm in arm to the elaborately tiled floor below, he had a handle on himself. Sort of.

They waited to one side while the herald introduced Flip's parents, Queen Constance and Prince Irfan—the only people important enough to be introduced after Flip and Brayden, which was, not to put too fine a point on it, a mindfuck.

Fortunately, once Flip's parents had made it down the stairs, flowing like water in a way that must have taken years to perfect, Brayden felt some of the pressure leave his shoulders. In an unrelated incident, he noticed a passing waiter carrying a tray of lemon wedges and nudged Flip's side. He gestured with his head. "Tequila shots?"

Flip turned to follow his gaze. "What—no, not tequila shots. Those are garnishes for the seafood frittura." He'd gone a bit pink.

Something about the way he said it…. "You've never done a tequila shot," Brayden said. That blew his mind almost as much as the opulence around him. "How old are you again?"

"Hey."

"I'm just saying. You're the crown prince. I bet if you ask nicely, one of the bartenders will find a bottle of tequila and a salt shaker."

"We do them with orange and cinnamon here."

"Excellent, we can do a taste test."

Flip groaned and led Brayden by the hand farther onto the floor. "Maybe later. First I have to play host."

"You never did get around to explaining that." It was a little too easy to let his fingers intertwine with Flip's. Maybe Brayden *should* have been an actor. "I mean, I know the whole thing is a fundraiser slash showcase… deal. What does a host do?"

"My first duty is to introduce the first act. In this case, the orchestra that will play the majority of tonight's music." They had crossed the floor to a raised stage area where musicians in tuxedos sat at rest, eyes on the conductor.

"That seems easy enough." Brayden didn't know why he had to come along for that. "What's the second duty?"

"Opening the dancing."

Brayden looked up sharply and narrowed his eyes. "You could have mentioned that at some point a little earlier in the evening. For example, when I asked for a rundown on how the night was going to go. Or, you know, when you asked me to this thing in the first place."

Flip grimaced. "I sort of forgot? If you're not comfortable, I can dance with my mother. It won't be a scandal. Do you even know how to waltz?"

Ugh. Brayden couldn't help the face he made. "A waltz? Really? All the variety in the world and you want to dance the world's most boring dance on national television. Are you trying to put your people to sleep?"

Flip started to smile. "So you *do* know how to waltz?"

Snorting, Brayden listed on his fingers, "Waltz, fox-trot, tango, salsa, cha-cha, swing, hip hop. I'm a passable belly dancer, but I never got the hang of the robot." Off Flip's incredulous look, he shrugged. "My grandmother owned a dance studio in Toronto. I taught there for the better part of a decade, until I finished university. Best after-school job ever. What, you think rich people are the only ones who can bust a move?" He still missed those days.

Next to them, a woman cleared her throat. "Your Highness… if I may?"

Oh Jesus, they'd been overheard and Brayden was already making Flip look bad. They both glanced over to see the conductor, who was smiling indulgently at them. "We have rehearsed a Viennese waltz, if that will suit."

Brayden looked at Flip, who lifted a shoulder as though it didn't matter. The Viennese waltz was twice the speed of the English style and could be fairly tricky, particularly with a new partner. Brayden smiled like a shark. "I'm in." Then he realized: "I supposed I'd better let you lead?"

"You can lead the belly dance," Flip promised him and ascended the stairs to a small podium to introduce the musicians.

Everyone else must have understood what Brayden had needed explained to him, because all around him, important people in gorgeous clothing had backed away around the perimeter of the dance floor. The lights dimmed and—Brayden wasn't exactly a wallflower, but he didn't think a spotlight was necessary either.

The conductor waited an interminable moment while a second spotlight followed Flip down the stairs to where Brayden stood. Then she raised her baton and Brayden raised his chin.

Flip's warm brown eyes were steady when he met Brayden's, and he put his hands on Brayden's body as though they had a right to be there—a proper hold high on Brayden's back, Brayden's right hand in Flip's left. Brayden settled his left hand on Flip's shoulder, conscious to keep his grip light. This close, he expected Flip to smell like some kind of heady, intoxicating, expensive cologne, but when he inhaled, Brayden smelled only a mild, pleasant-scented soap.

Flip mouthed, "Ready?"

"Born ready," Brayden answered.

Flip smiled, and the orchestra began.

Brayden forgot to be nervous and let Flip spin him around the dance floor.

If this were a competition, they would have angled their faces away from each other, the better to put on a display for the audience. But they hadn't rehearsed, and Brayden allowed himself the excuse that he needed to watch Flip for his cues.

He didn't. Brayden felt every move Flip made as he made it—every breath, every step, every turn. The space between them never widened, never shortened. Flip moved and Brayden followed him, half a centimeter away, in perfect time with the orchestra and the beating of his heart. That part—the physical steps—was as easy as any dance he'd ever done.

Holding Flip's gaze while they did it, though? That was nerve-racking. And yet he couldn't tear his eyes away. Flip was *smiling* at him—not because Brayden said something outlandish or ridiculous or because people expected it, but a warm, simple, content smile, like he was pleased to be here in this hall with Brayden. Like the mere fact of the two of them together made him happy.

Brayden strongly suspected he was going to panic about that later, but right now he only seemed capable of smiling back.

"Reverse?" Flip asked as they neared the end of the floor.

"Obviously," Brayden agreed, and they switched to a slightly more complicated step, one that had each of them crossing their feet every second rotation. Their positioning never faltered, and Brayden found himself smiling wider. They were *good* at this, and he'd forgotten how much he enjoyed dancing with a talented partner.

They breezed through another set of change steps, and then Flip suggested, "Fleckerl?"

That wasn't traditional for the Viennese. Maybe Flip watched too much *Strictly Ballroom*. But— "All right, show-off," Brayden teased, and Flip laughed as they spun in a quick circle. He dipped Brayden at the end of it, either to prove his point or just to be silly.

They almost missed a step on that change, and Brayden took control for a split second until they recovered. Then they were spinning the other way, back to the natural turn for the final bars.

The music died down, and for a moment, the ballroom seemed to hold its breath. Brayden's chest heaved with exertion, not from the physical exercise but from exhilaration. The last time he'd felt this alive, he was bungee jumping in Portugal. Flip's cheeks were flushed and his expression full of the same warmth that had suffused it throughout their dance, but he looked a little taken aback too. Maybe Brayden had surprised him.

Belatedly, Brayden realized the assembled crowd was applauding, and heat rushed to his face. The surprise slid from Flip's face and he dropped his right hand, spun Brayden out to the side, and told him to take a bow.

"You owe me a tequila shot," Brayden replied.

FORTUNATELY for Flip, he didn't have to endure an entire evening dancing with Brayden, who was far too charming and too attractive and too dangerous to get close to, especially with their arrangement expiring in just a few hours.

He wished he'd thought about that a week ago.

In the meantime he had elbows to rub and purse strings to loosen, so he left Brayden speaking with his aunt and let the scholarship administrator take him on a tour of the most generous donors. He tried not to think about how much he'd rather be dancing.

"Your young man is quite the dancer," said the heiress of a chain of upscale jewelry stores. "Is he an alumnus?"

Flip fought not to blanch. The last thing he wanted was for someone to draw parallels between his situation and his parents'. "No," he said too quickly, and then he reminded himself to take a breath before answering.

"No, his grandmother owns a studio. He's a former instructor." Thank God Brayden had told him that much.

"Really? Maybe he can teach my two left feet a thing or two."

"Maybe you should start with the macarena, honey," her husband said and kissed her cheek as though to soften the blow.

The heiress shoved playfully at his chest. "As if you're any better."

This was clearly either about to devolve into foreplay or escalate into an argument. Flip made his excuses and moved on to his next mark.

Perhaps three-quarters of an hour passed before Flip managed to find himself at a lull. Knowing he only had a few seconds in which to make his escape, he cast about for the nearest exit—

And yelped when an unseen hand dragged him behind one of the Doric columns. "Shh," Brayden said, eyes sparkling. "Come with me if you want to live."

Then he pushed Flip ahead of him into the service room behind the bar.

"Have you been drinking?" Flip asked, bemused, as Brayden continued nudging until they stood in front of a long plastic table serving as a prep area.

"Not yet," Brayden said cheerfully. "Now where's—there he is."

A tall blond man entered from the bar and offered a bow. "Your Highness," he said. "Your escort said you requested this specifically." He brandished a bottle of Don Julio Reposado.

Brayden beamed. "Isn't Sven great? Say thank you, Flip."

"Thank you, Sven," Flip said dutifully. One of the most important etiquette lessons his mother had drilled home was *Don't be rude to waitstaff.* Then he turned his attention back to Brayden, who had procured a pair of shot glasses and a plate of citrus, presumably from Sven. He placed them on the table.

Flip probably shouldn't. He had the distinct impression that tequila shots were the territory of frat boys and those who wished to be frat boys. But at some point in the past week, he'd gotten swept up in Brayden's enthusiasm. If he was going to give it up tomorrow, he wanted to indulge tonight.

"All right. How does this work?"

Sven had disappeared back to wherever he came from. Brayden took a salt shaker and a small canister of cinnamon from his jacket pocket—Flip silently vowed never to tell Bernadette—and lined them up next to the plate. "North American or European style first, do you think?"

Flip considered. "The lemon will taste extra sour after orange, so North American first, to be as objective as possible."

"Excellent choice." Brayden poured a generous amount in each glass. "So the order for the North American tequila shot is take the salt, drink the tequila, bite the lemon wedge. But you can't just dump salt in your mouth. You do it like this." He brought his hand to his mouth, licked a stripe across the back of it, and upended the salt shaker over his damp skin.

Flip sucked in a sharp breath.

Brayden looked up through his eyelashes. "What, too uncouth for you?"

Flip had a sudden flash of Braden licking the back of *his* hand like that if he hesitated too long, and the back of his neck went hot. He copied Brayden's actions almost defiantly.

"Now, in fairness," Brayden said, demonstrating how to hold the lemon wedge in the hand with the salt, "this tequila is way too good for this kind of treatment. But they didn't have any of the paint-stripping kind from my youth, so we're improvising."

"Because you're so ancient," Flip said dryly.

"My tequila days are many years ago now." Brayden handed him one of the shot glasses, his expression daring Flip to disagree.

"People years?" Flip queried blandly.

Brayden snorted, and they both had to catch themselves before they had a repeat of the ice cream shop meltdown. "Shut up. Okay, are you ready?"

Probably not. Flip clinked his glass against Brayden's. "Bottoms up."

"You're a menace," Brayden said, pink-cheeked, and Flip realized the double entendre.

The salt on his tongue made his mouth water, but the tequila went down warm and smooth. The lemon, though, puckered his whole face until he had to shake his head to clear it. "Ugh."

"Whew," Brayden agreed and wiped his mouth with the back of his hand. "All right, well, I'm awake now. Your turn. How do we do this the European way?"

Flip spread the cinnamon sugar on the plate, rimmed the glasses, and poured the shots. "There's no licking involved, I'm afraid."

"I bet you've never done a body shot, huh?" Brayden sighed.

Flip almost dropped the bottle. He'd seen Brayden mostly naked, after all, and he was seeing him again now in his imagination, laid out on his back with a line of salt on his stomach—

No. He turned to hand Brayden his drink. "A gentleman doesn't kiss and tell."

"You're not missing out on much. They're mostly just messy." Brayden threw back the tequila, hummed thoughtfully, and took his time with the orange. "I like that better. It wouldn't work half as well with crappy tequila, though."

Flip agreed and tried not to think about how getting messy with Brayden might not be so bad.

BRAYDEN would happily have spent the entirety of the evening in that back room with Flip, either shooting tequila or shooting the shit, but he knew they couldn't. He made sure they exited the room one at a time—he could only imagine the field day the Lyngria tabloids would have if someone thought the crown prince had snuck out of the party for a quickie—and resigned himself to an evening of schmoozing and maybe another dance with Flip if he got lucky.

Unfortunately it turned out he had made the dangerous mistake of underestimating his fake boyfriend's mother.

"Brayden," she said smoothly as she glided over to him not twelve seconds after he left the storeroom, leaving him almost certain that she'd seen Flip exit a minute before him and that she 100 percent thought they'd been boning. "There you are. I've been hoping for a dance."

Shovel talk! It's a shovel talk! Abort! Abort! shouted Brayden's hindbrain. But what was he going to do, run screaming from the queen at her own party? That seemed rude.

Dear Lord, if she's going to murder me, please ask her to make it quick. Amen. "Of course," he said, offering his hand and hoping his French accent wasn't

finished the last bite and wiped her hands yet
You're not like his other boyfriends."

t did *that* mean? Brayden looked down at
self-conscious. He thought he'd cleaned up
ut maybe he'd forgotten to tuck in a middle-
el somewhere. "Oh?"

y didn't dance like you. And they followed Flip
l night." Was Brayden supposed to do that? He
n't want to do that. "And they only wore black
." She said this last as though it disgusted her,
den realized her dress matched his vest.

sound like you didn't like them very much,"
arefully.

shrugged one bony shoulder. "They were
Flip likes you better."

den swallowed around a suddenly dry throat.
at makes you say that?"

ause you *are* better." She started ticking
on her fingers. "First there was *Armand*. He's
e a duke. But he didn't smile, and he smelled
e."

den took a moment to be fervently glad he'd
ed extra deodorant. "He sounds serious."

idn't even have fun at Midsummer. Midsummer
u get to drink elderflower wine and dance in the
lds and stay up all night. And he talked to me
a baby. I was seven and a half!"

ing seriously, Brayden agreed, "It sounds like
er off without him, for sure."

that, he didn't have a boyfriend for a long time.
e met *Adrian*." She inflected the name with the
quivalent of an eye roll as she ticked him off on
as well. "Aunt Constance said he followed Flip
a lost duck. Do ducks really get lost?"

too provincial. Speaking with Bernadette was one
thing; this was royalty. "Do you fox-trot?"

Queen Constance did, it turned out, fox-trot, and
while Brayden didn't enjoy dancing with her as much
as he had with Flip, she also didn't scoop out his liver
with a rusty spoon, so he was calling it a win.

On the stage, one of the current scholarship
students was belting a lively show-tune-type number,
and Brayden easily led the queen through the steps. She
didn't offer much in the way of conversation until they
were halfway through the dance, but perhaps she'd been
lulling him into a false sense of security.

"You're an excellent dancer," she commented as
he swung them expertly to avoid a collision with a
skilled pair of dancers. "When did you learn?"

"Kindergarten, more or less." He navigated them
through an easy spin. "My grandmother had a dance
studio, and I used to go there after school. Grandma
figured I might as well do the lessons too."

The queen tilted her head. "A shrewd woman."

"She would take that as the highest compliment."

She smiled. "How are you settling in this evening?
You seemed out of sorts earlier."

Ma'am, I was flat-out shitting my pants. He chose
his words carefully. "To be honest, meeting Flip's
parents, who happen to be the queen and prince consort
of a European country, and then being introduced to the
rest of said country as their crown prince's boyfriend was
kind of a lot to handle in five minutes." The song had
come to the key change. It would be winding down soon,
but not soon enough to get him out of this. "I should have
agreed to meet you earlier, when he asked."

"Why didn't you?"

Shit, he shouldn't have ad-libbed. Now he had to come up with an answer.

It shouldn't have surprised him that the truth fell out. "Deep-seated commitment issues." *Fuuuuuck.* No more drinking tonight. "It's a long story. But I'm glad I'm here now."

"Hmm," said Queen Constance. "Me too."

Oh God, she knows everything, Brayden thought, but fortunately the song ended, giving him an opportunity to escape. He bowed, and Her Majesty curtseyed and thanked him for the dance.

Brayden had sworn off more alcohol tonight, but he needed to do something with his mouth that wasn't talk, so he wandered to the outskirts of the room, found a server with tiny plates of some unrecognizable hors d'oeuvre, and took three of them to the first unoccupied table he found.

He was halfway through the second hors d'oeuvre—some kind of fish egg with cheese on toast? With capers? He had no idea, but it was delicious—when he realized that, in fact, he wasn't alone.

"Oh my God," he said automatically in English before switching to French. "I'm so sorry. I didn't see you there."

The blonde girl in the corner couldn't have been more than ten, and she was pushed as far into the corner as possible, as though she were becoming one with the wall. "It's okay," she said. "I'm used to it."

Brayden pushed his plate toward her. "You want one of these? They're weird but good."

She looked like she wanted to say yes but thought she shouldn't—fair, since she didn't know Brayden from Adam. But eventually hunger won out and she pulled the plate in front of her. "Thank you."

"You're welcome." Brayd
Where was this kid's guardian
things like this? Or maybe they ju
the exits and that was that? Or, sl
of the scholarship kids. Someho
horrifying. "So. Why are you sitt

She picked a caper off the
thing and ate it. "Why are *you*?"

Ouch. This girl knew wher
lot of people here that I don't k
do know are important and busy

Another caper. "Me too."

"Well," he said philosophica
other. I'm Brayden." He held his

She looked at him suspicio
hand on a linen napkin and sho

Clara—*Princess Clara*? H
impolite to ask. "Nice to meet

She ate another caper. I
deconstruct the entire thing and
if maybe she only liked the car
with Flip. You're a good dance

That answered his questi
leaving the *prince* off Flip's nam
she didn't think of him that way
of practice, starting when I was

Clara considered the remai
then took a bite of what remaine
When she had swallowed, sl
hands again. "Are you Flip's bc

"Uh… yeah. I am." Had
shovel talk to the nine-year-ol
devious. Brayden had agreed
realizing it would entail lying t

"I don't know. Maybe some of them do."

"Adrian smiled a little bit. More than Armand, anyway. But he was so boring. He didn't like anything except going to the beach. At least Armand liked cheese."

"Maybe too much," Brayden reminded her.

"Liking cheese is not the same as smelling of it." Clara pushed the empty plate to one side and leaned closer over the table as though to better examine him. "Now there's you."

"Now there's me," Brayden agreed, trying not to show fear. Curiosity, though—there was no help for that. "Why do you think Flip likes me better?"

"Because he smiles at you." He would have bet that if they'd been talking in English, she would have added *duh*. Brayden was torn between relief and disappointment at this simple answer, which didn't reveal much, but then Clara went on. "And he looks at you when he thinks you're not looking, like now."

Alarmed, Brayden moved his head to look, but Clara stopped him with her hand on his arm. "No, don't turn. He'll be embarrassed. Anyway. He always dances the opening dance with Aunt Constance, but tonight he danced with you. *And* he took you for ice cream."

Brayden felt a little faint. "He told you about that?"

"It's our spot," Clara said. "He promised he would only take special people there. So he must like you a *lot*."

Brayden had gone into the evening certain that no one would seriously believe Brayden thought he could be an appropriate suitor for a crown prince. And now here a nine-year-old had laid waste to his careful rationale. "Well," he said, and if it came out a little strangled, Clara had a pretty small sample size to compare it against. "I'm glad." Then, desperate to change the subject, he asked, "Do you want to dance?"

Clara's pleasant, open face shuttered. She frowned at the tabletop. "I don't know how."

Finally something Brayden felt equipped to respond to. "Then you're in luck, because it just so happens that I am a fantastic teacher." The orchestra was playing a leisurely waltz—boring under most circumstances, maybe, but perfect for a beginner. He stood and bowed, offering his hand. "Milady. Might I have this dance?"

For a second she looked at him, her lips pressed together in a tight line. Then she stood up and put her hand in his.

Brayden suspected Clara might have some musical training, because she had no trouble at all finding the beat. She watched with intent focus as Brayden demonstrated the natural step—first his part and then hers.

"The grip will be a little weird since I'm just a smidge taller than you, but we'll improvise." He put his hand on her shoulder instead of beneath it. "Ready to try?"

She pursed her lips in thought and then gave a decisive nod. "Okay."

"Count with me, then. We'll go on zero." Brayden counted down from nine, giving her three measures to get the rhythm. Then they were off, not exactly flying but not doing too badly either. Clara moved gracefully, though she was a bit quicker on her right than her left—a little practice would close that gap.

"You're doing great," Brayden said, noting a couple who appeared to have imbibed a little too freely heading in their direction. "We're going to try it going the other way now, okay? Or we're going to get run over." He indicated with his head.

Clara's eyes widened. "Okay."

He didn't want to push his luck by adding a leg cross on the fly, so he improvised a reverse step. It would have been perfect, except the drunk couple had sped up and changed course too. One of them bumped into Brayden hard enough to send him careening into Clara, though he managed to avoid doing her a worse injury than stepping on her toe.

"Oh my God," the woman who'd bumped into them said. She looked mortified. "I'm so sorry. Babe, I think maybe we should sit the next couple out and drink some water. Can I get you anything?" She directed this last to Brayden and Clara.

"I'm okay," Brayden said, hoping his protégée wouldn't be discouraged by their setback. "Clara?"

She shook her head that she didn't want anything, and the couple left.

"I'm sorry I stepped on your foot," Brayden said. "Even good dancers can't always avoid a collision if there's alcohol involved. Don't drink and dance. Are your toes okay?"

Clara looked at him as though he'd grown a second head. Then she smiled like the sun coming up and lifted the hem of her dress.

When she was standing, the hem went nearly to the floor. Now, though, Brayden could see that her left leg ended in a prosthetic just below the knee.

He shook his head and offered his hand once more. "Well, if your toes aren't hurt, do you want to try again?"

FLIP watched from across the room as Brayden sat down at Clara's table and struck up a conversation. He ached to join them, but he couldn't. Though the scholarship facilitator had taken over emcee duties, Flip had compatible people to introduce—dancers and choreographers, musicians and conductors, actors and directors—and hands to glad. Still, he did his best to move in that direction. Maybe he could steal Brayden for another dance. If not, at least Clara would regale him with her observations from people-watching.

He had made it halfway there when they got up to dance, and Flip stopped listening to the person he'd been speaking to. His aunt happened to be walking past, and he touched her arm as she went by and pointed discreetly to the lesson.

His conversation partner turned to look as well as Flip's cousin Clara took her first turn on the dance floor in Brayden's capable arms. Flip wanted to tell them to turn away and let her have this moment, since no one else seemed to be paying attention. But he didn't want to be rude.

"She's not bad for a first-timer," Flip's erstwhile companion commented.

Flip was still trying to pick his jaw up off the floor. Aunt Ines clutched his arm hard enough to bruise. "Did you put him up to that?"

He shook his head, not taking his eyes off them. "That's just... Brayden."

Ines dug her fingers deeper when the heiress and her husband got too close and then knocked into Brayden, pushing him into Clara. Flip's stomach knotted too. But the drunken couple ambled off, leaving—

Clara raising the hem of her dress to show her leg, *beaming*.

Ines sniffed. Flip wanted to sit down.

How was he supposed to pretend to end things between them when all he wanted was to begin something real?

"That's a good man," Ines said a few furious blinks later.

Flip couldn't disagree.

By the time he made it over to their table, the dancing seemed to have finished, and he interrupted a lively conversation about the merits of skiing versus snowboarding. Clara almost looked willing to entertain the idea of switching when she saw Flip.

"Flip!" She flung herself at his waist. "Brayden taught me the waltz."

He reminded himself she was too big to spin around, and she wouldn't like it in public anyway. "I saw. You didn't save your first waltz for me?"

"You were busy doing *prince things*. Brayden was bored."

Brayden sputtered and set down his water glass. "Hey, now—"

Flip grinned and leaned over their table. "I thought I might steal Brayden for a dance. If that's all right with you, Clara?"

Sighing exaggeratedly, she said, "I *guess*," and then burst into giggles.

Brayden let Flip pull him out of his seat and lead him back toward the dance floor. "Your cousin is a riot."

"Oh, believe me, I know."

The song wound down before they could do more than clasp hands, leaving them standing together somewhat awkwardly as the emcee introduced an entirely new group of musicians—and accompanying dancers.

"This is new," Brayden commented as a group of people in Nehru-style formalwear set themselves up at the back of the stage with a dhol drum, an ektar, and a sarangi. Then a man and two women took to the forestage, dressed in bright salwar kameez. When the musicians began to play, Flip was surprised to recognize a song his father had often played when he was growing up. Just as the emcee called on anyone who knew the dance to join in, Flip's father appeared through a parting crowd. He caught Flip's eye and smiled deeply.

Flip looked at Brayden. "I don't suppose you know how to dance a bhangra."

Brayden lifted a shoulder sheepishly. "Believe it or not, I do, actually."

Flip's father could never know. He'd have them married off inside a week.

"The instructors at my grandma's dance academy, we all used to take turns teaching each other. It was fun. I'm pretty rusty, though."

Clearing his throat, Flip gestured toward the space in front of the stage. All around them, the crowd had moved back to make room for the dancers. "Would you care to join me?"

Brayden looked torn, but he shook his head and squeezed his fingers around Flip's. He hadn't even realized they were still joined. "Another time. They're not doing this for some white boy from Scarborough. This is for you and your dad."

As though on cue, Irfan appeared over Flip's shoulder and gestured with both hands for him to join. Behind him the dance was already underway, with the three scholarship dancers forming the beginnings of a circle. Irfan moved to the beat as well, obviously itching to get started.

Flip cast a backward look at Brayden, hoping it didn't seem too longing, and then lost himself in the familiar movements as he shifted his weight from one foot to the other, kicked up his feet, and prayed Bernadette had left enough room for him to move without tearing a seam.

Tomorrow some right-wing blog would claim he was going to convert the entire country to Islam and outlaw eating beef—facts were not their strong suit—but tonight he didn't care. His father was in his element, moving with the practiced ease of someone who'd danced in a dozen Bollywood blockbusters, and his enthusiasm was contagious.

Flip spared a glance at Brayden as the song wore on and found him—consciously or not—dancing the same bedi step as Flip, clapping and hopping in place, several steps back from the action. Mostly, though, Flip needed his concentration for the dance, which was taken right from one of his father's movies. He had memorized it as a child, but that was a long time ago.

His father hadn't broken a sweat and didn't even huff for breath when he said, "Your Brayden seems like a nice boy."

Flip needed to copy his father's cardio routine. They traded places as the choreography called for, and Flip managed not to say *he's not my Brayden*. "I'm fond of him," he said, and wished he'd been able to agree with his father instead.

"And he can dance bhangra!"

Uh-oh. "Dad—"

Too late, though. He was dancing over to Brayden, still in perfect time with the choreography, only instead of the clap at the end of the bedi step he was making come-hither motions to get Brayden to join them.

Brayden protested for several seconds, long enough that the step changed to jhumar, but Irfan kept gesturing with his left hand even as he lifted his right, and finally Brayden gave in to the encouragement of the people around him and joined the dance for the last verse.

Flip's dad was probably composing the speech he'd give at their wedding.

Brayden obviously hadn't seen the movie—he moved just a split second behind the changes in the choreography. But his form was perfect—straight trunk, toes pointed up on dahmaal, low and wide on the chaal, arms at the perfect angle. And the way he smiled as he did it, broad and uncomplicated, oozing joy even as he shot Flip a vaguely sheepish expression…. Damn it. This wasn't what Flip had planned at all.

He hadn't meant to plate himself a perfect piece of cake and then deny himself the pleasure of eating it.

The dance wrapped up to boisterous applause and even a few whistles. Flip shook hands with the dancers and complimented their performance, flushed equally from the exertion and the attention to part of himself he normally kept private. He thanked the choreographer for inviting him to join in, but before the crowd could descend upon him, likely full of questions about bhangra, Brayden appeared at his elbow.

"I could use a water break," he said, sliding his arm through Flip's. Then he addressed the assembled guests. "Do you mind if I borrow him? I need someone to make sure I don't die of dehydration before I find a waiter. And maybe someone to double-check I didn't rip a seam."

Flip let himself be led away, not sure whether the emotion swirling through his chest was gratitude or dread.

BY the time Brayden climbed into the back of the car for Celine to drive them back to his hotel, he felt like he'd been through a meat grinder. He practically fell against Flip when the engine started.

It didn't help that their adventure together was coming to a close.

He took a deep breath, inhaling whatever simple soap Flip washed with, and made himself sit up. Just because he felt pathetic didn't mean he had to act like it. He had some dignity. "Is this the part where I tell you I had a really nice time tonight?"

Flip's smile looked as tired as Brayden felt. "Is that your way of letting me down easy?"

Brayden shrugged and turned to look out the window. The lamps were all lit and cast the streets in a sort of cozy, ethereal glow. Beautiful. "That's the story, right? I'm supposed to break your heart."

"That's what we agreed," Flip said softly.

The car rolled down otherwise empty cobblestone streets. It had to be two in the morning, if not later. Tomorrow—late; Brayden wasn't getting out of bed before ten at the earliest—he'd check out one of the hop-on, hop-off tours or maybe see about a trip into the countryside. He'd heard there was snow in the mountains, and a horse-drawn sleigh would make a great Instagram post.

It probably wouldn't be as much fun alone, though.

"After we fake break up, can we still be friends?"

Flip's silence was all the answer he needed, but Brayden turned to look at him anyway. His expression didn't give much away—he'd probably had actual lessons on maintaining a poker face—but his lips turned down at the corners, and the skin around his eyes was tight.

"Yeah," Brayden agreed quietly. "They're not going to believe we broke up if we keep hanging out together. It was a nice thought, though."

The car turned the corner onto his hotel's street. Finally Flip said, "It really was a good night. I've never had that much fun at the Night of a Thousand Lights before. And that's…. Thank you for that."

Brayden was about to tell him he should do it more often, that fun looked good on him, but he found himself focusing on the window past Flip's head. People seemed to have congregated on the street outside his hotel. At two o'clock in the morning on a misty, chilly December night. Were they trying to catch pneumonia?

The car slowed to a stop, and Brayden automatically reached for the door, too tired to remember he ought to wait for Celine. But when he popped it open, a bright light blinded him and someone shouted a question in French, too garbled for Brayden to hear over another, this one in English.

"There he is! Mr. Wood, how long have you and the crown prince been an item?"

"Is there any truth to the rumors of a secret engagement?"

"Mr. Wood, can you comment on Prince Antoine-Philippe's management of the Crown Mining Co.?"

"Over here, Brayden! How big is the prince's—"

A hand closed around his arm and jerked him back into the car. Over the voices of the reporters, he heard Flip curse and then instruct Celine to take them back to the ring road until otherwise instructed. Flip leaned over him to close the door, and Celine peeled rubber as they sped away, leaving Brayden's hotel in their dust.

The roar of the engine quieted some a few moments later, and a hand touched Brayden's arm. "Brayden? Are you okay?"

He took a deep breath and shook his head, which felt stuffed with cotton. "I think so. What *was* that?"

"Paparazzi." Flip's expression could have frozen the fires of hell. "The ball was televised. Someone at the hotel must have recognized you and leaked your whereabouts to the press."

Brayden's heart was still beating about twenty times a minute too fast. "Jesus. Well, that's inconvenient." All his stuff was there.

Flip slumped back in his seat and wiped a hand over his face. "I should have known this would happen. The press was always going to be interested in you, and then I introduced you as my boyfriend.... I shouldn't have done that."

"Hey," Brayden said weakly, too raw from shock to hide the sting those words evoked. Tonight was just an *arrangement*, and he'd let himself forget that. Flip wasn't the only one who'd lost sight of practical matters. "I agreed to this plan. I demand my share of the should-have-known-better blame. I was too dazzled by the whole... 1 percent glamor and charm and once-in-a-lifetime thing to stop and think."

That hung in the air for a few heartbeats before Flip said quietly, "The press attention comes with the territory, I'm afraid."

"I guess." Brayden leaned his head against the window and closed his eyes. God, he was tired.

They drove in silence for a few more moments, and then Flip asked, "What do you want to do?"

"Honestly?" He forced his eyes open again and glanced across the car. "I just want to go to bed and deal with this in the morning."

Flip nodded, straightened his posture, and knocked on the partition. It rolled down a second later. "Take us back to the palace, please, Celine."

The partition rolled up, and Flip turned his attention to Brayden. In the light from the streetlamps they passed, he seemed very human. "You can stay with me tonight."

Chapter Six

BRAYDEN woke up cradled in the embrace of the world's most comfortable mattress. For several moments he lay there with his eyes closed, stretching languorously. The sheets had to have a thread count in the thousands, and the comforter was the perfect weight. This hotel was worth every penny. He rolled over and snuggled his face deep into a fluffy, perfectly supportive pillow.

A pillow that smelled like Flip's soap.

Brayden's eyes shot open.

He was in a large, airy, yet somehow cozy bedroom, the walls a muted gray blue. Three floor-to-ceiling windows stretched upward fifteen feet or so. The heavy damask curtains remained undrawn, so weak sunlight filtered in. It had to be getting close to noon, if not later. Against one wall stood an antique writing desk, meticulously cared for and in perfect condition, with a scattering of documents on the surface. The bed was a king-size four-poster that could have been pulled straight from any child's picture book featuring a castle.

Aside from Brayden and a mountain of pillows, it was empty. The smooth coverlet on the other side indicated Brayden had stayed there alone.

Oh my God. Did I kick a prince out of bed last night?

No. Surely it was just one of Flip's many guest bedrooms. But then why did the sheets smell like him? And why the obviously-in-use writing desk?

Okay, so this was Flip's bedroom. Now that the fog of sleep had lifted, Brayden remembered Flip showing him in here, offering him a pair of pajamas to change into—which he was wearing, and they were awesome—pointing out the en suite bath, and then leaving him to settle in for the night. Brayden had been so tired and discombobulated he hadn't thought twice about whose bed this was.

Brayden sat up.

Someone had set out a bathrobe—simple but luxurious—and a pair of slippers, which he put on, because the floor was freezing. The perils of nineteenth-century architecture, probably. Then he went and got lost in a bathroom larger than his first apartment, standing under the spray of a shower that definitely did not rely on nineteenth-century plumbing.

Afterward he dried off on the most luxurious Egyptian cotton towel known to man and, faced with the choice of putting his pajamas back on or raiding Flip's closet, redressed in the pj's.

And then he had no choice but to face the music. With no small amount of trepidation, he crept to the massive wooden door to the bedroom and pulled. It opened soundlessly on smooth hinges, onto an enormous but simply appointed living room with the same towering ceilings as the bedroom. Flip sat on a comfortable-looking sofa, wearing a pair of wire-rimmed reading glasses, chinos, and a burgundy sweater over a collared shirt. He had his slippered feet propped up on a footstool, and a cup of coffee steamed invitingly on the end table next to him.

Brayden froze in the doorway, his stomach a rictus of knots. This was so... easily, comfortably domestic. He'd never expected to find himself here at all, never mind with a prince—a sweet, genuine, attractive prince.

A sweet, genuine, attractive prince whose parents and entire country thought he was dating Brayden.

Brayden tapped his fingers against the door and Flip looked up.

"So," Brayden said. "Good morning."

Flip set his newspaper down on a whole stack of newspapers on the couch. Brayden clenched and unclenched his fists.

"Good afternoon, actually." Flip moved the pile of papers to the side and gestured for Brayden to sit.

Brayden sat. "So. How famous am I?"

Flip cleared his throat. "Maybe we should have breakfast first. Well, lunch."

Oh boy. "That bad, huh?"

Grimacing, Flip gestured to the far wall, where a console table stood with a variety of electronic devices. "You plugged in your cell phone last night. It's been, ah, fairly active for the past hour and a half."

Brayden's stomach made a rude noise. At first he thought he might be sick—but no. "Okay, yes, lunch first and then... that." Which brought him to another salient point. "Uh, I don't suppose I can borrow something that's not pajamas?"

"No need, I think." Flip pointed out a familiar rolling suitcase that had been conveniently stashed out of the way just underneath the console table. "I took the liberty of asking Celine to retrieve that from the hotel for you. Let me know if there's anything missing. We can threaten them with legal action."

Now there was a scenario he hadn't foreseen. "You think someone wanted to get their hands on my Andrew Christians?"

"I think the staff at your hotel demonstrated a deplorable lack of respect for your privacy, and I wouldn't rule out further trespass." The hard edge to his voice made Brayden wonder which poor hotel manager had gotten an earful. "It was one of the employees who leaked your whereabouts on Twitter. Hence the impromptu welcome from the paparazzi." He blew out a breath and the tension in his shoulders relaxed. "That's really all you traveled with in that little bag?"

Brayden shrugged. "The hotel has a laundry service."

Flip shook his head. "You should see my father pack for a trip. It's incredible. Mother calls him *il divo*."

Brayden wondered where Flip fell on the packing scale. "They seem very…." He waved his hand, trying to encompass their general lovey-doveyness without saying it out loud. "My parents are like that too."

"It's wonderful and occasionally mortifying, isn't it?"

"That's an accurate assessment." Brayden stood and retrieved the bag. The light on his phone was flashing with just about every possible notification, and as he stared at it, it began to ring. Lina's face popped up on the call display. He sighed. "I might as well do this now, if you don't mind…?"

Flip shook his head and gestured to the bedroom. "Please, be my guest."

Brayden took the call sitting on Flip's obscenely luxurious bed. He didn't think his legs could stand the scolding. And he was right, sort of.

"*Oh my God,*" Lina almost yelled in his ear. "I've been calling you for two hours!"

That was hardly Brayden's fault. "Stop getting out of bed so early."

"Me? Tell that to *Grandma*, she's the one who woke me up. 'Brayden is dancing on my YouTube suggested videos,' she says." Oh hell. He wasn't looking forward to that conversation either. "Are you seriously telling me you neglected to mention your mystery sugar daddy is a legit prince? *A legit prince you're actually dating?*"

"I...," Brayden said and then stopped. He and Flip hadn't officially broken up as far as anyone knew. Not that there had been anything real *to* break up, officially, but—he glanced at the window. How good was spy technology these days? Was someone eavesdropping on his cell phone conversation through the glass with some kind of fancy laser listening device? "Sorry."

"Sorry? Good Lord." There was a thump. Brayden imagined Lina flopped over dramatically on her bed. "Tell me everything."

"What? No. I just got up. I'm starving. We're doing lunch in like ten minutes."

And didn't that sound incriminating. He held the phone away from his ear as Lina shrieked. "Where are you right now?"

"Uh. In Flip's apartment at the palace."

"*Flip?*"

"That's his name. I mean, his name is His Royal Highness Prince Antoine-Philippe, but that's a mouthful."

"I can't believe you didn't tell me. You are the worst brother ever."

"Hey!"

"Details," Lina persisted. "This is the guy who's got you dating again after ten years of slutty denial. *And* you lied to me about it. I demand compensation. What's he like?"

Sighing, Brayden crawled farther back on the bed and stared up at the hammered tin ceiling. The problem, he suspected, with telling Lina that Flip was kind and compassionate and warm and funny and generous and charming was that Brayden would have to acknowledge, at least to himself, that the primary problem with their relationship was that it was fake. "Handsome. Charming. Good dancer. Good with kids." He remembered how Clara looked at him like he hung the moon, and how obviously he adored her. "He loves his family, and he'd do anything for his people."

Yep. There they were—feelings. The worst.

"God, you have it bad, huh?"

Brayden swallowed. He recognized the truth, even if he didn't know what to do about it. "Would I be here if I didn't?"

"Bro." Lina's voice broke. Oh no, she was going to cry. "I know… I know things weren't easy for you after Thomas died. I know we don't talk about what he meant to you. And we don't have to. But I just… I'm so glad that you want to stop punishing yourself for something that wasn't your fault."

Shit, now *Brayden* wanted to cry—partly because Lina was right, and partly because she wasn't. He wasn't really dating Flip, and he hadn't stopped punishing himself, even though he desperately wanted to. He didn't know how. "I, ah… thanks," he said, voice thick.

"Uh-huh." She sniffled and then inhaled audibly in an obvious attempt to rally. "So, what's he like in bed?"

Brayden laughed in spite of himself, swiping at the single tear that had escaped. "A perfect gentleman," he said, which was true. Flip had let him have the entire bedroom to himself. "And that's all I'm saying."

"I hope he gets over that if he wants to keep you around."

She knew him way too well, but if he said anything else, she'd figure out they hadn't slept together at all, and then she'd *really* get suspicious. "I have to go. Twenty bucks says Grandma sent me a ten-page critique on our dance via text message, and I should probably call Mom and Dad. And have lunch. Seriously, I am starving."

Lina let him go, and he took a few deep breaths before thumbing open his texts.

Grandma had restrained herself to only four texts. His mother had sent seven.

Brayden went easy on himself and opened Grandma's first.

Brayden, sweetheart, what a handsome dance partner you found. That one wasn't so bad. Then, *You need to watch that footwork on the change steps, young man.* Fine, he probably deserved that; he was surprised she hadn't sent one admonishing him for not practicing enough. Next, *Did I read right that your partner is really your boyfriend? And he's the prince of Lyngria?*

Brayden scrolled down to the final message.

Tell His Royal Highness to let you lead next time.

He snorted in spite of himself. He loved his grandmother.

Mom, though—well, he loved her too, but she could be a little overbearing sometimes. Probably that had to do with her only son's heart being tragically broken at sixteen. With great trepidation, he opened her texts.

Grandma says you're dating the crown prince of a European country. At first I thought maybe dementia was setting in, like it did with your grandfather.

Brayden winced. His mother knew how to make that guilt trip hurt.

I know you're not interested in dating. You tell me so often enough. And where would you even meet a prince? But then I watched the video. When I saw the way you looked at him…. Oh, sweetie, I'm so happy. You seemed so determined to be alone, and I didn't want to push—

Brayden's throat closed up.

—but you've needed a friend these past ten years, if nothing else. I'm so glad you found that, even if I'm hurt you didn't tell me.

Fuck. He closed his eyes and bit his lip. How could he tell her the truth? Her heart would break for him all over again.

I'll let you be, since I bet you have lots to talk about with your partner this morning. Call me when you can, though, okay? I love you.

Brayden sniffed once, wiped his eyes on the sleeve of Flip's bathrobe, and then texted, *Thanks, Mom. Love you too.*

He dressed by rote—underwear, socks, jeans, T-shirt, sweater. Not knowing what else to do with them, he folded the pajamas and left them on the bed. Then he hung the bathrobe behind the door. The slippers he kept.

Now he just had to go out there and tell Flip—

What, exactly?

A quiet knock on the door. "Brayden?" Pause. Brayden imagined Flip saying *Are you decent?* and almost giggled. "May I come in?"

Time to face the music. He cleared his throat. "Sure."

Flip did, quietly, and closed the door behind him. He kept his voice low. "My parents are in the sitting room. I didn't want you to be unprepared."

"Oh. Right. Thanks, I guess." He ran a hand through his hair, the skin all down his back prickling. "I mean, we should probably decide what we're going to tell them."

Flip managed to imbue even a grimace with a sort of upper-class eloquence. "I want to apologize again. I shouldn't have let them think we were dating in the first place, and now I've dragged you and your whole family into a lie."

Brayden smiled weakly. "You're not the only one who had a hand in this. I could've said no." He blew out a long breath.

"I should have known better." He shook his head. "On top of it all, you've lost any anonymity you might have had. Anywhere you go in this country, people will know you. You'll be hounded."

Brayden swallowed hard and grasped for words. "I can change my vacation plans, go back to Paris, maybe try Copenhagen. I mean, my family will be pissed—they're already super invested in this fake relationship, but—"

Flip's head came up. "You didn't tell them the truth?"

Brayden fought the urge to squirm. "I didn't exactly lie either. But no, I let them think…. Past trauma, remember? They haven't even met you, and they already love you for healing my tragic broken heart." Whoops, a little bitterness spilled out in that last sentence.

At that, Flip's eyebrow and lip twitched. He was quiet for a moment. Then he said, enunciating each syllable, "Perhaps… I might suggest a solution."

Brayden flopped back onto the perfect mattress. "I'm all ears."

"I propose that we continue the charade."

And he sat up again. That sounded dangerous… and dangerously tempting. "Oh?"

Flip shrugged, looking only half as sheepish as Brayden felt listening to his explanation. "It's too late to undo what we've done. But if we continue seeing each other, you'll still be able to do some sightseeing unmolested—with royal security, but better than nothing. Our families will be none the wiser and can go on believing we've found happiness a little while longer. After your holiday is over, we can pretend to have a long-distance relationship that ends in an amicable breakup, which should satisfy everyone."

Everyone but me. "You're talking about me staying here with you for two and a half weeks… including Christmas."

Flip twitched again. "If you'd be more comfortable in your own rooms, I can arrange that. And I'll make your excuses for you at Christmas. No one will bother you if you wish to be left alone."

Damn it. He really *was* a prince. "It would look a little weird if we shared a bed one night and then just stopped. I mean, where did you even sleep last night?"

For a second, he would have sworn Flip was blushing. "The couch is comfortable enough in a pinch."

Shit, he really had kicked Flip out of bed. "Okay, no." *Don't do it don't do it don't do it.* "If we're going to do this, we're doing it. I'm not going to kick you out of your own bed again. So either you let me take the couch, and if someone catches us we'll just say I have insomnia"—Flip already looked mutinous at this idea, as though Brayden rejecting his hospitality offended him on a deeply personal level—"or we can share."

Well. He did it.

"You… wouldn't mind?"

Brayden gestured at the enormous bed he sat on. "I think there's room for two. Maybe four if you're friendly. We're adults, we're both gay, it's not like there's gonna be any surprises. You've already seen me mostly naked."

Flip almost smiled. "True… but the reverse isn't."

"You're right. I demand we share a bed so I can see you in a similar state of dishabille. Seems only fair."

Now Flip did smile—that slightly rueful one Brayden was getting very attached to and seemed to inspire on a regular basis. "Then I suppose it's settled."

"Good. Great. Awesome." Brayden's stomach growled. "So about that lunch…."

FLIP probably should have come clean, to his parents if not the press. But they had never taken so quickly to one of his boyfriends, and if he were being perfectly honest with himself, he wanted to keep Brayden around for selfish reasons. Brayden made him laugh, made him consider life from new angles.

Brayden made him *feel* alive, woke something in him that had been dormant so long Flip had despaired that it existed. Maybe he would only get to experience it for another few weeks, but that seemed better than nothing.

Of course, in the immediate present, their deception meant his whole immediate family, plus Brayden, was reading tabloids aloud to each other at Flip's dining table while they ate a tray of sandwiches and other finger foods. It was perhaps a tradition Brayden could have been introduced to more gently.

"The Brown Prince?" Brayden read from the pile of English ones. "Seriously?"

"Is it the racism or the bad wordplay?" Flip's mother asked as she glanced up from a German scandal sheet.

"I mean, both? I get that you're probably used to the racism part, which sucks." Brayden gestured with a tiny crustless cucumber sandwich. "But 'brown prince' is really bad. Like, are all the right-wing bloggers in your country just super lazy?"

On second thought, perhaps Brayden didn't need a gradual introduction to their peculiar brand of family therapy.

Flip's dad raised his newspaper. "Most of the zanier ones are in German or French. This one speculates on how many goats I'll demand for a dowry." He turned his attention to Brayden, expression serious. "Does your family have goats?"

"My parents have a cat. She does eat everything, though, so maybe she's part goat. Does that count?"

Irfan waved a hand. "I'm sure we can work something out."

Flip groaned and let himself put his face in his hands for just a moment. He rested his elbows on the table. "I knew you'd be like this."

Flip had originally planned to go into the Crown Mining Co. head office today and finish making inquiries about turning the company over to public interest. Instead he'd started the day getting Brayden's luggage retrieved from his hotel and reading about his own escapades in the press.

Prince Flips for New Man.

He was tempted to track down the rest of that bottle of tequila.

Funny. He'd invented the harebrained idea of taking Brayden as his plus-one to keep the tabloids off his back, and instead he seemed to have invited a scandal. And while he didn't enjoy being the focus of tabloid speculation, this felt different.

Maybe because his relationship with Brayden existed in print only.

On the one hand, he didn't want to complain that Brayden and his father got along so well. On the other hand, maybe if Flip's parents liked Brayden less, Flip could have just told them the truth.

"You'll have to make a statement, of course." Flip's mother addressed this to him, but she flicked her gaze over Brayden when she said it as well, as though to let him know she expected him to be there.

Flip had anticipated that, though he didn't look forward to it. "Of course."

"And I expect you'll want to rearrange your schedule to spend some time together." Flip's trips home always included a plethora of visits to schools and hospitals, charitable foundations, and so on.

"I don't want to take you away from anything important," Brayden protested. "I haven't been on an official palace tour yet. There are probably tons of things I can do to keep busy."

"I'm sure we can work out a compromise," Flip said, and suddenly his parents were looking at him as though he'd grown a second head. "What?"

"What?" his mother echoed, putting aside her tabloid and reaching for a legal pad and pen. "No, nothing, never mind." She shook her head and uncapped the pen. "Let's talk about this statement, shall we?"

The drafting itself didn't take long. The royal publicist—"That's not a real thing!" Brayden attempted to protest and was wrong again—revised it in a handful of minutes, but he took one look at Brayden's outfit and sent him away. "You can't appear on national TV dressed like that, not when you're representing the Royal House of Lyngria."

"We're hardly married. We've been dating for five minutes," Flip protested on Brayden's behalf. Who cared if Brayden looked like, well, a commoner? He was one. So were most people.

"Is he going to send me back to Bernadette?" Brayden stage-whispered.

"Perhaps I can lend him something appropriate," Flip suggested. Custom-ordering a new wardrobe seemed extreme.

Cedric blanched. "Good God, no. Do you know what people will say when they realize he's wearing your clothes? And they *will* notice."

Brayden raised his eyebrows. "That I'm sleeping in his bed?" he guessed. "Which I'm also doing."

Cedric appealed to Flip. "This man is not to speak into the microphone."

Oh no. Flip valued Cedric's expertise, but occasionally his snobbiness conflicted with his general good intentions. Flip didn't like to pull rank, but the situation called for it. Narrowing his eyes, he said, "This man has a name, and he will be treated with respect whether or not I am present. That includes the same self-determination accorded to anyone else in this family. Is that understood?"

Cedric flushed guiltily and cut his gaze back to Brayden. "Of course, Your Highness. Mr. Wood, I apologize. That was rude of me."

Naturally Brayden shrugged it off. "It's fine, dude, I definitely do not want to speak into a microphone about my relationship with the prince. Like, at all."

With that settled, Flip let his hackles lie flat again. "That said, perhaps an etiquette lesson or two wouldn't be amiss. Cedric, if you could arrange that?"

Brayden said, "Hey!"

Cedric allowed the tiniest fraction of a smile.

They left following Cedric's promise to have a selection of suitable clothing in Brayden's size sent posthaste to Flip's apartment in the palace. As they parted, Brayden leaned in, and his shoulder bumped Flip's. "Guess we better not tell him you lent me your pajamas."

Flip didn't bother to stifle his grin.

He made the official announcement just after four, with his parents behind him to one side and Brayden to the other in a smart navy cashmere sweater and wool trousers. But of course the press couldn't simply leave it at that.

"Your Highness, after your appearance at the Night of a Thousand Lights, many people are drawing parallels between your relationship with Mr. Wood and Queen Constance's romance with Prince Irfan. Can you comment on that?"

Flip's parents had gotten engaged three weeks after the ball and married a year later—hardly enough time, he remembered his grandmother complaining fondly, to plan a royal wedding. "As Brayden and I were well acquainted long before the ball, I'm afraid those parallels are rather divergent."

"Your Highness, you canceled an appearance at the Crown Mining Co. for later today. Can we expect more events to fall by the wayside as you spend more time with Mr. Wood?"

With the ease of years of practice, Flip bit back the *oh sod off, I canceled one event* that desperately wanted to slip out. "The mine appearance has been rescheduled to Monday to accommodate a necessary security check after Brayden's privacy was compromised at his hotel. I don't anticipate further emergencies."

A handful of other members of the press asked questions of varying levels of impertinence, but the whole ordeal was over by four thirty. They spent a few hours socializing in the palace common area with his whole family—Brayden challenged Clara to a game of Sorry!—but when Brayden's eyelids started to droop, they begged off a family dinner to eat at the table in Flip's rooms.

"Are you going to make it through dinner?" Flip asked, only half joking, the third time Brayden yawned into his water glass.

Brayden made a sheepish face. "Sorry. I'm mostly over the jet lag, but today's been all over the place, and I'm still not used to the whole 'gets dark at two thirty' thing."

"To be honest, I'm tempted to retire early myself."

Brayden raised his eyebrows. "Yeah? You don't seem that tired."

"I was raised not to show weakness," Flip said with no small amount of sarcasm. It worked—Brayden flashed a tired grin.

"I don't know, I think I've seen you fall asleep with your mouth open on the flight."

Brat, Flip thought fondly. He could have been embarrassed, but if they were going to pretend to be a couple for the next two and a half weeks, it seemed prudent to get over that embarrassment now. Likely it wouldn't be the last time Brayden found him catching flies. "Do I snore? I can send someone out for earplugs."

"You're good." Brayden finished his water and set the empty glass on the cart that the palace staff would remove later on. "I don't know about me, though. You might need them for yourself."

"I'm sure I can make it through one night." Most of the country's shops would be closed tomorrow, but Flip would be able to find earplugs if absolutely necessary.

They returned their dishes to the wheeled cart, and Flip called for housekeeping to come fetch it while Brayden took his turn in the bathroom.

Housekeeping came and went. Flip sat on the couch, but he was restless and jumped up again a second later. It had been only a few months since he'd shared a bed with Adrian, but that was different. They had dated for a year, and they were comfortable with each other physically.

Of course, physicality aside, Flip felt more comfortable with Brayden than he had with anyone since secondary school, so that excuse didn't hold water. He might as well admit to himself that he was attracted to Brayden—that he wanted their arrangement to grow beyond the charade they'd begun. He wanted to kiss Brayden, make him laugh, make him gasp, make him moan—

"Bollocks," Flip muttered aloud. He'd chosen a poor time to consider that train of thought.

A second later he heard the water shut off in the bathroom, and then Brayden poked his head into the living room. "You're up," he said, voice a little softer than Flip was used to—an intimate voice, part of him noted, for an intimate time.

Damn it.

It turned out that left to his own devices, Brayden slept in boxer briefs and a long-sleeved T-shirt, faded with years of use, that read *Maplewood High School Baseball Team*. Flip tore his gaze away from the name emblazoned across those broad shoulders and removed his own favorite pajamas from the wardrobe. Then he closed the bathroom door behind him to have a private, if very brief, crisis.

What was he doing? He was about to get in bed with a man he barely knew because, at the end of the day, he was too much of a coward to tell his parents the truth—

that Brayden had agreed to attend the ball as a favor and nothing more. Because it had been so long since his parents had been so full of anticipation, as though they'd known Brayden was special even before they met him. Because they were right, Brayden *was* special, only now Flip had gotten tangled up in the lie and—

Brush your teeth, he told himself firmly.

His brain was still spinning when he left the bathroom. Brayden looked up from his cell phone and cracked a tired smile when Flip opened the door. "What happened to the fancy pj's?"

Self-consciously, Flip glanced down at himself. These were his favorites, a decades-old set of flannel bottoms with holes in the hems and a college T-shirt. "They're in pristine condition because I never wear them except on Christmas morning. Don't tell my aunt. She gets me a new set every year."

Brayden crossed his heart. "Scout's honor." He set his phone on the bedside table. "I never thought—is this side okay? I'm a left-side-of-the-bed guy, but it's your bed, your rules."

Flip's brain took an abrupt turn into pornography, and it took him a split second too long to find his voice. "It's fine. I don't have a side preference, but I find it too drafty close to the windows."

Brayden grinned. "Good thing you found a nice Canadian boy to take the cold side of the bed, then."

"Nice? Is that what you are?" Flip slid between the sheets and automatically turned to face Brayden. He was right—there was plenty of room for two and little chance they would brush against each other by accident, never mind initiate anything inappropriate.

"Hey, I'm good enough to fake date you. What, Prince Antoine-Philippe doesn't date nice boys?"

Flip honestly thought about it and had to wince. "Not historically." He paused. "Actually, as a family, our track record for nonscandalous relationships is fairly terrible."

Brayden snuggled down across from him and faced Flip. "Oh?"

"Well, I told you about my parents. And my mother's younger brother—Clara's father—he's worse."

Now Brayden raised his eyebrows. "Present tense? I sort of assumed he was dead."

"No, just removed from the line of succession and banned from the country." Off Brayden's look of surprise, he elaborated. "He never approved of my father, but he didn't try to do anything about it until he had an heir of his own. His failed power grab coincided with the discovery of his affair with Clara's nanny."

"Jesus. Your family doesn't do anything by halves." His expression turned soft but still shrewd. "Clara said your exes were boring. She didn't mention any inherent evil…?"

He was fishing, but somehow Flip didn't mind. "The ones she's met weren't evil. She maybe had a point about the boring thing, though." He sucked in a breath and debated how much of the truth to give away. But then he decided that Brayden could find out nearly anything he withheld on the internet anyway. "Before Clara was born, though, when I was still at boarding school in the UK, my *first* boyfriend, he was a piece of work."

Brayden tucked his hands under his pillow. "Yeah?"

"I mean, we were children. I suppose it's possible he didn't grow up to be the Antichrist." That got a soft smile, but not the laugh he'd been angling for. Brayden could already read him too well for that. "I was a shy teenager. Miles was one of the 'in' group. Everyone liked him. Everyone wanted to *be* like him."

Somehow Flip half expected Brayden to say *but you're a prince*. But he didn't. He just shifted his body some and drew his legs closer to his chest. "And you?"

Flip shook his head slightly and tried to play it off, though he had a feeling Brayden would see right through him. "I fancied myself in love with him, of course. When he started wanting to spend time with me, I felt…."

Brayden waited.

"Included," Flip decided. Until then he'd felt so conspicuous—few boys at his prestigious school came from any parentage other than white—and his innate shyness made it difficult enough to make friends. Add his sexuality on top of that…. "Miles was out and proud, defiantly so. When he wanted to be my boyfriend…."

"You were pretty pumped, huh?"

"I'm surprised my teachers didn't have to scrape me off the ceiling."

"So what happened?"

Flip shrugged. This part of the story hurt the worst. "Oh, we dated for a little while, and then he got tired of me and sold his story to a tabloid."

Brayden inhaled a sharp breath. "Oh, Flip."

He suddenly felt the urge to turn away. "It's nothing near as awful as what happened to you—"

"What, because nobody died means it didn't hurt to be betrayed like that?" His voice was as soft as the pillowcase beneath Flip's head. "Come on. It's not a contest."

Flip inhaled through his nose, held it for a moment, and then let it out slowly. "I know that. In theory."

Brayden gave him a wry twist of a smile. "It's always the application that's the trick."

"Did you study psychology?" Flip asked a bit accusatorily, smiling a bit in spite of himself.

"Just the freshman 100 course. I majored in modern languages."

Of course he did. Of course Flip had been too blind to see how perfect Brayden was for him until he'd committed to pretend to date him, and trying to change the rules now would be not only awkward but inexcusable. "How many do you speak?"

"Six." He yawned and snuggled into his pillow. "Why, how many do you speak?"

"Five." Now he felt like he should be picking up Spanish in his spare time.

Brayden had closed his eyes, but he opened them again and smiled sleepily. "Hey. Something I beat you at. Imagine that."

Flip made a face at him, prompting a sleepy snort. "It's not a contest," he said, mimicking Brayden's line from earlier.

"Yeah, yeah." He yawned again, and it struck Flip how young he looked like that, wearing a T-shirt from his youth, curled up in bed and almost hugging his pillow. He was obviously exhausted.

"Go to sleep," Flip murmured, feeling suddenly protective.

"Mmm," Brayden agreed. "Turn off the lights, then."

With a quiet laugh, Flip turned to do just that. The room plunged into darkness. If not for Brayden's quiet breathing, he might have been alone.

"Good night, Brayden."

That steady breathing was his only reply.

Chapter Seven

BRAYDEN woke to the distant sound of running water. He stretched and opened his eyes, but with no light spilling from behind the heavy drapes, he couldn't guess the time. His body told him to keep sleeping, even if Flip wasn't, but he was overheating. In search of cooler sheets, he rolled into the middle of the bed and kicked the coverlet down. Perfect. Oblivion claimed him again.

The next time he opened his eyes, Flip was walking past from the bathroom, wearing only those ancient flannel pajama bottoms that clung to Flip's ass and hips—and nicely framed his cock, which Brayden discovered when Flip turned thirty degrees to grab something from the wardrobe. It wasn't Brayden's fault. The bed was at cock level.

No, Brayden told his own dick, firmly, and closed his eyes, knowing he was blushing and praying Flip didn't stop to notice he wasn't sleeping.

Finally he heard the door to the bathroom snick closed and he let out a long breath. It figured Flip would be just as gorgeous shirtless in ratty pj's as he was in a custom-fit tux. Brayden had better get used to that.

He was halfway back to sleep and getting cold—his shirt had ridden up his back and he was starting to goose-bump—and debating pulling up the covers again when the bathroom door opened again and he lost his chance. Flip's footsteps fell soft but sure nearly all the way to the door, and then he paused.

Brayden panicked, sure he'd been caught—though why that mattered when Flip was dressed and presumably not sporting morning wood, he couldn't have said. But he kept breathing as Flip approached the bed, made a soft *tsk*ing noise, and twitched the blankets up to Brayden's shoulders before he left.

Brayden's heart wanted to have feelings about it, but he fell asleep in self-defense.

When he finally crawled out of bed for good, his phone proclaimed it to be nine, and he quickly showered, dressed in Cedric-approved clothing, and went in search of Flip and/or coffee and/or food, in that order of preference. A note on the dining table informed him Flip had gone off for a rescheduled meeting with someone from the mining company and would likely not return until dinner. But it did give instructions for ordering breakfast, and a carafe of coffee sat waiting for him on the sideboard, so the morning wasn't a total loss.

Along with the breakfast instructions—which Brayden used to order yogurt, fruit, and scrambled eggs, and felt heinously awkward about—Flip had left a series of contacts Brayden might find interesting. He could call Cedric if he wanted to get started on that etiquette lesson (ha, ha, Brayden thought) or the palace private-tour operator (maybe), and so on.

He called the tour operator first. Her name was Louisa, she was a college student studying international relations, and if she gave a single crap that Brayden was allegedly sleeping with the crown prince, she didn't show it. She chatted casually with him while she showed him around the rooms on the usual tour, though "we're actually closed to the public today since it's Sunday."

That probably explained why Flip had suggested it for today, then—no chance of Brayden being mobbed.

Like any respectable royal family, Flip's had its share of bad blood and crackpots. "And this is where, in 1741, King Claudius pushed the archbishop out the window. He survived, and the king was excommunicated and replaced on the throne by his sister."

Brayden looked down at the drop. "Talk about having God on your side."

"Since that incident, Lyngria has maintained a strict policy of the separation of church and state."

Inevitably the tour also included a trip to the other throne room.

"You know, I never got why this is included in so many tours," Brayden said as he stuck his head into the royal bathroom—this one not in use since the early 1900s. "'Come and see the room where the ancestors of our nation's sovereign once took their morning dump.' I don't see the appeal."

"Me neither," said Louisa, "but you won't believe how many people I get taking selfies in here."

Brayden supposed the ornately appointed room, done in rich purple velvet and gold leaf, would make an interesting backdrop for an Insta post. And hey, there was a window for royal ventilation, so maybe the lighting was good.

The tour of the public areas ended, and Louisa handed him a map. "That wraps up my usual spiel. Any questions so far before we go on to part two?"

Brayden raised his eyebrows. "Part two?"

Louisa shrugged. "You're His Highness's official guest. He asked if I could show you around some of the private areas as well so you'll know your way around. None of the personal quarters—you'll still need an invitation for those—but the library, the gym, the conservatory—"

"Can we go now?" Brayden said, doing his best not to bounce on the balls of his feet. This was an opportunity few would have. Trust Flip to make sure Brayden got in a good day sightseeing even if he was sort of under house arrest.

"Well, we can," Louisa hedged, "but I'm supposed to take you to the kitchen for lunch first."

Flip had really thought of everything. "Lead on."

FLIP'S meetings ran late Sunday, and Monday threatened a repeat performance. He managed to squeak away just in time for dinner, with the promise that he would return to finalize things the following day. Celine would have to rearrange his schedule again, but at least the whole business would be over with, and then maybe he could find some time to show Brayden around.

He entered his apartment hoping to get Brayden's input, but no one answered when he called out. Brayden didn't answer his text message either. Frowning, Flip went in search—first the gym, then the library. Finally he followed voices coming from the common living room his parents shared with Clara and his aunt.

"K5."

"Miss!" Laughter.

Curious, Flip pushed open the door.

His father and aunt were arranged on the comfortable sofa, each with a pile of knitting at their side. Dad looked to be starting in on another pair of socks in his wife's favorite colors, purple and aqua. Aunt Ines was putting the finishing touches on a baby blanket for Bernadette. In the armchair sat Flip's mother, lips pursed over the Sunday *New York Times* crossword.

Brayden and Clara sprawled on the floor in front of the roaring fire, playing Battleship. From the look of things, Clara had finished toying with him and was about to go in for the kill.

"E8."

"Hit," Brayden sighed, long-suffering. "You sunk it."

"I hope you didn't go easy on him," Flip said as he closed the door behind himself.

Clara rolled to her feet and rushed him for a hug, half knocking the wind out of him. "Don't worry. I didn't."

"Yeah," Brayden agreed. "That's the third time she's handed me my uh—" He stopped, his gaze darting to Flip's parents and Ines. "Battle fleet."

"Nice save," Flip's dad said without looking up from his knitting.

Clara rolled her eyes. "I know the word *ass*. In three languages."

"Clara Elisabeth!"

"I mean, the word *butt*."

Flip and Brayden caught eyes and very carefully did not grin.

"Brayden is an excellent loser," said Irfan. "Even if his family doesn't have any goats."

"Irfan," Flip's mother laughed from her chair. "You need to get some new material."

Irfan looked at Brayden. "I don't think she understands how dad jokes work."

"Are you and Brayden going to stay for dinner?" Clara wanted to know. "Mom said you might want *privacy*. But you've been alone all day. You should spend time with us."

Now Irfan looked at Flip. "I don't think she understands how privacy works."

Flip's mother threw her husband an exasperated look full of amusement and affection, but it was Ines who intervened. "Clara, you've monopolized Brayden all day. Sometimes adults need to spend time alone together. Remember we talked about this."

Flip's cheeks heated. Nothing like your aunt casually implying, in a room full of family members, that you might like to whisk your fake boyfriend away for sex.

Brayden had gone red too and was rubbing the back of his neck sheepishly, as though for want of something to do with his hands.

"Well they have to stay now," Irfan said. "You killed the mood."

Flip wanted to put his face in his hands, but Brayden just shot his father a wry look. "Ye of little faith. But I don't mind staying for dinner if Flip's up—I mean, if Flip wants to."

Irfan looked delighted at the slip-up, but Flip stepped in before he could capitalize. "I do actually have a few updates on the diamond front for you," he said, grateful Brayden had given him the opportunity to collect himself. "It shouldn't take more than a few minutes, but I'd rather do it now while it's fresh. And then no work at the dinner table, I promise."

Family dinners were one of the things Flip missed most when he was based in Toronto—his mother insisted on them whenever possible growing up, to instill in him a sense of normalcy in a world that often wasn't. When Clara and Ines came around, the tone changed somewhat, but still, the rhythm of food and conversation and ribbing resonated with something deep inside him. With any subset of the five of them, it always felt like home.

Flip hadn't expected it to feel the same with Brayden there. Certainly it never had with any of the real boyfriends he'd brought home over the years. But perhaps he'd been dating the wrong men, because Brayden fit as though he'd always been there, riffing with his father and then turning around to ask insightful questions of his mother.

By the time they placed their dishes on the cart to be returned to the kitchen, Flip was almost expecting it when his father took him aside and said, "You know the goat thing isn't really a problem, right?"

He wasn't making a joke.

Flip kept his eyes on Brayden, who was across the room cleaning up the board game with Clara. "Dad. It's a little soon—"

"Sweetheart," Flip's mother broke in, touching her husband's elbow. "Let me handle this one."

Irfan kissed her cheek and went to help pick up the games, and Flip's mother led him away from the living area to her private office, where she sat him on the love seat. The very first time she'd invited Flip in there, he was fifteen and suffering public heartache, debating whether he should return to boarding school.

Remembering those days didn't do much for his composure now.

"Your father means well," his mother told him. She took the seat next to him but angled her body toward him. "But you and I are wired differently from him. We're quieter, less impulsive. More considered."

Already Flip found himself nodding, relieved as the tension released from his body.

"And as much as your father loves us, as much as he's part of our lives, he will never experience the stress that comes with being a country's figurehead."

It felt dishonest to agree to that—Flip's dad experienced plenty of stress related to being a member of the royal family, doubly so because his skin color made him a prime target. And every trial he and his mother went through, his father was there to lighten their burdens. But perhaps his mother had a point. "Being prince consort has its own pitfalls."

"I've done well in teaching you diplomacy." His mother smiled at him and reached for his hand. "Flip. You are my son, and I am so proud of the man you've become. I know that one day you will be a kind, compassionate, strong king."

His throat swelled with emotion, and he swallowed. Before he could answer, his mother went on.

"I have no doubt that whatever happens, you will be beloved by your people, and you will do right by them, and the country will be better for your guidance. I have never worried over your prudence or your judgment or your fairness in matters of state." She squeezed his hand. "But ever since you were a boy, I have worried over your happiness."

Flip swallowed the lump in his throat. "Mom—"

She raised her hand. "Let me finish. I know that Miles hurt you deeply, though you tried so hard not to let it show. I know that since then, you have been meticulous in choosing partners who would be suitable, respectable members of the royal family, partners whose qualifications no one could criticize. But sweetheart, let me ask you something. Do you think your father and I are happy?"

Disoriented by the direction the conversation had taken, Flip blinked. "Of course." His parents rarely fought, and most of their disagreements fell into the category of "playful."

"Do you imagine that foremost among his qualifications was 'suitable in the eyes of the tabloid press'?"

That brought Flip up short. "No, of course not."

His mother raised an articulate eyebrow, and Flip knew he was about to be crushed under the weight of motherly logic. "And yet you made it a qualification when you searched for a love of your own—to your detriment, I think. So you can imagine my joy when I realized you had set that expectation aside." She paused. "You *have* set it aside, haven't you?"

Oh. That was what she was getting at. Flip squirmed. "I don't know. It's—our relationship is so new. I didn't intend for it to get so serious so quickly. I…."

She was smiling, which brought Flip up short. "What?"

"Nothing, sweetheart." She let go of his hand, cupped his face for a moment, and shook her head. "Only that you remind me of myself thirty-some years ago, trying to make myself believe I was moving too fast when I knew exactly what I wanted."

Flip's throat went dry. "Mom?"

"People conveniently forget, you know, when they tell the story of how your father swept me off my feet— which he did. But people forget I was already queen then. Your father was hardly going to propose marriage."

She paused to let this sink in.

The penny dropped. "*You* proposed?"

Her lips curled into a satisfied smile that might have looked smug on someone with a less regal bearing. "Now, Flip, I know I've taught you about making assumptions based on gender."

"Gender nothing!" he said. "I never thought *you'd* be so impulsive!" Such a move seemed completely out of character. "Why have I never heard this story?"

"You never asked. But maybe you should have. You know no one proposes to royalty unless they're royal themselves." His mother shook her head. "And believe me, it wasn't impulsive. Sweetheart, I'm a smart woman prone to some amount of introspection. I knew your father was the one for me, and I acted. And all these years later, I don't have a single regret."

He felt as though the earth had shifted on its axis.

Would he have behaved differently if he'd understood why he'd effectively been sabotaging every adult relationship he'd ever had? If he'd understood that he hadn't needed to? Perhaps he'd cost himself a chance at happiness somewhere along the way.

Perhaps, a very insistent voice in his head told him, he had cost himself a chance at happiness with Brayden already, simply because he'd treated their acquaintance as a convenient sham relationship from the start. But then again, even more terrifying, maybe he *hadn't* ruined everything. After all, he still had a little over two weeks before Brayden had to go home. If his father could convince his mother they were meant to be in just three weeks, why not Flip?

"I can see I've given you something to think about," his mother said, a trace of laughter in her voice.

"I… yes," Flip admitted. "Thank you. I think."

His mother shooed him away. "Good. Now go get your man."

A VISIT to the diamond mine had been on Brayden's Maybe list, but once the opportunity came up to visit it with the nation's crown prince and get behind-the-scenes access, it jumped up several spots and landed firmly on his Must-see list instead. Especially since, though Clara was lovely, Brayden would go nuts if he spent another day lazing around the palace. What did spare royals do all the time, anyway? Surely they couldn't all be knitting.

Monday morning, instead of lazing around in bed until Flip left and then meandering to the gym and then tracking down Clara for some company, he got up when Flip did and ordered them breakfast—still odd but becoming worryingly less so by the day. He ate while Flip showered, and then they switched places.

Of course, everything became just slightly more complicated when Brayden realized that he'd have to dress with the assumption that he'd be in the public eye. People would critique his clothing. A telephoto lens might notice that bit of stubble Brayden hadn't quite managed to shave off.

He went back into the bathroom and shaved again and only realized he was in danger of making them late when Flip knocked on the door as he was standing half-naked in front of the wardrobe. "Brayden? Is everything okay?"

Brayden threw open the door. "What do I wear?"

For a heartbeat Flip just blinked at him. Considering their relationship was strictly, maddeningly fake, Brayden was spending a not-insignificant amount of time undressed in Flip's presence, he realized as

Flip carefully kept his eyes above Brayden's nipples. "Clothes?" he suggested. He indicated Brayden's boxer briefs and socks. "That's a good start."

"Give me a hint, here. I'm not used to being important enough for people to care what I'm wearing if I'm not at work. Well, Grandma doesn't care for plaid or T-shirts with profanity."

"What's wrong with profanity?" Flip approached the closet and sifted through it. "This isn't an official state visit, just a sort of business one, so the chinos will be fine. The ankle boots—we'll be out in the countryside, and there's likely to be snow or mud, so that's practical as well as fashionable."

Brayden filed these tidbits of information away as if he'd need them again beyond the next two weeks. "Okay, great," he said. "And then?"

Flip turned and gave him a once-over that left Brayden feeling like his pants were about to shrink. He shook them out and shoved one leg in immediately, hoping for some camouflage, as Flip reached into the closet and selected a shawl-neck sweater in heathered purple. "This one, I think. You'll be warm but not uncomfortable."

"I haven't worn this much purple since I gave up being a twink," Brayden half joked as he wiggled into the other pant leg. "But it's like half the clothes Cedric picked out for me are…."

Flip was blushing, looking away. Because he was embarrassed Brayden had lost all his modesty by age fifteen? Or…?

"I suppose there's some significance to the color?"

"It's the traditional color associated with the heir to the throne," Flip admitted somewhat sheepishly.

So essentially, Brayden had been walking around with a metaphorical "property of" sticker. He couldn't find it in himself to be upset about it. "Ah. Fortunately I look great in this color."

"Yes," Flip agreed simply. "It suits you."

They managed to make it to their appointment on time. Brayden stared out the window of the car as they approached, expecting an immense ugly hole in the ground to dominate the landscape. He knew the mine had been in operation for almost a hundred years. But though the grounds lacked much in the way of tree cover, the surroundings fell short of his bleak expectations.

"Is the actual mine elsewhere?" he asked, pointing. "This seems… I don't know, I expected something else."

"It used to be a lot different." Flip leaned over so he could see out Brayden's window and pointed to a spot on the horizon. Brayden suppressed a shiver at his warmth and tried not to be too obvious about breathing in his smell. "That's where the original pit was. Diamond mining… it's not glamorous, and it's bad for the environment in a number of ways. Chemical runoff can get into fields and streams, and we have such a short growing season here that we can't afford to have that affect soil quality. So we were early investors in lab-grown diamonds."

"So when you say 'diamond mine,' you actually mean 'diamond lab'?"

"Sort of. The scientists will explain it better than I can."

Inside, one of the managers absconded with Flip and left Brayden with yet another intern, Sam, a black man in his early twenties. "His Highness said you wanted a tour?" He handed Brayden a hard hat. "Let's go see the ugly part first."

They drove through the massive industrial building in an electric golf cart, sticking to pathways marked out on the concrete floor in yellow paint. Finally they came to the end of the factory, where a two-story window looked out on a field of dirt.

Brayden said, "Oh."

"This is what a diamond mine used to look like." Sam pointed to an eight-foot poster on the adjacent wall. An enormous dirt snail was scrawled into the bleak and desolate landscape. "For twenty years we have worked with the crown to restore the wildlife to this area. Slowly we can see our efforts have effect."

It was difficult to tell in the dim light, but Brayden thought he could see some young trees and scrub brush dotting the field. Now that he was looking for it, he could see a few birds overhead too. "Wow."

Sam clapped his shoulder. "Come. I'll show you the labs."

As they toured, Sam explained the principles of "synthetic" diamonds—which had all the same properties as regular diamonds, but without the environmental or social impact. Heat chambers containing raw materials and "seed crystals"—shavings from other diamonds or simply pure carbon—served as incubators.

"And this is the first diamond ever grown in the lab." Sam gestured to a small display case that seemed to have pride of place.

Brayden peered in. The diamond was a light, clear blue, cut princess style. A fissure marred the middle of the stone, though, presumably destroying its value. "What happened?"

Sam shrugged. "Trial and error. Diamonds have to be perfect, though, or close to. Something with a flaw this big is essentially worthless. But creating it in the first place was still a big deal, and we're proud of it."

They both looked up as Flip came through a door across the way, led by the manager of the facility, who spotted them and smiled. "Admiring our first failure?"

Brayden looked back at the diamond. "I like it. It feels like a metaphor, though. Things aren't worthless just because they're not perfect."

Flip met eyes with Brayden, and then they both looked away. Brayden felt like perhaps he shouldn't have said that out loud, at least not with witnesses, though he couldn't have put his finger on why.

And yet somehow they met eyes again afterward, and Flip smiled as he said, "I appreciate your outlook, Brayden. Well put."

Brayden flushed at the unexpected praise—with an audience, to boot. He couldn't think of anything to say, but fortunately he didn't have to, as the operations manager motioned Flip to continue through the lab.

"We should be finished in a half an hour or so," Flip said on his way out. "I'll meet you in the lobby?"

Brayden nodded. "Okay. I trust Sam can get me there."

"Of course."

Flip and the manager left, but another scientist entered—a woman nearly as pale as her lab coat, with braided pigtails and goggles on the top of her head.

Sam waved her over. "Julia. Come over here." He said something in Polish a little too fast for Brayden to catch.

Julia turned to Brayden. "You want to plant a diamond?"

It was the coolest tour ever.

BRAYDEN'S enthusiasm for the diamond factory made it very easy to invite him along for the rest of Flip's commitments for the week.

"What's on today's agenda?" he asked Wednesday morning over their usual eggs, yogurt, and fruit.

"Barracks visit." Flip looked up from his coffee in time to enjoy Brayden's double-take.

"Really?"

"Like a lot of other European countries, Lyngria has mandatory military service. Well, you can choose civil service instead. I wasn't allowed to join the military."

"Too gay?" Brayden asked, head cocked.

"No, Mom sorted that before it became an issue. But they're shockingly unwilling to let you serve in the military if you're the first in line to the throne, especially if you don't have any younger siblings. Even in peacetime."

Brayden nodded and stirred his yogurt. "Makes sense. So you did civil service. Let me guess, in an embassy?"

Flip acknowledged this with a tilt of his head. "It seemed prudent."

"Cool. So mandatory military service. Explain that to a liberal Canadian?"

He put his fork down and took a moment to gather his thoughts. "We're a small country. And you may have noticed how large and close Russia is."

"Fair." Brayden traded yogurt for coffee. "How do the citizens find it?"

"Well, they're paid. And they learn skills that are generally applicable outside the service. They have the option to defer until after university if that's the course they want to take, or if they're an elite-level athlete or what have you."

At that Brayden sat back in his chair, his gaze calculating. "So job security and job training during what can be a really difficult transition time for young people. All right, that doesn't sound draconian."

Flip gave him a wry look. "I do my best."

Unlike the mine, the next official visit involved PR, which meant they had a camera crew trailing them as they toured the facility. At first Brayden seemed distracted—he kept turning and watching them watch him, rather than paying attention to the tour. Flip supposed it would be a bit strange to someone who wasn't used to it.

He elbowed Brayden as discreetly as he could. "Stop looking at the cameras."

"Easy for you to say, Mr. My Dad Was a Movie Star Prince." Brayden huffed, but he looked up at Flip instead of at the film crew, at least. "Some of us didn't grow up under this much scrutiny. What if I get a wedgie?"

For a moment Flip had nothing to say. Then, "You do realize I have veto power over the footage released?"

That knocked the wind out of Brayden's sails. "Oh thank God." Then he glanced at Flip out of the corners of his eyes, coquettish and sly. "So hey. Want to really stick it to the paparazzi?"

Flip did, but he wasn't supposed to admit it out loud. "What did you have in mind?"

"Just follow my lead," Brayden said, and he slipped his hand into Flip's and laced their fingers together.

It turned out Brayden didn't care much for the shooting range—he flinched whenever someone fired and claimed it was too loud even with hearing protection—but his eyes lit up when they toured the obstacle course. Flip didn't even feel a little bit guilty about asking the CO if Brayden could borrow some workout gear to compete against someone in basic training. The young woman—her shirt said MOREAU on the back—beat him handily, but she grinned widely and shook his hand when he made it to the end.

"He doesn't seem to mind being beaten by a woman," the CO commented approvingly.

Flip allowed himself a controlled smile. "Well, he's been playing board games with Princess Clara all week. He's used to it by now."

The film crew was getting the footage of their lives.

That night when he climbed into bed, he was surprised to find his sheets already warm. Brayden must have been watching for the expression of surprise on his face, because he turned onto his side and smiled. "You fidget when your feet are cold, did you know that?"

Flip did know that. It had driven Adrian crazy. Flip hated it too, since he couldn't sleep with cold toes. He fished around at the foot of the bed and pulled out a Magic Bag that Brayden must have found in one of the cupboards and stuck in the microwave. "Your doing, I presume?"

"Just riffing on an old classic." Brayden grinned. "I mean, I don't think they put coal warmers in people's beds anymore. Even if they're princes."

In truth, Flip used to do this himself, but he'd been spending so much time in Toronto he'd forgotten he had it. "Thank you. I appreciate it."

Friday Flip visited the children's hospital.

"You don't have to come," he told Brayden. "This visit… I do it because I love the children and it does cheer them, but it isn't fun or easy. I don't expect you to come."

"I've come with you everywhere this week," Brayden pointed out. "All of a sudden I'm going to bail because it's not fun? What kind of message does that send to kids? I'll end up in the gossip blogs as a callous, heartless gold digger."

Flip rolled his eyes. "Since when do you care what the gossip is?" Other than the bit where he insisted on sappy expressions and hand-holding.

"All right, that's fair. But I'm still not backing out on the kids. I like kids."

That was what Flip was afraid of. He just hoped Brayden and his big, soft heart came through the day intact.

Their visitor coordinator showed them how to scrub in for the general wards first—for this part of the visit they could wear their own clothes. Brayden followed directions assiduously, but he was largely silent while Elin went through a list of dos and don'ts. He almost seemed to be bracing himself for something. At least this time he paid no mind to the film crew.

Flip wanted to put a hand on his back for comfort, but he'd been listening to Elin's directions too, and he was trying not to touch things if he didn't have to.

The first children they visited weren't chronically ill, just laid up with tonsillitis, appendicitis, a broken leg, or another relatively minor childhood affliction. Flip chatted with them and posed for selfies while Brayden played video games with them or charmed their parents.

"He seems like a nice young man," Elin commented as Brayden started a rock-paper-scissors tournament with the twin five-year-old siblings of one of the patients.

People kept saying that like it surprised them, but they approved. "He is," Flip agreed, and he wondered if it weren't his own heart he ought to worry about.

As Elin led them down the hall to the next ward, Brayden fell into step next to Flip. "So health care in this country," he began.

"Single-payer, tax-funded. Sometimes the lines in the waiting rooms do get long." He glanced over. "We do have astronomically high taxes here, or so the Americans would say."

Brayden shrugged that off. "You get what you pay for, right? I mean, the security of knowing your medical bills won't bankrupt you—that's worth it for your people, so it's the right thing. And hey, I'm Canadian. I'm used to lines."

The children in the next ward were very ill, which meant a longer scrubbing-in and actual gowns, masks, and gloves that had to be changed between each room.

"No outside cameras for this part, huh?" Brayden said as he tied the back of Flip's robe. "I'm kind of relieved. This is not my color."

"I don't know that anyone can really pull off this shade of yellow. What would you call it? 'Pastel vomit'?"

Brayden finished tying and turned around so Flip could do the same for him. "We should ask Bernadette."

"Mmm," Flip agreed.

This part of the hospital tended to be pretty bleak. Flip didn't like to ask people to fake hope they might not feel for the sake of PR.

They started with the children who couldn't get out of bed. Flip had years of experience putting on a brave face, so he did most of the talking. He even blew up a latex glove into a silly balloon animal, a trick made possible via an amenable nurse who'd seen him do the trick before and a nearly empty oxygen tank. By the third room, though, they found a groove—Flip played Brayden's straight man, and Brayden made the kids laugh.

Flip didn't know how people did this every day. Many of the kids were in good spirits, but not all of them.

Finally they finished with the toughest cases and moved down the hall to a common room. The kids there had more energy—they sat playing video or board games, coloring, or building with Lego. Flip took a seat across from a little girl in pajamas with pink unicorns on them and asked if he could help build her castle. He wondered if Brayden might join him, but instead he took a seat next to the kids playing an ancient version of *Dance Dance Revolution* using the handheld controllers.

"Hey, I remember this game," he said. "I used to play when I was a kid."

The children exchanged glances. Then one handed over his controller. "Think you can beat Jess?"

Flip's companion, whose name was Zoe, turned to look over her shoulder. "No one can beat Jess at this game."

Having no idea of Brayden's prowess at video games, Flip only offered, "We'll see."

Jess won the first round, but Brayden begged for a rematch. "I haven't played this in fifteen years. Come on. Give me one song to knock the rust off." And sure enough, he squeaked out a win in round two.

Jess's companion whooped, and Jess looked like she was trying to be sour but couldn't quite manage it. "Beginner's luck."

"Old man luck is more like it." Brayden handed the controller back. "I used to have the dance pad that came with this game—you know, so you could play with your feet."

Jess narrowed her eyes and scrolled down to another song. "Show me?" She passed the controller to her friend and wobbled once as she slowly stood up.

Brayden cast a quick glance at Flip, then Elin, as though to verify it was allowed, but when no one intervened, he shrugged. "Sure. Okay, so the trick is when you're just learning, try using one foot for all the up arrows and the other for the back arrows."

They didn't have a dance pad, but that didn't seem to matter—they went through two different songs on Easy before Jess started to visibly fade, and she raised a hand to her face to rub her eyes. "I always wanted to learn to dance for real."

For a second Brayden looked heartbroken, as though his face were about to crack down the middle. But he composed himself, cleared his throat, and offered, "Well, as it turns out, I used to teach kids how to dance. So if you all want… we can do that."

Zoe got up to join the lesson as Asher's partner, but that left the boy who'd been coloring alone as Brayden partnered with Jess. "Do you want to learn too?" Flip asked, holding out his hand. "I can do the girl part."

The boy considered for a minute and then let Flip help him to his feet. "We can take turns," he said diplomatically.

Brayden led them through the basic steps of the paso doble—a good dance with big, slow steps that were easy for beginners to learn and easy to count. "Don't forget that the first count is just to bend your knees," Brayden reminded them. "And remember, always to the right first, if you're going forward. That means if you're following, you're going back and to the left. Ready? Let's try one more time before we add the music."

Not surprisingly, the kids' energy levels flagged before they really mastered the basics. Flip handed his partner off to an orderly, who put him in a wheelchair to go back to his room. Asher and Zoe were glassy-eyed and pink-cheeked, but Flip didn't think they would tear themselves away from the visit until he and Brayden left. He made eye contact with Elin, who nodded and gestured at Brayden to wrap it up.

"All right." Brayden held out his hands to Jess. "We're going to do this one last time. And because it's important that you get a feel for it so you can practice when I'm not here, I want you to stand on my feet, okay?"

Jess looked down at the plastic coverings on his shoes. "Really?"

"I won't let you fall, I promise."

They got situated, and then Asher hit Play on "Another One Bites the Dust."

Flip had to look at the ceiling a few times as Brayden carried Jess through the whole song. Jess never stopped smiling.

Later, they stripped off their gowns and waited for Celine to bring the car. Brayden was quiet, and Flip didn't want to interrupt whatever was going on in his head, so he kept silent too. But he worried. Uncharacteristically, Brayden had his head down. He was shuffling his feet. And—

Brayden's voice was very small when he lifted a face writ with grief. "Hey Flip?"

Flip didn't have words either. He opened his arms and Brayden fell into them, clung tight, and pressed his face into Flip's shoulder. Flip took a deep breath and wrapped him up, trying desperately not to memorize the scent of him, the way his body fit with Flip's, and failing miserably.

Eventually Brayden took a deep, shuddery breath, pulled away, and wiped discreetly at his eyes. "Thanks for taking me with you."

Flip swallowed hard. "Thank you for coming. It meant a lot to the children… and to me."

"You know, I enjoyed it." He huffed at himself a little disbelievingly. "Even though it's not easy. You normally do this alone?"

For the nth time that day, Flip found something fascinating about a light fixture. Fortunate that hospitals had so many of them. Kept things nice and cheerful. Lighting-wise, at least. "Yes."

Brayden let out a breath and shook his head. "Not while I'm here, okay? I want to come too."

It was definitely his own heart Flip should have been worried for.

"All right," he agreed. "Now come on. I think we deserve hot alcoholic beverages in front of a toasty fire."

"That sounds like a pastime I can get behind. Or in front of."

And get in front of it they did. Flip ordered them a light supper, and then they both changed into lounging clothes. Brayden lay in front of the fireplace, absently eating a plate of vegetables and hummus while he scrolled through something on his phone. For the first time since he could remember, Flip sat on the floor with his back to the couch, his legs outstretched with his feet toward the fire, and worked his way through a crossword on actual paper.

"This princeing thing is more difficult than people give you credit for," Brayden said around a yawn. He tossed his phone away and rolled over, presumably to heat his other side. The motion made his high school T-shirt ride up almost to his rib cage. With Brayden's face turned toward the flames, Flip stared at that stretch of skin with impunity, imagining what it might feel like under his hands.

Or his mouth.

After a moment Flip remembered to respond. "Thank you. You're keeping up admirably."

But he didn't drag his eyes away from Brayden's stomach until Brayden turned his head toward him. "Thanks for taking me with you to everything. You didn't have to do that."

Flip shrugged, the muscles between his shoulders tightening. "You didn't have to be my escort to the Night of a Thousand Lights. But you did, and that put the kibosh on your solo sightseeing trip. This is the least I could do."

For some reason that made Brayden's mouth tighten in a false smile. "Yes, true. You owe me."

Damn it. Flip rewound the conversation and backtracked. "And it's nice," he said, "having someone around to do things with. I've never…. I was mostly in Canada, and I didn't have a lot of princeing to do, as you put it, the last time I was with someone." And before that, he'd never really been serious enough about someone to trust them to come along. Which he should have noticed earlier, and he realized now that they would have been awful at it. "Clara's too young to come along, and my parents have their own appearances to make." He briefly glanced away from Brayden's face and into the fire. "It'll be difficult to go back to doing it alone."

Brayden let out a slow breath. "Yeah." Then he half sat up and looked at the forgotten newspaper lying near Flip's knee. "Okay, enough being maudlin. What're you working on?"

Flip picked up the paper. "My mother's crossword." He shook his head. "Before I moved into my own apartments, we used to squabble over who would get to it first. I could get my own newspaper subscription, but it wouldn't be the same as sneaking hers. Sort of a running joke."

Brayden grinned. "Yeah, it's the same in my parents' house if I ever visit in the morning. My mom's an English teacher, so she's got an edge, but I speak more languages and I'm better at the travel stuff. And Dad gets up earlier and he's pretty good at them too. It can get cutthroat."

Flip could easily imagine Brayden partaking in a morning of shared coffee and newspaper subterfuge.

The mental picture made him smile. "Competitive crossword-stealing. A pastime for arseholes."

With a sly look, Brayden tilted his head to indicate the paper. "Sure. But what about cooperative crossword-*solving*? You look like you're having trouble."

Flip looked down at the puzzle. "Got stuck," he admitted. "It's been a long day and I guess my brain's had enough."

Brayden lifted his head a fraction of an inch, a partial smile on his face.

"What?" Flip asked.

"Just… you do this thing, you know? When you're not comfortable, you get very formal. And then, all of a sudden, you start dropping words and saying 'arsehole' and I know you're happy." His cheeks went rosy as though he were embarrassed at having made the observation.

Flip felt himself go red too, because he was aware he did it but hadn't known it was so noticeable. And he hadn't considered what it might tell Brayden about him.

"Anyway." Brayden crawled over to look and leaned his head against Flip's shoulder. "Gimme a clue."

"Fifteen across," Flip said, tapping his pen. "Renovator, eight letters."

"Mmm. Restorer."

Flip filled it in and Brayden pointed to the fourth-last letter. "There, starts with *o*. What's the clue?"

He scanned over the Down list and… stopped. He needed a moment to silently curse the world.

Brayden nudged him. "Well?"

Nothing for it. "Lubricate." *Why* hadn't he filled that one in? Three letters—it was obviously *oil*, only now he wasn't thinking about squeaky wheels.

"Seriously?" Brayden craned his neck, giggling. It made Flip want to laugh too. "Is this the naughty crossword or something?"

"Perhaps if you've a fetish for home repair," Flip said dryly, writing in *oil*.

"I do like a man who's good with his hands." Flip didn't have to look to know Brayden was wagging his eyebrows. "What about this one? Thirty-seven across. You don't even have any hints for that one." He'd pulled Flip's hand with the paper close enough that he could read it himself. "Bottom's master."

For God's sake. "I think I might have to throw this paper in the fire when we're done so the press don't get hold of it."

Brayden shook against his side. "*Bottom's master.* God, what do you think, does 'power top' fit in there?"

Flip couldn't hold in the laugh any longer. "If he puts his back into it."

Thirty-seven across turned out to be a reference to *A Midsummer Night's Dream*, but they were still laughing as they got ready for bed. Flip came in with his Magic Bag heated up to find Brayden snickering, and that set him off again.

And then Brayden snorted. Flip really wished he could stop finding that so endearing—and also so hilarious.

When they finally calmed down, Brayden asked, "God, did we have too much to drink?"

Flip smiled at the ceiling. "I'd say we had just the right amount."

Sleep came swiftly, each of them on his own side of the bed. But even though it had never happened before, Flip couldn't say he was surprised when he woke up in the middle of the night to find they had gravitated together, Brayden's head, hair fragrant with Flip's mint shampoo, tucked under his chin.

Flip decided to worry about it in the morning and went back to sleep.

Chapter Eight

BRAYDEN had to stop waking up like this.

Ever since Friday night, when it seemed like some kind of dam had broken between them, he and Flip had been behaving like heat-seeking missiles. They went to bed firmly on their own sides, and then Brayden woke up clinging to Flip like an octopus, or, for a fun twist this morning, with Flip plastered against his back.

Brayden hadn't ever spent a real morning after with a boyfriend—largely because he didn't have boyfriends. But that wouldn't have been like this anyway—it wouldn't have carried this sort of illicit thrill, seasoned with equal parts shame and self-indulgence and a liberal sprinkling of *what do you think you're doing*.

What Brayden was doing was holding very still, hoping Flip didn't realize he'd woken up.

What he *wanted* to do was wiggle around a little to see if he could get a better idea of what Flip was packing under those pajamas—though with the way Flip was pressed against him, his hips flush with Brayden's ass, it wasn't like he didn't have some idea.

And it was a *good* idea.

Even if Brayden had wanted to go anywhere, he probably couldn't have managed it without waking Flip, whose breath he could feel on the back of his neck and who had slung his arm around Brayden's stomach to boot. Brayden was so hard that if Flip moved his hand a half inch lower, he could steal third. *I guess I'll just stay here, then.* And think about… all the things he'd been avoiding.

About how easy it was to be around Flip, even though his life *wasn't* easy. About how welcome Brayden felt in the palace, with Flip's family. About how he fit into their lives just as seamlessly as he fit in Flip's arms.

About how good it felt to be there.

You've been doing so well until now. Don't fuck it up by falling in love, for the first time in ten years, with the prince you're fake dating, you absolute idiot.

On the other hand, wasn't it good penance? If Brayden fell in love with Flip and had to leave when his vacation was over and go back to his life, wouldn't that heartache cancel out the one he'd caused when Thomas died?

The idea was stupid. Brayden knew there were no cosmic balances. Nothing he ever did would make up for Thomas being gone, and if he were honest with himself, he knew that it wasn't his fault and that he had nothing to make up for. But knowing those things intellectually didn't make a difference.

Brains were dumb.

"Stop thinking so loud," Flip rumbled, an inch from Brayden's ear, and Brayden's upstairs brain went offline entirely.

That was just not *fair*. A handsome prince who wasn't stuck-up, who danced like he'd been taught by Brayden's grandmother, who had a sharp wit and a warm embrace and a frankly ridiculous body—maybe Brayden should join him and Irfan for yoga?—and his morning voice promised exquisite debauchery of the slow and painstaking variety.

"Sorry," Brayden rasped. "I was trying not to wake you." He wondered how long Flip had been lying there and whether he'd been afraid to move too… perhaps out of politeness.

"Well, now that we're both up—"

Brayden felt himself go scarlet. He thought he could feel the heat from Flip's face too, as he blushed. "Nice choice of words," Brayden managed.

"You're a terrible influence," Flip said, mostly into the pillow. Then he rolled away and left Brayden with a suddenly cold backside. He turned to face Flip.

"On the plus side, that was a great icebreaker. 'Good morning, I'm definitely thinking about your dick right now.'"

Flip muffled something into the pillow that might have been a very quiet scream of frustration. Then he raised his head. "Good morning, Brayden. You're in fine form this morning."

"What can I say? You're an excellent straight man."

"I live to serve." He slung his legs over the side of the bed, and Brayden didn't bother to pretend not to watch. Flip was obviously still hard as he slid into his slippers and reached for his bathrobe. "You should get up and get dressed. We don't want to be late."

"Oh yeah?" Brayden copied his actions, grateful for the bathrobe hanging on the hook on the side of the bedpost. The weather had turned cold—but not cold enough to dissuade his dick just yet. "Where are we going?"

"We're going to do something we haven't done before," Flip said a bit mysteriously. He reached into the wardrobe and withdrew Brayden's rolling suitcase. "We'll be gone two nights. Pack warm." He slinked toward the bathroom.

Brayden's jaw dropped. "But where are we *going*?"

Flip turned from just inside the door and stuck his head out. "Sightseeing."

FLIP knew there was a slight chance he was about to fuck everything up forever. But he thought—he was pretty sure—Brayden really cared about him. Maybe it wasn't love yet, but it could be.

Now that he was ready to make final decisions on the Crown Mining Co., he didn't have to fly back and forth to Toronto anymore, and if he didn't make a move sooner or later, he'd lose Brayden by default. That was unacceptable.

If things turned awkward, he could always claim he was making things up to Brayden by making sure he got to tick something off his bucket list.

"Private jet, huh?" Brayden said as they buckled themselves in.

This one had eight seats, but they were the only ones on board—an extravagant expense Flip wouldn't normally have gone for, especially considering the environmental impact, but it was a special occasion. Or so he hoped. He simply nodded.

"Trying to impress me?" Brayden continued.

"If I wanted to do that, I could have let you stay home and play with the heated floor in the bathroom."

"True."

"There's no flight crew, though," Flip said apologetically. "Tough to get staff this close to a holiday, I suppose. So if you want anything from the minibar, you'll have to get it yourself."

Brayden rolled his eyes and then bent his neck to peer out the window as though he could divine their destination from their position on the tarmac.

Flip was pretty sure even a very seasoned traveler couldn't do that.

"Sounds like work," Brayden commented. "How long's this flight?"

He was fishing, but Flip indulged him. "Two and a half, three hours?" Brayden hadn't asked the aircraft's top speed yet, so that information likely wouldn't be enough for him to guess. "Are you going to ask questions the entire flight?"

"Would you prefer I put on my work uniform and serve you?" Brayden said wickedly.

Flip shuddered. "Lord, if the pilot ever spoke to the press, they'd have a field day wondering whether I'm an arsehole or if we're just very into weird role play."

Brayden fluttered his eyelashes. "What's weird about it?"

"I can't imagine it would be much fun for you role-playing your day job."

"Eh." Brayden shrugged, but he still had that gleam in his eye that foretold mischief. "I've never gotten to join the Mile High Club, for example. Lifetime regret."

Oh God. In that moment Flip was deeply thankful for his years spent schooling his expression into something more neutral than—how had Brayden put it earlier?—*good morning, I'm thinking about your dick.* "Maybe on the way home," Flip deadpanned.

Brayden's eyes widened and he opened his mouth, and for a second Flip wondered if he was going to have to clarify whether he was serious, which would be difficult, since he didn't know. But then the pilot came on the speaker system and directed their attention to the in-flight safety video.

"Oh, man, I've seen this one." Brayden sighed and shot Flip a sly smile.

Grateful for the reprieve, Flip rolled his eyes on cue.

For the first quarter of their flight, Brayden kept his nose pressed to the window. Unfortunately for him, today was the darkest day of the year—this close to the north pole, the sun's light cast barely more than a match's glow over the landscape, and it burned out nearly as fast.

Even if Brayden could have recognized landmarks by lit-up streets and buildings, there wasn't anything to see. The plane was crossing the Baltic.

"The suspense is killing me," Brayden grumbled, but he didn't seem to have his heart in it. A constant smile played on his lips, and he jiggled his leg as they ascended to cruising altitude.

When the plane leveled off, he got up and went to the minifridge, laughed, and returned with three bags of peanuts for Flip, which he dropped in his lap. "Individual servings of wine," he commented as he set the tiny bottles on his seat so he could return for the glassware. "It's just like I'm at home."

"In that case, maybe I should pour." He did, and they touched glasses.

"What are we toasting?" Brayden asked.

Good question. "Clear skies, I think." Otherwise the whole trip would be—well, it would be a blatantly romantic overture but without the distraction of fulfilling an item on Brayden's bucket list.

"To clear skies, then."

Brayden took a picture of their glasses next to each other on their trays, presumably to post to Instagram later.

When they deplaned, the airstrip lights illuminated a little halo around them. The wind whipped into Flip's face and froze the hair in his nostrils, and his breath hung in the air. He'd put on his gloves and scarf and changed into heavy boots on the plane. Even so, he wasn't used to weather this cold—even in Toronto.

"You weren't kidding when you said to pack warm." Brayden shivered despite the thick parka Flip's stylist had picked out for him.

Flip wanted to put his arm around him. *Soon.* With a little luck, anyway.

Their SUV pulled up just a moment later, followed by another. The first driver handed Flip the keys to the Range Rover, loaded their luggage into the boot, and got into the second vehicle. All perfectly mysterious and designed to keep Brayden in suspense.

"I'm dying here," Brayden said good-naturedly as he climbed into the passenger seat. "Where are we going?"

Flip pulled up the GPS, which was already set with their destination—not that it would mean anything to Brayden, because—

"Actually, scratch where we're going. Where are we *now*?" He raised his eyebrows at the screen. "That's a lot of vowels. And consonants. And umlauts." He paused. "Are we in Finland?"

So much for the surprise. Flip should have known better than to underestimate Brayden's language skills.

"Looks that way," he said as he followed the directions to exit the tiny airstrip.

The landscape outside the bright bubble of the airport might as well have been a different planet. Though the sky was a clear, dark indigo scattered with stars and only a quarter moon, every candela of light reflected tenfold off a perfect, gleaming layer of snow.

Brayden licked his lips. "Is it—is this…. I mean." He glanced at the clock. "Just before six," he murmured to himself. "So, what, the sun's been down for a few hours?"

"The sun hasn't come over the horizon in a week," Flip corrected quietly. Theirs was the only car on the road. Twelve minutes to their destination.

"So we might see… I mean, we're here for the Northern Lights, right?"

"I booked us a room for two nights," Flip confirmed, a little disappointed Brayden had spoiled his own surprise. He still had the hotel itself up his sleeve, at least. "If we haven't seen them by then, I'll extend our stay."

A few kilometers passed in relative silence, the only sound the Range Rover's tires on the road.

"You didn't have to do this," Brayden said at last. He was looking out the window, his expression a mask of wonder. If Flip could get Brayden to look at *him* like that…. "But I'm glad you did. This is… this is more than I could have asked for. So. Thank you."

Flip swallowed hard and pushed down *I don't want your gratitude.* It wasn't true exactly, and Brayden was a gracious person by nature, even if he expressed that in nonstandard ways.

But oh, he didn't want Brayden to act out of appreciation. Not tonight. Flip wanted so much more than gratitude.

He curled his fingers tighter around the steering wheel and said, "You're welcome."

BRAYDEN couldn't tell much about the hotel from the lobby, partly because Flip had instructed him to stay in the car while he checked in and procured their keys. A well-bundled woman knocked on his window and asked him to open the trunk so she could deliver their suitcases. Apparently that would happen via snowmobile sled. Brayden didn't know why they couldn't take the bags themselves, but perhaps it was a fancy hotel thing.

"Thank you," the woman said cheerfully, and she zipped off into the night. A number of glowing lights in the distance seemed to indicate the rooms were separate cabins of some kind, or at least in different buildings. Brayden couldn't tell from there.

Brayden couldn't tell a lot of things.

What *was* this trip, really? Could it just be a makeup for the unchaperoned sightseeing Brayden had given up? Surely they could have done something similar in Lyngria, without all this trouble. But maybe Flip thought that wasn't good enough, and since he had a fair amount of wealth at his disposal, he decided on a grand gesture?

Or maybe Brayden's instinct that morning had been correct and Flip wanted to get in his pants.

The door opened, breaking Brayden out of his contemplation, and Flip buckled in and put the car in gear before glancing over at Brayden. "Ready?"

No. Brayden's heart was beating too fast. Out loud he said, "Absolutely."

The hotel was located at the top of a fell dotted with snow-covered pines. They passed the snowmobile on its return trip, and then Flip slowed the SUV in front of a small building with the number 3 embossed on the door. He pulled into a parking place that mostly consisted of a spot of cleared-away snow and turned off the engine.

Then he handed Brayden the key and briefly curled Brayden's hand around it before he let go. "After you."

The wind outside was as bitter as it had been at the airport. Fortunately, though, the key turned easily in the lock, and Brayden stepped inside.

The little cabin was warm enough that Brayden immediately unzipped his coat. He left his shoes on the drying rack near the door. Off to one side was a small, modern kitchenette with a sleek coffee maker that looked like it cost more than the snowmobile he'd seen earlier. To the other was a wooden door that smelled of spruce.

A thick curtain separated the small entry area from the larger space, probably to keep anyone still in bed warm should the exterior door open. Brayden swept it aside—

And raised his hand to his mouth.

All of Lapland and half the sky seemed to spread out in front of him—snow-covered trees and twinkling stars and the quarter moon. A huge glass dome formed an igloo over a luxuriously appointed bed, and an intimate seating area framed a fireplace set into one of the walls. Rich, thick area rugs covered the floor.

Brayden let it pull him in and trailed his fingers over surprisingly warm glass. The walls featured unobtrusive curtains, currently pulled back to make the most of the view, but they didn't reach all the way to the ceiling—someone could watch the aurora while lying in bed and still have complete privacy. Though really, the igloo was angled such that even standing in the middle of the room, Brayden couldn't see into any of the neighboring buildings.

That would come in handy if he wanted to take a bath, since the giant tub stood just a few feet to the left of the fireplace. No point in modesty here. If someone brought you to this place, they definitely wanted to have sex with you.

Brayden swallowed that thought and continued exploring.

The bathroom was just off the kitchen—a toilet and glass shower stall, with a sturdy vanity made of the same solid spruce he'd noticed earlier, its countertop stained a rich brown and lacquered until it gleamed.

Brayden touched that too.

When he looked up, he saw Flip behind him in the mirror. He'd taken off his parka and gloves and boots, and now stood in a burgundy sweater and fine gray wool pants, staring at Brayden with naked affection and no small amount of desire. Brayden could relate.

Time seemed to stretch out. This was his moment—whatever he did next would dictate how far he fell and how hard. He could still turn and run. Flip would give him space.

But God, Brayden didn't want it. He wanted to feel it all—every moment, every rush of oxytocin and the inevitable crush of heartbreak. He wanted Flip to crowd him in here and turn him around. He wanted to be kissed on that bed, on the floor in front of the fireplace. He wanted to go back to Lyngria and spend his life on Flip's arm, at Flip's side, across from him on the dance floor. He wanted—

"Brayden," Flip said, halfway across the tiny bathroom now, and Brayden turned around and kissed him.

Right away Flip made a noise of frustrated desire into his mouth. His hands went first to Brayden's face and cupped it while he teased open Brayden's lips and swept his tongue inside. Then, while Brayden's brain lit up at the thorough exploration, while he tried to keep his feet as his knees wobbled, Flip ran his hands down his shoulders and up underneath Brayden's sweater.

Brayden's coat still hung open, and he shrugged it off. A second later those hands smoothed down his ass, kneaded once, and then hooked under Brayden's thighs and lifted.

Brayden wrapped his legs around Flip's waist and his arms around his shoulders as Flip walked the two steps, set Brayden down on the bathroom counter, and released his mouth to fasten his lips to Brayden's neck. Cursing under his breath, Brayden tilted his head against the wall and scrabbled at the back of Flip's sweater to pull it up. "This *sweater*," he said, and then he lost his words on a cut-off groan when Flip scraped his teeth up to Brayden's ear. "This sweater has been tormenting me *all day*."

He got it rucked up to Flip's armpits, but Flip didn't seem to want to stop what he was doing long enough for Brayden to have his satisfaction. Brayden kneed him gently in the side, shoving him away, and finally Flip lifted his arms and stripped off the sweater, somewhat imperiously. It dropped unlamented to the bathroom floor.

For the first time, Brayden got to drink his fill, unworried about being caught. Flip's smooth brown skin covered lean muscle, a dancer's build—strange for Brayden to think, as he was broader across the chest than Flip was. Cut hipbones—Brayden licked his lips—a dusting of wiry chest hair—

"*You've* been tormented?" Flip enunciated, stalking forward again with a predatory gleam in his eyes. "Your cursed high school baseball T-shirt has lost all its shape, and you're always flashing *this* at me." He slid his hands under Brayden's sweater and ran them up his flanks. He kept going until Brayden had to raise his arms so the offending garment could join its fellow in ignominy.

Brayden put his hands on Flip's obliques and traced his thumbs up toward his nipples. Flip kissed him again, pressing closer between Brayden's thighs. There was no mistaking the hard line of his cock as it pressed against Brayden's, or the possessive way he kissed, or the shiver that went through Brayden when Flip bit gently at his lower lip. Breaking the kiss, Brayden fumbled for the button of Flip's trousers. "I can't believe—you brought me all the way to *Finland*—" Flip kept interrupting with more kisses. "—to *seduce me*. I was—a sure thing—"

"Shut up," Flip said warmly and kissed him again. But he seemed to have developed a taste for Brayden's throat, or else he had noticed that kisses there made Brayden gasp and squirm, because he worked his way south again. "I wanted to."

Brayden shuddered and finally eased Flip's fly open. He slid his hand into the opening and palmed Flip's cock through his absurdly expensive underwear. He was hard and thick, and Brayden could feel his foreskin sliding beneath the fabric as he worked him. "Please tell me you have—" Flip sucked a mark over the tendon in his neck. "—*fuck*, please tell me you have condoms and lube somewhere on your person, I swear to God."

Flip broke away and rested his head against Brayden's for a moment. "Bernadette would kill me." Then he reached to his right and dragged over what Brayden had assumed was a basket of complimentary bath products—which he supposed they were, since technically they were about to get good use in the bathroom. "Fortunately the hotel has provided."

Thank God. He shoved Flip's pants down. Bernadette could retaliate however she liked—it'd be worth it. "I am leaving such a good Yelp review."

Flip helpfully stepped out of his trousers, but before he stepped close for another kiss, Brayden saw a look of consternation cross his face.

"What?"

"I'm trying to work out how to get your pants off without letting you off the counter." He mouthed down the other side of Brayden's neck and then lower. He swept his tongue over Brayden's collarbone, then his pectoral muscle as he slid Brayden's zipper down.

"Teamwork?" Brayden gasped. Reluctantly he released his grip on Flip's dick, braced himself on the counter with both hands, and lifted his lower body enough for Flip to yank his pants and underwear down. Brayden kicked them off and promptly wrapped his legs around Flip's hips again.

"Don't tell me if this is the kind of teamwork you got up to when you played baseball," Flip huffed as he smoothed his palms up Brayden's thighs.

Brayden hooked his fingers in the waistband of Flip's underwear and pushed it down the rest of the way with his heels, freeing his dick just as Flip took him in hand. Then—at a horribly inappropriate moment—he started to laugh. "No." He shook his head before Flip could get the wrong idea and kissed him quiet. "But I did play catcher."

Flip groaned into his mouth, but he cut off when Brayden pushed him away. "What—"

"As hot as this is, I'm pretty sure you can't fuck me and kiss me at the same time on this counter. That's not a challenge," he said quickly as Flip narrowed his eyes. "It's an observation that there's a giant bed in the next room, and I bet you could have my ass on it in ten seconds. Which is something I'm interested in. If you are?"

Flip stared at him. "If I am?" he repeated.

Brayden batted his eyelashes.

That was all it took. Brayden darted out a hand for the basket of necessities as Flip lifted him again. Their bodies rubbed together as he moved, and he teased Brayden's crack with his fingers until he almost dropped the lube.

The mattress rushed up to meet him, and Flip followed, pushing the basket farther up the bed to safety while he ravished Brayden's mouth, his body cradled between Brayden's hips. "I want to do this right," he murmured, almost shyly.

Damn it. Now was no time for *feelings*. Definitely not the bittersweet kind, at least. Brayden couldn't think about Flip being sweet to him knowing that in a few weeks they'd be parting. "Let's settle for doing it fast and then doing it again?"

"God, you'd be a terror in politics."

Brayden laughed as Flip pressed one last kiss to his chest and then sat up and reached for the basket. He pretended his breath was steady when Flip pressed a slick finger inside him, but his heart was beating in trips and stutters, and his fingers curled into the blankets when Flip found his prostate with two. "What," he gasped, "you're not intimidated by flight attendants?"

"Shut up," Flip told him again, just as fondly as the first time, and withdrew his fingers. "Ready?"

"Long past."

The first push of Flip's cock inside him didn't break his world apart. It seemed to click together instead. Their eyes met and held, and then Flip exhaled quickly and shifted his hips and Brayden's nervous system lit up like a Christmas tree.

He was right, it didn't last. Flip kissed his shoulder, his mouth, his neck, and Brayden dug his heels and fingers into Flip's back, needing everything more, now, harder. Flip seemed to know just where to touch him, or maybe it simply didn't matter—a fleeting touch on the inside of Brayden's upper arm got a shudder.

"Flip," Brayden cried, shutting his eyes as Flip nailed his prostate, then again. His stomach tightened. He couldn't remember the last time he'd gotten this close, this fast. Then again, they'd had a week of foreplay. "I—"

"Me too," Flip said, though even Brayden wasn't sure what he'd been about to say. His face was close, their noses brushing. Brayden tilted his head until their mouths touched again.

He didn't even have time to gasp out a warning when Flip's hand, still slick with lube, curled around his cock. One second he was ready, body thrumming with *almost*. Then that simple touch, Flip's thumb rubbing under the head of his cock, and he cried out again, wordless this time, pleasure bursting through him.

Flip shook against him, breathing shallowly against Brayden's mouth, hips still thrusting minutely, wringing out every little aftershock.

Finally they stilled, and Flip rested on his elbows and then reached down to hold the condom as he pulled out. He curled on his side next to Brayden, loose-limbed and, if Brayden were any judge, sated.

Brayden opened his mouth, hoping for a smart remark, but before he could get anything out, Flip kissed him, languid and slow, his faint stubble scraping against the hypersensitive skin around Brayden's mouth, which already felt raw. He shivered—not entirely from pleasure—and goose bumps rose on his upper arms.

Flip pulled away, flicking his gaze down Brayden's face, trailing his finger over Brayden's shoulder. "We should clean up," he said regretfully.

Brayden was about to counter that they should get dirtier instead, but then he remembered the room's setup and pushed up onto his elbows. "I agree. Think we can both fit in the tub?"

FLIP woke up to quiet music playing on the alarm clock. At first he didn't know why. He was still muzzy from sleep and warm with Brayden tucked against him, sleeping the sleep of the sexually exhausted. At least, Flip liked to think so.

Then he looked up.

It seemed he wouldn't have to extend their stay. He was almost disappointed.

"Brayden," he murmured, carding his fingers through Brayden's hair. Irina had cut it into a more European style—short on the sides with a few inches of length on top. It was already growing in, though, returning to his former all-over disheveled waves. Flip looked forward to it. The unruliness suited him infinitely better.

"Mhhhh," Brayden answered, somewhat muffled by Flip's chest. "I need at least another hour before round four."

Idiot. "Should I tell Mother Nature to wait on you, then?"

Something of this seemed to register, because he took a deep breath and then another, tickling the skin of Flip's neck, and raised his head, brow furrowed. "What?"

Flip moved his hand from Brayden's hair and tilted his chin toward the sky. "Look up."

Finally comprehension registered, and Brayden turned onto his back and snuggled close against Flip's side.

Above them, the Northern Lights glittered through the Milky Way in shades of green and blue, chasing each other in some otherworldly dance. As they did, they cast their colors over the landscape, a nearly pristine canvas of white. Then a wave of fuchsia swept in, arcing across the sky before yielding to green.

And then suddenly the whole sky was alive with color, pulsing in spiked, concentric ribbons of lime and viridian and scarlet.

The two of them remained silent for countless minutes, taking in what felt to Flip to be an intensely private, personal show. And then Brayden drew in a shuddering breath, and Flip tore his gaze from the sky to take in the play of color over Brayden's features, and found that his eyes were glassy bright. "Brayden? What—"

Brayden raised a hand to Flip's lips, and Flip kissed the tips of his fingers. "It's beautiful," Brayden said. "It's the most beautiful thing in the world."

It turned out he didn't need the full hour after all.

With permission to take his time, Flip put everything he hadn't said into his touches—a soft kiss at the corner of Brayden's eye, one at the edge of his jaw, a third above his heart. He'd been a fool to believe anything about their relationship could be pretend when Brayden was his perfect complement in every way. But if he voiced his feelings now, would Brayden believe him? Surely even Brayden, who did nothing by half measures, couldn't fall in love in a week.

You did, said a tiny voice inside him, but Flip hushed it and laced his fingers with Brayden's. The beautiful glass bubble that let the sky in kept the real world out just as well.

Chapter Nine

AS Flip had expected, Brayden made an excellent travel companion—when he could be convinced to leave the igloo.

"We need breakfast," Flip pointed out when Brayden's stomach growled at nine thirty the next morning. The night before, they'd missed dinner, eating only off the snack tray the hotel staff had thoughtfully packaged away in the refrigerator.

Brayden leered and gave Flip a once-over. Flip threw a pair of underwear at him. "No protein-shake jokes."

"Spoilsport," Brayden teased, but he put the underwear on, followed by the rest of an appropriate Nordic winter outfit, and let Flip lead him to the main building for breakfast.

Over slow-cooked oats topped with nuts and preserves and crispbread with thick-cut cheese and paper-thin lox, Brayden flipped through the hotel activities guide and exclaimed every second page. Perhaps Flip might have an excuse to extend their stay after all.

"I'd love to check out the snowboarding, but—oh, a dogsled tour! I've never done that." He looked up abruptly. "Uh, what about you, though? What do you want to do?"

As far as Flip was concerned, the trip's sole purpose was to be good to Brayden. "Everything you've mentioned so far sounds good." Flip enjoyed skiing, which was what he'd do if Brayden wanted to snowboard, though he'd rather spend the time doing something cozy. Perhaps he could nudge Brayden in that direction. "Do you think it's too much to do the dogsledding and then the sleigh ride/barbecue?" That was, to put it delicately, a lot of sitting.

"Probably, but that's why there's coffee and Advil." He grinned. "Let's do it."

The dogsledding was exhilarating, though cold. Flip marveled at the athleticism of the animals and their sheer joy for the task, but his favorite part of the trip came before and after the dogs were hitched, when Brayden was baby-talking to them and thanking them for a job well done.

But the sleigh ride. If Flip lived to be a hundred, he would never forget it—tucked next to Brayden in a sleigh behind a snowmobile, while overhead every color of the rainbow fought to prove itself the most beautiful. Brayden spent most of the ride with his head tilted back against Flip's arm as he took in the sky. They were both going to have sore necks tomorrow, because Flip couldn't tear his own gaze from Brayden's face.

They stopped for a barbecue under the endless sky and drank blueberry tea to keep warm. When they at last stumbled back to their igloo, even Flip was sore and tired and cold. He was contemplating the fireplace, and maybe a call to the front desk for a hot-water bottle for his feet, when he leaned against the door to the sauna to take off his boots and noticed it was warm.

"Surprise," Brayden said. "I asked the hotel staff to start it for us so it would be ready. I am a genius."

In the small, hot, humid space, Flip let him prove it with his hands and mouth and then returned the favor, Brayden straddling his lap and writhing as Flip stroked him and kissed his neck. Flip's spent cock twitched hopefully when Brayden came, spattering Flip's stomach with release, but neither of them had much energy left. They rinsed off in the shower, fell into bed, and sleepily watched the remainder of the show.

Eventually it clouded over enough that Flip could close his eyes without guilt. He drifted off to sleep with Brayden half sprawled on his chest and thought if he could spend the rest of his life like this, he would die the happiest man in all of Lyngria.

BACK at the palace on Wednesday, Brayden realized he had a problem.

"You want to go shopping," Flip repeated.

"I'm not going to be the guy who doesn't have Christmas presents for his boyfriend's family." Fake boyfriend. Whatever. It was probably splitting hairs at this point. Either way, he wasn't going to be that guy. "Clara would never forget it."

Of course she might have plenty of reason to hate him anyway, because even if there was something between him and Flip, Brayden would eventually have to go back to work, and then what? But there was no reason to disappoint her prematurely.

Flip sighed. "I can't go with you today. State business with my mother."

"Two days before Christmas?"

Flip's cheeks colored a bit. "In fairness, I did just sneak off with you for two days. We probably could've done this then, but the weather forecast…."

It had been snowing when they left Finland. "All right, you get a pass." Brayden sighed long-sufferingly, but it was only partially put on. He was all too aware that their time together had an expiry date. Now every day felt precious.

Flip kissed the side of his head, a habit he'd picked up on their trip. "The crowds won't be as bad here as they are in Toronto, but it won't be a picnic. You sure you don't want to shop online?"

He shook his head. "I need to get out and browse. Unless that's inconvenient?"

"We'll make it work." He trailed his fingers over Brayden's shoulder and then took the seat next to him. "I think my dad's planning to go out. Would you mind doing your shopping together? We've got a skeleton crew for security around the holidays."

"Oh my God, a few hours alone with your father? Good thing there'll be half a dozen chaperones."

Flip sighed, put upon. "Of course you think my dad is hot."

"No, I think your dad is *scorching*. I'd use the acronym but I'm afraid you'll never speak to me again because of the trauma."

Flip's expression turned wry. "Thank you for considering my feelings. I appreciate it." Then he pulled his chair closer to the table and folded his hands, and it was like a switch had flipped. Brayden paid attention, and he noticed things. Flip got formal when he felt emotionally vulnerable—probably some kind of PR training he'd had drilled into him. Brayden wished he didn't feel the need for it when it was just the two of them.

"My spidey senses are tingling," Brayden said before Flip got the courage to open his mouth. He hoped a little humor might help Flip relax. "What's up?"

"I'd like to talk to you about extending your visit."

A little thrill raced down Brayden's spine, but he quashed it before he got too excited. That didn't have to mean what he thought it meant. "Oh?" He tried to keep his voice neutral, but a certain amount of hope must have slipped out, because Flip almost smiled.

"I think—I hope—we can both agree that for the past few days we've been... operating outside the bounds of our original arrangement."

Brayden cleared his throat as his ears went hot. "That's one way to put it," he agreed.

"Yes, well." Flip smoothed his hand over the back of his neck and then seemed to realize he was fidgeting and put it on top of his other one. "I thought—a few weeks hardly seems like enough time for us to get to know each other properly."

I don't know, I felt pretty well-known last night. For once in his life, Brayden bit his tongue on the instinctive quip. His heart skipped a beat. Could this really be happening? "I... could think about taking a leave of absence," he suggested cautiously.

Flip broke into a wide grin and his posture relaxed. "Yeah?"

Brayden would do a lot for a Flip who loosened up enough to grin like that and use slang to boot. "Yeah."

Holy shit, his *life.*

"Then it's settled." He rose from the table, and Brayden did too—just in time to be caught in a kiss that felt almost unfamiliar, full of warmth and hope and joy. He could get used to being kissed like that.

Of course, they were still new enough that the kiss turned lustful quickly enough, and a few seconds later Brayden was humming in pleasure as Flip squeezed his ass. But no sooner did he offer this promise than he pulled away, looking regretful. "I really have to go or I'll be late."

Brayden sighed and rested his head against Flip's chest for a moment. "I get it. Duty calls." Then he cheered. "Rain check?"

"Of course."

BRAYDEN did not have the slightest clue what to expect from a shopping trip with Prince Irfan, but he certainly didn't expect it to begin with Irfan insisting on driving.

"Unless you want to?" he asked as he dangled the keys in front of Brayden's face. "What's the point of having expensive cars if you don't get to be the one to drive them?"

"Oh, uh." Brayden hadn't anticipated needing to confess something to Flip's dad before he mentioned it to Flip. "I actually don't have a driver's license."

Irfan accepted this without explanation. "Oh well. More fun for me. Come on, get in. The front has massaging seats."

Brayden was tempted to look to Irfan's bodyguards for guidance, if only because this seemed like a safety issue. But ultimately he decided they were probably used to going along with Irfan's whims, whatever they happened to be. One of them got in the back seat, and two more got in the SUVs parked in front of and behind

Irfan's. "What is this, anyway?" Brayden boggled at
the array of seat controls.

"Fun," Irfan answered, and revved the engine.

Unfortunately for Irfan, the security team boxed
him in and never let him get more than ten kilometers
above the posted speed limit, a fact Irfan lamented at
length as he drove.

Brayden missed sitting in the back with Flip. Since
Thomas's accident, he mostly avoided sitting in the
front seat.

Perhaps Irfan noticed he was nervous, because
after a few moments, he slowed down and seemed to at
least pretend to pay more attention to his surroundings.
"So, Christmas shopping, yes?"

"I mean, obviously it's last-minute, which isn't ideal."
Shit, how was he going to explain he hadn't brought gifts
for Flip's family? They were supposed to be dating.

"Flip says you were nervous about meeting us,"
Irfan prompted, as though offering Brayden a lifeline
out of his own lies.

"Yeah. Uh, it's not every day you not only have to
meet your boyfriend's parents, you have to meet your
boyfriend's parents, who govern a small European nation."

"We do okay." Irfan preened.

Brayden held back a smile. "Sorry, that should be
'your boyfriend's mother, who governs a small European
nation, and her husband, who used to be a movie star.'"

"I'm like Grace Kelly."

Why had Brayden been nervous about this outing,
again? "Exactly."

Lyngria didn't have much in the way of shopping
malls, having escaped the widespread damage of World
War II that paved the way for such developments in
neighboring countries. Instead, Irfan parked in an

underground lot, and their security detail led them to a set of pedestrian-only streets with small shops lining each side.

"First stop," Irfan said with his characteristic cheer. But instead of entering one of the shops, he walked up to a small newspaper stand run by a smiling woman with a bindi.

Oh God, Brayden realized as Irfan and the woman exchanged words in Hindi. Irfan had come to collect gossip rags and newspapers. The racks at the stand were full of them—English, German, French, Polish, even a couple with writing systems Brayden couldn't identify. He ran his fingers over the covers and front pages of a few and marveled at the absurdity of it all while Irfan talked to his friend. UFOs on this one. Bigfoot on that one. Speculation as to the true parentage of some Greek aristocrat. The next rack over was a bit more tame, featuring nonbonkers headlines about the financial market, a jewelry heist that got busted, the latest of various political goings-on.

And then he saw his own face. He tilted his head, and his heart sank as he read the headline.

Glass Houses—Inside Prince Flip's Secret World

With a sick feeling in his stomach, Brayden hastily looked around, but the street seemed miraculously empty. Maybe Irfan's guards had cleared it out prior to their trip, or maybe people had deduced that the thick gray clouds overhead portended a thick, fierce snowstorm. Either way, Irfan was busy, and there was no one else to watch him as he discreetly reached for the tabloid and flipped through it so he could read the article.

Could Prince Flip's new suitor be offering a window into the private life of Lyngria's most (in) eligible bachelor?

It certainly seems that way. Savvy Instagram users have ferreted out the secret handle of Brayden Wood, Flip's brand-new beau—so new, in fact, that as recently as October, Wood tagged a picture of a drink at a Paris establishment well-known for its hookup culture with #noboyfriendnoproblems.

Brayden's stomach dropped. How had they found him? He didn't use his real name on Instagram, and he certainly hadn't taken any pictures of the royal family or used them in hashtags. His handle was @whatwoodbdo. A little corny, maybe a bit suggestive… but not something that should've been picked up unless someone was specifically looking for it.

Of course someone went looking for it.

Since his arrival in Lyngria, Wood has treated his followers to a unique glance inside the world of our future monarch—and it looks a lot more familiar than one might think. The collection of Lyngria-based photographs includes a shot of poutine ice cream from Virejas's own Temmel Eis (aptly captioned "lunch fit for a king"), one of Wood's ensemble for the Night of a Thousand Lights Ball ("#notasugardaddy"), and a set of wineglasses from what seems to be a surprise romantic getaway.

Brayden felt sick. On the one hand, he hadn't posted anything damning. On the other, the idea that he might have inadvertently allowed the whole world to spy on their intimate stay in Finland made him want to throw up and then toss his phone in the canal.

The tabloid had run a few of the pictures as well and included a note that it had archived them on its own site in case he locked down his Instagram. Which he should have done two weeks ago, clearly.

While little is known about Brayden Wood aside from his occupation and his skill on the dance floor, it seems his social media may have much to tell us. We can only hope that his future posts will be as enlightening as these.

Brayden put the newspaper down, his ears hot with shame and his stomach a burbling mess. The tabloids they'd read the day after the ball had made him laugh. But back then there'd been no stakes. Now?

Now everyone was going to think Brayden was a gold digger—he'd as good as implied it in his own words. Now the whole world knew he and Flip had gone on a quiet retreat together, and they'd assume— well, most of the truth, that they'd spent a great deal of time naked in bed together.

He needed to be more careful. What would Flip think? Brayden hadn't asked his permission to post those things—he'd figured that since Flip wasn't in them or mentioned by name, it wouldn't matter. He'd been naïve.

"What's this?" Irfan asked, stepping away from the shopkeeper. He plucked the paper from Brayden's grasp. "Oh, I have that one already." He gave it back and patted the paper bag he held. Not a single comment about the contents of the article. "Ready for the next stop?"

Brayden took a deep breath and replaced the paper on the rack. "Yeah," he said, trying for unconcerned. He missed by several tones. "Let's go."

They walked side by side, flanked, preceded, and followed by bodyguards. "So, Christmas shopping," Irfan said. "Last minute. I like your style."

"I bought my family's gifts at the beginning of November," Brayden confessed.

Irfan chuckled and gestured to his right. "Let's go in here."

From outside appearances, the shop seemed to be a bookstore. But inside, Brayden also found shelves of toys and board games—the old-fashioned kind that didn't need batteries. Some of them were not just old-fashioned but *old*. Secondhand, maybe, but in good condition.

He glanced at Irfan. "I don't suppose you know which games Clara already has in her cupboard?"

Irfan held up his phone. "I have a picture."

That was as far as they got before someone recognized them—or at least recognized Irfan, who seemed happy enough to pose in a few selfies. Brayden mainly managed to escape notice, perhaps due to Gilles the bodyguard, who was almost seven feet tall, had the most intimidating resting bitch face Brayden had ever seen, and was sticking close to Brayden's elbow. Considering Brayden's extremely recent brush with internet fame, he was grateful.

Finally Irfan disentangled himself from his admirers and made his way over to Brayden, who held up an ancient English version of Clue. "Think she has this one?"

"I think that's perfect."

Brayden paid for his purchase and they moved along, wandering in and out of various shops. Clara turned out to be the easy one. Brayden tried not to wonder what each shop's employees might say about him after he left or whether they'd read that tabloid article. Maybe they were now following his Instagram.

Surreptitiously, he took out his phone and deleted the account.

"Do you celebrate Christmas?" he asked Irfan finally as they continued down the street, needing something to distract himself. "I know Flip said the two of you are going to spend the day meditating because it's Gita Jayanti, but I mean usually."

Irfan popped a handful of candied nuts he'd bought from a street vendor and chewed before replying. "I'm not a Christian. But I like Christmas as a secular tradition—charitable acts, time with family." He shot a sideways look at Brayden. "Presents."

Brayden mentally put him on the Yes list for gifts. No big deal. Just find a suitable gift for a reigning monarch, her husband, a crown-prince boyfriend, and his aunt. Also maybe Celine. All while not panicking about being accidentally famous.

Easy.

He took a deep breath. "So. Any hints?"

They chatted idly as they shopped. Brayden picked out a colorful silk scarf for Aunt Ines and, when Irfan wasn't looking, a set of knitting needles and yarn in Constance's favorite blue.

Three down.

They were meandering through a department store when inspiration struck—except there were enough people around to make Brayden nervous. He stood staring at a purple plaid flannel pajama set, high-quality material, softer than a kitten.

Irfan must have guessed the direction of his thoughts, because he said, "Ines gets him pajamas every year, you know."

Brayden caught the slightly wry note to his voice and lowered his own. "Yes, fussy silk ones, and instead he wears the ones he must've had since he was a teenager. A few more washes and they'll disintegrate."

Irfan laughed. "You noticed."

"Hard not to." He looked around. "But, uh. How do I buy pajamas for the crown prince without the whole country finding out about it?" And putting it on the internet?

"Leave that to me."

In the end Brayden picked out a pair of slippers too, on a whim—in a matching amethyst, with removable inserts that could be microwaved. Irfan gave him a bemused smile, but he spoke quietly to one of the shop attendants, who nodded and took Brayden's credit card. They wandered over to a display of sweaters while a different attendant boxed up the appropriate-sized gift and bagged it, and then the package, receipt, and credit card were delivered to them as they left the store.

"Buying underwear must be hell," Brayden observed.

Irfan waved this off. "We just buy them online like everybody else."

Brayden wondered about the name on Flip's credit card. Would it say Antoine Philippe like the entry on the passenger manifest? Or maybe Antoine-Phillipe of Lyngria? That probably wouldn't fit on a single piece of plastic. "The royals," he mocked, referencing a hundred memes. "They're just like us."

"Only when we're not swimming in piles of money."

"Or holding audiences with—who was Flip off to talk to today?"

"The prime minister of France." Irfan shot him a sideways look, and something in his tone shifted slightly to the left. "My son is a skilled diplomat, you know, and a passable actor. Those are related."

Brayden didn't know quite where this was going, but he nodded anyway. "Sure. That makes sense."

"But not as good as me," Irfan went on. He stopped at a roadside stall and bought a mug of hot cider for each of them. He handed Brayden his and then blew across his own and started toward the antiques shop on the corner. "And I'm his father. I always know when he's putting on a show."

The penny dropped. Brayden sloshed apple cider over the rim of his mug and onto his fingers, but he hadn't even hissed at the pain before Irfan handed him a napkin.

What could he say? *Sorry? You caught us? I know what you think, but actually we're together for real now?*

"Flip is a stubborn man. He doesn't do things he doesn't want to do." Great, so at least Irfan didn't think Brayden had blackmailed Flip into anything. Probably he wasn't about to get locked in the royal dungeon. "The question is, what are you getting out of it?"

Brayden looked at the cider, which didn't hold any worthwhile replies. When he looked up, Irfan was still watching him.

"You don't have to answer. Whatever is going on with you and Flip is your business—for now." He sipped his cider. "But if I discover you acted in bad faith with him, I will have the palace chefs bake you into the Christmas pie."

He let that hang in the air a moment, and Brayden was left wondering if Irfan thought Brayden had only wanted to get internet famous. He was scrambling for something to say when Irfan shook himself and said, "Ooh, I gave myself chills with that one. Come on. Constance loves antiques. I bet you find something good in here."

Brayden trailed helplessly after him.

As they shopped, he mulled over what he'd say to Flip. Then, back at the palace, between wrapping gifts, he jotted things down on some stationery from Flip's desk—phrases like *I'm sorry* and *I feel awful for letting you down* and *I don't want you to think I'm not taking our relationship seriously.*

But Flip never brought up the article, and Brayden didn't know how to broach the subject. *Hey, just FYI, someone internet stalked me and found out things about us, and oh by the way, your dad is totally onto us?*

That night he lay awake in bed, trying to sleep with Flip's cold feet pressed against his calf because they'd forgotten the Magic Bag.

If Irfan had guessed the truth about their relationship, who else might know? Who could guess? Celine, probably, and Bernadette. Maybe some of the palace staff, if they realized Flip had slept on his own couch that first night. More people than Brayden cared to think about, anyway.

Flip hadn't brought up Brayden's Instagram. Either he didn't know—he'd been busy all day, after all—or he didn't want to start an argument. Brayden couldn't blame him, this close to the holidays. Maybe he thought Brayden had already learned his lesson.

And he had. Perhaps it had all started as a charade, but it was real now, and that meant Brayden had something to lose. It was time to start acting like it. He didn't care what people thought about him, but Flip was good and kind and sensitive. Brayden wouldn't give anyone a reason to think anything else.

FLIP wasn't much for Christian religious celebration, but the church in oldtown Virejas hosted a prize-winning choir, so he cajoled Brayden into dressing in slacks and an amethyst sweater—Flip couldn't help being the slightest bit possessive—and they went downtown, with just Celine to look after them. He laced his fingers with Brayden's and led them up to the highest seats in the gallery, overlooking an altar painted in vivid blues and gold leaf.

"How traditional of you," Brayden said as they settled on the hard bench, their fingers still entwined.

"Hush," Flip admonished and squeezed his hand. "Just listen."

The choir performed Handel's *Messiah* with little fanfare, but Flip liked the meditative nature of it, the ritual. Most of all he liked that it seemed like something he could do with Brayden next year and the year after and the year after that. The performance might change, but the important details—the way Brayden's hand felt in his, his thigh pressed next to Flip's, the acoustics of the building, the sense of peace—those would remain the same.

It was possible he'd been dwelling on his plans for the future a lot in the past few days. He'd barely had time to think about Brayden's unfortunate second baptism into tabloid fodder. He was too busy building castles in the sky.

They kept a comfortable silence on the drive home, though they had the partition up. Brayden kept his fingers laced with Flip's until Celine pulled up outside the palace.

Flip kissed Brayden's cheek and squeezed his hand. "Go on inside without me? I'll be a few minutes. I need to talk to Celine about something."

Brayden gave him a curious look, but he got out of the car when Johan opened the door. "All right. Don't be too long, okay?"

"I won't. I just need to talk to Celine about holiday coverage," he lied. "Put the kettle on for me?"

Brayden always put the kettle on. "Of course."

When he'd closed the door, Celine rolled down the window to the back seat. "What's up, boss?"

Flip took a deep breath. "I want you to set up internal interviews—someone who's looking for a long-term commitment but who already has a solid amount of experience as head of an individual security team."

Celine paused. "Your Highness?"

"Brayden's going to need a permanent detail." The idea still seemed impossible, but he couldn't deny how right it felt. He knew that sometimes their duties would separate them, and Brayden would need his freedom when Flip was occupied elsewhere. "We'll start looking in the New Year."

Celine broke into a smile. "Yes, Your Highness. And… congratulations."

When Flip entered his apartment, he spotted his tea mug right away—one with antlers for a handle that Brayden had bought in Finland at the hotel gift shop. It was already steeping with his habitual nighttime blend—something with lavender and rosehips and absolutely no caffeine.

He had every intention of starting that conversation about social media—he needed Brayden to know he wasn't angry and that Flip would put a whole team of Cedrics at Brayden's disposal if he wanted to have an official account—but he heard the water running in the shower.

Serious conversation could wait. Flip skipped the tea and went straight to the bedroom, following Brayden's trail of stripped-off clothes and leaving his own.

Brayden had left the bathroom door only partially closed, and he looked up when Flip opened the shower door, eyelashes clumped together, skin rosy pink. "What's a guy have to do for some privacy around here?" he teased, stepping back unnecessarily to make room. "These are the prince's private rooms, you know."

Flip could have bantered with him for hours. Instead he kissed him and stepped under the spray to take his face in both hands and taste his smile. Brayden spread his palms on Flip's chest, tangling lightly in the hair there, but he went easily when Flip nudged him back against the shower wall. "We'd better hurry up before he catches us, then."

Brayden's breath rushed out in a whoosh as Flip trailed kisses over his chin and jaw. "Is that... is that so?"

Flip hummed into the juncture of his neck and slid his hands down Brayden's back to the curve of his ass. "Think you can be quick?"

"I...." Brayden exhaled shakily as Flip eased himself to his knees. "...think that won't be a problem."

Flip didn't bother taking it slow. Tonight he wanted to take Brayden apart hot and dirty. He pinned his hips to the wall and swallowed him down, teasing his thumbs over the tops of Brayden's thighs. Brayden cursed as though he hadn't expected that, and his cock went from half-hard to fully erect against Flip's tongue.

"Oh my God," Brayden moaned. He had one hand braced against the wall, the fingers balled into a fist, but he raised the other, brought it to Flip's face, and traced his orbit and then his cheek before thumbing at the corner of his mouth. "Fuck."

Flip had never given head in a shower before, and the thrill of it superseded the ache in his knees and the difficulty of breathing without getting water in his nose. His own cock bobbed between his legs, wanting attention of its own, but Flip focused on the sweet salt of Brayden's skin, the minute trembling in his thighs. Everything was slick and hot and steamy, and when Flip wet a finger and pressed it between Brayden's cheeks, he moaned and curled his fingers tight into Flip's hair and said, "God—sorry—*fuck*," and came, salt-sour on Flip's tongue.

Flip licked his lips and swallowed. Then he looked up, trying desperately to suppress his laughter. "*Sorry?*" he echoed, getting unsteadily to his feet.

"Shut up, Your Highness," Brayden said, taking him by the elbows and pushing him against the wall.

But Flip couldn't help himself, and the laugh started to take over. "That's so *Canadian*—"

Brayden cut him off with a kiss and a hand around his cock, sliding the foreskin forward and back, and Flip had a bright, heart-stopping moment of clarity that this was it, this was the man he would spend the rest of his life with, before pleasure took over.

They dressed in their pajamas and went to sit on the couch in front of the fire, Flip with his tea and a paperback he'd been meaning to finish for months, Brayden with one of Flip's mother's crossword books. Flip tucked his feet under Brayden's thigh when they got cold, and Brayden put the throw blanket from the back of the couch over Flip's lower legs without looking up.

I love him. Flip let himself consciously use the word for the first time. It felt right, as cozy and warm as the fire and the blanket.

"Zany, six letters?"

"Madcap," Flip murmured, flexing his toes.

His mother had been right. He couldn't let Brayden slip away from him. Flip would wait until Christmas was over, with all the negative associations it held for Brayden. And then he would do something the opposite of impulsive.

CHRISTMAS morning Flip woke Brayden with a soft kiss on the cheek. "Morning, love. Merry Christmas."

Brayden was still mostly asleep, warm and happy to laze around in Flip's bed. Better still if he could get Flip to laze with him. "Mmm. Happy Gita Jayanti. Come back to bed."

Flip chuckled and ran his fingers through Brayden's hair. "My father's expecting me. But there's breakfast in the family room in a few hours if you want to come."

Brayden mumbled in agreement and went back to sleep.

When he woke again, his stomach was rumbling. A glance at the clock showed he wouldn't be late for Christmas breakfast if he hurried, and he wanted to be there when Flip's family members opened their presents, so he brushed his teeth, put on his own nicest jeans and one of the beautiful amethyst sweaters Cedric had procured for him, and hustled off to the common rooms.

"Brayden!"

For a moment he almost didn't recognize Queen Constance. Today she wore her hair down instead of in a no-nonsense bun, and she'd eschewed makeup and her usual pristine suit, instead favoring flannel pajamas with reindeer on them. She kissed Brayden's cheek. "Merry Christmas, darling. Are you hungry? We're making pancakes."

They did actually seem to be doing the work themselves—Ines and Clara stood in the kitchenette area of the suite, bedecked in holiday-themed aprons and wielding spatulas.

"Merry Christmas," Brayden replied. He missed his own family, but he was profoundly glad to be included in this one. "Pancakes sound great."

"Irfan and Flip should be along shortly." Constance went to the cupboards and took down plates. "Not that they're any better in the kitchen than these two," she added conspiratorially and passed the plates to Brayden so he could set the breakfast table.

As she said that, Ines, at Clara's urging, attempted to flip a pancake without a spatula. She managed to catch half of it, leaving the rest splattered down the outside of the pan, on the floor, and on their feet.

Brayden looked from the mess to Constance. "Maybe I should lend a hand."

He ended up working three frying pans while his sous chefs transferred finished pancakes to a warming dish. Clara told silly jokes all the while, and Brayden laughed at every one.

He didn't realize Flip and Irfan had come in until arms wrapped around his waist and a familiar mouth found his neck. Casual PDA in front of the family. Was that where their relationship was now?

Flip bestowed a quick, quiet kiss and then withdrew. "Can I help with anything?"

"No," Brayden said wryly and warded him off with the spatula. "I've been warned about your kitchen skills. Go have your mother put you to work."

They sat down to breakfast as a family, and then Flip and Irfan were directed to cleanup duty while Clara was finally allowed to begin sorting the presents under the tree into piles by recipient. Constance made tea, and everyone gathered on the sofas. It was nothing at all like Brayden's typical family Christmases, but it felt homey and authentic, even though they were nestled in one of the grander buildings in the country.

Ines added a log to the fire and then settled in an armchair and looked at Constance. Before either of them could say anything, Clara piped up, "Can we open them *now*?"

Now *that* refrain Brayden was used to hearing at family holidays. He pretended to scratch his nose to cover his smile.

It wasn't until he was settling into bed next to Flip that he remembered that today was also the tenth anniversary of Thomas's death.

He inhaled sharply at the realization and rubbed his hand over his breastbone until Flip reached up and gently clasped his wrist.

"Okay?" Flip asked quietly.

Brayden let the breath out again, slow and steady, and exhaled the worst of the pain along with it. It still hurt, but at some point over the past few weeks, he'd let go of the guilt. "Okay," he agreed. "Thank you."

Flip kissed his forehead. "You're welcome."

BRAYDEN was still in bed when Flip got up on the twenty-sixth, determined to accomplish as much of his lengthy to-do list as possible before noon so he could spend the rest of the day with Brayden. They could have a long chat and still have plenty of time to celebrate if things went well, which Flip hoped they would.

First, though, he had to get through the morning. Which meant putting on a very patient face for the cabinet minister in his public office, who was droning on about how much Flip's support for his bill meant and never mind that Flip wasn't supposed to have a public opinion on how the democracy worked.

"I really think that if you just talked to Counselor St. Louis and explained your position," the man was saying, completely disregarding all of Flip's diplomatic attempts to point out that he wasn't going to do it.

For God's sake, man, parliament isn't even in session until January. Go away, I intend to propose to my boyfriend today and I don't have time for this.

When, after nearly forty minutes, the man still hadn't gotten the hint, Flip was forced to resort to less diplomatic tactics. "Minister Bechard, I appreciate your dedication to your cause, but to intervene in the course of democracy is a serious breach of protocol and one that I will not be committing over a bill that defines how much pesticide can be used on organic produce."

Minister Bechard looked taken aback. "Oh—well, of course, Your Highness, I wasn't suggesting—"

Yes he was, and Flip was done listening to it. "I apologize for my bluntness, Minister, but I'm afraid I have a very busy day scheduled"—large portions of it in bed, with any luck—"and I really have to make my next appointment. I'm sure you have your own matters to attend to." *Read: fuck off.*

Minister Bechard left in a bit of a huff, but Flip couldn't bring himself to care.

He caught up to Brayden in his apartment, where Brayden was sitting at the breakfast table, idly tapping a pencil on a pad of paper. He looked up with a smile when Flip came in. "Hey." The tension melted away from Flip's shoulders and his incipient minister-induced headache receded, all because Brayden looked at him and smiled.

Oh God, what if he said no?

Flip pushed the door closed and let himself lean against it for a moment, for strength. Then he drew himself to his full height. "Good morning. I… wish to talk to you about something."

Smooth. He grimaced at himself as the smile faded from Brayden's face. "Okay. What's up?"

Flip could do this. His palms were sweating, but how many times had he made a public address? Hundreds since he was a teenager. He'd even insisted on speaking at the press conference after Miles's account of their relationship was published. "When we first began our arrangement, I needed your help, and you rose admirably to the task."

Brayden said nothing, only tilted his head as though he were confused where this was going.

Flip pushed on. What was the saying? You couldn't make a cake without breaking a few eggs, right? "But very soon it wasn't only my parents whose scrutiny we had to endure. Once the media became interested in our story, everything became... regretfully more complicated." He wished for Brayden's sake that they'd had more privacy to get to know one another, though in truth, he couldn't find it in himself to be upset at the outcome.

"If this is about my Instagram account being discovered," Brayden ventured cautiously, "I just want you to know I deleted it. If I'd thought anyone would find it, I never would've...."

Damn it, Flip should have talked with him about that. Now his train of thought had been derailed. "This isn't about that," Flip said in what he hoped was a reassuring manner. The whole conversation had gotten away from him. He put his hand in his jacket pocket, closed it around the ring box, and clutched it like a talisman. Just a few more sentences and they could celebrate. He hoped. "Some more critical members of the press might have dubbed you unsuitable a match for me. But while you have conducted yourself well—"

Frantic knocking on the door at his back interrupted. Bollocks. Flip closed his eyes and took a deep breath, trying not to let his agitation infect his voice. "Yes?"

"Sir, I'm afraid it's an emergency." Cedric's voice put Flip instantly on alert, and he spun around and opened the door. "I'm sorry, Your Highness, but we've just gotten word—your uncle has been arrested. Your mother has requested your presence right away."

Sod everything. Flip looked beseechingly at Brayden. "Brayden, I'm so sorry. I really do have to go."

Brayden nodded, pale-faced. "Sure. I understand."

"*Thank you*," Flip said fervently. And with that, he hurried into the hall after Cedric.

WHEN the door closed behind Flip, Brayden inhaled deeply. Or he tried, at least. The breath got stuck halfway and hitched, and he had to swallow down a wave of emotion.

He hadn't expected their relationship to end like this. Though maybe he should have.

The press have dubbed you an unsuitable match for me, Flip had said. Well, he wasn't wrong. Brayden wasn't exactly bred to be a royal. He'd thought maybe that didn't matter to Flip, but obviously he was wrong. Brayden couldn't even blame him, considering Flip's history with the press. Brayden wouldn't want to be reminded of his past indiscretions every time his current relationship was mentioned either.

Everything became regretfully more complicated. Yeah. Brayden agreed with that too, but he couldn't fully bring himself to regret the past few weeks. Even if it wasn't going to work out between them, at least he knew now, and he could move on with his life. He could fall in love. He could be brave.

It would take him some time to work up the nerve to try it all again, though.

In the meantime, he should pack. He didn't really want to wait around for Flip to come home and finish breaking up with him. Brayden could spare them both that. Flip had obviously been uncomfortable.

He'd reverted to the stilted, formal language he used whenever something had him wrong-footed.

Brayden left his pencil on the table. Quietly, he packed up his things and tried not to look at the bed they had shared. But he couldn't just stop *breathing*, and the room smelled a little like Flip—warm and woodsy from the fire, crisp and clean under that. It smelled comforting and welcoming and familiar. Maybe one day it might have smelled like home.

Goddammit.

Brayden put on his boots and coat and slipped out of Flip's rooms and into the palace corridors.

Louisa's tour had been informative. He'd learned that a driver was always on duty to take the royal family and their guests anywhere they wanted to go. And since a taxi would certainly not drive through the gates without attracting undue attention, he trudged across the frozen crushed gravel to the drivers' lounge next to the garage.

Brayden knocked, and when someone called out in French for him to enter, he pushed open the door to a well-appointed area filled with comfortable overstuffed couches, a desk and computer, a TV showing soccer highlights, and Flip's driver, Celine, looking up from a tablet with a dumbstruck expression as Brayden came in.

"Uh," Brayden said. "Hi."

Damn it. He hadn't expected *her*. He'd been sure she had the seniority to merit the day after Christmas off. Not that a driver he didn't know would have been much better.

Celine scrambled to her feet and dropped the tablet onto the couch. "Sir. Does His Highness need something?"

If Flip had needed something, they could have called the lounge extension to ask. Brayden shook his head. "No." And then he lied, and the words fell as smoothly from his tongue as anything he'd ever said. "There's been a family emergency at home. I was hoping you could drive me to the airport."

"Oh. I'm sorry to hear that. Of course. We'll leave right away."

If she thought it was odd that Brayden was leaving alone, without Flip for moral support, she didn't mention it. Perhaps she knew Flip was dealing with a family emergency of his own or thought Flip too important to be whisked away from his country at a moment's notice to comfort a man he'd been seeing just a few weeks.

Brayden sat in the back seat and traced his fingers over Flip's monogram. It was for the best. Sooner or later things would have ended. Brayden couldn't play house with a prince forever.

He wondered where his family was. Would they be in Aruba by now? Or maybe they were still in Kingston. He couldn't remember. But maybe if the flights worked out, he really could meet them in port somewhere.

Then he thought about their questions, their pity, the inevitable whispers and walking on eggshells they'd do if he showed up now. Yeah… maybe not.

Brayden closed his eyes and imagined he was curled up next to Flip. His eyes burned.

At least he could tell Lina the truth. He settled back against the seat and counted the miles to the airport.

Chapter Ten

FLIP returned from police headquarters exhausted, with a splitting headache and a heavy heart. He hated seeing the toll dealing with her brother took on his mother, and he was glad he didn't have to explain the man's sudden reappearance to Clara. It would be up to Ines to decide what to tell her.

All he wanted was to relax by the fire with Brayden and maybe a stiff drink. Never mind the proposal for now—after the day he'd had, the mood hadn't just been killed, it had been hanged, drawn, and quartered. He could try again tomorrow.

But when he pushed open the door to his apartment, something felt off. "Brayden?"

No Brayden on the couch, by the fire, or at the table. Flip left his shoes on and ventured into the bedroom to change—no Brayden there either. His parents had both been with him deciding what to do about his uncle. Ines and Clara wouldn't want company.

Maybe he'd decided to try out sightseeing on his own?

In his socks and underwear, Flip dug his phone out of his jacket pocket and turned it on for the first time in several hours. Nothing from Brayden... but he did have a message from Celine.

Taking Brayden to airport. He says family emergency. Everything okay?

Oh God. That didn't sound good. Why hadn't Brayden called him?

He had wandered back out to the living room to check if he'd left a note when the next message, timestamped a few minutes later, pinged on his phone—*Something seems off, though. Too quiet. Why aren't you with him?*

And finally—*Did you break up?*

Flip's heart hit the floor. He could feel the blood rushing from his face, and he dropped onto the couch before he could get lightheaded. Had Brayden guessed that Flip was going to propose and decided to spare him the indignity of refusing to his face? But that seemed unlike him.

Perhaps he really had an emergency and had to leave. But if so, why no message? He must know how important he was to Flip. Flip had been in the middle of telling him as much when he had to leave.

Ignoring the pit opening in his stomach, he started a new text message to Brayden. *Where are you?* He should get all the facts before he started to panic. That seemed like the rational thing to do.

So, of course, that was when his father dashed into the room without knocking, breathing hard, the suit he'd worn to the police station in disarray—jacket open, tie flung over his shoulder. "Flip! I made a— What are you doing? You have to get dressed."

Flip stood, knowing he needed to act, but something in his father's tone made him suspicious. "You made a what?"

Irfan waved a hand. "It doesn't matter right now. Brayden's gone and you have to go after him."

"Yes, I know. Celine messaged me. But I don't know where, or why, or what any of it means—"

His father pushed him into the bedroom. "He asked Celine to take him to the airport. He said he had a family emergency." Irfan made a scoffing noise. "An obvious lie. If he'd had an emergency, you'd have gone with him."

"Yes, I *know*," Flip repeated, automatically putting on the sweater his father thrust at him. "How do *you* know? And what else do you know that I don't?"

I should have talked to him. Something must have spooked him. Flip had been so sure Brayden felt the same way he did. He didn't think that had changed, not judging from how sweet Brayden had been since they returned from their trip, how tender. "Why would he…," he mumbled, half to himself, as he put on the trousers Irfan held out.

He couldn't have said exactly how he knew. His father was an excellent actor. But *something* gave him away, and Flip whirled. "What did you do?"

"Nothing!" Irfan protested, taking half a step back with his hands raised.

Flip wasn't convinced.

"Okay, maybe I tried to nudge him a little bit while we were out shopping," Irfan admitted. "I thought maybe if I hinted that I knew your relationship was fake from the beginning, he'd sac up and tell you he's in love with you and you would make the whole thing real before he went home and left you with a broken heart!"

Flip froze with his hand on his fly. "I'm sorry, you did *what*?"

"It works in the movies!"

"Dad!" Flip finished zipping and ran his hands through his hair. *What a disaster.* "You're going to tell me everything on the way to the airport," he said darkly. Then another horrifying thought occurred to him. "Oh no, did you tell Mom?"

"What do you take me for? Of course I didn't tell your mother. I love you and I don't want you to die." Irfan pushed him toward the door. "That doesn't mean she didn't find out on her own, so for both our sakes, let's hope you can fix this before she stops pretending she doesn't know."

Shit. "All right, good point, let's—" Flip stopped abruptly. "Okay, but that was days ago. Why would he leave now?"

His father paused and stood up straight, his hands dropping to his sides. "Hm. Good question. What were you doing when you last saw him?"

Panic clawed at Flip's throat. If he said it out loud, it became a real possibility—that Brayden had left to avoid having to say no.

If he *didn't* say it out loud, though, he would have to try to puzzle out the meaning behind Brayden's disappearance alone, and he didn't think his head was clear enough for that.

"I was about to ask him to marry me."

The words seemed to suck all the sound out of the rest of the world. For several long seconds, silence reigned. Finally his father said, "I think you'd better think about your exact words. What did you say? How did you say it?"

Flip swallowed and thought back. He'd been nervous, and not just nervous but thrown off from his interactions with Minister Bechard, and he'd started setting up his proposal like he would an argument—points against first, so he could refute them.

Everything became ... regretfully more complicated.

That sounded bad.

Some more critical members of the press might have dubbed you an unsuitable match for me. But while you have conducted yourself well.... What? He'd never finished that sentence. That could just as easily be leading up to *it's not good enough for me, please pack your things.*

"I am an utter wanker." How could he have bollocksed this up so completely?

His father clapped him on the shoulder. "It's okay. Your mother needed two tries too."

For fuck's sake.

Flip picked up his momentum again and exited the bedroom into the living area. He needed shoes and a coat. His passport, maybe, if he was going to have to fly somewhere. Where had he left his gloves—on the table?

He hadn't, but while he was looking, his eyes caught on a square of white paper—his own stationery from the desk in his bedroom. Was this the note he'd looked for? Or—

"Read it in the car," Irfan ordered. "Come on, let's go."

Flip let himself be hurried. His father was right. But before the door closed behind him, he ran back for one more thing.

He wouldn't be caught unprepared this time.

BRAYDEN had purchased a coffee and a pair of sunglasses—not easy to find at Virejas Airport in the dead of winter—and spent the remainder of the time before his flight in the first-class lounge, an indulgence he paid for with some of the money he's saved from his refunded hotel stay. For two hours he hid behind a week-old copy of the *Guardian*, nervously bouncing his foot up and down.

Miraculously, it went even worse than he'd feared.

He'd hoped that the first-class lounge would be less crowded, perhaps populated only with a few well-to-do patrons who would be too polite to stare or at least to talk about him when he was within earshot. Maybe they'd even be jaded—surely they rubbed elbows with Europe's wealthiest on the regular. Who would even care about the brand-new (ex-)boyfriend of Lyngria's future king?

Clearly some deity somewhere had seen Brayden's incredible hubris and was acting to correct it.

Though many of the passengers seemed to be traveling alone, that didn't prevent them from turning to each other, or the lounge staffers, and whispering to each other.

"Isn't that…?"

"Why isn't he with the prince?"

"He's not as handsome in person."

"Do you think they broke up?"

"Should we ask him?"

Brayden felt lucky that his flight was called for boarding before anyone gathered the courage to make inquiries to his face. But his luck didn't hold. As he buckled into his seat in economy class, his neighbor squinted over at him. "You look familiar."

"I get that a lot." Brayden pasted on a plastic smile. He'd never been airsick a day in his life, but his stomach felt as though it might revolt at any moment, and he felt a hair's breadth away from a breakdown. He put his headphones on before takeoff, hoping to telegraph how much he didn't want to speak to anyone.

His neighbor kept glancing at him from the corner of his eye and then texting frantically until the flight attendants asked that everyone put their phone in flight mode until they reached cruising altitude.

His stomach fell away along with the ground as the plane took off. That was it. It was done. He'd left.

Now he had another week and a half of his leave of absence to heal his broken heart before he had to go back to work, a thought that filled him with dread. What would Joanna and the others say? Luis? Would they ask about Flip? Would his passengers recognize him?

Maybe this was the kick in the ass he needed to finally quit his job. He'd spent enough of his life traveling. He'd gotten over Thomas's death. He didn't need an excuse to keep him from settling down anymore. He could get a regular nine-to-five, have a family, find someone to come home to every night the way he had for the past three weeks.

Compared to the way he'd felt in Flip's arms, that was cold comfort. But it was all he had, and he clung to it as the plane swung north.

I'M so sorry, read the paper, just one line among several disjointed ones, some crossed out, others underlined.

Flip's stomach lurched as his father turned onto the highway. Their bodyguards usually kept his speeding to a minimum, but today they didn't have any, and Flip couldn't complain. The flight to Paris—the one Brayden would be on if he was going home—was scheduled to begin boarding in twenty-five minutes.

I should have been more careful about social media. I don't want to—

Here several words had been scratched out and written over each other to the point of illegibility.

The past few weeks have been perfect. I hate that my actions led to more media garbage for you when

When what? The line ended without a conclusion. Flip rubbed his suddenly damp palms on his trousers and huffed in frustration.

"If you're not going to read that out loud," Irfan said, "stop making those noises. You're making me curious."

Flip flushed and consciously reined himself in.

I know I don't belong in your world. I'm always afraid I'm going to embarrass you, and I hate the idea of disappointing you.

"For fuck's sake," Flip half shouted, and ended up reading that part aloud because he needed to vent about how stupid Brayden was.

"Is this a Hallmark movie?" Irfan asked as he took the exit for the airport. "I didn't know he was such a hand-wringer. He's perfect for you."

Flip wasn't sure whether to be insulted. "Hey." But that reminded him. "What did you say to him, anyway?"

His father kept his eyes on the road and passed a slow car in the right-hand lane. "I perhaps… mentioned… that you were a good actor but not as good as me, and I knew you were lying."

"Yeah, you said that already," Flip said impatiently. "That wasn't all of it. There's something else."

Now he squirmed and flicked his gaze from the signage overhead to the one marking the nearest exit. He had to be feeling pretty guilty if he was betraying this much emotion. "Okay, so maybe I asked him what he was getting out of it."

"*For fuck's sake*," Flip repeated.

"In hindsight, it was not a good idea."

"No shit." Flip rubbed the bridge of his nose. He was getting a headache. "What were you doing when this happened? Was this when you were shopping?"

Irfan took the exit for the airport, and his face went slack. "Oh—oh shit, we had just stopped to pick up the stupid tabloids—the one where some internet creep found his Instagram—"

Reflexively Flip crumpled the note. "That's it, then. You were going for 'maybe you should talk about your real feelings' and he heard 'someone's going to use you to make Flip look stupid.'"

As if Flip cared about that. As if it mattered the slightest in the larger picture of things—the picture where Flip went to bed with Brayden every night and woke up with him every morning.

"Flip." Irfan reached over and put a hand on his arm. "I'm so sorry."

"You were trying to help." And maybe, just maybe, Irfan's interference would allow Flip to head this off early, before it became the issue that would destroy them. The flight to Paris hadn't left yet. There was still hope.

He had to believe there was still hope.

They squealed into the airport departures lot with fifteen minutes to spare. Irfan pulled up in front of the main doors and slammed the car into Park. "Go get your man," he said with gravitas.

Flip was already out the door.

At this early hour, the security line was just starting to form as weary business travelers in work suits shuffled blearily along until they could get their tepid airport coffee. But Flip had a diplomatic passport, security clearance, and no carryon to check through.

"Everything in order, Your Highness," the security attendant told him as he handed back his phone with the mobile boarding pass he'd downloaded in the car. "Have a nice—"

But the second Flip had his phone back, he was sprinting down the terminal, cursing his stupid expensive shoes for having the type of sole that slid precariously on smooth floors. Gate A7—he needed to get to A7—

He skidded around the corner just in time to see an airline employee open the door to the Jetway. "Wait."

The passengers in the seating area turned toward him, faces painted in mirror images of mild surprise—surprise that turned to shock when they recognized that the disheveled man with the mismatched ensemble and unshaven face was their crown prince.

At least three people took out their phones.

"Wait," Flip repeated dumbly, and then called on all of his reserves to project an aura of calm as he approached the desk so he could speak more privately. Several other passengers watched him avidly, and perhaps they could read lips, but he couldn't help that. He needed information. "I'm sorry," he said quietly to the desk attendant. "But could you tell me, please, if Brayden Wood is on that plane?"

"Your Highness," squeaked the freckle-faced young man who had just opened the Jetway door. He must have batlike hearing, or else the acoustics in there were incredible. Damn it. "It's not our policy—"

"Oh shut up, Stefan," said the woman at the desk. Her nametag read Danielle. She looked back at Flip. "He's not on my passenger manifest, sir."

Right. Of course. "Thank you very much," Flip told her, trying not to let on that his world was crumbling.

The sympathy on her face let him know he hadn't fooled her. "Would you like to board, sir? Our VIPs are always allowed priority boarding."

He shook his head. "Thank you, no. I won't be traveling today. An urgent matter has come up."

"I understand. Have a pleasant day, sir."

He didn't know quite what to do when he walked away from the desk. His chest felt tight, and panic bubbled below the surface. This wasn't how he'd envisioned this going. How could he be too late?

He swallowed hard and forced himself to accept the possibility that Brayden might be gone for good. The airport was almost empty. He felt sure that if Brayden were there, he'd have seen him. Which meant Brayden's flight had already left.

But it was a very small airport, and Brayden had a window of only a few hours. If Celine had dropped Brayden off here, and if he'd gotten on a plane instead of, say, taking a taxi somewhere else—

A screen above him showed the day's scheduled departures. One was boarding now, with three more scheduled throughout the day.

Five were marked DEPARTED—ON TIME.

And suddenly Flip knew where Brayden had gone.

EVEN when he rolled his suitcase under the double bed in his hotel room, Brayden couldn't quite believe he'd gone through with it. For the first time since he'd begun traveling, he'd actually followed through on that promise to himself—*if I can't stay where I am, I'll go back to someplace I loved.*

This wasn't exactly the place, of course. Brayden couldn't afford to stay in a glass igloo overlooking a valley, especially not if he were really going to quit his job. He had a view of a snowy parking lot, and considering the occupancy rate of the hotel around the holidays, he was lucky he had that. But the room was clean, and the hotel had a package that included ski or snowboard rental. He'd spent the afternoon on the slopes, losing himself in the hush of snow under his feet and the sting of powder on his face, pushing his body until everything ached. No one recognized him with his goggles on. It was practically paradise.

He'd have had a lot more fun if Flip were there too.

Maybe he should have just gone home, but his family wouldn't return until after New Year's, and he couldn't face his empty apartment.

At the moment, though, his empty hotel room wasn't any more appealing. He didn't want to talk to anyone, but he didn't want to be alone either, especially not alone and cold and wet.

Fortunately Brayden's travels had taught him one thing—ski resorts always had a bar. And a strong drink by a roaring fire sounded like heaven.

THE bar was a bust. Sitting next to a crackling wood fire with a hot toddy only made him long for the evenings he'd spent with Flip, and the ache inside him deepened.

He'd thought the sauna would present the same issue, but it wasn't intimate like the one at their glass igloo. The quiet drone of conversation—mostly in Finnish—soothed him. He leaned his head back against the wall and let the heat and steam loosen his aching muscles.

The door opened and a hotel employee stuck his head in and said something in Finnish to the guys sitting next to the door. They exchanged looks and got up to follow.

Brayden closed his eyes and tried to plan for his future. If he quit his job, what would he do? He could probably find work as a translator, either for the government or privately. But his heart wouldn't be in that any more than it was in his current job, and he wouldn't have the travel benefits to keep him happy enough to fake it. He could get a teaching degree, but then what? Teaching jobs weren't exactly easy to come by, even if he had nepotism on his side.

One by one the other bathers filed out, leaving the room silent except for the occasional hiss of steam. Caught up in self-pity, Brayden didn't move.

Maybe he could return to his grandmother's studio. She might consider selling the place to him when she retired, not that Brayden had much saved to give her for it.

Of course, every time he taught the waltz, he'd think of Flip's sure grip and warm eyes, the steady pressure of his hand on Brayden's waist, the way their bodies moved together. It had taken Brayden ten years to get over teenage heartbreak. How long before he could imagine a future for himself—one he *wanted*—that didn't have Flip in it?

He'd been foolish to ever believe he could pretend to be involved with Flip and walk away with his heart intact. He should have known better from the first time Flip rushed off to be his cousin's knight in armor. From the first time he shared that sometimes he ate ice cream for lunch. From the first time Brayden made him laugh.

He should have known, just as he should have known Flip couldn't be for him. He didn't blame Flip for wanting to break it off. Even if all he wanted in the world was to go back to Lyngria right now and beg him to reconsider.

"Brayden."

The hair on the back of his neck rose. He opened his eyes.

Flip stood in the doorway to the sauna, cheeks flushed, his normally coiffed hair in disarray. That, paired with his expensive mismatched clothing, lent him a sort of hopeless air. He looked like a wealthy man who'd just come off a bender—or a prince who'd suddenly discovered his lover absent from his life.

Brayden's mouth worked without his permission, and he wondered if he was seeing things. "What are you doing here?"

"Coming after you. Obviously."

That didn't make any sense. "*Why?*" Not that he was complaining.

Flip went on, just as calmly, as though he didn't already have sweat beading at his temples, "Tell me you don't love me and I'll let you go."

Brayden swallowed hard. "What does that have to do with anything? You're the one who wanted to end things."

"I wasn't breaking up with you."

Brayden waited a few seconds for that to sink in. It didn't. "I'm sorry, what?"

"I wasn't breaking up with you," Flip repeated, flushing either with the heat or embarrassment or both. "I wanted to talk about our relationship, but it wasn't anything bad. I was nervous and flustered, and that made me sound... formal and distant when I meant to be affectionate. I started badly and it got worse from there, and then I got interrupted...."

"Started badly." Brayden rubbed his eyes and looked up again, but Flip was still there. Unless Brayden had been sitting there long enough to start hallucinating. "And got worse from there. And then I thought… and I left." He winced, but his heart was lifting, and he managed half a laugh. "Jesus, we're a pair."

"Maybe we can make a New Year's resolution to communicate better," Flip offered with a soft smile. "I'll start now, though. You are far too kind, charming, and good-natured to cause an international incident."

Brayden's hands were trembling. "The press… they're so awful to you. And I remember your face when you talked about what happened with Miles. I don't ever want to be the reason you get hurt like that. My Instagram account could have been so embarrassing for you."

"Brayden. I was born brown and gay. To the worst of the press, I'm already the scourge of the country. Do you really think I take anything they say to heart? Especially when it's about the man I love?"

The man I love. Brayden's throat worked. Flip loved him—now, still, after everything he'd put him through. How had he misunderstood something so fundamental to Flip's life? "But after the ball… you were upset. I thought…."

"Yes—for you," Flip said. "You didn't sign up for that level of scrutiny, and I was angry with myself for subjecting you to it without preparing you. And embarrassed—not *of* you, but because I…."

Brayden waited. He was still reeling from Flip's confession and had no idea what he might say.

"Because I knew I wanted to pursue a real relationship with you, and I'd just made it very complicated for myself."

"Oh," he said in a small voice. A smile began to tug at the corners of his mouth, but it seemed too early to give in to it. Surely things could still go sour? Brayden had an excellent track record of fucking things up.

Flip kissed the back of his hand. "My dad told me what happened on your shopping trip and that he might have scared you off. He was extremely contrite." Then he shook his head. "But that's partly my fault too. Apparently he was trying to give us a nudge in the right direction. If I'd told him the truth earlier…."

"I mean, let's not discount the fact that I jumped to conclusions and left the country instead of actually talking to you." Brayden swallowed hard thinking of what he'd done. "There's plenty of blame to go around."

Flip sat next to him on the bench. He had to be sweltering in the heat of the sauna, but he didn't betray the slightest bit of discomfort. "I'd like to start our conversation over, if that's okay with you?"

"After making you chase me to Finland, I think hearing you out is the least I can do." He felt really stupid. "I'm so sorry. I was so preoccupied thinking I'd fuck things up for you. Or that someone would find out the whole thing was fake…."

Flip huffed softly and leaned his forehead against Brayden's. "You idiot. Not a single moment has been fake."

Brayden leaned back and let Flip hold some of his weight, the last of the tension melting from his body. "Yeah." He blinked slowly, enjoying the moment. "Okay. This conversation. You have my attention. I promise I'm not going to run out before it's finished and get on a plane this time."

"And I'm going to be casual and affectionate instead of formal and cold." Flip laced the fingers of their left hands together and briefly pressed a kiss to Brayden's knuckles. "I don't care what people say about you or about us in the media. I know who you are. You're kind, compassionate, and smart, and you make me happy. Almost since we met, I've wanted more from you than I thought I could ask for, but you proved me wrong last time and maybe you'll do it again."

Brayden swallowed, but he wouldn't let himself look away from Flip's eyes. He could feel his heart beating in his throat.

"I want you to come back with me—to come *home*."

Brayden exhaled shakily, overcome with relief. "I don't know how I thought I could stay away." He belonged with Flip. That Flip was a prince would occasionally be a minor inconvenience to overcome. "Though I don't know what I'm going to do. I'll have to quit my job, but I don't think I'm cut out to sit on my hands all day."

"Oh, I can think of a few positions that need filling." Flip's eyes were laughing.

For fuck's sake. They really were a pair. Brayden held back an incredulous laugh. "Was that an innuendo? Right now? I thought we were having a moment."

"I was thinking the head of the Thousand Lights charity committee," Flip protested innocently. "Maybe some work developing dance classes and other activities for hospitalized children? Senior citizens' homes too, if that doesn't keep you busy."

Damn him. He *had* thought of everything. "That sounds like it could be in my wheelhouse."

Flip smoothed his thumb over the back of Brayden's hand. "You have no idea how happy it makes me to hear you say that. But I hope that won't take up all your time, because there's one more role I had in mind."

"Oh yeah?" Brayden said, wondering what ridiculous thing was about to come out of Flip's mouth. "What's that?"

Flip slid off the bench and knelt on the sauna floor. From his pocket he produced a small jewelry box, which he opened. It held a simple white gold band and an enormous familiar-looking flawed diamond. "My husband."

Brayden raised his left hand to his mouth.

Flip took his right. "Will you marry me?"

Brayden's mouth got ahead of his brain. "What if I accidentally tell a dick joke to the Pope?"

Flip shrugged, ignoring entirely the absurdity of the question. "He's eighty-one years old. You think he's never heard a dick joke before?"

Brayden managed a watery smile. "Not one of mine." Flip squeezed his hand again and Brayden remembered his next thought. "I've known you for three weeks."

Flip smiled and slid the ring on his finger. Apparently he could tell that was not an actual objection. "So we'll have a very long engagement. Family tradition. Anyway, I hear it can take years to plan a royal wedding." He curled Brayden's fingers around his own. "But I'm not going to change my mind."

Brayden laughed and pulled him to his feet, and Flip wrapped both arms around him and kissed him until all he could do was hold on.

When Flip pulled back, eyes soft and warm and full of love, it was like stepping off a cliff. He knew he couldn't go back. But that was okay. Life was a gift, and now, finally, Brayden was living it to the fullest.

Besides, he thought as their lips met, Flip would be there to catch him the next time he fell.

Epilogue

"I COULD'VE driven," Brayden grumbled as the car slushed down the damp streets of downtown Scarborough.

In the front seat, their driver, Geoff, didn't comment. Flip felt no such compunction to hold his tongue. "Yes, you could have," he agreed, "except *someone* asserted that he didn't want special driving privileges. He wanted to go through the same licensing process as anyone else, and so someone only has a learner's permit. And there's no reciprocity agreement for learner's permits."

Brayden sighed, long-suffering, because all Cedric's etiquette lessons went to hell when Brayden wasn't in the public eye. Thank God. "It would've been so cool to show up driving James Bond's sugar daddy's car."

In truth, Flip suspected Brayden was putting on a show to distract him. He'd drunk too much coffee on their flight and now he felt ready to vibrate out of his own skin, just in time to meet Brayden's extended family, which apparently included fourteen cousins and cousins-in-law and ten cousins once removed.

Flip wasn't nervous per se. But—

"Flip." Brayden brought his hand down to rest gently on Flip's knee, stilling the reflexive jiggle.

Okay, he was a little bit nervous. "Are you sure there's no diplomatic crisis I shouldn't be attending to?"

"There might be one here, if Brian eats all the rolls again."

Geoff stopped the car and got out to open the door for Brayden, who waited outside while Flip dragged himself out of the back seat.

"Thanks, Geoff," Brayden said to the driver. "See you at eight thirty?"

"I'll be here with bells on." Geoff nodded to Flip. "Your Highness."

He got back in the car and drove off, but despite the prewinter chill in the air, Brayden didn't usher Flip inside right away. He slid his hand into Flip's and squeezed his fingers.

He was right—Flip was being silly. Everything would be fine. And anyway…. "They'll be calling you that before long."

"Sap," Brayden accused fondly and turned his face up for a kiss.

Inside, the restaurant's private dining room looked much as Flip had imagined it—wood-paneled walls, tiled floor, two long tables set with plain plates and cutlery, a Christmas tree set up at one end. Over the cacophony of half a dozen children playing and twice as many adults conversing, no one noticed them enter, so Flip had several seconds to gather his bearings.

This was a family, he reminded himself, not unlike his own, and not unlike Brayden himself. Just on a larger scale. Flip loved Brayden, and these people also, presumably, loved Brayden, so they already had something in common. And—

"Brayden! You made it!"

Brayden let go of Flip's hand as Lina vaulted into his arms and sent him staggering back a few steps. "Hey, sis."

"*Hey, sis*," she echoed. "I thought you weren't going to be able to make it. You said you had a conference in London or something."

Brayden put her down and glanced at Flip, the corners of his mouth turning up to match the smile in his eyes. "Yeah, but it sucked, so Flip got us on a last-minute flight."

For the first time, Lina tore her eyes away from Brayden and looked at Flip. Other family members were coming over too, waiting their turn to say hello, and Flip reached for the manners his teachers had instilled in him from a young age—

And almost cursed out loud when Brayden stepped on his foot.

Right. This was family.

Lina sized him up. Flip had met their parents over their March break and again in the summer, when they were off work, but Lina hadn't been able to get time off. He extended his hand. "It's nice to meet you."

Lina flung her arms around his neck. Somewhat bemused, Flip cast a glance at Brayden, who just lifted a shoulder. Eventually he managed to hug her back. "*Hi*. Welcome to the family."

Flip's throat went suddenly thick, and he looked at Brayden again, half-panicked.

This time he intervened. "All right, we all appreciate that Flip's willing to put up with me on a daily basis, but maybe you could let him breathe a little? He's turning blue."

The rest of the family came up to make their introductions. Brayden stood by Flip's side the whole time, offering a running commentary no one seemed to think was the slightest bit strange. The names got a little meaningless halfway through the cousins, until Brayden introduced Seana and Brian and something twigged in his brain. "Is he the one who brought the live lobsters, or the vegan?" Flip asked, sotto voce.

"The lobsters," Brayden said, rolling his eyes as Brian flushed. Seana swatted his arm. "And Julie's the one who opened them—she's the vegan."

"My reputation precedes me," Brian said and shook Flip's hand firmly. "Good meetin' ya."

"Likewise." Flip leaned in. "I don't suppose you brought lobsters this year?"

The gift exchange—a chaotic swap whose objective seemed to be stealing whichever present made the most people squawk—didn't happen until after dinner, when Flip was pleasantly full and coming down from his caffeine buzz. He and Brayden hadn't had time to purchase gifts, which suited Flip fine because he was going to need a year to study the strategy of white-elephant exchanges. Instead they sat back at the table and watched the madness unfold.

And then, when all the presents had been opened and the wrapping paper collected for recycling, Brayden tugged Flip to his feet. "I know you're probably all disappointed we didn't participate in the gift exchange this year, because who doesn't want the chance to steal something from under a prince's nose"—Flip rolled his eyes on cue—"but I think we brought something almost as good."

Flip reached into his jacket pocket and withdrew a number of small envelopes and passed them to Brayden, who took out several of his own. "These were going to go in the mail," Flip said, "but we thought it might be nice to hand them out in person."

He had just turned to hand an envelope to Brayden's grandmother when Brayden added, "I hope you're all free the second week of July?"

For a moment you could have heard a pin drop. And then chaos broke loose. Someone shouted, "You set a *date*?" so high-pitched Flip assumed it had to be Lina, but when he looked it turned out to be Brayden's dad, wide-eyed and grinning.

As the friendly horde descended for another round of hugs, Brayden's grandmother put her hand on his arm. "Congratulations," she said warmly, holding her wedding invitation close to her chest. Then she leaned into him and raised her eyebrows meaningfully. "Maybe let Brayden lead the dancing this time."

Coming in July 2019

Dreamspun Desires #85
Come Back Around by BA Tortuga

Can two divorced dads get a second chance at a redneck wedding?

When Reid Porter agrees to be his best friend's man of honor, he never considers that his ex, Mateo, will be there too. Which is ridiculous, because Jennifer is marrying Mat's brother. Reid would never let Jen down, though, so he finds himself at the Leaning N Ranch with his two daughters and a whole lot of baggage about seeing Mat again.

Mat loves his baby brother and would do anything for him, including face the love of his life, whom he's has moved on. When he and Reid come face-to-face after more than two years apart, they realize they've never let go. Now they have to do what they never could before—balance work, home, and children, while finding a way to come back around to each other's love.

Dreamspun Desires #86
Warm Heart by Amy Lane

Following a family emergency, snowboarder Tevyn Moore and financier Mallory Armstrong leave Donner Pass in a blizzard… and barely survive the helicopter crash that follows. Stranded with few supplies and no shelter, Tevyn and Mallory—and their injured pilot—are forced to rely on each other.

The mountain leaves no room for evasion, and Tevyn and Mal must confront the feelings that have been brewing between them for the past five years. Mallory has seen Tevyn through injury and victory. Can Tevyn see that Mallory's love is real?

Mallory's job is risk assessment. Tevyn's job is full-on risk. But to stay alive, Mallory needs to take some gambles and Tevyn needs to have faith in someone besides himself. Can the bond they discover on the mountain see them to rescue and beyond?

Love Always Finds a Way

ꕔREAMSPUN DESIRES
Subscription Service

Love eBooks?

Our monthly subscription service gives you two eBooks per month for one low price. Each month's titles will be automatically delivered to your Dreamspinner Bookshelf on their release dates.

Prefer print?

Receive two paperbacks per month! Both books ship on the 1st of the month, giving you *exclusive* early access! As a bonus, you'll receive both eBooks on their release dates!

Visit
www.dreamspinnerpress.com
for more info or to sign up now!

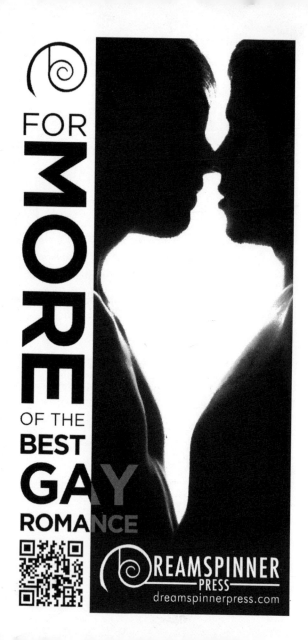